FOREVER STARTS TONIGHT

A Wilder Family Novel

KARLA SORENSEN

To the wonderful readers who've been waiting patiently (and not-so-patiently)
for Poppy and Jax.

Their story is yours now, and I hope you love it like I do.

Prologue
Jax

Twenty-five years ago

My mom's favorite flowers were red roses, but by the time I walked to the grocery store—the money I'd been saving from chores for the past two months wadded up in the pocket of my jeans—they were gone. It was my own fault, really. I waited until Valentine's Day to get them, and by the time I got out of school and waited for her to fall asleep while she watched *General Hospital,* all that was left at the store was an almost empty black bucket with a sad looking bunch of daisies drooping in the corner. The crinkly paper around them was bright pink, and I tried bunching them together as I walked home, to see if it made them look a little bit nicer.

It didn't. I found a big box of chocolates though, and threw that in my shopping basket, and then wandered down the next aisle and checked the prices on a new basketball because mine had gone flat. I was careful not to squish the flowers with the ball, because they were already small enough as it is.

But I still bought them though, with my own money, because she was always talking on her birthday and Valentine's Day about how the only thing she wanted was someone to bring her something pretty, for someone to be thinking about her.

I thought about her all the time, but maybe most kids were like that with their moms. She was silly and young and all my friends at school thought she was a fun mom, or the jackasses in the grade above me said she was the hottest one too, probably because she was only sixteen when she had me. And I guess she was fun sometimes. When we had ice cream for breakfast, and chocolate cake for dinner. When she let me skip school when she felt like sleeping in. That stuff was cool. But usually she was just tired at home, because she worked two jobs. That kept her busy enough, but her most important job, she said, was trying to find me a new dad.

Hadn't worked yet, but she sure tried hard.

Some were nicer than others. Some made me want to punch them in the balls. Most ignored me, and that was fine, too. But usually, they weren't around long enough for me to get used to them. When they were gone, she'd mope for a while—that's when we'd have cake for dinner—because she had to see them at the grocery store or at church or at the coffee shop. After a few weeks, or a month, she'd snap out of her funk, and try to find someone else. But it hadn't worked this time. According to her, they were all assholes or married, or both.

That's why on this Valentine's Day, my mom didn't have anyone to buy her flowers. She'd cried for days because she didn't have someone to take her for a nice dinner.

That's when I thought, *I could buy her flowers.* I'm almost eleven. That's practically a teenager.

So I saved up my money. I asked neighbors if they had chores that needed to be done, and most gave me something little, even if they got a sad look in their eye when they paid me a buck or two. Definitely wasn't enough for a nice bouquet. Thankfully, Mr. Henry across the street gave me the good paying jobs.

I got ten dollars to pick up sticks in his yard after a storm blew through. And he gave me fifteen dollars to help him wash windows. Another ten when I helped him wash his car. I spent some of that already, because I needed a new helmet for riding my bike, and Mom kept forgetting to buy me one. But the best was the twenty-five bucks I got when I helped him paint the railing on the back porch.

"It's important this looks nice," he said, showing me how to turn the brush just right so I didn't spill paint everywhere. "I spend a lot of time in this backyard, young man."

He had a nice one too, with a big deck covered in expensive furniture, and a big, pretty meadow as far as the eye could see, bursting at the seams with wildflowers. All the kids in the neighborhood were allowed to play back there, as long as we respected nature, he said.

I probably could've picked her flowers from the field, but I knew her well enough … she'd want the fancy ones.

When I finally finished at the store and walked home—the smallest one on the street—I puffed my chest out and smiled a little when I thought about how excited she'd be that someone got her flowers. It may not be as good as jewelry or some big fancy dinner, but I was still the man of the house, right? Carefully, I unlocked the door and walked in. The couch was empty, so she'd woken up from her nap.

"Mom?" I called. She didn't answer, but I heard noises coming from her bedroom at the back of the house. Before she could come out of her room, I dragged a chair over to the front of the fridge and pulled open the cabinet where she kept the vases. We only had a couple, but with my tongue tucked between my teeth and really careful movements, I could reach the pretty green one with the wavy edges. It was her favorite. She'd love them even more in that. Maybe she'd even put them right in the middle of the table, where we'd see them every time we ate. Clutching it to my chest, I climbed down from the chair and set the vase on the edge of the kitchen counter.

I scratched the side of my head, because I didn't know how the heck to make them look nice in there, especially not such a dinky little bouquet.

Her bedroom door flew open, and she rushed into the kitchen, her red robe tight around her body and her hair wrapped in curlers.

"Where'd you go?" she asked.

"Went to the store," I told her, wiping under my nose. "I got—"

"You're gonna need to feed yourself tonight, Jax," she interrupted, her attention on the mirror on the wall above the circular table where we took our meals. She started pulling the curlers out, her blonde hair falling in big circles around her shoulders. "There's stuff to make sandwiches in the fridge, or you can order a pizza with all that money that old man's been giving you." She eyed me in the mirror. "You got enough for pizza?"

My belly tightened nervously. "No. I spent it."

Her brows dipped. "On what?"

I edged behind her and clutched the edge of the pink, crinkled paper. "Happy Valentine's Day, Mom." I swallowed when she didn't look right away. "I bought you these, because you said you wanted some."

She froze, glancing down at the flowers tight in my sweaty hand. Her eyebrows dipped again. "Why'd you spend your money on flowers?"

"You said you wanted some," I said quietly. "Didn't you?"

Mom gave me a tight smile. "I wanted some from a boyfriend, or a husband. It's nice you thought of me, but I think you wasted all your money, bud. That's not really what I need from you, if that makes sense. I just need you to be a good boy and take care of yourself tonight."

Something heavy in my stomach dropped down into my

feet, and my eyes felt like I'd rubbed sand in them. The daisies looked even smaller in my hand. "Oh. Okay."

She pulled the last curler out. "I called Sally next door, she said she'd be home tonight if you need anything. Maybe you could give them to her as a thank you."

I tried to hide my grimace. Sally always smelled like heavy perfume and she pinched my cheeks like I was a stupid little kid. I didn't want to give her flowers.

"You're going out?"

Mom nodded. "I got a call from the guy I met at the store in Redmond last week. The one I told you about, I think he was a banker or something." Leaning in toward the mirror, she fluffed the curls, running her fingers through them like she always did. "If he knows what's good for him, he'll have a gift for me," she muttered. "Won't go very far if he doesn't."

I wasn't sure what to say, so I just stayed quiet, setting the daisies on the counter.

Mom turned, setting a hand on my shoulder and giving me a slightly warmer smile. "Some day, I'll find the right man, I just know it. And he'll bring me flowers every week. Maybe this is the one, yeah?"

Slowly, I nodded, because I knew that's what she wanted me to do. Mom kissed the top of my head and rushed back into her bedroom to finish getting ready.

Ten minutes later, she was gone in a cloud of perfume and a promise she'd be back by nine to put me to bed.

The flowers were still on the counter.

I stared at them for a while, that sandy feeling still in my eyes, no matter how hard I tried to blink it away. Before I could do something stupid, I carefully filled the vase with water, and set the daisies—still wrapped in paper—into the light green glass.

The vase went onto the center of the table, and they looked stupid and small, but I didn't know how to fix them, so I stomped out of the house and let the door slam behind me so loud that the windows shook. It felt good. Since it was something I could never get away with if Mom was home, I opened the door and slammed it again.

"You know how to fix that if you break it?" a voice from across the street called.

I pinched my eyes shut, heat flooding my cheeks.

Slowly, I turned around and shook my head. "No, sir."

Mr. Henry was washing his car. "Why don't you come help me with this?"

With shuffling feet heavy from embarrassment, I crossed the street and picked up the soap bucket without making eye contact.

One of the things I liked most about Mr. Henry was that he never made me talk if I didn't want to. He just let me help him, and if I felt like talking—which I usually didn't—he'd listen.

The water in the bucket was cold, but I refused to complain, so I finished soaping up the side and he pulled out the hose to start rinsing it off.

"Saw your mom leave," he said.

I nodded. "Got a date for tonight."

Henry gave me a shrewd look. "You buy her those flowers you were carrying home earlier?"

Thinking about that pathetic bunch of plants in the too-big vase, I had to swallow really hard before I could answer, but I nodded with my eyes locked on the side of the car. "Waste of money. She said she wants some from a husband or something." I dumped the sponge into the bucket, and suds splashed out onto my tennis shoes. "That's all she ever cares about," I said, anger creeping into my voice now. "Wants someone to buy her things and get her pretty presents, and I hate it."

Henry sighed, crouching down so I had no choice but to look at him.

"Some people think finding love will solve all their

6

problems." His face was slightly wrinkled, and I wondered again how old he was. "It won't though. You just take your problems into that relationship with you. There's no person in the world who can carry all that weight, it's up to your mom to figure out why she hates being alone so much."

"I love being alone," I stated, my chin lifting in a dare. "I don't need anyone to fix me."

He smiled. "So do I, kid. Why do you think I never married? Being a lone wolf doesn't suit everyone, you know. But it suits me just fine."

A lone wolf.

"You probably never have to buy anyone flowers, do you?" I asked.

The laugh he let out was quiet, but real. He never pretended I was funny, or gave me those fake-smiles that some adults did with kids.

"No, I don't."

That sounded pretty damn nice to me.

I studied his face again, then looked up at his nice big house, with the perfect lawn and the clean windows and the nice, sturdy furniture that filled each room. Sometimes he let me watch football games with him, as long as I promised to pick up after myself.

"I could be a lone wolf too." I gave Mr. Henry a shy look.

"You think so?"

Puffing my chest out with a deep breath, I nodded. "I don't need anyone to make me happy."

He hummed thoughtfully. "Hmm. You're pretty young to know that for sure, kid."

I finished soaping up the tires, standing back he sprayed off all the bubbles. His car was always perfectly clean and shiny, probably because he washed it a few times a week, no matter what the weather was like. Today was warm for February, the sun peeking out a little.

7

"I won't change my mind," I told him. "If all girls want is big shiny gifts, I don't want anything to do with that."

Under his breath, he laughed quietly. "Some do. Some don't. But taking care of someone isn't all that bad if it's the right one."

I twisted my lips to the side. "Did you ever find someone like that?" I asked.

He shook his head. "I was married to my work, Jax. Liked exploring when I was your age. Any time I felt that itch for a new adventure, I had the freedom to do it."

"Yeah," I whispered in awe. "That's what I want."

Instead of doing that stupid adult thing where he waved me off or told me I was being ridiculous, Mr. Henry gave me a long look, like he was studying something in my face. "You know, I think I believe you, kid."

The way he said it had my chest feeling warm, and I tried to keep my face serious, instead of smiling like I wanted to.

He finished rinsing the last of the soap, then nudged my arm, gesturing toward a clean towel. We finished drying the car, and I liked the way it gleamed under the sun.

Mr. Henry tossed the damp towels onto the driveway, still crouching in front of the tires. "Come on, little pup, let's order some pizza."

"Really?"

Henry jerked his chin toward the house. "Yeah. Can't let the wolf pack go hungry, can we?"

I ran into the house, allowing one small whoop of excitement that had Henry laughing.

8

Chapter 1
Jax

Four years ago

"I'm not sure the beer is worth this," I yelled to my friend Cameron. The music was so loud in the bar, he couldn't hear me, though.

He tilted his head, cupping a hand over his ear. "What?"

I managed a slight eye roll, shaking my head in a *never mind* gesture. Tipping my beer back, I grimaced when the last swallow was lukewarm. Holding it up, I tilted the bottle toward the bar. "Want another one?" I yelled.

When he furrowed his brow in confusion, I said it one more time, and his features lit with understanding. Cameron shook his head. "I'm good, thanks."

"Why are we here again?" I asked.

"What?" he yelled.

I sighed. "Never mind."

Under normal circumstances, my best friend and I stuck closer to home if we were going to go out for a drink or two. In our hometown of Sisters, Oregon, we had a handful of options if a couple of beers sounded good on a Friday or Saturday night, but he'd dragged me to the neighboring town of Redmond. The list of options was slightly longer, and the present faces were slightly less familiar, which was always my preference for a night out anyway.

Especially when I felt like this.

A restless sort of energy built under my skin, a rolling, slightly unpleasant warmth, seeking an outlet.

Finding someone to leave with would be the best option to save my night. I'd been busy at work, pulling longer than normal days because Cameron was short a few guys, and even though my body was tired, it had been a couple of months without evening companionship.

That was all it ever was, really.

The evening.

It was almost like this giant barrier in my head to the possibility of more than that—something invisible to the naked eye but thick and impenetrable all the same. No matter how that energy spit and hissed when it was ready to be unleashed, I never, ever wanted more. There'd never be any fruitless searching for something I wasn't even sure existed. No twisting myself—my life—up in knots over the idea of some soulmate who could solve all my problems simply by existing.

Thanks for that, Mom, I thought dryly. Not that she could hear me. She was somewhere on the East Coast, living with her latest husband in some giant mansion that made her blissfully happy. What was his name again? Rick? Ron?

It was Ron. I'd met him at their wedding—his big, dopey smile and overly large ears gave the appearance of an overgrown child who was happy to have someone pretty at his side.

A new song, loud and boisterous, interrupted any thoughts of husband number four.

The live band playing on a small stage was good, doing covers of popular eighties and nineties songs, but it would likely take my eardrums a week to recover. Slowly, I approached the bar, weaving through a group of college-age kids with giant arms, big mouths, and backward caps, then a whooping line of bachelorettes, holding hands, wearing bridal veils with ropes of beads around their necks.

One of them eyed me as she passed, but despite the inviting smile, the giant ring on her finger and slightly glassy expression had me keeping my face impassive when she brushed past my chest with an intentionality that was best ignored.

The line at the bar was easily three people deep, and I let out a slow, deep breath when the reality of another cold beer was at least fifteen minutes off yet.

"Fuck this," I muttered.

I was just about to turn and tell Cameron he was on his own when I saw her.

She stood all the way down at the end, elbows braced on the bar and leaning forward to be heard by the bartender. Her sleek pale blue dress showed a considerable amount of toned legs and firm, tan thighs. I tilted my head, eyes trailing over the dip in her waist, the curves of her backside, the straps crisscrossing over her back. An inviting amount of skin was visible when she shifted on her dangerously spiked high-heeled feet. Her hair—a mass of dark, messy waves that hid her face—was long and thick, and a hot curl of interest unspooled immediately through my gut.

Her.

Her.

The slightly unpleasant warmth under my skin turned lava hot in less than a heartbeat.

My feet moved before I clocked the decision to head in her direction, and the graceful line of her arm waved in the air as she spoke to the bartender. No ring.

Show me your face, pretty girl, I thought.

The bartender finished making her drink, a fruity-looking concoction paired with a light green shot on the side that raised my eyebrows. If she was shit-faced drunk, this would be a short conversation and a quick return to my friend.

To her left, the couple parked against the bar gathered their drinks and walked away. I slid immediately into the spot they vacated, my arm brushing slightly against her shoulder as I kept my eyes forward on the bartender and settled in against the bar. She wasn't short, thanks to the heels boosting her height, but still, I could probably tuck her head underneath my chin.

Next to me, she'd gone unnaturally still, and even in the crowded bar, I caught a whiff of something clean and citrusy. The band finished a song, and after the applause died down, they said they'd be back after a ten-minute break.

Thank God.

The bartender caught my eye, and I held up the bottle. "Another one of these, please. And I'll pay for what she just ordered," I said smoothly. My hand tightened into a fist on the bar when she raised a hand to gather up her dark hair and pull it over the opposite shoulder. The bartender handed me my beer, taking the cash I'd held out in a deft move. "Keep the change," I told him.

Beside me, the woman sucked in a quick breath, then slowly angled toward me. Her head was down for a moment, but in my peripheral vision, I caught a glimpse of perfectly mouthwatering cleavage—high and firm—pressing against the low neckline of the dress, and ignored the screaming impulse to stare.

One of us would have to speak eventually, but given I'd just bought her drinks, I'd know within a few seconds if there were any possibilities here.

God, I hoped there was.

An insistent, screaming instinct had my body fighting the urge to turn toward her, and I pulled in a slow breath through my nose, locking my muscles to stay in place.

Next to me, her head finally lifted, and anticipation had my pulse racing.

Finally, finally, she spoke. "Happy birthday to me, I guess."

Her voice hit my eardrums, and I froze, my chest icing over immediately.

No.

There was no fucking way.

Moving slower than I ever thought possible, I turned my face toward hers, eyes taking in the sex-bomb hair and the gloss of heavy makeup, the likes of which I'd *never* seen on my best friend's little sister.

"Poppy," I said evenly even though that wild, fierce energy now screamed at me to run the fuck away. Jaw tight, I let my gaze track over her face. "When did you get here?"

"About fifteen minutes ago. We came in through the back," she answered. "I knew Cameron was here somewhere, but he didn't say you were coming too."

And she smiled up at me, bright and happy and so fucking earnest that I wanted to scream. I knew why she was here, so I didn't even have to ask. It was her twenty-first birthday, something I'd heard about all week at work.

From my best friend Cameron.

Who was her *brother*.

I wanted to punch myself in the fucking nuts for ever walking up to this bar. Gritting my teeth, I stared down at her, keeping my facial expression even.

She picked up the mint green shot and knocked it back, licking at her bottom lip when she set the shot glass back down on the bar with a decisive clack. I kept my eyes firmly on hers and nowhere near her mouth or that tiny flash of her tongue.

"Yum. Thank you," she said.

I grunted, backing away from where she stood. "Your brother's back there," I said, tilting my head in the direction of our table.

Poppy picked up the other drink and took a sip from the straw, her big, dark eyes locked on my face in a way that had my heart thudding uncomfortably.

Leave.

Leave now, something screamed in my head. Probably my conscience, currently working overtime trying to get me the fuck out of that mess.

The last person in the entire fucking world I should buy drinks for was Poppy Wilder.

Because she was too young. Too pretty. And too … in love with me.

Had been for years. Every time I walked in the room, from the day she turned fifteen, that girl looked at me like I hung the fucking moon.

I swallowed. Hard. Then gripped the reins of my sanity and let out a deep exhale.

"Happy birthday, Poppy," I told her, giving one last glimpse at the front of her fucking dress that got us into this mess.

Where were her jeans? Her T-shirt and tennis shoes? The ponytail?

The Poppy I knew didn't wear skintight dresses and have sex-messy hair and look like a motherfucking model.

The image of her legs and ass would be burned into my brain for a solid month, and God, there was no escaping the truth of that.

As I walked back to the table, I could feel it. The need to run. The need to clear my head of anything unwanted.

And a lot of unwanted thoughts were running wild at the moment. About perfect tits and long legs. Pink lips and soft tongues. The crack of a whip in my mind had me corralling those baser instincts.

All the things I actively avoided? The forevers and the I love yous and the open-heart search for something lasting. Those were all the things Poppy wanted. Which is why it didn't matter what was under that dress or how good she looked or how she turned my stomach into knots with a single look.

Cameron was typing on his phone when I got back, and he gave me a nod. "My sisters are in the back," he said.

"Yeah, I know," I answered grimly. "Thanks for telling me that's why we came here, by the way."

His eyebrows rose. "You saw them?"

"Just one." I took a long drink of my beer. It was the ominous way I answered that told him exactly which of the sisters I'd seen.

Cameron grinned. "Oh, I bet that made her happy."

I glared, which made the asshole laugh heartily. "It's not funny. I thought she was ... not her. I bought her a drink before I realized it."

His laughter faded immediately. "Poppy?"

I gave him a short nod, my gut churning with unease.

Cameron eyed me, a healthy dose of brotherly protectiveness sparking in his gaze. "Do I need to worry about that?" he asked lightly.

"No." I met his look steadily. "No. I promise. I'll never ... I would *never*."

His expression eased. "I know you wouldn't. Poppy is just ... she's got stars in her eyes, man. She wants the fairy tale. Always has."

There was no need to respond, but I knew that too.

I wasn't in the business of delivering anyone's happily ever after unless their happy ending came in the form of one really great night. I didn't want the fairy tale. I just wanted my freedom.

Cameron knew that too.

"Why don't you go find someone?" I said, voice tense and tight.

Cameron laughed under his breath. "I'm too damn busy to date anyone."

I gave him a look. "I didn't say date."

"I know," he answered easily.

Wilders didn't do casual. It was like embedded in their DNA or something.

I couldn't pinpoint what was embedded into mine. Never really wanted to.

But when I took a drink of my beer, I closed my eyes, and stamped on the back of my eyelids was a blue dress, long hair, chest-tightening smile, and great fucking legs.

No.

No.

I set the beer down, a plan formulating in my head before I had the chance to think it through. "I, uh, think I might get away for a bit," I told him. "I was thinking about heading up to Washington for a couple of weeks."

Cameron nodded. "No problem. Just let me know when you'll be back."

I slapped him on the back, smiling when he winced. "That's why you're the best boss ever," I told him.

Cameron rolled his eyes. "Give me a break. You and I both know you're doing me the favor in this situation."

"True. I am a very benevolent friend."

He snorted. "I'll remember that the next time you piss me off."

"That won't take long," I said.

His sisters arrived at the table in a loud, giggling blur of dark hair and big smiles, dragging Poppy behind them, who was now wearing a twenty-first birthday sash over her blue dress. I kept my facial expression even, noting the pink tinge to her high cheekbones when she glanced over at me.

On second thought, maybe I'd leave for Washington now. Because I should've been out of this bar ten fucking minutes ago. At the moment, it felt like being in the same state as Poppy Wilder was a horrible idea.

"Drunk already, Pops?" Cameron asked his little sister.

She laughed. "Getting there."

Adaline, the middle Wilder sister, slung an arm around

Poppy's shoulders. "She made a list of all the drinks she wants to try. What kind of sisters would we be if we didn't help her?"

Cameron sighed. "Good ones, I'd reckon, depending on the size of the list."

Poppy laughed. "Three checked off already! It's gonna be a good night."

Looking desperate for a subject change, Cameron lifted his chin at the gift bags that Adaline set in the middle of our table. "What did you guys get her?"

Poppy hissed something under her breath. Adaline merely smiled. "Greer got her a vibrator," she proclaimed loudly.

The people at the table next to us swung their gaze in our direction immediately.

Cameron and I froze. He pinched the bridge of his nose while his other sister Greer laughed. Poppy picked up another brightly colored shot from the table and knocked it back. The motion made the length of her hair sweep down her back, and all the blood rushed between my legs as I registered it.

No.

No.

I closed my eyes and took a deep breath. "I'm out of here," I told Cameron under my breath.

"Take me with you?" he begged.

I slapped him on the back again. "Not a chance. You have to stay and babysit."

I said my goodbyes, leaving my unfinished beer on the table, and even though I could feel Poppy's gaze on me as I weaved through the crowds, I ignored the fact that I could breathe just a little bit easier when she wasn't in sight.

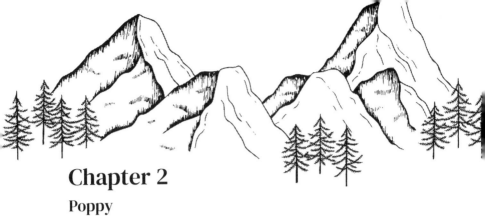

Chapter 2
Poppy

Present day

Some day, in the very distant future, I might blame all of what happened next on my propensity for making decisions through a pros and cons list. It wasn't that the system was flawed. Lists were *good*. I loved making lists on paper. Seeing things in black and white with the ability to cross off what was already done was very helpful. In this case, the list was titled *A confrontation with Jax to be able to move on.*

The list was a solid one too.

Pros:

-Life is short. If I died tomorrow, I refuse to feel regret that I didn't at least try, and regrets are bullshit.

-My mom is out of town, which means there will be no roommate interference. (side note: start a new list re: because I'm twenty-five and my MOM is my roommate)

-Jax isn't expecting me, so the element of surprise is on my side. He won't be able to talk me out of it.

-Seeing him in his home element could negate my feelings for him. Maybe he's messy, and it looks like a frat house. (check for posters of naked women on the walls)

-I've had an out-of-control crush on him since I was fifteen. Zero clarity has been gained in that time. Confrontations gain clarity.

-Clarity will allow me to finally move on.
There was really only one con. And sure, it was a doozy, the sort of crusade-killing truth that would negate all of the above.
Cons:
-Jax will never let me in his home because he refuses to be alone with me. Which means the risk of mortifying embarrassment is high. I would never be able to show my face in front of him again once it's done. If he laughs, I might consider moving away and starting a new life.
If I'd been sober, there was a high possibility that I never would've made the trek.
As it turned out, drunk Poppy had questionable decision-making skills.
Which is how I ended up getting relationship advice from my twice divorced Uber driver while she safely transported me to the home of my longtime crush, who'd never given me a single moment of indication he wanted me. There was one moment, right before she turned onto the road that led to his house, when I tried to read the list again but couldn't see my chicken scratch handwriting. I shrugged, wadding it into a ball and shoving it in my purse.
It would be *fine.*
"You figure out what you're gonna say to him?" Patrice asked. She had frizzy red hair and the raspy voice of someone who smoked *many* cigarettes in her life, but damn if she wasn't good for a drunk pep talk. Fifteen minutes in her car and I felt like I could take over the world.
I nodded, my head still very filled with wine, so all my movements felt slow. "Yeah. Maybe. I think so?"
She laughed. "Just rip your top off and kiss him. That always worked for me."
My laughter came out with the slightest edge of hysteria, but I wasn't sure she heard it. Mainly because the only thing currently filling my head was, how the hell did I get here? List or no list, this was almost undoubtedly certifiable.

It's not necessarily the kind of story that painted me in a good, flattering light, but I couldn't do much about that.

I should probably start with how I ended up drunk in the first place.

There's a special kind of intoxication one wants to achieve at the end of a spectacularly bad date. I hadn't experienced it often, and I was thankful for that, but this bad date? Not enough bottles of wine in the fridge at home.

On a normal night, a couple of glasses was good enough for me. If I really wanted to feel that fuzzy, floaty feeling, I'd go for the harder stuff, but it had been a long time since anything had happened to make me crave that.

Apparently, it took one handsy finance guy with an ego the size of a small planet and a rejection complex. When I politely yanked his hand off my leg, I told him I'd stab him with my steak knife it he tried feeling me up again. Dude wasn't a fan of that.

He left me with a lesson in the creative use of swear words, the expensive bill, as well as a sneaking suspicion that there were no solid relationship prospects for a hundred square miles. I finished my giant glass of wine, then his, before heading home.

I'd met nice men. Kind and funny and sweet. I'd met a few asshole men, like the handsy dude who was fortunate enough to keep his fingers. And I'd met a few others who honestly defied categorization.

Months of going on dates to uproot Jax from my head, and what did I have to show for it?

Abso-fricken-lutely nothing.

The guys were never quite right, and as I yanked the first bottle out of the fridge at home—thank the Lord for a screw top because I was not sober to wrangling a corkscrew—I knew why.

I didn't want to think about why they weren't right or enough or why a date or two never quite progressed past more. The first drink I took was straight from the mouth of the bottle because trying to find a cup felt like a ridiculous waste of time and energy.

The house itself was empty when I arrived—which I was prepared for—and my trusty roommate was gone for the night. As referenced in the list, the roommate was my mother, newly widowed within the past few months. I'd stayed home longer than I ever intended so that I could be there while my dad was sick and then in the aftermath of losing him. It wasn't like I was embarrassed to be in my mid-twenties and still living at home, but I had a sneaking suspicion that it didn't really help my love life either.

I had a good job working for our family's construction company, and between my mom and my sisters, I could legitimately count my family as my best friends. It was a good life.

I should be happy. Happy-ish, at least.

But I wasn't.

I missed my dad, gone only for a few months, and in the wake of that gnawing, empty hole in my chest, I just wanted *something*. But I couldn't, or wouldn't, pinpoint exactly what that was. And being alone tonight wasn't helping.

I was never the impulsive one. At least not with my own life. I had plans. Good plans. Organized, color-coded plans.

And tonight, I was just building to a killer hangover and another disappointing night.

Usually, the empty house didn't bother me. I could crank the music she hated, I could waltz around naked if I wanted to (I didn't because honestly, who *wanted* to walk around naked, but that was beside the point). But tonight, as I plopped on the couch and took another healthy swig of the wine, the quiet pressed in on me like a vise. Like someone invisible turned a giant metal crank and walls closed in, inch by inch by inch, until the air felt thin and my rib cage was tight.

If I closed my eyes, the room might spin just a little bit, but if I breathed beyond that, I knew what I'd see. I'd see the reason that all these dates felt like a giant waste of time, why no one gave me butterflies or goose bumps or fantasies of more.

What a glutton for punishment I was, because closing my eyes is exactly what I did. Sure, there was spinning of the walls, and as soon as it settled, there he was.

Jax Cartwright, the bane of my existence the past ten years and the only man who'd ever made my head go twisty turny in the way that no bottle of wine ever would.

"Fucking Jax," I muttered, taking another swig of wine.

He was everything you'd think of in a man who'd held your attention for a decade of your formative years. Handsome, of course, with all the rippling muscles and big biceps that made me lose a few IQ points. Mysterious and quiet, with the kind of soul-searing dark eyes that always made me lose my breath a little. And no matter how hard he tried to hide it, he was kind underneath it, even if he had the conversational skills of a potato.

And most unfortunately, he was ten years older, the best friend of my brother Cameron, and had never given me a *single* lingering look. Not even a little baby one that could be misconstrued as one. There was no lingering. Ever. Honestly, he kept his distance so thoroughly that sometimes I questioned my own intelligence that I couldn't quite shove him out of my mind.

And why, on nights like this, when I'd threatened violence and got left with a massive bill at the nicest restaurant in the neighboring town of Redmond, I kinda just wanted to get drunk and wish for the day that I'd stop comparing every man to him.

It wasn't fair.

Maybe if he'd been a dick to me, it would be easier. But he wasn't.

Angrily, I took another drink. A big one, too. More wine was definitely the answer to this problem.

But problems had solutions, right?

Tapping my fingers on the glass bottle, I tried to think of what that solution might be. There had to be a way to purge one stupid man from my head. I wasn't silly enough to think I was truly in love with him after all these years of nothing from him, but I couldn't quite rip the hold he had on my head away either.

What better way to do that than just confront him. The racing of my heart was the first indication I was on the right track because I was not the confrontational Wilder in the family. I was the cheerful youngest sister; I was the optimist. The one who listened and encouraged. But never once had I stood face-to-face with Jax and asked him *why*. Or why not, I guess.

Why not me?

He wasn't married. Wasn't in a relationship. Hell, he'd never been in a serious relationship.

I was nice. People liked me. And I was attractive, in that girl next door kinda way. No, men didn't usually trip over themselves when I walked into the room, but son of a bitch, I was a fucking *catch*. And I wasn't a kid anymore.

Before I could talk myself out of it, I was off the couch, slamming back another drink of wine and yanking out my phone to pull up the rideshare app. With vicious taps of my thumbs, the address was in, and I submitted my request with the smug-ass grin of a drunk girl who was feeling a little too feisty for her own good after putting planet-ego man in his place.

And to my luck, Patrice was the one driving.

"Where're we headed tonight, honey?"

I toppled into the back seat and yanked the door shut when a gust of wind lifted my floaty skirt up. "Jax fucking Cartwright's house," I said. Her eyebrows popped up, but she didn't say anything, verifying the address I'd entered into the app. "He doesn't know I'm coming, so I'm sure he'll be thrilled. He's ignored me for *ages*," I said, only the teeny tiniest slur to my voice.

"Ignored a pretty girl like you?" She clucked her tongue. "He married?"

"He's painfully and perpetually single, which almost makes it worse. He won't even sleep with women from town so he doesn't risk seeing them again."

Patrice whistled. "I had a husband like that once. It's kinda fun to be the one to have them coming back for more."

"I don't have Jax coming back for anything. First or seconds." Slumping in the back seat of the car, I fiddled with the hem of my skirt. "And I just don't understand why. I've never straight out asked him to go out with me, and the only thing I can think of is that he's afraid of my brother."

"You got a protective one?" she asked.

I blew out a short laugh. "I have four brothers who are varying degrees of protective and two sisters. One of those sisters is the most terrifying of all my siblings, and they'd all admit it too. But yes, Jax is my brother Cameron's best friend." My tone turned glum. "They're older than me by, like, ten years. I think that's why he always blew me off. But how can I *know* if I don't ask him, right?"

"Ten years ain't nothing," Patrice said with an encouraging smile. "My second husband was twenty years older than me."

"Twenty?" I whistled. "Damn, Patrice."

She chuckled, a low, throaty sound. "He croaked after a few years, and I got a nice little house out of the deal. He wasn't so bad. Not my favorite, though." Her eyes glinted in the dark interior of the car. "Husband three is my favorite. He's the best in bed and always lets me do whatever I want."

My cheeks heated.

"You know there's an ice storm rolling into tonight, yeah?"

she asked, eyeing me warily through the rearview mirror. Rain started hitting the windshield in big, fat strikes. Suddenly, the sight of them looked very ominous.

It was a very good thing I wasn't sober, because man, this shit might make me turn back around.

"Huh," I said, only the slightest wobble to my voice. "Is there?"

She hummed. "Be a damn shame if you got stuck out there in the woods with your mystery man, wouldn't it?"

Nerves erupted in my already roiling stomach, and I pressed a shaky hand there. "You think I will?"

"No doubt," she said easily. "No one should be driving on these roads when it gets icy like this. Will your family be looking for you tonight, honey?"

"No," I said on a sigh. "My mom is visiting my sister in Salem. No one else will check on me until tomorrow afternoon."

"Hot damn, you can do a lot in a twenty-four hours."

I covered my face with a groan. "Oh my gosh, you're going to make me chicken out."

"You got good underwear on?" she asked.

Slowly, I pried my fingers apart and caught her eye in the mirror, giving her a slight nod.

Patrice hooted. "Good girl. Always gotta be prepared."

"I'm not going out here to get *laid*, Patrice. I just want to talk to him while I have the courage. My brother is always around when I see him, and…" My shoulders slumped, the weight of feeling stuck hitting me from a dozen directions. "I'm sick of doing nothing," I whispered. "I want to do *something*. I want to know for sure, so that I can move on from him."

As she took the final turn toward his house, she asked if I knew what I was going to say, and the answer to that, no matter what came out of my mouth, was an unequivocal no. Hell, just the sight of his house had my legs trembling a little.

I knew where he lived, but I'd never been inside. It was a small white house tucked back in the trees, hidden from the road. Because he was farther out from town, the houses were spread apart, so he had total privacy, and even though the sky was dark and the rain pelted the car with increased intensity, it was still a beautiful drive. In the daytime, at least.

The headlights from Patrice's car sliced along the front of his house—white siding with wooden shutters, and underneath the carport was the black and chrome motorcycle he loved. A zap of nerves had my tummy rolling again, and I let out a deep breath when Patrice told me to just take off my top and kiss him.

It wasn't worth arguing with her anymore because she had her heart set on naked shenanigans, but that was about as likely as getting struck by lightning as I walked to his door. Patrice gave me a thumbs-up. "Good luck, kid. You look hot."

Quietly, I exhaled a laugh and nodded. "Thanks. I promise I'll give you a good tip for bringing me out here in this weather."

She winked. "Don't you worry about that, honey. Husband number three waits for me at home, and he'll take good care of me."

I smiled, then tugged my purse over my head to shield me from the freezing rain as I huddled under his front porch. My entire body trembled from nerves and cold because my drunk ass didn't even think about grabbing a coat. I hadn't knocked yet. Maybe I could still head home, and he'd be none the wiser.

For a moment, I pinched my eyes shut, running through a quick list.

Pros:

He never knows, thereby I don't have to move away in embarrassment.

Cons:

I'll know. And … something with regrets. No regrets, right? Yeah.

26

That was it. And not dying without asking his grumpy ass why he always ignores me.

But it was so *cold*. And my shirt was wet. And I started shivering just long enough that the first one on the list won out. Avoiding mortification was a hell of a motivator, as it turned out. With a raised hand, I turned to flag down Patrice, but she was already turning the car out of the driveway.

"Dammit," I whispered. I wrapped my arms around my middle in a pathetic attempt to stay warm, then blew out a slow breath. "Being impulsive is bullshit," I hissed. "Why do people like this?"

Before I could get up my nerve to pound on the front door, it was yanked open.

The wine wasn't enough.

Not a dozen more bottles.

No list in the world could prepare me for this moment.

Because framed in the light of the doorway—a white T-shirt stretched over his broad chest, towering above me with his dark brows furrowed in confusion and his dark eyes locked on mine like he couldn't believe what he was seeing—was Jax Cartwright.

His gaze tracked down the front of my rain-soaked body, and somehow, impossibly, his glare intensified.

I lifted my hand in a pathetic little wave. "Hi."

"What the fuck are you doing here, Poppy?"

Chapter 3

Jax

In the back of my mind, the place where I shoved down all the things that I refused to think about, I think I knew this would happen eventually.

There was no way it wouldn't happen.

It would've been too easy for me to just wait it out. Let her find someone else. No, because not a single person in that fucking Wilder family could let something go easily when they believed in it strongly enough. Poppy Wilder—though she came off as sweet and kind and innocent, everything I should avoid—was so fucking stubborn because you *had* to be the worst kind of stubborn not to let go of whatever her misplaced feelings were for me.

And a stubborn woman, a sweet and kind and innocent one, with big brown eyes and long eyelashes and a smile that lit up every fucking room she walked into, was the most dangerous thing in the world. Letting her walk into my house while it was dark and stormy and I'd been drinking, with a shirt damp from the rain and a skirt swishing around her thighs, was an awful lot like setting a grenade on the floor and hoping it didn't blow the whole damn place down.

My hands tightened on the frame of the door as I stared

her down. Her chin edged up, and that slight show of challenge had my lungs tightening.

Don't do this, I begged silently. *Don't put me in this position.* If I closed my eyes, I could only imagine what her *six* older siblings would plan to do with my body.

We stood there for an impossibly long moment that could've been seconds, could've been minutes. I wasn't even fucking sure. She slowly dug her teeth into that lush bottom lip before speaking.

"Can I come in?" she asked.

The rain was coming down sideways now, and the ominous, clanking sound of water turning to sleet as it hit the side of my house intensified my glare.

"I don't know if that's a good idea. I've had a few drinks," I admitted.

She smiled—the bright, sunny smile that did things to me, and I had to tear my eyes away. "Perfect, me too."

Then Poppy ducked underneath my arm, leaving a warm breeze of a sweet, clean scent that had me slamming the door shut. The walls trembled, and she was, naturally, completely unfazed.

Hands clasped behind her back, Poppy studied the main living space of my house. I found myself watching her reactions as her eyes tracked over the wood burning stove in the corner, the oversized couch and chair, the wood beams that ran across the ceiling, and the L-shaped kitchen where I usually ate takeout or something simple.

I'd never needed much. It was a place to lay my head and had a pretty view while I drank my coffee. The preserve behind my house reminded me of the meadow behind Henry's yard.

But beyond the flowers and the meadow and the space, I was able to be alone out here, just the way I liked it.

Never, not once, had a woman wandered this space.

For it to be *this* one, I had to clench my teeth and prepare for whatever the hell she had planned by showing up here.

"It's nice," she said finally. She gave me a wry grin over her shoulder, a tiny dimple appearing in her cheek. "I can't really see you in it anywhere, though."

All she got in response to that was a low grunt of concession.

I tore my eyes away from that dimple, the whiskey in my veins making my head swim dangerously. Why, *why* did I think I could have a quiet weekend at home and enjoy a few drinks while I listened to the rain?

Poppy swayed slightly on her feet, and I resisted the urge to reach out to steady her. I kept my arms crossed over my chest, my eyes locked on the wall just past her when she started twisting all that dark, long hair into a knot at the top of her head.

It fell in a wavy curtain around her shoulders when she let it go, and with a sigh, she sat on the couch, crossing one leg over the other as she met my gaze head-on. If I looked, I'd see the slight flex of muscles in her upper thigh, so I didn't look because I didn't *want* to look.

"What do you want, Poppy?" I asked. God, why did my voice sound like I'd chewed glass? "Did something happen?"

She licked her lips and took a deep breath, her chest rising and falling along with that small bit of fortification. "I had a bad date tonight," she said, her eyes big and wide and soft. "I've had a lot of bad dates recently, but this one might have been the worst."

Don't ask.

Do not ask, you asshole.

"Why was it bad?" The words crawled out of my mouth without permission from my stupid brain. This was the problem with whiskey. I'd never touch it again after tonight. I'd never be *alone* with her after tonight, if I could help it.

She sank back into the cushions but kept her slightly

unfocused gaze very focused on me. "He tried to feel me up under the table, and when I told him I'd stab him with a steak knife if he tried that again, he left me with a huge bill."

Whenever I was around her, safely buffered by her family, there was always a low hiss of a lit fuse in the back of my head.

I ignored that too.

Sometimes, especially moments like this, it was like someone dumped gasoline right on top of that fucker and my insides lit up in flames. My jaw twitched slightly before I unlocked the tension holding my teeth clenched together. "Name?"

All she did was smile. That was soft too. "I'm not telling you anything." Then she leaned forward, the neckline of her shirt gapping so that the lush swells of her breasts pressed together. My throat went dry, and I kept my eyes right on hers, not dropping so much as a fucking inch. "You have no reason to want to know anything about my dates, right?" she asked lightly. "No reason at all."

This was punishment. I wasn't sure *why* I was being punished, but someone sitting up in some big, fluffy fucking cloud was undoubtedly laughing their ass off at my predicament.

Having her in my space, looking like that, smelling like that, I felt that screaming impulse again. It was always there, like a burner set so low that you can hardly tell if it was on. And the moment, the precise moment that my awareness of Poppy clicked into place, some giant, invisible hand turned the lever and the flames shot sky high.

Get out.

You need space to let this pass.

Go somewhere else. Anywhere else.

It's all I ever wanted to do when my notice of her got to a level that was hard to ignore.

Her gaze was this glowing, otherworldly kind of thing. "I made a list," she said.

I blinked. "For what?"

"Why I should come out here and talk to you."

I scrubbed a hand over the lower part of my mouth. "You need to keep that list to yourself, Poppy."

The line of her throat moved on a hard swallow. "I don't know if I should, though."

No.

No.

Whatever tension pulled tight across the room, binding this strange little moment together, I snapped it when I strode toward the door. "You need to go. I'm leaving on a trip soon," I said, not even thinking about the words as they tumbled out of my mouth, "and I don't have time for this."

She tilted her head. "When is your trip?"

My eye twitched. The trip didn't exist yet, and boy, she didn't need to know that. "Soon. Call your Uber back."

"Patrice can't come back to get me," she said on a sigh. She didn't sound all that upset, and I pinched my eyes shut while my composure tried to claw itself back into place. Fuck, what I wouldn't give for some magical pill that would make me sober. Poppy kept talking. "Plus, she said there was an ice storm coming in. I don't think anyone will venture out tonight."

No shit.

The rain pelting the side of the house had gotten louder, and when I marched to the kitchen window and looked out, it was already starting to form a silvery film on the glass, sticking ominously. Ice was the quickest way to shut anything down, even in places equipped to handle winter weather.

And I, at the moment, was not.

My work truck was at the shop, and even if I was sober, there was no way I could drive her back home on my bike in this kind of weather. The grip of my hands on the edge of the counter was so tight, I was surprised I didn't grind it to dust.

"You plan it that way, angel?" I asked dangerously. Her eyes widened at the nickname, unconsciously spoken.

Fuck me, *why* did I go and say that? I held my breath while I waited for her to ask, to press, to push. And she didn't.

"Nope." She stood and joined me at the kitchen counter. Her bare shoulders brushed mine as she stared out at the storm, and my jaw tightened dangerously. "Admittedly, this whole thing wasn't very well thought out, but no one will be looking for me tonight if that's what you're worried about."

My early demise at the hand of her brother—my best friend—was what I was worried about.

A harsh laugh escaped my mouth. "You shouldn't be here, Poppy. This is a very, very bad idea."

With a too-innocent tilt to her head, she glanced up at me. "Why? We're friends, aren't we? Of a sort. And if we're friends, why is it a very, very bad idea for me to be here?"

Why the fuck did she smell so good? She was so small. If she stood in front of me, I'd be able to notch her right under my chin. I thought that once before, too. A long time ago. I hated that I was thinking it again.

"No, we're not," I answered curtly. "You're Cameron's little sister, and that is it."

"Does this mean you won't answer my questions?" she asked.

Slowly, I turned, hitching my hip against the counter while I stared down at her.

Okay, so we were doing this. After years of knowing she was watching me. Years of very much *not* watching her, we were going to nip this shit in the bud. Unease curdled in my belly, mixing dangerously with the whiskey.

"So you like lists, huh?"

Her cheeks flushed pink, but she didn't look away. "Yes.

Th-they help me think more clearly. Sometimes I can't..."
Her fingers wiggled by the side of her head. "I can't calm my
thoughts long enough to make sense of what I need to do."

"Sounds logical," I told her. "Maybe I should try it
sometime."

Her brows furrowed.

"Like now, maybe," I said smoothly. "I'll give you a list of
why this is a bad idea." I started ticking off points on my
fingers, voice calm and steady. At first. "You're too young for
me. I don't want a girlfriend. I don't want to get married. I
don't want a family. And you are too fucking young for me," I
finished on a yell. "You know all those things, yet you're still
here."

By the time I finished, I was breathing hard, well aware
that I was answering questions that she hadn't yet asked.
Every fucking time I was around Poppy, for years, the
questions were stamped all over her face, buried deep in her
eyes.

Why not me?

She'd been on the sidelines at bars when I found someone
to go home with, the same kind of women I'd indulged in
throughout the years. The kind who weren't looking for
anything serious, the kind I'd likely never see again. It was a
Band-Aid, of sorts, to staunch the flow of blood temporarily.
To drown out whatever creeping sense of loneliness hit me in
the middle of the night, the kind that snuck up on me in my
sleep and had me rolling over in bed, searching for someone
warm and sweet, only to find a cold fucking bed.

Why not me?

God, I'd seen in it in her face for years. As soon as she
turned twenty, really. Five years later, and her questions still
lingered. I could see them linger right in front of me now, in
the painfully small confines of my house.

It didn't matter that she'd never said them out loud.
Sometimes it felt like she was screaming them for how

painfully the weight of those questions fell on my shoulders. We both damn well knew why she was out here, and part of me wished I could yank open the door and send her out in the rain without caring what happened to her.

I did, though.

No matter how stupid it was, no matter how long the list grew for all the reasons I was terrible for her, because every damn thing I said to her was true, no matter how much I locked it up in the back of my head and tried to ignore it, I cared far too much.

As my list of reasons hung in the air between us, Poppy's pink cheeks flushed deeper, a sign of embarrassment maybe. But there was no argument, not like I'd expected.

I thought maybe she'd point out that the ten years between us wasn't such a big deal, not now that she was in her mid-twenties. She wasn't a teenager. She was a woman—a beautiful one, maybe even more beautiful than she even realized. But I felt each one of those years like a blow to my chest because mine were steeped in building a quiet life by myself, a staunch refusal to budge even a single inch to allow someone space.

Even someone like her.

It was so much easier that way.

Eventually, the silence stretched into something uncomfortable the longer we stood there. Never the one to fill silences with pointless words, I simply stared down at her and kept my face even. The graceful arch of her brows dipped into a thoughtful V, and I found myself fighting the urge to fidget under the astute gaze of Poppy Wilder.

Before tonight, I could always feel the weight of her eyes on me, but this was different. There was no hiding from her, no distraction to tug between us. It was simply me and her and an endless stretch of hours while we waited for the storm to pass.

Who was I kidding? Poppy was the storm I needed to wait

out. Eventually, she'd figure out that I wasn't the guy for her. That she needed someone good and kind just like herself.

The clouds would clear, and she'd go back home and realize what a mistake this was. What a mistake I was.

Everyone regretted me, eventually. Except Henry. There was only one other woman in my life before Poppy, the one who taught me exactly what I didn't want out of life, and she thought I was a mistake too. Something to move on from in search of a better, easier life.

Poppy's sigh was deep and dramatic, and to my utter shock, her pink lips edged up in a crooked, amused smile. "Well, I guess that settles it then," she said breezily, waltzing past me to start pulling open cabinets, letting out a noise of satisfaction when she found the whiskey and a few other bottles. "Nothing left to do but play a drinking game with a sort-of friend who's too old and grumpy for me, and then pass out so that I can allow my hangover tomorrow to be punishment for my stupid idea."

I blinked.

"What?"

She fluttered her lashes as she passed. "Catch up, Jax. We're drinking to moving on from old crushes. Right? You're too old, too grumpy, too stubborn, etcetera, etcetera."

My head reared back. "I never said I was too stubborn."

Poppy snorted. "Those words may not have come out of your mouth, but believe me, you did."

Absently, I rubbed at my chest because fuck, was it bad that I was praying this was all a drunk hallucination? "I don't have an old crush. What am I drinking to?"

She sat down at my kitchen table and opened the bottle of whiskey, pouring us both a generous serving into two glasses. Then she knocked one back, shuddering as she coughed. She waved her hands in front of her face as her eyes watered, hunching over to curse through the burn in her throat.

"Oh, that's terrible," she gasped.

I tried to lock down my smile at the pinched look on her face, managing it just as she was able to pry her eyes open as the coughing settled down.

Hooking one of the chairs out from the table, I turned it around and sat down backward. "Where do you think you're passing out, exactly?"

She waved her hand somewhere in the vicinity of the back of the house. "Guest bedroom."

I snagged the glass meant for me and took a leisurely sip, enjoying the heat as it went down. "Don't have one of those. Unless you plan on sleeping on my weight bench."

"Oh." She blinked. "Well, I guess we'll figure that out before it's bedtime, huh?"

Bedtime.

Bedtime in my home with Poppy underneath my roof.

It would take the authorities *ten years* to find all the pieces of my body.

I grunted. It was the only possible sound I was capable of.

Poppy set her chin in her hands, and even with the clear glaze of alcohol in her eyes, she studied my face leisurely like she had all the time in the world. The warmth of that hit my bloodstream like another shot, which is why I set the glass back down.

"Not agreeing to any games just yet," I said as steadily as I could manage. "You eat dinner?"

Slowly, she shook her head. "Didn't have much appetite on my shitty date."

I took one more sip of the whiskey, stood and opened the fridge, frowning when I saw the meager options on the empty shelves. "I have some leftover pizza. A couple of eggs. And cereal."

She laughed. God, what a sound it was. Light and delicate, another punch to my already swimming senses, and I shook my head slightly to try to shake that off.

"Surprise me," she said.

Forever Starts Tonight

I took a deep breath, steeling myself for the fact that she was here, she was *staying* here, and I was about to face the greatest threat to my sanity I'd ever experienced: an entire night alone with Poppy Wilder.

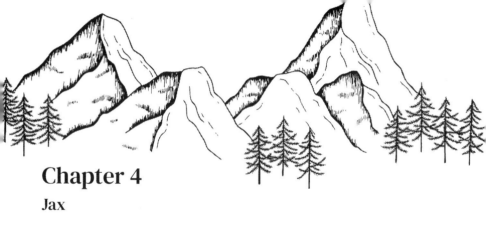

Chapter 4
Jax

"This isn't exactly what I had in mind when I suggested a drinking game." Poppy's eyebrows had a challenging arch to them.

I took a minuscule sip of my drink, gesturing to the game board. "We're drinking. It's a game."

"It's *checkers*," she said, enunciating her words as clearly as someone drunk could. "How is this the only game you have at your house?"

It was the only game Henry liked to play, and the hours we spent staring at each other over that checkers board were some of my best memories. Sharing that, anything, with her was firmly on the list of *Lines Not To Be Crossed with Poppy*.

Instead of answering, I merely held her gaze. "You wanna play or not?"

She let out a dramatic sigh that had my lips fighting the urge to smile. "Fine."

With her chin resting in her hand, Poppy tucked one leg up against her chest and studied the board with slightly unfocused brown eyes. Her hair dried slightly curly after getting wet in the rain, and she had a blanket wrapped around her shoulders.

The rain pelted the windows outside, and her attention kept bouncing between the board and the storm.

"What is it?" I asked begrudgingly.

The line of Poppy's throat moved on a visible swallow. "You won't, like, lose power or anything, will you?"

"I have a generator if that happens." I moved one of the black pieces, waiting for Poppy to take her turn, but she was still staring at the front of the house. Inexplicably, she smiled.

"What's that look for?"

She shook her head, snapping herself out of whatever memory she'd been wading through. "I hate storms," she murmured. "Always have. When I was little, I used to be afraid of the trees all around our house. That they'd fall and crush my bedroom ceiling while I was sleeping." Gingerly, she moved her red piece, sitting back in her chair when she finished. "I woke up one night, terrified to stay in my room, and my dad heard me crying. He was still up watching TV. Came into my room and when he saw how upset I was, he let me get out of bed and come downstairs for some ice cream. As I got older, we just kept doing it. Every time it stormed, I'd stay up late with him. He'd put on a movie and we'd eat ice cream straight from the carton."

Throat tight, I tapped my thumb along the edge of the board. "You still scared of storms?"

Her eyes locked on mine. "Not when I'm not alone, no. But if you had ice cream, I wouldn't turn it down," she said wryly.

"You'd have to call your Uber back if you want to get some of that," I told her.

Poppy didn't answer, content to watch my next move carefully.

We played silently for a few minutes, moving our pieces around the board. It wasn't uncomfortable silence either, much to my surprise.

In all the years I'd known her, since she was a fifth-grade

toothpick with braces, this was the most time I'd ever spent alone with her. The conversation over reheated pizza was easier than I thought it would be. We talked about work—the place we crossed paths the most. Her brother was also my boss, even though I had more freedom than most of the people who worked for Wilder Homes. If she questioned that, I'd never heard about it.

Poppy managed the office, and as the family construction business was on the cusp of expanding into a physical store, that would be her domain as well. We talked about her brothers—or she did most of the talking, I did most of the listening—and more than once, just like now as she moved one of her pieces, I caught myself staring.

"What?" she asked. Her eyes flicked up to mine. "Something on my face?"

How honest did I want to be? The whiskey loosened my tongue, that was for sure, and I chose my words carefully.

"I've avoided being alone with you for years," I said gruffly. "Everyone in your family is so damn stubborn, I shouldn't be surprised you pulled this off."

She smirked. "I noticed. Did you think I'd tie you up on the bed and never let you leave?"

I gave her a long look. *No one* would ever be tying me up anywhere, no matter what their smile did to my insides. That would also go unsaid, locked up in a dark, dark place never to see the light of day.

A slight eye roll was all I allowed in reaction, but she grinned all the same. "No," I responded patiently. "It just didn't seem ... prudent."

Everyone in Poppy's family knew about her crush on me. And there was a strange sort of relief when she decided she was going to start dating. It lessened a pressure banded around my chest that I'd never wanted to dig into. It was also, not so coincidentally, the longest stretch I'd gone without any last-minute trips in the past five years.

If she'd ever put that one together, I'd give her a fucking medal.

"Tell me about the worst date you've ever been on."

I took a slow, slow sip of my drink because the addition of alcohol to this evening was … unwise. If it took me an hour to drink this one, all the better. The truth was, it didn't really matter how slow I drank, because already, the pressure of having her there morphed from *something that might get me murdered* to *maybe this wasn't so bad*.

That's how I knew I was fucking buzzed.

Poppy had laughed, more than once, at something I said. I wasn't funny, had never been funny. And maybe it was a testament to her blood alcohol level that she found me as amusing as she did, but no matter where it came from, it was … pleasant. Enjoyable.

Inside, at least.

Outside though, the storm raged, ice coated the windows and the howling gusts of wind elicited creaks and groans from the house. It was a ruthless type of storm, the mere sound of it had me feeling cold, so I'd lit a fire while Poppy toed off her shoes and tugged a blanket off the couch.

By silent agreement, we'd ended up at the table. Sitting on the couch, for me at least, felt too informal. Too comfortable. And nothing about this was comfortable.

"I don't go on dates," I admitted, holding her gaze unflinchingly as I answered. "Which you know."

She conceded that with a soft hum. "I guess I'm curious then," she said. "They're not dates. But you have drinks with them. Or meet in the grocery store and then have drinks. Or you just … meet someone and decide, 'this is the person I want to have sex with tonight'?"

"Poppy," I ground out. "This is not a conversation I will have with you."

"Why not? Maybe I'm curious about your approach. I'm a

42

grown woman who lost possession of her hymen *years* ago, and—"

My tortured groan, the kind dragged from the pits of my black soul, cut her off. "Holy shit, do not talk to me about your hymen."

The second thought was nipping quick at the heels of what I'd just said; Who did you have sex with for the first time? I'd bite my fucking tongue off before I asked *that*.

Poppy continued as if I hadn't said a word. "I could totally be a one-night person, I think."

All manner of dark thoughts clouded my head, and I pressed the heels of my hands into my eye sockets.

"This has to be a nightmare," I muttered under my breath. "It's the only explanation. I got drunk, passed out, and I'm having a nightmare right now."

"I am very real, I assure you."

My hands dropped, and I pinned her with a heated glare. "I'm fucking aware."

Poppy's cheeks flushed a soft-pink color, and this time, she looked away. Her questions signaled a clear and obvious shift. One I wasn't sure I'd ever be ready for. It was the shift I'd avoided for years, when she grew from a gawky teenager with stars in her eyes to an undeniably beautiful woman who, under any other circumstance, would be exactly my type.

Keeping the truth of that was the thing I never really even admitted to myself. It was tucked so far back in the recesses of my mind. I didn't think about it when I saw her at work, I didn't think about it if we were with a group having drinks at the bar, and I certainly wasn't sitting at home pining.

But across the relatively small stretch of my kitchen table, with a weakened verbal filter and a violent storm outside that felt like an omen, I decided it didn't really matter if I admitted it to myself. The risk of any dangerous truth came with action, and there'd be none of that. Not if I could help it.

But while she sat there and tried to decide whether she

wanted to push this topic with me, her graceful fingers toying with the glass in front of her, the desire to indulge that whisper of a thought was there before I could stop it.

It was like pulling on the end of a thread, batting it around until more of it could be seen. The thought grew and grew, clouding my head until the fog cleared, and all that was left was an admission I couldn't deny. If I imagined myself sitting across from Poppy at a bar, I'd want her.

I'd want to go home with her for a night, and it wouldn't have taken me long to admit it either.

Once admitted, the truth had a cunning way of clouding my head with images of how that would play out.

With a slight tilt of my head, I studied the height of her cheekbones, the straight line of her delicate jaw, the arch of her dark eyebrows, and the impossible length of her eyelashes. When she smiled, it was like a spotlight on her lips—pink and soft-looking.

And this was just her face.

Anything below her neck had me shifting in my seat with an immediate hardening in my pants because my eyes traveled lower. And lower.

Oh yes. I'd want her. And I might not even be able to wait until we found a bed. In the back corner of a dimly lit bar, if the chemistry bubbled up between us anything like it was right now, I'd tug her into a hallway, the back of the parking lot, push her into the back bench of my truck, lift her skirts and find all the ways to make her scream my name.

I'd never had a type when it came to the shape of a woman's body. I loved curves, and I loved sleek, toned bodies. Whatever Poppy was, it fucking worked. Slender through her waist and hips, trim legs and toned arms, and the slope of her cleavage had my mouth going dry. A luscious, tempting mouthful. They were high and firm, and if someone stuck a gun to my head, I'd bet every single red penny to my name that they were tipped with a soft-pink nipple that tasted like fucking candy.

She cleared her throat, and I blinked sluggishly. My brain tripped over the uncivilized fantasies, and I took another sip of the whiskey to yank myself free of them.

"I'm still going to call them dates," she said primly, and based on the heated look in her eyes, she saw exactly where I'd been staring. "And I'm sure you still have stories, even if you don't feel like telling them."

What the fuck was wrong with me?

I had a hard-on that could be seen from space, and saliva pooled under my tongue from the thought of my mouth on Poppy Wilder's tits and my hand under her skirt.

With a clench of my jaw, I tipped the remainder of my whiskey back and swallowed it, even though it burned like hell, and I was the biggest fucking idiot in existence.

Slamming the glass down, I pinned her with a hard look. "You know exactly why I shouldn't be telling them," I snapped, an unmistakable roughness to my voice that she should've heeded as a warning.

It was supposed to intimidate her.

She was supposed to back off. But no. She'd been raised in a family that taught her differently, and those fucking Wilders were all so fucking stubborn, she met that hard look with an undaunted, slow arching of her brow, and fuck if that didn't get me even harder.

Poppy tipped her head back, finishing off her drink in a far more graceful fashion than I managed, and the glass settled back on the table with a delicate clink.

"All this time, I thought you avoided me because you were uncomfortable with my attention. Because I was an annoying kid in your eyes. Or you were being respectful of my brother." She slowly stood from her chair. The lithe movements of her body as she shrugged off the blanket had my hands tightening into helpless fists on my lap. Then she braced her palms on the table and pinned me with a stare so direct, so open in what she wanted from that it sucked every fucking ounce of air from my lungs. "But you are terrified of me, aren't you, Jax?"

If I moved my eyes even a single inch, I'd be able to see straight down her shirt. I'd be able to see the color of her bra, so I kept every growling instinct focused on keeping my gaze right on hers.

"I'm not scared of anything, Poppy," I said as evenly as possible. "Least of all you."

Her eyes narrowed slightly, not in anger or distrust, but like she was weighing the truth of my words and found me coming up short.

I was too drunk for this.

My head was swimming dangerously, and I needed her away from me. Now.

Pushing my chair back from the table had her straightening to her full height, still so much smaller than me. But damn if she didn't raise her chin in a dare.

"Should we switch to truth or dare?" she asked lightly.

That didn't deserve an answer. Crossing my arms over my chest, I prayed to whatever deity who would listen that my hard-on wasn't too visible. Thank God I was still wearing jeans from my workday. If I'd switched to my normal gray sweatpants, I'd be in trouble.

"I think it's time for bed, Poppy," I growled.

A mischievous smile hovered at the edges of her lips, her eyes glittering in the dim light of my kitchen. Why didn't I have every fucking light on in the house? Why did I start a fire?

What an idiot I was.

None of this was harmless, no matter what her plans were when she showed up shivering at my front door.

I jabbed a finger in the air. "Don't you smile at me like that. This isn't funny."

"It's a little funny," she said airily. "In a million years, I never thought I'd have Jax Cartwright running scared."

Was my eye twitching? It had to be because the tension in my face felt like my cheekbones would shatter, like my molars would be ground to dust.

"I'll get you a blanket and a pillow for the couch," I ground out.

"I need something to sleep in too," she added casually. My eyes slammed shut, the mental image of Poppy wearing one of my T-shirts had me swallowing down a groan.

"Fine."

As I yanked a blanket out of a basket in the family room, she took a few steps closer. "If we'd played truth or dare, you know what I would've chosen?"

"Nope, and I don't care," I snapped.

"Truth, first, because I know you well enough that you'd never dare me to do anything," she continued as if I hadn't morphed into some grunting entity incapable of pleasantries. "Eventually, I would've dared you to kiss me. Just once. Just so I know what it's like. So you do too."

Slowly, so slowly, with the blanket clutched in my hand, I turned to face her, my brows high. "You must be drunk off your ass if you think I'd do it."

The words were harsh in my head, something I yelled so loudly that my voice filled every corner of the room. But in reality, in that dark, fire-lit room, they came out differently. There was a distinctly uncertain edge to what I said, and my voice was choked, squeezed tight from the images bombarding my whiskey-addled brain.

Poppy didn't respond, merely stood there with a patient, understanding look in her eye, just barely masking the banked heat in her chocolate-brown depths.

This night had turned us both into entirely different versions of ourselves. This confident, sexy version of Poppy was my nightmare, and I couldn't even pretend to be polite anymore, the fear of her effect on me filing down any civility I had left.

I leaned closer, my voice rough and low and just on the edge of cruel. "What makes you think I kiss any of the women I fuck, Poppy?"

Her throat moved in a delicate swallow, and she blinked a few times. "You don't?"

"Don't need to," I told her. "No one's complaining, trust me."

She sucked in a slow breath. "Too intimate for you, I'm guessing."

Kisses created feelings. A false sense of what was possible and what they expected. It was easier, years earlier, to make that distinction in my head.

"Something like that."

Poppy tilted her head. "And what if you fall in love someday?"

I sucked in a short breath through my nose. "Okay, fine, in the catastrophic event that pigs are flying and hell freezes the fuck over, then sure, I'd kiss that person. But I won't ever do that, so it's a moot point."

The pink of her tongue flashed when she licked her lips, something quick and fast, and I wasn't sure she did it consciously. All the blood rushed south ... immediately.

"But sex is ... safe?" she said quietly. "You can fuck them and move on, and there's no attachment because you didn't do this one, little thing."

Poppy saying *fuck* did strange things to my insides, the tightening of a screw and the lifting of the hairs on the back of my neck.

I made a small noise of concession, probably because I didn't dare speak for fear of what might come out. The room already felt like it was on fire with this change of subject. My brain defiantly conjured a host of vivid images, and no matter what I did, I couldn't stop them.

What would happen if...
What if. What if. *What if.*

If my hand snaked around the back of her graceful neck, fingers digging into the mass of her dark hair, and I licked into that soft-pink mouth to see how she tasted and what she'd do. If her body would arch into mine and if she'd moan helplessly while she wrapped her arms around my shoulders and pressed up on tiptoe to get closer.

I could wreck her with a single kiss. Drag us both into some fiery pit where the only way out was through naked, writhing skin and the kind of release that split the world open.

Fuck.

Fuck.

We held like that for an impossibly long moment, her chest heaving as she breathed deeply, an anxious tell that she was just as stunned by what she'd said as I was.

Her eyes searched my face, a desperately confused sort of wrinkling in her brow.

Did she know? Could she guess what I was imagining? That I could immediately recognize how good it would be, and that I wanted it so badly that my hands shook from the restraint needed not to touch her?

"What if I was a one-night person?" she whispered. In the dark room, firelight danced off the graceful features of her face. "What if that's all I wanted from you, and I promised we could walk away tomorrow unscathed?" Underneath the cage of my ribs, my heart thundered wildly. The hesitation was damning, and she knew it as she took a small step closer, eyes glowing, her tongue darting out to wet her lips. "I want you out of my head, Jax."

Again, my eyes pinched shut, and fuck, my throat dried out so thoroughly that I couldn't force a denial. The words were anchored heavy in my stomach, and I couldn't push them up and out.

Then, then, a whisper-soft brush of her fingers over my forearm had my eyes snapping open.

Why was she so close to me? The sweet scent of her had my head swimming, and I sucked in a slow breath, desperately yanking on every shred of discipline buried deep under my skin.

"One night," she said again. "I think you want it too. But if you tell me you don't want me, I'll never speak of it again."

Why couldn't I lie to her?

They were just words—easy to speak out loud. *It didn't matter whether they were true or not*, I told myself.

I don't want you.

I don't *want you.*

Say it, I screamed in my head. *Say it.*

But I could imagine the pain flashing in her eyes, and I'd sooner pluck my skin off than cause her any more hurt than I already had over the years with my forced indifference. I shoved the blanket in her hands.

"Good night, Poppy."

She sucked in a quick breath, clutching the blanket to her chest.

"Bathroom is across from my room if you need to use it. I'll set a shirt on the counter for you." Then I glanced down at the floor, cursing every single thing about this whole night. She swayed slightly, running a visibly trembling hand through her hair.

The reminder of our mutually lowered inhibitions, the millions of reasons touching her was the worst thing I could possibly do was exactly what I needed to brush past her and walk away.

Chapter 5
Poppy

About an hour after I lay on the couch, the fire in the hearth dimmed from dancing flames to bright orange coals, and the room held a chill to it that I hadn't felt when I first curled up under the blanket and attempted sleep. My brain raced too fast for any sort of rest. And now … I was cold. I turned, pressing my back into the back cushion, trying to seek warmth from the stupid piece of furniture.

The effects of the alcohol still swam in my head, but as I edged closer to sobriety, I knew I needed water and some painkillers. With the blanket wrapped around my shoulders and Jax's too-large T-shirt draped around my body, I shuffled into the kitchen and found a glass in the cupboard, filling it with lukewarm water from the tap.

I drank the whole thing and sighed, leaning my weight against the counter while I filled the glass again. Maybe it was the wine or whiskey or the looming threat of a killer hangover, but I couldn't drudge up a single shred of regret for any of the things I'd said or done.

Too long, I'd sat back and let my feelings for Jax hold the reins. Too long, I'd felt unseen and unnoticed by this person with such a visceral hold on my brain. Something needed to be done, even though it was drastic and rash, and I'd soon face consequences I didn't like. I wanted to move on from this man—quite desperately. But it wasn't always that simple, was it?

To make a decision to leave them behind, even if they've never given you any hope. He had, though, even if it was inadvertent. There had always been moments when I felt him watching me, but the instant my eyes moved toward him, his focus was elsewhere.

Tonight, though ... he was looking. Each one of those looks, longer and more intense than anything he'd given me in the past, was like fire spreading over my skin. And the thing that made my tired brain race as I lay on his couch and struggled to get comfortable was, yet again, what he *hadn't* said.

I gave him a clear opportunity to tell me he didn't want me. Yet those words never crossed his lips. When my heart started racing, I rubbed at my chest.

What if he did want me? What if this was my opportunity, and the moment I walked out the door in the morning, he disappeared for one of his long trips?

He did it often, packing his bags and heading off to who knows where for weeks or a month or two. Cameron never told me where he went, and I didn't ask either.

The timing was perfect, really. There'd be breathing room if this entire thing crashed and burned, and my ass ended up back on the couch.

I was never the impulsive one, but so far, nothing horrible had happened by showing up here. If anything, Jax was far more conflicted than I ever realized, based on the searing heat in his eyes before he stormed off to his bedroom.

If looks could conjure naked orgasms, then the one he gave me would be the big daddy winner of all time. It wasn't the way you looked at a friend or someone you pitied.

It wasn't the way you looked at your best friend's little sister.

Not unless you wanted to screw her into the mattress but refused to admit it.

Heat licked up my spine, and I blew out a slow breath.

Deep in the back of my still-tipsy brain, I knew I'd only be considering something this drastic because of the helping hand of alcohol.

Sober Poppy wouldn't march into a man's bedroom and climb under the covers with him.

Tipsy Poppy was a bit less concerned with consequences. Tipsy Poppy felt a little desperate to exorcise this man from her head, and at the moment, it felt like the best way to do it.

Just once. Then I could know and take the memory to my grave as the risky, impulsive thing that I did because I knew he wanted me but wouldn't act because of my age and my brother and whatever arbitrary list he'd conjured.

This unexpected night felt safe. No one knew I was here. No one saw me arrive, and whether he realized it or not, Jax and his no-kissing rule gave me a surprising sense of security.

Was I capable of no-strings with a man who'd been at the center of every fantasy I'd ever had? Especially if I went into it with my eyes wide open. I wasn't trying to change his mind or magically make him a romantic Prince Charming. That was something he'd never tried to be.

What he could give me, though, as Jax Cartwright—imperfect and completely upfront about it—was a night I'd never forget.

I ran a hand through my hair and stared down at the second glass of water, waiting for reservations to come clawing to the surface. Waiting for reason to prevail and sideline what insanity had gripped me.

It didn't pass. And the longer I stood there, the more I didn't want it to pass.

Pros:

The kind of sex I'd only ever heard about. Headboards banging and multiple orgasms (God, please let there be multiples) and dirty talk because if the look on his face was any indication, Jax was capable of excellent dirty talk.

Freedom from this thing over my head for years. A crush that could be left safely in the past because he was always honest about how he didn't want anything serious.

Cons:

He might turn me down. He might toss my ass out of his bedroom and tell me I was a stupid little girl. See previous note about moving away from embarrassment.

But he might not. Maybe he'd curl his arms around me and say I could stay in the bed, but nothing would happen. The bittersweet ache in my chest was my answer.

I wanted that too.

Just once, for one night, I wanted to know, even if it sated only a small corner of my burning curiosity.

Decision made, I chugged more water and dug into my purse for painkillers, tossing two back to help ease the headache I'd likely have in the morning. Then I tugged the blanket off my shoulders and left it in a heap on the couch while I crept down the hallway.

His door was unlocked, and I eased inside as quietly as I could manage. Seeing the details of the room was impossible, but in the middle of the space was a king-sized bed. Light filtered weakly from the hallway, and I tilted my head to the side as I studied the way he slept.

Jax was on his back, his massive body filling the middle of the mattress, one big hand on the muscled expanse of his broad chest. A sprinkling of dark hair covered his pecs, and my mouth watered as my eyes tracked down the flat, chiseled stomach and the line of black hair that disappeared underneath the blanket bunched around his waist.

His chest rose and fell on deep, even breaths, and I felt my first moment of indecision. God, wouldn't I murder someone for doing this to me?

Not him, I thought immediately.

If it was him climbing into my bed after our evening, my legs would open for that man *so fast*. I'd Venus Fly trap that shit, locking my thighs around him so he couldn't move, and roll on top of him in the next breath.

I took a deep breath and eased the blanket up to slide underneath it. Jax didn't move as I carefully edged closer toward his big, warm body.

Once I did, oh, the heat of his body had me melting into the mattress. It was like laying next to a furnace, and an involuntary shiver wracked my frame. For a moment, I curled onto my side, pressing my face into a pillow that smelled like him.

This was heaven. Clean and crisp and masculine— sandalwood and citrus and a sharp, delicious note that had my toes curling.

It was when I took a second deep breath and curled more fully into the pillow that Jax moved. He turned onto his side, one arm slipping immediately around my waist and tugging me closer.

My mouth fell open on a quiet gasp. I didn't dare breathe because this was the part I hadn't quite figured out. Some gentle touching to wake him, perhaps, but this was like an unexpected gift. The solid weight of his arm over my waist was glorious, and I snuggled closer into his embrace, my nose pressing into the skin of his chest.

God, if this was all I got for the rest of the night, I'd die a happy woman. I'd never ask for anything for the rest of my life. The size of his body dwarfed mine, and it would be so easy to tuck myself next to him and let the smell of his skin lull me to sleep.

This time, my inhale was greedy and deep, and let out a shaky inhale when his arm tightened slightly, the muscles in his biceps moving against my waist, his legs tangling with mine under the covers. His big thigh was between mine, and my jaw tightened to hold in a panicked laugh when I imagined a different way to wake him up. The shirt I wore bunched up around my hips, adding a sleek, wicked feeling to this relatively innocent embrace.

More. Oh, I wanted more.

My skin tingled as I registered it, and I found myself rocking forward slightly—a pervading emptiness that I wanted to chase away. His thigh was just far enough away from me that I couldn't get any friction, which was probably for the best.

Without a single drop of more alcohol, I was drunk again in an entirely different way. Now, my blood swam because of *him* and how good it felt to wrap myself in his arms. The erratic thump of my heart was undeniable, and it stemmed from years of wanting this man. Something as simple as him holding me was enough to make my eyes burn and the bridge of my nose tingle.

I'd wanted this for so long, a quiet moment to pretend Jax was mine, and now that I had it, I wanted to tattoo it into my brain for the rest of my life. Something permanent to remember this night.

My hips shifted restlessly again. Jax made a low rumbling noise, his body shifting around mine, and I froze, waiting for him to jump away from me. I waited for the inevitable, *what the fuck, Poppy?* Waited for anger and embarrassment that he'd wrapped his body around mine like a giant, muscled python.

But he didn't do any of those things.

His nose dropped into the crown of my hair, and his chest expanded on a slow, focused inhale as my eyelids fluttered shut. It wasn't something unconscious because his hand slowly fisted into the back of my shirt, and his hips rocked forward then too, bringing our bodies closer.

My eyes flew open when they did.

Granted, my carnal knowledge of men's bodies was … limited.

But for him to be hard that quickly was impressive. The

size of him against my thigh had me shivering again. Why couldn't he have just been average? It was some cosmic joke that Jax would be well above average, and now I knew it. Watch … he'd know what to do with that thing too. If he could get me off with just that and no other help, I'd probably end up crying sad, sad tears at the end of this because no man would compare, and I'd be so much worse off for knowing it.

My head tilted back as I pulled in a sharp gasp. Should've added this to the cons list.

Jax Cartwright is too good at sex, and I'm ruined forever.

The hand fisted in the back of my shirt unclenched, sliding up underneath the cotton and curling dangerously around my hip, fingers denting my flesh while I struggled to keep my head clear.

This was getting out of hand. I needed to wake him up or back away to a safe distance.

Slowly, I pressed my hands against the warm, solid wall of his chest and tried to push back. Jax let out a discontented, growling noise that raised the hairs on the back of my neck. I froze, waiting to see what he'd do next.

"Stay," he whispered, rough and deep and tortured.

I let out a shaky breath, short puffs against his skin. "Jax," I said quietly.

"Why do you smell so good?" He turned, shifting even more closely to me, arms tightening, hands pressing harder into my hips, his nose dipping to the skin beneath my ear. "So fucking good. I wish to God you didn't."

The hands on his chest meant to be pressing him away softened, and I dragged the tips of my fingernails along his skin. The muscles around me tensed, and he groaned, the edge of his teeth scraping the line of my jaw.

"Holy shit," I breathed out. His tongue slipped to the shell of my ear, and when he sucked it into his mouth, I whimpered, rocking my hips along the muscles in his thigh.

"That's it," he ground out, his hands turning demanding

on my skin as he mapped the line of my back, the curves of my thighs and backside with the rough skin of his palms and fingers. The edge of his fingers toyed with the elastic of my underwear, dipping beneath the light pink cotton, and I shivered.

"Jax," I said again, louder this time. "I need to know you're awake."

Instead of answering right away, he placed a hot, sucking kiss on my neck, dragging his lips to my cheek, then the edge of my mouth. I was panting embarrassingly loud, but God, if he stopped now, I'd curl up in a ball and *weep*.

The temptation to turn my mouth toward his and take a kiss was screaming loud, an instinct that had my pulse racing, but I barely, barely kept it in check.

"You think I'm sleeping right now, Poppy?" He hissed when his impossibly hard length, barely contained behind the tight fabric of his boxer briefs, dragged over my thigh. "You crawl into my bed smelling like a fucking dream and feeling like sin, and you think I wouldn't know it's you?"

We hadn't even kissed yet—wouldn't kiss, based on what he told me—and I was ready to vanish my clothes with a snap of my fingers. I wanted them gone, wanted him over me, in me, and God, how I wanted this night to be as good as I always imagined it could be.

My chin tipped back helplessly at his voice in my ear. Everything went fuzzy in my brain, wiping out any reservation, any worry that this might not have been a good idea. All doubts and fears were swept away in an instant because nothing mattered in the entire world except this. Him and me in a dark room while a storm howled outside.

Electricity gathered between my legs as I pressed down on his hard body, and with his hands guiding the slow back-and-forth motion of my hips, he ghosted his lips over the line of my jaw.

"I might burn in hell for this, angel, but tonight, you're mine."

I continued rocking against his body, getting closer, closer, closer. That was when he wrenched the edge of my panties to the side and slid two big fingers between my legs. The shocked gasp at the sudden intrusion had him groaning into my skin. His tongue was hot and wet against my jaw, and the soft scrape of his teeth against my neck had me panting. Then he curled his fingers, and I let out a decadent, loud moan as a burst of heat skittered over my skin.

Good.

So, *so* good.

He pressed his palm against me, the perfect pressure as he rocked his hand between my legs, and I kept chasing, chasing, chasing what was just out of reach.

"Feel like heaven," he said against my skin, then pulled his face back to watch me. "Don't fucking deserve this, do I?"

"Harder," I begged.

I could feel his gaze searing into mine in the dark room, and oh, how he gave me what I wanted with a deceptively simple twist of his wrist and a press of his palm.

Just before my back arched, before the crest of sensation cracked over my skin, Jax sucked on the side of my neck, his hot tongue laving over the skin.

And it was in that almost, not-quite-a-kiss, through the skillful way his mouth and hands worked my body, that the sharp, keening sound of my first orgasm escaped.

Deep from his chest, he grunted in satisfaction, never breaking his lips and teeth from my neck as my heart rocketed in my chest and my pulse shot to the sky with wave after wave of bliss.

He'd bruise my skin. He was holding my hips so hard as he rocked me through it. I wanted them. If this was my one night with Jax Cartwright, I wanted proof on my skin that it happened. His tongue swept over my jaw, his teeth scraping the skin there, and as my arms snaked around his neck, our bodies were so tightly wound together that there wasn't even a paper-thin amount of space anywhere between us.

My hands wedged between us, scrambled to tug off my shirt, and he cursed as his own hands tore at his boxer briefs, immediately ducking down to run the flat of his tongue over my breasts when I threw my shirt onto the floor. He sucked hard, and I whimpered, his hands pulling at my underwear until I could shove them down my legs.

Frantic, greedy movements felt so very, very right. Because we both damn well knew that this was a stolen moment in the dark, something we hadn't earned and nothing we could repeat.

It was only happening because inhibitions were lowered, and we'd both had enough of dancing around it for so long. I'd had enough.

An ache built in my chest when he dragged his nose over the hard edge of one nipple. It was so gentle, so opposite of what we'd done so far.

"So sweet," he whispered.

He did it again, blowing a soft line of air over my impossibly tight skin, then dragging his nose across my sternum to give the same treatment to the other breast. Jax raised his palm, dragging it in ghost-like circles, whispering over the hard tip until my hips arched, and I sobbed his name for more.

"God, you're pretty, angel," he said, kissing the bottom curve of my breast, sucking on it in the next breath. "Could taste these all night."

I couldn't handle gentle from him. I couldn't handle sweet and slow because then all the reasons this might hurt me would come rushing back to the surface. So I gritted my teeth and wrapped my hand around him, his hefty, hot weight in my palm slightly intimidating.

Before I said something stupid like, *Are we sure this is going to fit?* I decided to turn the table, dropping sucking kisses along his neck as my hand worked up and down. He folded a big hand around mine.

"Like this," he whispered. He squeezed harder than I ever would've dared, and his answering moan had my toes curling.

He bit out a curse, sucking at my chest, his hands going hard and demanding again once they were back on my body. His teeth scraped my breast, and I cried out, Jax rolling us so he was wedged between my legs, his hands gripping my wrists to anchor them to the bed.

I tightened my thighs around him as he rolled his hips, teasing me until I shook.

"Oh fuck you," I groaned.

He chuckled, dark and dangerous, and I felt it like a shock of lightning under my skin. Jax ducked down and spoke against my lips. "I will, pretty girl. You knew what you were doing climbing in here with me, didn't you?"

I nodded frantically, gasping when he ducked his head down again and licked at my chest like an ice cream cone melting all over his hand. He sucked one tip into his mouth, and I cried out.

"Please, I want you. Please."

Jax froze, his forehead resting on my sternum while he bit out a curse.

"What?" I asked, frantically wiggling my hips. Just … a couple of inches lower, and we could be having so much more fun.

"Fuck," he muttered. "I don't have any fucking condoms. It's been … months."

My eyelids fluttered shut when the tip of him dragged between my legs. "Jax," I pleaded. "Oh, I'll die if you keep doing that."

"Are you on birth control?" he asked, then tugged on my nipple with his teeth.

"Y-yes. For years."

He wrenched my thigh tight against his side, his eyes burning into mine. "Dammit, I've never done this without one. Poppy," he warned, "tell me this is okay."

"Please, please, please," I begged, digging my fingers into his heavily muscled back. "Jax, *please*. I need you."

The veins in his neck stood out while he clenched his teeth, fisting himself as he pressed his hardness into me. The groan he let out as he slid forward had my toes curling and the breath locking in my lungs.

Forward, forward, an endless, slow thrust until he bottomed out completely.

My chin tipped up, teeth gritting as I fought not to work myself against him. The delicious, perfect fullness was almost too much.

He got as far as he could, then pulled back, sliding forward again with a tortured sound that tightened the skin on my scalp. It was so, so good that every inch of my body filled with relief.

Jax pushed forward again, and I widened my thighs, hitching them up against his side. He sank like a stone, and my back arched, a helpless sound escaping my mouth at how full I was.

"God, Poppy," he groaned into the skin of my neck. "You're so good, angel. You feel so perfect."

More. I needed more. When I shifted my hips, grinding against him just right, he braced his elbows on either side of my head, and oh, he gave me more.

Jax was relentless—long, even strokes, and he was so big, it was almost painful, riding that edge until I was gasping his name. The bed rocked forward, knocking into the wall as he gritted his teeth and pulled me into the endless wave of pleasure that built and built. I could hardly breathe through it, and it was so *big*, so big and overwhelming that it threatened to drown me.

My pulse thundered in my ears, and I think he was saying

things to me. Filthy things about how tight, how wet, how incredible I felt.

He's going to wreck me, I thought, the thought disappearing almost immediately with another ruthless snap of his hips. Jax was going to obliterate my heart with this one night, and I damn well knew it. And I'd welcome that destruction with open arms. I'd sit in the rubble for the rest of my life if it meant I could feel like this just once.

The head board slammed against the wall, and he gripped my thigh, wedging it against his chest, the angle had me seeing stars while he screwed me absolutely senseless.

My hand gripped the sheet, my heart rate impossible to sustain, and I just kept saying his name over and over while he rearranged every piece of my fucking soul inside my body.

The build climbed under my skin, a gathering of some invisible, crackling ball of energy that had my back arching.

"Come on, angel," he said between gritted teeth. "Come on."

He wrenched my thigh away from his chest, dropping down close to me again. My breasts pressed to his chest, and oh, I wanted to kiss him so badly, but I sank my teeth into the meat of his shoulder and felt the muscles in his back tense. With one hand, he gripped my hair and tightened his fist, and I clenched around him. It felt so good, and I couldn't help but feel like the way we touched each other felt just shy of angry —maybe because we both knew this was just one night. Maybe he felt it too, the dangerous gathering at the base of his spine.

Jax snapped his hips again, grunting into my skin and his hand coming down in a sharp crack on the side of my ass.

Bliss—white and clear and endless.

The shattering of that ball of energy split into a million pieces over my skin, and I mouthed the edge of his jaw while I sobbed through my release. Another thrust, another pivot of

63

his hips, then one more—even harder—and Jax tipped his chin up and groaned my name.

I wish I had that sound locked in a vault somewhere because it was the most amazing thing I'd ever heard.

He milked what was left, a slow rolling of his body as we both came down from the dangerously high highs, from the edges of the universe we'd created in this room.

I memorized all of it. The taste of his skin, the way he kissed my shoulders and chest as we lay there panting, the way he shivered when I dragged my hands over his back and sides and arms and shoulders. The way he pressed into my touch when I pushed my fingers into his dark hair.

And I memorized the way he curled me against his chest, one arm anchored around my back and my thigh slung over his. I fell asleep that way, the steady pounding of his heart under my cheek, and my heart aching because I knew that tomorrow, he'd probably never come near me again. Maybe it was better that way.

Chapter 6
Jax

It was rare for me to sleep until the sun came up, and the moment I stirred to wakefulness, my body went eerily still.

Everything around me was warm, soft, that heavenly fucking smell enveloping the entire bed, and in my arms was Poppy Wilder—naked as the day she was born and tucked into my side like she was meant to be there. Her breathing was deep and even, slow puffs of air from her mouth on my chest, and her arm was slung around my waist, precariously close to a very telling morning hard-on that was inconvenient. Inconvenient because she was there, and I damn well knew if I rolled over, she'd take me. She'd let me do anything.

Images from the night before rushed into my brain, each one better than the last.

The first time, I could blame the haze of sleep and alcohol. That I found her there next to me, smelling and feeling like she did.

The second time, though, that was pure indulgence. We slept for a couple of hours, and I woke with my thumb brushing along the bottom curve of her breast and my aching hard-on resting right between the perfection that was Poppy Wilder's ass.

That second time was slow and quiet.

I brought her awake by sliding my hand down the flat line of her belly, coasting between her legs while she started panting, arching her back with a gasp when I found her slick and ready. With my mouth on the back of her neck and her leg slung up over mine, I took her that way, with my chest pressed tight against her back and my hips moving in slow, short thrusts.

She made the best noises, breathy little gasps when my movements changed, got harder, longer. Whimpers when I plucked at the hard tips of her chest. A decadent, keening moan when my teeth sank into her shoulder as we crossed the peak together, my arms locked tight around her body while I pinched my eyes shut and let the heat of the release slip through my veins like a drug.

Poppy turned her face toward me, my forehead resting on her cheek while we breathed in the dark. I stayed inside her, unable, unwilling to force myself to pull out just yet.

God, I'd been so close to kissing her. Not because I was in love with her or wanted some happily ever after with a girl who deserved someone better than me, but because it felt like I should. That the sex would somehow be better if I had.

And even without it, the sex was incredible.

With the morning light coating the room, I waited for a rush of shame, for an ounce of regret, and shockingly, I came up really fucking short on both of those. A slight headache was blooming at the base of my skull, and my mouth was dry, but even my hangover wasn't that bad.

The truth was, I didn't deserve any of these things. Poppy was so good, so innocent, she'd wanted the fairy tale of her parents' marriage her entire life, and God, she deserved it. Who was I? Fucking no one who should be touching her, that's for sure. My arm tightened where it was anchored around her back, and I inhaled her shampoo again.

I wasn't good. I definitely wasn't innocent. The times in my life when I'd gone home with someone, gone to a hotel, full well knowing I'd never see them again was more than I could count. Fewer, maybe, than a lot of people assumed, but still a lot. It wasn't like I'd never slept with someone more than once because I had. But there were lines I'd never crossed.

No kissing.

No one married or engaged.

And no one in my bed.

Only once. Just her.

Gorgeous and naked and probably the best sex I'd ever had in my life. The kind you wanted more of. The kind you thought about when you were alone and couldn't have it—a pale memory and my own hand would never give me that same high.

Was it better because I knew it was wrong? Was it hotter because I knew that I shouldn't be tearing off her underwear and letting her ride my fingers, all that tight, hot perfection clenching around me in a way that had me losing my fucking mind?

"Fuck," I whispered, bringing my free hand up to pinch the bridge of my nose.

Maybe I had lost my mind.

Insanity by Poppy Wilder's perfectly tight—

I stopped myself short, jaw tight with sudden tension, because she wasn't perfect. No one was. Calling her angel in my head had always been a mistake because it built her up to something untouchable and unfair.

One night didn't erase anything. Not for me.

I gave her one last look, studying the peaceful way she slept, half on top of me, and then gently eased my arm from around her. Instead of waking, Poppy curled up on her side when I moved out from under her, turning her face into the pillow while her breathing evened out again.

I exhaled quietly, carefully pulling the blanket up to cover her delectable, bare body. Once all that flawless skin was out of sight, my head felt clearer, and I went into the kitchen to drink some water and start a pot of coffee. While that was brewing, I checked the weather forecast and stared out the kitchen window, a rolling barrage of memories from the night before weighing my chest down.

Not because the memories weren't good.

They were too good.

If noticing Poppy had me leaving town to clear my head, then what the fuck was I supposed to do with this? My hands tingled, and my throat felt tight as signs of anxiety crawled up over my body.

Get out.

Clear your head.

It was always the same. A glimpse of her big brown eyes. A flash of her smile sent off a pang of … something … deep in my chest.

Don't name it.

Don't feel it.

I drummed my fingers on the counter and took a few deep breaths, feeling like I'd lost an anchor somehow. Lost the thing grounding me for so many years. Scrubbing a hand over my face, I thought about what felt best when direction and clarity were in short supply.

Fresh air. New sights. And a challenge to exhaust me to my core.

The one trip I'd hesitated making pushed up through last night's memories. *It was too long*, I thought. Even though he'd never done it before because of how well he understood me and my situation, Cameron might push back on this one.

I just might have to push back.

Because this … this I needed. The consequences of decimating those barriers always surrounding Poppy grew bigger and bigger the longer I stood there.

If I stayed, I'd fool myself into thinking I was capable of ignoring her. And right now, with the scent and feel of her fresh in my mind, I knew what bullshit that was. There was no lying to myself. Not right now.

I pulled out my phone and sent him a text about the trip, hoping he was too busy on his weekend away to answer until later. His name flashed on the screen immediately—an incoming call that I probably should have expected. Blowing out a slow breath, I glanced down the hall to make sure the door was shut before I answered.

"Morning," I said.

"What happened?" he asked, bypassing pleasantries altogether.

Wincing, I rubbed at the back of my neck. "Something needs to happen for me to go do this?"

Bullshit. What utter bullshit.

Cameron was tellingly quiet on the other end of the phone. "You can pull together that big of a trip in such a short time?"

"I think so," I told him.

He made a small noise of concession. "You've been talking about doing this trip long enough. Probably good you're finally doing the thing."

I pinched the bridge of my nose. I did the thing all right.

The thing being his sister.

"Yeah, it's about time."

He sighed. "You still have that international phone for emergencies?"

"Of course. If I used my own phone, Wade would text me daily with how much he misses me."

My friend snorted, and my smile faded fast. The deception sat bitter on my skin, but there was no avoiding it.

"Yeah, go ahead," he answered after a long moment. "You promise you're okay, though? You'd tell me if something happened?"

Covering my mouth with one hand, I wrestled that

screaming part of my conscience with my eyes pinched shut. The hand dropped. My conscience went quiet.

"Nothing happened, Cameron," I lied smoothly. "Just don't want to push this off any longer."

"Okay. Just keep me updated with your travel dates."

"I might be gone a while for this one," I said quietly.

"I know. We'll be all right without you. And maybe Wade will be in a good mood without you here."

Even with the disquiet hanging over my head, I managed a smile. "Sure he will," I said dryly.

Cameron laughed, said his goodbye, and disconnected the call.

My chest seized, and I hung my chin down into my chest while I fought the crawling sensation pushing up my spine. It wasn't just Poppy, of course. I mean, it was mostly about her. But in the moments when I most felt the need to escape, I could hear my mom's voice in the back of my head.

God, Jax, that's not what I need right now. I know you think you're helping, but just … can you just leave me alone, and I'll be able to figure this out.

If the Wilders were characterized by their dizzying sense of loyalty, an unwavering belief in what they thought was right, and the way they loved each other without reservation, then I'd learned entirely different lessons.

Go.

Leave.

Peace and quiet and solitude were the only way to keep up those necessary barriers in my head.

Thoughts of my mom had the throbbing in my head increasing, and I strode down the hall to the bathroom, cranking the knob on the shower to hot. When it was ready, I stepped under the spray and let the scalding water beat down on my head and shoulders. I stood there for a long time until my skin was red, and my head was slowly clearing.

As the water cooled, I soaped up quickly, drying myself off

with a towel from a hook on the wall. The door to the bedroom was still shut, so I assumed Poppy was still sleeping. I had a pair of sweatpants hanging on the hook on the back of the door, and I tugged them on before running the towel over my hair to dry it off enough to go make some eggs for breakfast.

That was what I was doing when the door to the bedroom creaked open and soft footsteps padded down the hallway. I braced myself for the sight of Poppy in my T-shirt, but when I glanced over my shoulder, she'd pulled on a pair of my pants, far too long for her. A ghost of a smile tugged at my lips because the end of the pants kept covering her feet while she tried to walk, tripping as she entered the living room.

"Morning," I said, steeling myself against an almost primitive rush of affection at the sight of her.

The barrier went back up in my brain, brick by brick by brick, sealing off any remnants of the night before.

Her cheeks were flushed, and her eyes bright in her face. "I think maybe your pants are hazardous to my health." She gave me a wry grin and picked up her outfit from the night before where she'd folded it on the couch. "I'm gonna go, uh…" She hooked a thumb back toward the bedroom, and I nodded.

"Eggs will be ready in a few minutes," I told her. "Want some toast?"

Poppy shook her head, her dark hair in tangles around her face. Probably from the way I manhandled it the night before. My stomach tightened at the memory of fisting it in my hand, and I tore my gaze away as she disappeared down the hall again.

As I divvied up the eggs onto two plates, the simple domesticity of it knocked the breath from my lungs. But I ignored the implications, focusing instead on pouring us coffee and setting everything on the table.

Poppy smiled gently when she returned, her hair pulled

off her face and her slightly wrinkled outfit a much better fit than anything of mine. "This looks great, thanks."

I shrugged. "Can't make much, but I'm good at scrambled eggs."

She took a seat, sipping the coffee first, and then digging straight into her food. When the first bite hit her tongue, she closed her eyes and made a small noise at the back of her throat that had me shifting in my seat.

It was kinda like the noise she made when I put two fingers between her legs.

I cleared my throat and tucked into my breakfast.

It was quiet as we ate, and after she finished, she set her fork down before giving me an impish look. "Eggs were almost as good as the sex."

I choked on my last bite, and Poppy laughed when I had to get up for a drink of water.

"Sorry," she said.

After draining half the glass, I glared at her over my shoulder. "Somehow I don't think you are."

"I told you I'd be fine with one night, Jax." Her words were direct, but she'd shifted her gaze down to her empty plate. Her fingers toyed with the handle on the fork. "And that one night was a great one," she added.

Instead of answering, I let out a slow breath and took my seat again. Her eyes tracked over my bare chest, and I wished I'd taken the time to sneak a shirt from my room. I wanted to snap at her not to look at me like that, but hell, if she was topless, I'd be staring too.

I wanted to tell her that it was a great night for me too, but those words lodged in my throat just like the food, cutting off my air supply until I swallowed them down. It would be easier to redefine the lines from before now that the air was calm outside and the sun shone. We'd slept in long enough that the temps rose above freezing, and with the addition of the bright sun, I knew the roads would be fine for her to get home.

Telling her anything would only make it harder for her to leave.

"Do you need me to drive you home?" I asked.

Her gaze moved over my face, and eventually, she shook her head. "I called an Uber while I was changing."

My jaw clenched, and I nodded. "And if you get Patrice again?"

Her mouth curled into a smile. "I'll have a great story for her, won't I?"

I grunted.

Poppy glanced at her phone and then brought her plate to the sink. She turned, pinning me with a searching look. "When do you leave on your trip?"

"Uh..." I grimaced. "Need to buy my tickets yet."

She rolled her eyes. "Soon, huh?"

"I didn't lie," I said defensively. "A couple of weeks is soon."

Sort of.

Her lips quirked in a tiny smile. "Where are you going this time?"

I let out a slow, measured breath. "Spain. It's a hiking trip I've always wanted to take. Never figured out the best time to do it."

Her eyebrows rose slowly. "Spain? That's … a long flight."

"Long trip, too."

She shook her head and smiled. "You must have triple the vacation time as everyone else at Wilder Homes."

I pushed my tongue into the side of my cheek and didn't say one fucking word.

The tense silence that built between us had my chest squeezing uncomfortably. There was no one to say goodbye to when I disappeared for weeks or months on end. No one who needed to know my comings and goings. No one who cared enough to pay attention, at least. I had a lifetime of practice for that.

And I waited to see what Poppy would do—if she'd ask to see me when I got back or how long I'd be gone. But she visibly straightened, her gaze direct and her resolve iron-strong. "Well, if I don't see you before you leave, be safe," she said.

I nodded. "Always am."

Her phone dinged, and she glanced at the screen again. "My ride is almost here." She tucked her phone in her purse. "I should go."

Why did I feel an anxious tingle in my hands, a buzzing in my ears at the thought of her leaving like this after a night like the one we'd had? Frantic thoughts crawled through my brain like a line of ants, and I couldn't squash them, no matter how hard I tried.

"Are you," I said, "are you okay after last night?"

The rough sound of my voice made it sound like someone else was speaking. Someone with a pinched throat. A ragged sort of desperation there that I didn't recognize.

Poppy softened, and she closed the remaining steps between us, lifting her hand to cup the side of my face. My heart thundered wildly at the gentle touch. In her eyes, there was something I couldn't define, and trying to only would've led me further down into that insanity I'd already felt.

"More than okay," she told me. "I would never regret you, Jax."

The words, so casually spoken, speared through some unseen weak spot between my ribs, slicing straight into the pit of my chest. With my chest thundering, she rolled up onto the balls of her feet and placed a featherlight kiss on my cheek, resting her forehead against my face before pulling away.

My hands curled into fists at my side to keep from snagging her wrist and pulling her close. I could hardly breathe the way I wanted to.

Was this easier for her than for me? And how? I was always the one walking away.

Poppy hooked her purse strap over her shoulder and gave me another long, unfathomable look before she opened the door.

"Thank you," she said simply. And then she smiled, bright and wide, and I felt it like a blow to my chest.

Somehow, I managed a nod and watched her disappear through the door, then walk out to a dark blue sedan idling in front of my house. The woman behind the wheel gave me a thumbs-up through the windshield, and I muttered a curse under my breath.

Then they drove off, and I wondered when the lingering ache beneath my ribs would disappear.

Chapter 7
Poppy

Patrice dropped me off at home with a high five and a mischievous gleam in her eye. Half our drive home was her begging me for salacious details, and I only gave her the bare bones (*no, he didn't kick me out; yes, things happened; no, I am not telling you my sex story; you're a stranger*), which seriously compromised our friendship, according to her.

"So it was worth it?" she asked as I opened the door to exit her car.

My answering grin had her laughing heartily.

God, I floated all the way to the front door. My body was the best kind of sore, and to my utter delight, I didn't feel any embarrassment or regret. This was no morning-after walk of shame, I'll tell you that.

I felt *liberated*, strutting my hot ass back into my house after a night of epic, atom-scrambling sex. I got good and railed, which I could confidently say had never happened before.

I felt *empowered*.

"Where *were* you?"

With a squeak, I dropped my keys, whirling at the sound of my sister's voice in the kitchen.

My mom and my oldest sister sat in the kitchen, staring slack-jawed at my sneak arrival.

I *felt* like a kid who got caught sneaking in after curfew.

"Holy shit, Greer, you scared me."

Her eyebrows rose slowly. "Imagine how Mom and I felt when we got back to the house, and you weren't here. I thought you got murdered."

"Why didn't you call me, then?"

"Have you checked your phone in the last twenty minutes?" she asked, enunciating her words in that incredibly annoying older sister way that had me narrowing my eyes.

"No." I shifted uncomfortably. "I was talking to my Uber driver. She's very nice." I glanced around the room. "Where's Olive?"

Olive was Greer's stepdaughter, and dammit if she wouldn't be the perfect distraction right about now. What good was it to have all these kids coming into our family if they didn't deflect when nosy people wanted to know about my night?

"She's in the barn checking on the cats," Greer answered.

My mom watched me over the rim of her coffee mug. "I take it your date went well."

The skin on my cheeks was probably a thousand degrees, and I cleared my throat primly. "It was … fine."

Greer snorted. "You're coming back home the next day in the same clothes from the picture you texted me yesterday when you were getting ready for said date. I *bet* it was fine."

Oh.

Oh.

They didn't know I'd been home and left again. The wrinkled hem of my skirt brushed my legs as I slowly moved into the kitchen. If I told either of them about my little jaunt out to Jax's, they'd lose their ever-loving shit. Then my brothers would be called, and it would be a whole thing. A thing I very much wanted to avoid.

My one night with Jax would go safely into my memories, to be played on repeat when I lay in bed for the next couple of weeks. Then I'd get back on the saddle—metaphorically—and find a nice, kind, funny, emotionally available guy.

Easy peasy.

"Is there more coffee?" I asked.

"Didn't get much sleep?"

"Not really," I muttered. With my back turned, I poured a generous mug of steaming black coffee, then wrenched open the fridge to get the creamer. When I turned around, Greer and my mom were trading sly grins. "Oh my gosh, stop it."

With a laugh, Greer stood and wrapped her arms around me in a tight hug. "I can't help it. Look at our little baby growing up and having sex on the first date!"

My mom sighed. "Greer…"

"What? She did." Greer's arm stayed around my shoulders as she steered me over to the couch. "Do I get details?"

"Dear Lord, not while I'm in the room," Mom said firmly. "I love you girls, but I have limits."

Greer laughed, but I kinda wanted to crawl under the couch and hide.

"I'm not going to share, Mom. Don't worry."

Greer pouted as we sat on the couch. She tugged a blanket up to cover our legs like we used to do when we were younger. She was married now, living with her husband and stepdaughter outside of Salem, so it was an easy drive when she wanted to come visit.

"How was your sleepover at the Coleman house, Mom?" I asked, quite desperate for the subject change. Greer's eyes narrowed because she knew exactly what I was doing. I merely smiled back.

"It was wonderful," Mom said. "Olive and I had the best night. She's an absolute angel."

I choked on my coffee, barely keeping it from coming out of my nose. Greer gave me a strange look. "You okay?"

You're so good, angel, he'd said. *So perfect.*

I rolled my lips together, nodding frantically as I tried to breathe through my nose. "Totally okay," I managed. "Swallowing is hard, you know."

She smirked. "Have a little practice with that last night?"

I swatted her leg while Mom groaned. "Greer," I hissed.

Mom raised her hands and left the room. "That's it. I'm going to unpack. Greer, thank you for driving me home. You sticking around today?"

My big sister settled into the corner of the couch and pinned me with a thoughtful look. "Yup. At least through lunch."

I pretended her look didn't exist, sipping my coffee and ignoring the slightly stinging ache I felt between my legs. If she only knew. Even if my brothers knew about what happened, they weren't the ones Jax would need to worry about.

Greer would destroy him if she thought he'd taken advantage of me. A slightly hysterical laugh threatened to climb up my throat. If she only knew. One person was climbing into a bed in the middle of the night, and it sure wasn't Jax.

I still wasn't entirely sure it wasn't me taking all sorts of advantages.

Mom disappeared into her bedroom, and we sat quietly for a while.

"So," Greer drawled. "You gonna make me beg for information?"

"Maybe. I didn't make you tell me about your sex life when you married Beckett."

"More's the pity. It's a good one."

I gave her an incredulous look. "You didn't *have* a sex life when you married him, he was basically a stranger."

She waved that off. "Not for long, and we had very good reasons for that. Plus, he wasn't a total stranger, he's Parker's teammate. I knew who he was. Sort of."

It was the truth. Before our dad passed away, Greer overheard him telling Mom he'd never get to walk any of his girls down the aisle. Naturally, this translated to my slightly impulsive sister to conjure a husband to be able to fulfill that wish—one of the teammates of our brother Parker, who played professional football for the Portland Voyagers.

Luckily for Greer, Beckett was perfect for her. The calm to her … not calm. They were a perfect fit, and there was no other way to describe it. Watching them together was the thing that made me question my longtime crush on Jax. Whether it was time to let it go and find someone who completed me in that same way. Who completed me in the way our parents had completed each other.

What I wanted was a soulmate. Someone who *saw* me. The real me. That was always the reason that dating had been hard for me—looking for that one perfect person where they may not exist. Clinging to a crush on someone who was so incredibly not perfect, but I still couldn't dig him out of my head, no matter what I tried.

"Anyway," Greer continued. "Who did you go out with last night? Do I know your mystery date man?"

I could do this. I wasn't lying. I was just … subtly bending the truth.

I blew out a slow breath. "Umm, no, I don't think you do. We went out to dinner in Redmond. He's … he's in finance or something."

She gave me a soft smile. "You had fun?" she asked lightly.

Before answering, I licked my lips and chose my words very carefully. "Dinner was fine, like I said. But after…" My eyes closed, and I took a deep breath. "After was amazing."

"Are you going to see Mr. Finance again?"

"No," I said. Her brow pinched slightly in confusion, but I continued before she could ask why. "It was a fun night. I don't regret it. But … that's all it was. One night. And he and I both knew it."

Again, Greer studied my face, and I worried that the things I'd left unsaid were stamped all over my features.

You know, something like *I had sex with Jax Cartwright* stamped in neon letters on my forehead. But for once in her entire life, Greer didn't push, and she simply smiled.

"Well, that's okay too. Sometimes we need nights like that."

I nodded. "Sometimes we do."

She glanced at the watch on her wrist. "Parker and Beckett's game is starting soon."

"Playing on the East Coast?" I asked.

She nodded. "New York. Cameron and Ivy decided to fly out for that one," she said.

Cameron and his girlfriend had been traveling a bit more since she moved in with him, and it was good to see my brother—who normally sacrificed so much of himself to take care of the rest of us, especially before our dad died—do some fun things for himself. Also … it meant he wasn't anywhere close for Jax to accidentally let something slip.

Like, *oh FYI, I got your sister off three times last night. Hope that's all right.*

"I'm going to go change," I told her. "But I'll watch it with you."

With her attention diverted, I breathed a small sigh of relief, escaping upstairs to slip into comfy pants and a Voyagers sweatshirt. Before I left my bedroom—the same one I'd lived in my entire life—I couldn't help but notice how young I looked in the mirror above my dresser.

Leaning forward, I brushed a fingertip along the edge of my jaw, looking for any marks that Jax might have left, but only the slightest abrasion marks had my stomach curling pleasantly.

Despite how much last night shifted things, I was still me. That wouldn't change. Everything else in my life seemed to be changing at a head-spinning rate. My siblings were getting settled and falling in love, finding that thing that had always seemed so elusive to me.

Within the past four months, we buried our father, and that hole wasn't any easier to fill now than it was on the day he died.

Our company was growing and expanding, offering opportunities I was excited about.

And here I was, still mooning over the same man, staring at my reflection in the same mirror with the chip in the corner from a particularly epic fight between Parker and me when I was in fourth grade. I ran my finger over the chip and took a deep breath, meeting my own eyes in the glass.

"Okay now, Poppy, your one night is over, and it's time to move on." I nodded firmly and walked out of the room, feeling lighter than I had in years.

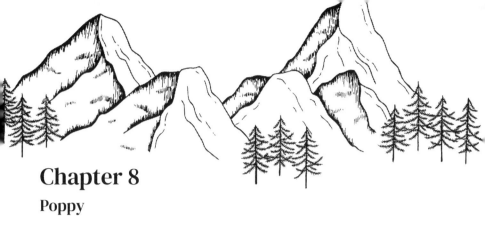

Chapter 8
Poppy

One week later

"No, I can't wait too much longer for those fabric choices," I told my rep. "We need to make our decisions on the summer throw pillows by next week, and you've already pushed us back twice."

"I'm trying, Poppy," she told me. "There was some shortage of the blue thread, and they had to pivot to a new distributor. I should have them to you by the end of the day. Tomorrow morning at the latest."

With the phone wedged between my shoulder and my cheek, I waved at my brother Ian when he slipped through the door of the shop.

"Great, thank you. Once I have those in hand, I'll email you as soon as we decide. Shouldn't take long." Pen in hand, I filled in the empty space next to *Call on Pillow Designs* with a neat little X.

Ian hooked a chair from the corner and, after sitting, plopped his big booted feet on the surface of my desk. I gave him an annoyed look, and he dropped his work boots down with his hands raised. "Looks like a ghost town in here."

I blew out a slow breath and sank into my seat. "I know. Ivy said she's sending a couple of guys over soon to take the rest of this."

The office where I spent most of my time was empty except for the desk and two chairs, boxes stacked neatly in the corner for my move to the new shipping warehouse across town where our new home decor business had set up shop while Cameron and his crew worked on the physical location that would be opening in the summer.

I always kept my office tidy, but it was strange to see it stripped bare.

A stack of papers and my to-do list for the day were on my desk. Now that I'd finished my calls and paid outstanding invoices to our subcontractors for plumbing and electric on the last job, I glanced at what came next.

-pick up Larry from the vet at three

"You unpacking at the new office today?" he asked.

In response, I gave him a small shake of my head. "Gotta pick up Larry in about an hour."

"Who's Larry?" Ian asked.

I arched an eyebrow. "Larry the barn cat? The black one with the white patch on his chest. He was the only one we kept this round."

My brother's face bent in confusion. "Who named him? That's a terrible name for a cat."

"I believe Olive was in charge on this last litter," I answered.

"Ahh. That makes more sense. Why's he at the vet?"

"Poor Larry got snipped," I said, picking up the stack of invoices and clacking them into a straight line. The moving box on the top hadn't been taped shut yet, so I pried it open and tucked the papers away, then yanked the tape dispenser across the top with a loud zip.

Ian grimaced. "Poor guy indeed. I hope they give him good drugs afterward."

"I will be sure to ask the vet for a male-approved painkiller. Lord knows you need them stronger than we do." I smiled sweetly.

With a dry look, Ian ignored my jibe. "Why isn't Mom picking him up? I saw her car at the house."

I sighed and rolled my eyes slightly as I sat back down in my chair. "I think Mom is playing matchmaker. She's told me seventeen times in the past month how cute the new vet is."

"Seventeen, huh?" Ian asked.

"Close enough." The door outside my office pushed open again, and when I heard low voices, I called out, "Boxes are in here, guys."

One of the younger Wilder Homes employees came in first, tipping his head deferentially. "Poppy."

I smiled. "Hey, Rob, thanks for moving these for me."

His cheeks reddened, and Ian snorted quietly. I narrowed my eyes in his direction. Rob glanced behind him and nodded when the person behind him spoke.

All it took was the sound of his voice, and I sucked in a quick, sharp breath at the immediate pounding of my heart.

Jax's eyes swept the office when he walked in, and my throat went dry at the way his black shirt stretched across his chest and the dark line of stubble across his knife-sharp jaw. When his gaze finally settled on mine, I couldn't help but wonder if my cheeks had turned bright red too. What an inconvenient time to replay what my name sounded like in his sex voice as he came.

News flash—it sounded really fucking good. I'd only allowed myself to indulge in that memory twice over the past week when I couldn't sleep. Okay, fine. Three times.

Get it together, Poppy, I hissed in my head.

"Jax," I said coolly.

There was no hidden heat in his eyes. No lingering glance loaded down with subtext. Jax Cartwright, the absolute master of keeping his emotions in check, gave me a short nod. "Poppy."

Rob took the first two boxes and left the office, and Ian asked Jax a question about the jobsite they'd just left. After answering, he took one of the heavier boxes and walked out.

Was that it?

Was that … all we'd be now?

I hadn't really taken the time to form any sort of expectation, not enough that warranted this kind of empty disappointment.

This was what one night was like. And why he'd always been so careful in who he slept with. Because of moments like this.

The three of them emptied the boxes from my office in less than five minutes, and when Rob came back in for the last one, he gave me another smile. If he wasn't fresh out of high school—seventeen, if I remembered right—it might have been sort of sweet.

Probably not the time to remember that the span of years between Jax and me was only one year different from the one between Rob and me. I blew out a slow breath through puffed-out cheeks when that math bomb dropped in my head.

With my arms crossed on the desk, I let my head settle on top of my stacked hands.

"This is too dramatic for me," I whispered. With a sigh, I lifted my head and slid my hands over the marred surface of the solid wood of the desk.

With all the boxes gone, it was just me and the desk in the large, empty office. I wasn't taking it because the shop would still get used, just not by me. Cameron and I decided it needed to stay right where it was, in the place it had been since Dad built it so many years ago.

I ran my hands over it, thinking about everyone who'd worked here and how much of our family's history was embedded in this shop, office, and desk. My dad worked in this exact spot when he started Wilder Homes. There were scrapes on the surface. Nicks and dings from the rough treatment us kids had given it when we were younger.

I found pencil marks in the middle where I used to do my homework, and if I looked closely enough, I could make out letters and numbers. My eyes fell shut, only the slightest burn of tears pressing at the backs of my eyelids.

Memories of Dad sneaking his calculator out to help me with math, winking when Mom asked us if we got it figured out. I fought a hard swallow, emotion clogging my throat.

I hadn't seen him sit at that desk for years, but the image was so clear in my head when I conjured it. All of this was his first, and we were just trying to steward it successfully and turn it into something that would last. That would make him proud.

Time passed, no matter what we did or how it refused to conform to our expectations.

My dad thought he'd be alive to watch us all start families and watch his grandkids grow. And he hadn't.

But the heartbreak for all of us didn't stop the days from turning into weeks, months, and years. I couldn't let this stop me either, to wedge me into place in my own life.

I was *not* going to let this thing with Jax make me feel stagnant.

This part of my story was a whole new list to process, and I didn't even need to write it down.

Pros:

I had experienced the kind of sex reserved for really well-written romance books.

A full week had passed, and I still had no regrets, because as previously established, regrets were bullshit.

Cons:

I had experienced the kind of sex reserved for really well-written romance books, and now he could hardly look at me.

I sighed, my chest feeling a little heavy. Expectations were a bitch, weren't they? Jax had always been so very, very clear about what he wanted and didn't want. There was no blurry communication, no words that could be misconstrued. And I'd been clear in return.

I could do one night, I told him. And this was the fallout of that promise. A stilted moment that made me wonder if I'd dreamed the entire thing.

No dreaming. No fantasizing. This was the real world, and I was perfectly capable of moving on if he was. So I fixed my ponytail, pulled a compact out of my purse, and checked my reflection before I went to get Larry, the testicle-free cat.

And honestly, I was glad I did because when Dean Michaelson—the new vet, the one I'd heard about seventeen times—walked into the exam room to talk to me about Larry's post-surgical care, I about fell off my fucking chair.

Mark down a point for Sheila Wilder because holy bananas, he might have been one of the most beautiful men I'd ever seen.

Ever.

He was tall, easily a couple of inches taller than my brothers, with a wiry, muscular build that had all those really sexy veins roping over his forearms. His hair was a dark gold color, cropped tight to his very nicely shaped head, and the man had a jaw crafted by the gods.

And when he smiled at me—all those straight, blindingly white teeth—I actually went a little speechless.

"You must be Poppy," he said. His bright blue eyes traced over my face, that smile deepening until a dimple popped out. A *dimple.* When he shook my hand, I managed a swallow and a stammering sort of hello. "Your mom has told me all about you."

"H-has she?" I asked. "Hopefully all good things."

He laughed, the sound rich and deep, and I felt the beginnings of a tingle in my belly. "Excellent things," he murmured.

I eyed him, crossing my arms over my chest. "Don't the vet techs usually handle these appointments?"

His answering grin was completely unrepentant. "Yes."

Dean was easy to talk to. He was kind and sweet with the cat as he explained exactly what we should watch for over the next week. He was funny, his eyes gleaming as he handed me his card with his cell phone added in black ink on the bottom right underneath his name. My cheeks felt warm when he pointed it out.

"You know," he said slowly. "I do have one problem with what your mom told me about you."

My eyebrows rose slowly. "What's that?"

"She said you were pretty, but that's just not an accurate statement."

Honestly, this wasn't even fair. Dean was just sitting there with a *purring cat* in his lap, one of his big hands petting down Larry's arched spine, and I swear, I couldn't find words. The symbolism of how he was handling that normally feral pussycat was about to make my brain explode.

"It's not?"

Slowly, Dean shook his head. "She should have said you're stunning. Far too beautiful to go out with someone like me, but I think I'm going to have to take a chance and ask anyway."

The sound that came out of my mouth—part laugh, part shocked gust of air—was by far the most graceless articulation I'd ever made in my entire life, but Dean the vet thought it was hilarious, tipping his chin back and laughing, deep and rich and oh my word, how was every single woman in this town not dropping their panties at the sight of him?

They had to be.

Single men in Sisters were hard to come by.

Single, hot men were even more rare.

But single, hot, gainfully employed, good with animals,

and even better with casual compliments men? Forget about it.

I didn't need a pros and cons list to make this decision. Not even close. Because there was only one con I could think of.

He wasn't Jax.

And that wasn't enough of a reason to say no anymore.

So I took a deep breath and notched my chin up, daring myself not to get stuck in this place of pining and wanting and waiting for someone who might never want me in the same way.

"I'd love to go out with you," I told Dean.

And I meant it.

He called me that night to set something up because he told me he couldn't wait another day. And the following evening, as I pulled on my best date dress—a sleek pale pink number that dipped low over my cleavage and skirted my thighs—there was only one fleeting moment when I thought about Jax getting on a plane and being gone for months. Just once.

There was no point in lying that the one thought wasn't painful. Where my ribs felt a little too tight, and my heart squeezed uncomfortably. But I forced that thought to be short, taking my time with my makeup and hair for a first date that I was excited about.

My mom was damn near giddy as she watched me leave.

Dean was, in no uncertain terms, the perfect first date. He opened doors. Pulled out my chair. Brought me to an expensive, romantic restaurant. Asked excellent, thoughtful questions. Laughed easily and often. Treated the server with kindness, leaving a huge tip at the end of the night.

And when he brought me back home, he walked me to the door and stared down into my face. There was no hiding that he wanted me. It was practically screaming from his eyes, the way they locked on my lips when I thanked him for a wonderful dinner. I waited for the eruption of nerves, the butterflies in my belly and lungs and veins, and even if it wasn't powerful, I did feel something.

"So your mom might have told me that you've had trouble finding the kind of guy who warrants a second date," he said smoothly.

I breathed out a quiet laugh. "My mom talks too much when she sees you."

Dean grinned, that dimple popping again. "I do like a challenge," he admitted.

One eyebrow arched slowly. "Is that what this is? See if you can win me over because others couldn't?"

His eyes locked on mine so intensely that I lost my breath a little. "Maybe," he admitted. "And maybe I think you're worth chasing if no one else has been able to catch you yet."

I bit down on my bottom lip to stem the immediate smile that threatened to bloom. He reached his hand up and pulled lightly on my chin, my lip escaping from my teeth.

"I'd love to kiss you good night, Poppy," he said, his rich voice causing the slightest of shivers along my spine. Then he leaned down, and at the last minute, he turned his head and brushed a whisper of a kiss along my cheek. "But I think I'll wait until our next date, if that's okay with you," he whispered against my skin.

Oh.

Oh he was *good*.

I managed a drowsy nod as he backed away.

"Can I call you tomorrow?" he asked, gaze searing into mine. "Not sure I can wait until the weekend to schedule that second date."

My smile, and yes, was easy. And as I lay in bed that night, my fingertips brushing over my un-kissed lips, I wondered if moving on from Jax was as simple as this.

A good first date and the promise of a kiss from someone new.

Maybe it was, I thought, entertaining only the briefest of thoughts about what he was doing right now.

No. Not maybe. It was that easy, I told myself.

As I drifted off to sleep, I believed it, too.

Sort of.

Chapter 9
Poppy

Four weeks later

"You look like shit."

"I'm exhausted," I snapped. "I think I'm getting sick, okay?"

"I can tell. Dr. Dean keeping you up too late these days?" He took a huge bite of his sandwich. "I like him. Did you see his face when Ivy beat him at chess last night?" Parker chuckled under his breath. "If he sticks around long enough, he'll realize that's a lost cause."

"No, he's not keeping me up too late. I've been on maybe four or five dates with him," I said. "And one of them was dinner here last night. What am I supposed to do, sneak him upstairs into my bedroom? Put a sock on my door so Mom doesn't interrupt?"

Parker raised an eyebrow. "Do you not remember how bad it was with Adaline and Emmett when they first got together? No one could go in the house for hours because we were afraid of what we'd walk in on."

All he got in agreement was a pathetic sort of moaning

sound. "Why are you here again? I thought you lived in Portland?"

As was his way, he shrugged nonchalantly, taking a leisurely sip of his giant glass of milk.

Milk. Like he was still a little kid. My stomach roiled unpleasantly at the sight of that glass in front of him, but I forced another bite of the leftovers I'd heated.

"Just needed a break. Felt like I haven't spent more than a weekend here in forever."

"Because you haven't spent more than a weekend here in forever," I pointed out. He'd been here a week, and every day that passed, Mom and I watched him with increasing concern. "And I don't think you should be lecturing me on looking like shit."

Even with dark circles under his eyes—a matching set to my own, thanks to the perpetual exhaustion I hadn't been able to shake in days—Parker was one of those guys who was just … stupidly good looking. All my brothers were in their own way.

Erik and Ian were tall, dark, and broody with personalities to match.

Cameron and Parker were both tall too, but had the golden good looks they got from our dad. Tan skin, strong jaws, and big smiles. Since Parker started playing professional football, he'd added more muscle to his frame, and even though he still had the golden hair and jaw and all that went with it, the smiles didn't come as easily since our dad got sick.

In fact, since he'd come home, I'd hardly seen it once.

"Can't sleep," he admitted gruffly.

I picked at my food, eyeing him underneath my lashes. "Is it Dad?" I asked.

His jaw clenched. "No." Then he pinched his eyes shut. "Maybe. I don't fucking know, Poppy. I just can't get my head clear."

Parker and I were the youngest in the family, even though

he was quite a few years older when I was born. It was a second marriage for my mom and my dad—they both brought three kids into it with them when they tied the knot. I was the only biological child from that second marriage, which only added to that whole older, protective thing my siblings had going.

I was the baby by a lot.

One thing I'd learned throughout the years was that very few people confided in the baby of the family. They continually operated under the delusion that I was a child and couldn't handle their shit, even though I'd been through loss, same as them.

Parker had a hard time watching our dad in his last round with cancer when he'd chosen not to do any treatments that would ravage his body. Parker made his peace with Dad by the end, but it still felt like we were tiptoeing through raw grief, all of us dealing with it in our different ways, even months later.

I couldn't say my grief was any healthier than Parker's, given my impulsive night with Jax still had me all shredded up inside. Turned out, ignoring that one night wasn't as easy as I thought.

"Is it the game?" I asked quietly.

Now his jaw didn't just go hard. His whole face went stony. No one had talked to him about it yet, probably because his face did the same intimidating thing it was doing right now, even though the replays made the rounds for weeks after the Voyager's last playoff game.

But as I held his gaze, that stoniness faded with a slump of his big shoulders, and Parker leaned forward, rubbing his forehead as he sighed. "You mean the playoff game I dropped the fucking pass in the end zone as time expired? And because of that dropped touchdown we lost the chance to go to the Super Bowl?"

I winced. "Yeah, that one."

He didn't answer right away as his eyes locked onto the

95

table for a few minutes. "You ever feel like … you don't know what the hell you're doing in life? Like it's just moving forward all the time, and you're scrambling to stay caught up with everyone around you."

My eyes pricked with tears. "Sometimes, yeah. I didn't know you felt like that, though. You've been off living your dream for years, Parker. And we're so proud of you."

Parker gave me a sad smile. "Ignore me, I know I have nothing to complain about. Just a rough ending to the season. I'll get over it."

"You can have good things in your life and still feel sad or overwhelmed. It doesn't lessen what you're going through." I set my chin in my hand and studied him. "We have a great family, right? I have a beautiful place and a job I enjoy. But I feel … stuck, too, sometimes. You and I are the only ones who haven't found that one person, you know?"

Parker snorted. "Could've fooled me. You've got the vet wrapped around your fucking finger, and don't tell me you don't. What did Mom say? He's *smitten*."

My cheeks felt warm. "I know he is. I like him," I said simply. "I think maybe I was a challenge to him at first, but … he's nice. And funny. And there's a lot of potential there, but I can't say he's my soulmate."

At that term, Parker rolled his eyes. "Soulmates aren't a real thing."

"Yes, they are," I argued. "Look at Mom and Dad. And you know what I mean about our siblings. They're all building lives, and I'm still sleeping in my childhood bedroom." I let out a short, dry laugh. "Sleeping a lot these days, actually. So now I can add stuck and lazy to my résumé."

Parker's eyes finally glinted with humor. "You've never been lazy a day in your life, Poppy. It was annoying because anytime I slacked in school, I had your punk ass showing me up."

"Someone has to keep you on your toes."

At that, his mouth edged up in a grim smile. "Indeed. I could use a little less of that, to be honest."

I sighed, folding an arm on the table and laying my forehead down. "Ugh, I slept twelve hours last night, I took a nap this morning, and I feel like I could go back to bed. What is wrong with me?"

"You're not pregnant, are you?"

He said it jokingly. Lightly, with an edge of teasing. And right along with the light teasing edge, I felt the world drop out underneath me.

My head snapped up. "What?"

He took a huge bite of his sandwich, eyeing my face. "When Mom got pregnant with you, I remember her laying her head exactly like that on the table during dinner once. First sign she was pregnant, actually."

My heart had stopped beating. Completely. When it restarted, I lifted a shaky hand to my forehead while I started counting the days in my head. I was late, but honestly, I'd been so tired I just didn't think about it.

Parker's eyes widened, his jaw falling open at whatever he saw on my face. "Holy *shit*, could you be pregnant, Pops?"

My gaze locked on his, eyes blurring with immediate tears. "M-maybe," I whispered.

"I heard you and Greer talking yesterday, so I know you haven't slept with Dean yet," he said.

No, there was *zero* chance it was Dean's. In truth, our dates had been a little high school-style pent-up sexual frustration. Lots of making out in cars, and some under-the-clothes action that had felt nice, but nope, nope, nope, there was zero impregnating happening from that beautiful man.

"The finance guy? The date you went on?" he asked.

"How did you know about that?" I snapped.

"Greer told Cameron. Cameron told me. And Ian told me, actually. Basically everyone knows."

"This fucking family," I hissed under my breath. "No one

can ever have any privacy." I stood from the table, pacing back and forth in the kitchen. "Oh shit, shit, what if I'm pregnant?"

Parker stood too, gripping my shoulders and bending down to make sure I was looking at him. "Stop. Breathe. What do you need?"

My chin quivered. "A pregnancy test?"

He nodded. "Okay. I mean, I've never bought one, but how hard can it be?"

"You can't go buy me one," I yelled.

"Why not?"

My hand waved in a wild gesture. "You're, you're *you*. You're ten feet tall, and everyone knows you, and the last thing you need is some tabloid headline that Parker Wilder is out buying pregnancy tests for a mystery woman."

He rolled his eyes. "I'll wear a hat."

"Oh, because that'll disguise who you are."

Parker merely raised his eyebrows. "Would you rather walk into the drugstore to get your own?"

At the mental image *that* conjured, all eyes in the entire town zeroing in on me in the pregnancy test aisle, I whimpered, and my stomach roiled dangerously.

"That's what I thought." He squeezed my shoulders. "I'll be right back, okay?"

"Get the digital one," I called out as he hustled out the door a few minutes later, Voyagers hat tugged low on his forehead.

He waved a hand over his shoulder as the door slammed shut behind him. When the sound of his truck engine disappeared, I curled up under a blanket and tried to steady my breathing.

I didn't even need the test. Deep down, I knew. I *knew*.

Jax Cartwright and his super penis couldn't just give me one night of good sex. He had to *impregnate me*. God, it was unfair. Of course his sperm would be stronger than birth control.

Frantically, I thought back to the week before I'd gone to his house, my throat closing up with the realization that I'd been sick and taken antibiotics to knock out a nasty head cold. Shit. That messed things up, didn't it? Immediately, I wanted to call Greer. Or Cameron's girlfriend, Ivy. Or my mom.

But they'd freak out. Like level ten, code red panic. They'd want to avenge my honor.

They'd march into every bank in Redmond trying to figure out who the guy was. And oh *fuck my life*, when they found out who did the impregnating.

My stomach bottomed out, and I took a deep breath to try to keep myself from dry heaving. I wouldn't, *couldn't*, tell them anything until Jax got home. I snatched my phone and immediately pulled up his number.

> I need to talk to you. Please call me when you have a chance.

I pressed send, holding my breath, and then lost it in a gust when a red exclamation point showed up next to the text. Undeliverable. With a growl of frustration, I threw my phone onto the couch and waited for Parker.

He was home in record time, bursting through the door with a bag in his hand. When he dumped it over, seven or eight boxes fell in a pile.

Brows high on my forehead, I glanced up at him. "How many do you think I need?"

Parker tugged on his hat, twisting it backward on his head so I could see his face. He looked about as frazzled as I felt. "I don't know, but you said digital, and there were like four kinds, and I panicked and grabbed one of each kind."

For a long moment, I just stared at the pile of boxes, unsure of what to do next.

Once I knew, there was no going back. My skin prickled ominously, the telltale signs of a panic attack creeping up to the edges of my vision. I took a minute, steadying my breathing, reminding myself that it would be fine, and no matter what, I would be okay.

I snatched one of the boxes and marched to the bathroom.

After the test was capped and set down on the counter, I leaned up against the edge of the vanity and closed my eyes, listening to the whooshing sound of my pulse in my ears.

Pregnant.

Pregnant.

Pregnant.

Jax was going to lose his mind. I'm the one who told him we were fine without a condom. Mr. *I don't want a family* would probably hate this.

My chin quivered again, and I could hardly see the painting on the bathroom wall while I tried to get my emotions under control. When I was sure a couple of minutes had passed, I opened the bathroom door with the test gripped in my hand.

Parker was pacing in the hallway, his face tight with worry. "Well?"

"I haven't looked yet," I whispered. "I'm scared."

My brother straightened his massive shoulders, sucking in a deep breath. "Do you want me to look for you?"

I shook my head, feeling very much like I was going to toss my fucking cookies right there in the hallway.

"And it's not Dean's, right?" he asked.

Eyes wide, I glanced up at my brother. *"Parker."*

"Right."

I sucked in a deep breath. I'd count down from sixty and then look. Miserably, I answered, "Besides, Dean plans on waiting to have sex until he gets engaged. Something about his college years and being an athlete, and it felt meaningless sleeping around so much or something. He's ... he wants to wait."

Parker blew out a slow breath, eyebrows high on his forehead. "Your boyfriend is regenerating his virginity?" he asked slowly.

I pinched his arm. "Does this feel helpful right now?"

He raised his eyebrows. "No, but I'm just imagining telling someone that story with a straight face on the first date."

"Second," I said glumly. "Second date. It was a little awkward, and I almost laughed because I thought he was kidding. Have you *seen* him? But..." I shrugged. "It's not the worst thing in the world, right? Like, there are worse things than dating a man who looks like him, and he won't sleep with me?" My breath was coming in short, choppy pants. "Let's think about what those things are. Maybe we can make a list?"

My brother attempted a smile, but it fell quickly. Probably because my freaking out was so big that he was absorbing it by osmosis.

"Poppy," he said gently. "I think it's time to look."

"Right, right. Not the time for a list."

Heart thrashing in my chest, I joined him in the hallway, and we stood side by side while I lifted the test with shaking hands and focused on the screen.

Pregnant.

A sharp exhale left my mouth, my heart pinwheeling down into my feet, and my whole mind going blank and fuzzy while I stared at the tiny little screen.

I'd imagined having a family. Someday. But not like this.

I'd imagined a partner who loved me, who I loved in the same way. I imagined a nice little home we made for ourselves, and a big white wedding surrounded by all our family and friends. Maybe it wasn't very modern of me—to want such simple things, love and marriage and then babies after—but there was no ignoring the way my heart hurt from removing so many of those foundational pieces from the equation.

"Holy shit," I whispered, the first tear sliding down my cheek. "*Holy shit.* What am I going to do?"

"I mean, you might want to tell your boyfriend first," he muttered. "Shit, he's gonna think you had an immaculate conception."

"Parker," I wailed. "You're so bad at this."

He huffed out a soft laugh. "Sorry. This is ... new."

"What am I going to do?" I said again.

My big brother gentled his face and gently gripped my shoulders. For just a moment, he looked like the old Parker with his eyes fixed on mine. "I'll tell you what you're going to do. You're going to let your family take care of you. That's what we're here for."

The hurt in my heart broke open into something sharper, something unnamed that I felt down to my toes. The grief of so many different things was too big to fit into my skin, and I felt it like a tear through my bones. "That sounds like something Dad would've said," I said in a trembling voice.

In the next heartbeat, Parker had me wrapped tight in his arms, and while my brother held me, I let myself cry.

Chapter 10
Jax

Three months later

"This is stupid. Do I have to do this?"

My table companion was remarkably unfazed. She sipped her coffee, eyes trailing over the courtyard thick with tourists. Some, like us, had finished their pilgrimage and had the unkempt look to prove it.

"You do," she said calmly, her English accent familiar and kind. "You turn your mobile on yet?" she asked.

I shook my head. "I already told you, not until I land Stateside."

Margot eyed me over the rim of her cup of coffee. "How the bloody hell does your boss let you do things like this and not sacked you yet?"

Steadily, I held her gaze.

She blew a raspberry. "Now he stops talking," she muttered. "You're full of secrets, young man, and it's not nice to keep secrets from your nosy friends."

I'd done so much of this trip alone, but in the past few weeks, I'd linked up with her and her husband, there to complete their own journey after losing their son. We walked together for twenty-four days, taking two rest days in a small town with open rooms, taking turns washing our socks, resting our legs and stopping to listen to choirs singing in beautiful old church buildings. Cobbled pathways and bridges and mile after mile at the end went much easier with their steady companionship.

In front of me was a piece of paper she'd conjured from her backpack, stacked on top of the certificate saying I'd completed the arduous trek. Never in my life had I felt the twinge of every single muscle in my body like I had in the past few months.

It wasn't even pushing past the physical discomfort. It was the feeling of being completely disconnected from anything familiar. And through that tiredness, through the isolation, I was craving home for the first time in my life. Craving familiar.

The pen in my hand felt like an anchor though, and I pressed the tip down onto the paper, then yanked it back. "I don't … I don't know what to say."

Margot made a small humming noise, waving at two little girls playing in front of our table. They raced in circles around their parents, giggling at the birds as they chased them. Behind them, the spires of the Santiago Cathedral stretched tall, the blue sky behind them a stark backdrop for the age-blackened edges.

"Robby wrote a letter to himself," she said, nodding her head to where her husband was wandering in front of the church, camera against his face and aimed at the peak of the impressive building. "A reminder of how he felt being at the end of this."

I sighed, watching her face as she talked. They were in their sixties, and kept impressive pace along the walk for their age. Some days, she was the one who kept me moving on target, if I was being honest.

"And yours?" I asked.

She smiled, her eyes misting over slightly. "I wrote a letter to our son. Telling him about our trip. What he would've liked. How I wish it could've been him accomplishing this marvelous thing like he'd always planned." Margot blinked rapidly, the tears disappearing like they'd never been there, then she patted my hand absently. "Write what's on your heart, dear. If you want to remember what you feel like right now. Or maybe something you know needs to be said, even if that person might never see it."

Just like it had every day I woke with the sun on this trip—every single day—her name was the thing that materialized in my head. Just a whisper. A reminder.

What did I feel right now?

I felt haunted.

Felt like I couldn't tear her from my chest even though the thought of seeing her again sent a dizzying sort of anxiety racing down my spine. Years of avoiding Poppy, years of lying to myself that she was nothing, and I had to face the truth that I couldn't escape her. Going halfway across the world and pushing myself to every physical and mental limit in existence, and she was still there—locked deep in a corner of my ribs that I couldn't pry open.

If I pinched my eyes shut, I'd see her wrapped in a blanket, playing checkers, choking on her whiskey, and the soft, patient look in her eye when she kissed me on the cheek and walked out the door.

I *wanted* to tear her loose. I wanted this feeling gone. Because no matter what I felt right now, I still knew I wasn't built to make someone like her happy.

"That girl," Margot continued quietly, eyes still on her husband. "The one you told us about. You could write to her."

"I still can't fucking believe I told you about her," I muttered, scrubbing a hand along my jaw, now fully covered with a beard. "I swear, you put something in that sangria."

She laughed loudly. "Oh, my boy, you had those words locked and loaded. You had one drink before you were spilling your guts, and there's no point in lying about it."

I grimaced, which made her smile.

She wasn't wrong, unfortunately. Maybe it was the days, weeks, and months of hardly conversing with anyone beyond a hello on the path, ordering food in a café when I stopped, or getting a room when I took a break. When Margot and Robby came alongside me on that last stretch, I felt like a shaken-up bottle of champagne, and they knocked the cork loose with their warmth and kindness.

"What would I say?" I said, voice hardly more than a rough whisper.

Margot took another sip of coffee. "Oh that's an easy one. Tell her how you feel. That you walked hundreds of miles, and she was with you every step of the way."

Elbows braced on the table, I sank my head in my hands and stared down at that blank piece of paper. "And what if how I feel is a giant, fucking tangled mess? I'm not cut out for serious relationships, Margot. I've spent my *entire* life avoiding them, watching the absolute fucking misery that comes from chasing and chasing some idea of perfect that I don't even know if it exists." I lifted my head and gave her a look. "How many kids do you know that felt like that? That being in love or trying to make someone else happy was a fucking death sentence to any sort of freedom or independence. Do I want to subject her to that? That's rooted just as deep inside me as anything else. Cynics don't make for very romantic partners."

"Bollocks," she tossed back. "What do you think I am? Robby's the one always making us stop to look at the beautiful views, wasn't he? The one chatting with you that first day because he thought you looked lonely. It wasn't me, was it?"

My eyebrows arched. "Not at first, no."

"Trusting people isn't just about letting them see what's inside you," she said, leaning forward to settle one of her wrinkled hands on top of mine. "Sometimes you have to trust that they can show you a different view of the world than the one you thought to be true. A different view of love and friendship and life. Do you think she's one of those people?"

My hand tightened on the pen, my chest heavy and my brain racing.

Could I do this?

I closed my eyes.

I could never regret you, Jax.

Soft lips and sweet smile, and the noiseless sound of my aching heart getting ripped from my chest to follow her when she left. And she didn't even know.

"Yeah, she is," I answered immediately.

"Well then," she said with a satisfied smirk. Margot tapped the paper. "Get to writing, young man. That way if you die on the way home, they have something to bring her a little bit of comfort."

I gave her a long, steady look. "That's fucked up, Margot."

She laughed. "We've all got a bit of darkness in us, Jax. No point in trying to hide it."

Picking up her coffee, Margot took a moment to squeeze my shoulder, then go off in search of her husband. Pen in hand, I watched them trade a quick kiss, then Robby showed her some of the pictures on his camera. The little girls darted past the table again, chasing pigeons in search of their next meal.

The busyness around me—people and sound and smells—felt a bit like the inside of my brain. Too much to filter through. But if I took a step back and pushed past the defiant stubbornness circling my feelings for her, I found some clarity.

My lips inch up in a small smile, thinking of her standing in my kitchen with wet hair and big eyes. I took a deep breath and started writing.

Chapter 11
Poppy

"Poppy, come *on*, we're going to be late."

"I had to pee, okay? I'll be right down." I blew out a short breath, tugging my leggings up and turning to the side to study my profile in the mirror. "Geez Louise," I muttered. "There's no hiding it now."

The little nugget was no longer making me puke up all my food, which was *lovely*, but I also couldn't really hide the bump anymore either. Not that I was hiding it from anyone that mattered. My family had known since the beginning. My mom came home about an hour after Parker made The Great Pregnancy Test run, and my tears started afresh when I told her. She cried too, but hers were happy tears, not *holy shit existential crisis* tears like mine.

"More grandkids is *always* a good thing," she told me, holding my face in two hands and kissing my forehead. "Don't you worry about a thing, sweetheart."

My sisters were cautiously ecstatic, babying me even more than normal, and being surprisingly not-pushy when I didn't make any clear leaps to announce paternity. My brothers gave big, tight, supportive hugs—something they'd always been good at.

Cameron's girlfriend, Ivy, was the only one who straight out asked the thing no one dared ask.

"So are we not going to talk about the sperm donor in this situation?"

It was at a family dinner a few weeks after I'd told everyone. Cameron held my gaze after Ivy said it, and Ian traded a quick look with his wife, Harlow.

Harlow's daughter Sage raised her hand. "What's a sperm donor?"

Ivy grimaced. "Sorry. Maybe I could've phrased that differently. Was there a turkey baster involved or an actual human being? Because I'm pretty sure I heard it was the latter."

Harlow's eyes widened. "Ivy."

"*Sorry,*" she said again. "I'm just asking what everyone's thinking. Shouldn't the guy be involved? Or aware?"

Cameron sighed, rubbing a hand over her shoulders. Even with the blunt delivery, I knew Ivy was just worried about me. They all were. But the absolute last thing I was going to do was tell a flat-out lie about the father. Because it was only a matter of time before Jax reappeared—any fucking day would be great—and I couldn't exactly press my brother on when that would be.

And Dean. Dean was just … weirdly so okay with me being pregnant with another man's baby that sometimes I questioned whether he was real.

Like I'd conjured him, my phone buzzed on the top of my dresser.

"Good morning," I said.

"Be a better one if I'd seen you before work, but maybe we can rectify that later."

The warm, deep sound of his voice had me smiling. "Possibly. How late will you be today?"

Dean hummed, and I heard the click of keys in the background. "I have a block in my afternoon in case I need to head out to Redmond. One of my client's horses is due to give birth any time, and her last one didn't go very well, so I'd like to be there if she starts labor. So I'll either be done by three today or elbow deep in horse fluids by dinner."

My nose scrunched. "I really appreciate the visual, thanks."

His laugh was just like his voice—a soothing comfort bled through even the most stressful of mornings. "You leaving for your appointment soon?" he asked.

"Probably should've left five minutes ago, but I can't decide what to wear." I tugged at the hem of my shirt. "My burrito baby is looking less burrito and more … baby."

"You'll look amazing no matter what you wear," he answered.

I turned to the side and studied my bump. "I'm going to be huge soon. You might retract that statement when my ankles are the size of my neck."

He hummed. "Thanks for the visual."

I laughed. "Will you help me put on my compression socks if that happens?"

"I can't imagine anything else I'd rather do," he answered gravely.

With a lingering smile, I shook my head. How many men would find out their girlfriend was pregnant by another man and just … go with it? The night I told him, he asked some questions about the father, and I evaded those like a fucking champ, managing to avoid any outright lies by saying the father wasn't in town, and he didn't want a family. He simply hugged me and told me that any child of mine was lucky to have me, and as long as I wanted him around, he wasn't going anywhere.

Then he kissed me. Dean was a good kisser. He knew when to use tongue and not too much of it. He knew when to kiss sweet and soft and slow. I definitely got butterflies when he kissed with an edge too, like he was holding on by a thread.

And that thread had to be *short*. With the *hey surprise I'm pregnant* announcement, I was oddly relieved for Dean's second attempt at virginity. I was too busy puking and feeling like death for the first ten weeks to even consider bedtime activities. The thing he'd done, though, unfailingly, was make me feel beautiful. Supported. And loved.

He hadn't said it yet, which I was oddly grateful for, but there was no hiding the way he looked at me. Every single day, I prayed to wake up and feel it like a lightning bolt. To feel like, *Yes, this sweet, perfect man was it for me, let's ride off into the sunset together*. But so far, it wasn't so much a lightning bolt of love as a sweet wave of happiness and contentment.

That was good though too, and I knew it.

"Poppy," my mom called.

"Dean, I gotta go. Sheila's head is about to explode if we don't leave."

He clucked his tongue. "I told you I'd use the wand in my office if you wanted an early ultrasound."

I snorted. "The same wand you used on the feral, flea-infested cat yesterday?"

"The very one. You're missing out."

"As much as I'd appreciate you using your *wand* on me," I teased, "I think I'll pass for now."

"Go," he said gently, and I could hear the smile in his voice. "It would be very messy if your mom's head exploded."

Dean disconnected the call with a promise to check in later, and again I tugged my pale purple T-shirt down over my leggings and let out a long sigh at just how *pregnant* I looked.

It was a warm day—spring was still a ways off—but even in March, we were getting some warmer, sunnier days after a colder-than-usual winter.

Cold winters made for excellent pregnancy hiders, as I'd learned. I could hibernate at home, watching movies and football underneath big fuzzy blankets, my handy puke bucket never very far from reach.

For a while, baggy sweatshirts and big coats were my friends, especially any time I went into town.

The double-edged sword of being from a well-known family in a very small town was that everyone knew your business. Sometimes that was good. We felt so taken care of, so loved when my dad was sick and when he passed away.

But with something like this? I snorted softly, rubbing a hand over my little bump.

"Can't keep hiding forever, can we, nugget?" I asked quietly.

"Poppy," my mom snapped, the sharp tone of her voice had me jumping. "Let's *go*."

I stuck my feet into some slip-on shoes and wrangled the mess of hair into something a little neater as I skipped down the steps.

"Sorry, sorry," I said. "Dean called while I was trying to decide whether big and baggy was a thing of the past."

Mom eyed my bump with a wry grin. "I'm thinking yes."

I sighed. "Let the rampant gossip begin, huh?"

She slung an arm around my shoulder. "Let them talk, sweetheart. The people who matter don't mind, and the people who mind don't matter."

It was such a mom thing to say. But it helped, no matter how cliché of a statement it was. Inside the protective bubble of our family, this life curveball didn't seem so daunting. I had a good-paying job that I loved, a roof over my head, and a mother who seemed to take this whoopsie of a pregnancy so well, I could only imagine it's because it gave her a new little person to fret over.

We buckled ourselves into her car, and I eyed the clock nervously when I realized how close it was to my sixteen-week appointment. "Oh shit, no wonder you were yelling."

"Mm-hmm. I don't break out that tone for very much now that you guys are grown."

I smiled, then gripped the handlebar above the car door

when my mom roared down the driveway, taking a corner with a squeal of the tires. "Easy, turbo. We're not that late."

"You heard the woman last time. They'll reschedule you if you're even five minutes past the start time." She gripped the steering wheel, her eyes focused on the road. "I want to listen to my grandchild's heartbeat for the first time, and I am not giving her the satisfaction of canceling us because I know she was just waiting to knock us down a peg."

I snorted. "Is she part of that, *those who mind don't matter* thing?"

Mom clucked her tongue. "Don't sass me, young lady. I can still be bothered by someone clearly judgmental. I saw the way she eyed your belly when she came out of church last week even though it was hidden under your sweater. Don't think I didn't." She cut someone off as we blew through a yellow light, and I tightened my grip on the handle. "And not like she's perfect. She left her first husband for her son's best friend. I oughta put her right back in her place one of these days."

"Mother," I said on a shocked gasp of laughter. "What would Dad say if he heard such things come out of your mouth?"

She let out a small snort. "He'd probably make some fuss about not having a violent reaction and extending grace, blah, blah, blah, but deep down, that man would have me going for the jugular if anyone was making you feel bad about yourself, and you know it as well as I do."

Absently, I rubbed at my chest, trying to soothe the dull ache. It was getting easier to talk about him as the days turned into weeks, and the weeks turned into months. I'd had many nights where I laid awake wondering what he'd think of all this.

When I stared up at the sky and wondered if he somehow knew what was happening since he left.

Where I cried myself to sleep, because even though my

brothers gave good hugs, and my mom and my sisters were amazing and supportive, I'd never be able to hear my dad's voice tell me that it would be okay while he wrapped me in his arms. That he'd love the little nugget no matter how much of a surprise they were.

I blinked away the sudden wetness in my eyes before my mom could see it because even though she was doing really well, it didn't take much to tip her over into the cry-fest with one of us if we started it.

So I held it together. For me and for her.

We made it to my appointment two minutes early, and damn if my mother didn't give the woman behind the desk a smug little smile when we checked in. She held my hand while I lay back on the table and answered the doctor's usual questions. Then the doctor pulled up my shirt and placed the wand over the bump, pressing into the skin just a bit.

Instantly, the room filled with a loud, fast whooshing sound. A smile broke open over my face, and my mom cried silently as she clutched my hand even tighter.

"Hey, baby," I whispered, my fingers spreading over the part of my stomach still untouched by the wand.

It was magic. Maybe one of the purest kinds we could experience on this earth, and I closed my eyes and let the sound of it wash over me while love—perfect, strong love— knocked me over like a giant wave.

And right on the heels of it, a dull pang of longing, wondering where Jax was and when he might show his face. Wondering what he'd say or do. I blew out a slow breath, forcing any of those stresses out of my mind. I took a few deep breaths, lest my blood pressure rocket sky high at the mere thought of him.

"Sounds good," the doctor said, a wide smile on her slightly wrinkled face. "Nice and strong. You're looking great, Poppy. Your blood pressure is excellent. Weight gain is right on track. Keep doing what you're doing, and I'll see you next month, okay?"

I nodded, tugging down my shirt while my mom wiped her face with a handkerchief. "Thank you, Dr. Beal."

My mom was quiet as we left the office and walked back to her car. I snuck a glance at her profile as she slowly pulled the seat belt around her.

"You okay, Mom?" I asked.

She blinked, but when she looked over at me, she hadn't quite gotten rid of the lingering sadness I could see there. I reached over and grabbed her hand, squeezing tight while she took a deep breath.

"I was thinking about my appointment with you, actually." Another tear slid down her cheek, and she dashed it away with a flick of her fingers. "Your dad walked on air the whole week after we heard your heartbeat. He was convinced you were a boy."

I smiled. "Really? You never told me."

"That's because once you were born, and that man heard you cry and the doctor said it was a girl, he was wrapped right around your little pinky." She smiled, a little bit happier this time. "We all were, honey. You were just what our family needed."

Something unspoken hid between her sweet words, and I tried to figure out what it was. "What's making you sad, though, Mom?"

For a moment, she didn't answer, her gaze pulling away from mine while she stared out the windshield. Her chin quivered for a moment, but she swallowed, then looked back at me.

"This baby is something our family needs too," she said. Then she took in a big breath. "But I wish you had someone here with you that would walk on air just for hearing that perfect little heartbeat. I hate seeing you do this alone, honey.
"

The heavy press of truth clogged my throat and kicked my heartbeat higher.

How long could I keep going without telling them? I'd made a dozen lists, and each one ended up in the same place, with me reaching the same conclusion.

No one could know until I talked to Jax. It wasn't fair to him.

So I leaned forward, flinging my arms around her shoulders while we both sniffled quietly. "I'm not alone," I told her. "Not even a little."

She pulled back, wiping at her face. "You're right."

While she gathered herself, fixing the mascara under her eyes, I settled back in my seat and wondered for the millionth time when Jax would ever show his damn face. I'd texted him one other time, another plea for a phone call, and it went undelivered, just like the first.

He'd never been gone this long, and the only comment I heard from Greer was that it was some months-long mountain hike thing that Jax had always wanted to do, and Cameron told him to take as long as he needed and see some of Europe while he was there if he wanted.

Thanks a lot, brother. Give the man a free pass to gallivant all around the world while I stayed at home, guarding the biggest family secret in … forever.

"Want to pick up some cookies or something and go out to the jobsite? Greer said she'd be there all day. We can tell her about the appointment."

Visiting their build sites wasn't something I did much of anymore either because I couldn't stop looking around the corner, hoping I'd see a dark-haired, dark-eyed man appear out of the shadows. And he just didn't.

With two dozen cookies in hand for the always hungry crew, Mom and I headed downtown to where they were working on the Wilder House store. As our primary investor, Ivy had snagged a prime piece of land just on the end of the main street that ran through downtown Sisters. The frame was up, roof on, drywall in, and they were working on trimming out the interior. The loud buzz of machinery had me smiling as we walked up the front porch and through the wide double doors that would serve as the main entrance.

It was built to look like a barn-shaped house, with tall ceilings and a loft-style upstairs overlooking the bottom level. Ivy's plans, much like everything else she did, were immaculate, and I couldn't help but grin at how much it had all changed in the last month since I'd visited. Tucked back into the far corners would be two model kitchens, each with a long stretch of counter to display some of the home goods we were carrying—cutting boards, flatware, plates, and artisan glasses. Right now, they were framing out the skeleton of those kitchens, building in the custom cabinets that would also serve as a sample of what Wilder Homes—our branch dedicated to building custom homes—could do for their residential clients.

Greer popped her head out from a hallway at the back, which led to a couple of offices, the bathrooms, and a private space to meet with clients. Her grin spread wide. "Oooh, cookies. I love when you bring us things." She yanked off her safety glasses and pulled me in for a sidelong hug. "How was the appointment?"

"Good."

"Amazing," Mom corrected. "We heard the heartbeat."

Greer's face lit up. "Aw, you did? Can they tell if it's a boy or a girl yet?"

"Definitely a boy," my brother Ian said, appearing from behind me to snatch a giant chocolate chip cookie.

I swatted his big, dumb hand away when he tried to grab a second one. "Next appointment, if I want to."

"What's at the next appointment?" Cameron asked, dropping a kiss on the top of my head and snagging a cookie from the box. When he finished half the giant cookie in one bite, I rolled my eyes.

"Ultrasound," I told him. "Oh my gosh, did you even chew that? Don't you have any manners?"

"I'm starving. I haven't eaten since breakfast."

One of the loud machines from upstairs turned off, so I no longer had to raise my voice to speak over it. "They'll be able to tell the gender at the next appointment as long as nugget is cooperating." I ran my hand over my stomach, wishing desperately I could feel them move. "But honestly, I'm not sure I want to find out."

Greer let out a disappointed groan. "You're not going to find out? How am I supposed to plan the most epic nursery of all time?"

I fluttered my eyelashes. "Any good interior designer can work with gender neutral, right?"

She gave me a withering stare in return.

A few guys walked past, taking cookies and saying thank you. Only one of them glanced down at my bump with slightly widened eyes.

Sigh.

Here we go.

One of the younger ones gave me a grateful, slightly flirty smile, which had Greer clearing her throat pointedly.

Cameron smothered a laugh with another bite of his cookie. "Can someone go tell Wade and Jax we've got cookies?"

My chest turned into a giant block of ice, something almost impossible to breathe through. "Jax?" I whispered.

Cameron gave me a guarded look. "Yeah, he, uh, got back last night. Showed up this morning without any warning, of course."

Oh good. This was *great*.

My vision went a little spotty, and I vaguely registered just how fucking horrible it would be if I passed out right there at my brother's feet.

Some heavy boots came down the stairs from the loft

space, and I rubbed at my belly, an undoubtedly nervous gesture. Maybe I could run. Sprint the hell out of the house and figure out a better time to have this little reveal.

Yes. Running was great. Sure, I hadn't run voluntarily in about five years when an angry swarm of bees was chasing me, but I could easily break that streak with the icy-cold panic coursing through my veins.

I needed out. *Now*.

My hands fumbled with the box as I tried to push them off at Cameron, but he wasn't paying attention, and just as a big, broad body came into view in my peripheral vision, the box fell to the floor.

"Hey, watch the cookies," Cameron said, leaning down to snag them.

My heart was in my fucking throat, thrashing at a rate that could not be good for my blood pressure. Jax hadn't seen me yet since he was deep in conversation with his coworker Wade.

It wasn't too late, right? If I hid behind my sister and then bolted through the back, maybe he wouldn't see me.

Maybe there was a way for me to communicate wordlessly. Just project very strongly with nothing but the power of my gaze for him to *keep his cool*, and I'd talk to him later when half my family was not in the room with us.

In my head, panicked laughter crowded my brain.

He was *here*.

Right after my mom gave her big emotional speech about wishing the father was around to experience this with me.

We were about to have an experience, that was for sure.

I couldn't help it, my eyes drank in the sight of him, greedy for even the slightest bit of how he'd changed in the past few months. His hair was slightly longer, the usual stubbled jaw thick with a dark beard. Like usual, he wore a black T-shirt and worn-in work jeans that molded to his thick thighs. The toolbelt slung low around his slim hips jangled when he came to the bottom step.

He looked *good*. Heart-stopping, lung-squeezing, if-I-wasn't-pregnant-already,   him-looking-like-this-would-probably-knock-me-up-all-over-again good.

That's when his gaze snapped to mine.

I couldn't breathe.

"Hey," I whispered, my voice trembling only the slightest bit. Everyone around us went suspiciously quiet. I felt my sister's gaze heavy on my face, but I couldn't possibly look anywhere but Jax.

Those dark, dark eyes traced over my face first, then slowly tracked down to where my hand rested on my stomach and narrowed. His big frame expanded on a sharp inhale and an equally sharp exhale.

"What the *fuck*, Poppy?"

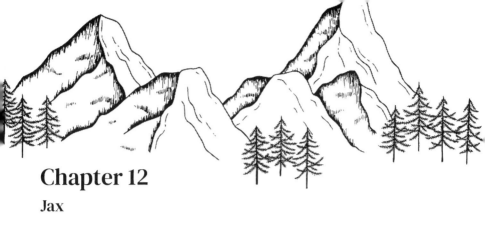

Chapter 12
Jax

There were probably a million better, smarter, calmer ways to handle this, but every single fucking option flew out of my fucking head the moment I saw her hand on her obviously pregnant belly.

Pregnant.

Poppy was pregnant.

I didn't know much about pregnancy, or when a woman started showing, but no matter how much I avoided her over the years, I knew Poppy Wilder, and all it took was one solitary glance at the way the color drained from her face, the way her eyes were full of shock and apology, and I fucking knew that baby was mine.

"You're pregnant?" I said again, voice raspy and low in disbelief. "You're *pregnant?*"

No one moved.

If a single nail fell on the ground, the echo would've sounded like a gunshot.

Slowly, Poppy nodded, and a hint of pink crept into her pale, pale cheeks. Next to her, Cameron narrowed his eyes.

"Why do you sound so pissed right now?" my best friend asked quietly. It was a dangerous sort of quiet too, and I struggled not to give anything away on my face.

Poppy's eyes fluttered closed for just a moment. At her side, Sheila Wilder kept her face impassive, but she gently wrapped an arm around Poppy's back.

"That's why you texted me?" I shouted.

After a visible swallow, Poppy nodded again.

Ian Wilder let out a sharp gust of air, rubbing a hand over his jaw.

"I think we need to go talk somewhere," I said grimly.

"Jax, why do you sound so pissed off right now?" Cameron asked again, his voice rising loudly.

Wade, our longtime foreman, stood behind me, and I heard his muttered, "Fuck me sideways, I did not see this coming."

The first person to move was Greer Wilder—the oldest Wilder sister, the one I'd worked with for over a decade, and at the moment, quite possibly the scariest woman in the world. Slowly, she looked down at the worktable next to her and picked up a hammer, hefting its weight in her normally very graceful hand.

"Greer," I warned.

She nodded sharply. "Yup, this'll do just fine."

Sheila Wilder covered her mouth with a visibly shaking hand, and Poppy gave her sister a frantic look. "Greer, wait—"

And then, with every man in the room watching with a slightly terrified widening of their eyes, Greer brushed past Poppy with a ferocious look on her face, hammer gripped tight in her fist, and she strode toward me in a way that had me backing up with my hands raised.

"Greer, hold on," I shouted.

She did not hold on.

People behind her were shouting—Poppy yelling at Cameron, and Cameron was yelling at Ian, but no one was overly concerned with the angry, armed woman bearing down on me.

"Can't someone grab her?" I asked frantically.

"You asshole," Greer hissed.

I tried to back up again but bumped into Wade, who did me no favors by blocking my exit back up the stairs.

God, Greer probably would've swung that hammer straight up at my balls too, but Ian Wilder took pity on me, darting forward to snatch his sister around the waist, yanking her back just before she could do any permanent damage.

She kicked her legs out. "Put me *down*, Ian."

"Everyone, outside. *Now*," Ian bellowed. Any yelling stopped immediately. With Greer struggling against his grip, Ian gave Cameron a quick, hard look. "You too, Cameron."

As the crew shuffled out, curiosity clear in the way they glanced between Poppy and me and Cameron. I tried to reconcile the way my entire life had flipped on its axis in the span of about three minutes.

I couldn't, though. There was no reconciling this. Not yet.

Greer finally finagled out of Ian's hold, but instead of trying to murder me with a hammer, she dropped it on the ground, immediately wrapping her little sister up in a tight embrace and whispering something to Poppy that I couldn't hear.

But Poppy nodded, and I heard a pitiful sniffle that had my gut churning.

Alone. She'd been alone for months while I was off hiking fucking Europe and watching sunsets and completely disconnecting from the world. It hadn't been a self-centered trip, but the timing of it now held an oil-slick feeling of exactly that. Selfishness.

What if something had happened? What if she'd lost the baby, and I wasn't here?

A baby.

A fucking baby.

My hands started shaking, and I crossed my arms, trying

to stem the beginnings of a panic attack as it crawled over my skin.

What do I do?

What do I do? I thought frantically.

My eyes locked on Poppy, taking in the pale color of her face because I wasn't the only one stunned right now. God, she had no idea I was back, and judging by the complete explosion of her siblings, I wasn't the only one getting their world rocked.

She clearly hadn't told anyone it was me, and the two unread texts that popped up on my phone when I turned it on last night suddenly felt like a lead weight hooked into my stomach. She *tried*.

When you spend a life crafted around emotionally safe decisions, moments like this felt like walking across a canyon on nothing but a flimsy thread for support. Nothing on either side of me but air. My pulse skipped dangerously, and I pulled in a slow breath through my nose.

What do I do?

Self-loathing was a foreign feeling, and I hated the way it climbed around my ribs and took root in my stomach. It was dark and bitter, something you couldn't erase quickly or easily. That was the thing about any feeling born in shame. Those roots went deep, and pulling them out alone was almost impossible.

Eventually, Greer pulled away from Poppy, and she cupped her sister's cheek, then said something else. Poppy gave her big sister a tiny smile, then nodded again. The color was coming back into her face.

Cameron, however, still hadn't budged. His eyes seared into my skin, and when I finally tore my gaze from Poppy to his, that self-loathing grew into something else.

His disappointment left me feeling so ice cold, I could practically feel the frost climbing through my veins. Hadn't I promised him that I'd never? Could never. *Would* never.

Promises were flimsy foundations when you didn't really know what your future looked like. Or what hers looked like either. Years ago, it felt simple enough to say that because one look was nothing. Years ago, it was impossible to believe that she'd still look at me like I was something, someone, vital to her.

"Cameron," Poppy snapped. "Knock it off."

His eyes dropped to the floor, his arms tightening as he crossed them over his chest.

"Tell them to come back inside," Poppy called out to Ian's retreating back.

I blinked.

So did Cameron.

Poppy took a deep breath. "There's no reason for them to stop working. We can go outside and talk," she told me.

With a tight jaw and a racing heart, I nodded. How different this was from the last time I was close to her—sleep-rumpled in my kitchen while she gave me the sweetest, softest fucking kiss on my cheek. Even after she left, I caught whiffs of her shampoo.

I didn't count our brief exchange in her empty office. I'd been so locked down, refusing to show even the slightest flicker of how fucking unhinged I felt being in her presence again. If I'd looked at her too long or said more than her name, I would've lost it. As it was, that one tiny moment—a polite hello and those questions in her eyes—had my hands shaking from the desire to shove her against the wall and have her just one more time before I left, something, anything to prolong that one night into something neither of us would forget while I was gone.

And look at that. I'd succeeded without realizing it. Because there was definitely no forgetting it now. Just thinking it had my chest feeling tight, a giant invisible screw straight through my sternum.

There was a back entrance to the store, so I held my arm out and gestured for Poppy to precede me.

The heat from Cameron's gaze bored into my back as I followed Poppy outside. Of course, I'd have to talk to him eventually. Hopefully, he wouldn't go for any sharp-edged tools like his sister. Knowing him, he'd just need one good punch, and we'd be fine.

I rubbed at my chest, praying we'd be fine.

As Poppy walked in front of me, I couldn't help but stare. From the back, you couldn't tell anything was different. Her waist still nipped in at the sides, and there was no change in her hips or backside.

Not yet, at least.

The door was held open with a wedge, and behind the building were piles of dirt from the initial dig. A small picnic table and some camping chairs sat in the shadow of the roofline, where the crew normally had lunch.

Neither of us sat.

My hands were in tight fists, my arms crossed over my chest as I watched Poppy turn in a slow circle before finally meeting my eyes.

"I tried to text you while you were gone," she said. "I didn't … I didn't realize you'd be away for months when you left."

I slicked my tongue over my teeth and tried to pick out one, just one, single rational thought. It was impossible, though.

Poppy Wilder stood in front of me, her eyes full of apology and worry, pregnant with my fucking child. God, what a mess.

"Your text didn't come through until I landed last night. I keep an international phone just for emergencies. Your brother has the number, but…" I answered.

"He didn't know," she finished quietly, her hands wringing nervously in front of her.

"You told me we'd be okay," I said, and the words came

out harsher than I intended. Her brow furrowed at my tone. Already fucking this up. I clenched my teeth together, willing down the strongest of my emotions until I could speak again. "What happened?"

Poppy sucked in a quick breath through her nose. "I was sick the week before I saw you, and I ... I didn't know antibiotics messed with my pills. It lessens the effectiveness."

I swiped a hand over my mouth and managed a tight nod.

A child.

A child with Poppy.

"Are you okay?" I asked, studying her face, noting the slight dark circles under her eyes. "Like, do you feel all right?"

At first, Poppy just stared. Then her chin quivered.

"Shit," I muttered when the first tear slipped down her cheek.

A heartbeat later, she sank on the picnic table, dropped her head in her hands, and started crying. Her shoulders shook, and I stared at the sky because me and crying women were never, ever a good combination.

I eased myself down into a crouch in front of her and gently patted her shoulder while she purged all the things she must have been holding in while I was gone.

"I didn't know what to do, Jax," she said, lifting her head, making no effort to wipe the wetness off her face. "You were gone, and I wasn't going to tell them it was you when I couldn't even tell *you* it was you. And I had that date that night, you know? They all assumed it was him."

"Oh great, so they think the father is the banker douche who got stabbed in the hand?"

Poppy's eyes flashed, the spark of anger so hot that I almost backed away. "What other option did I have? I couldn't tell them the truth! I couldn't tell them it was you before you came home. And I didn't know you were back. You think I wanted you to find out this way?" My hand was still awkwardly patting her shoulder, and she smacked it away, standing to pace the small area in front of the picnic table. "Stop patting me. I'm not a little kid."

Because I wanted to keep my limbs intact, I stood a safe distance away and let her unload.

"I was going to wait for Cameron or Greer to tell me you were home, and I was going to call you," she said on a frustrated rush. "And then, then I could finally tell you and move on because I'd know for sure if you didn't want to be involved or—"

"Why would I not want to be involved?" I interjected.

That stopped her short. Her hair was a mess, the ponytail from earlier had slipped out of its tie, the dark hair falling over her shoulder while she gaped at me. "You do?"

"You thought I'd make you do it alone?" I asked.

"*I don't want a girlfriend, I don't want a wife, I don't want a family*," she tossed back at me, eyes still blazing. "I don't want a *family*, you said. Your exact words. So no, I wasn't assuming anything. For all I knew, you'd hear the news and bounce the hell out of town, never to be seen again," she said in a wobbling voice. "Lord knows you do it enough."

My skin was crawling. Anger and frustration and regret on a sickening loop in my head.

"Fuck," I ground out, kicking at a small rock by my feet. "Yes, I said that, but—"

"Do not tell me you didn't mean it because I know better than that," she said hotly. "I *know* you, Jax Cartwright. Don't pretend I don't. I walked into your house that night with my eyes wide open." Poppy covered her face with her hands. When she dropped them, the look in her eyes about did me in, carving my chest hollow. "You don't get to be mad at how I handled this, okay? You were gone, and I did my best."

How ugly it was to face the consequences of all your choices like this. For years, I refused to put too much thought into why I avoided serious relationships. Even semi-serious.

If I tried hard enough, I could still hear my mom chatter

on and on about how she'd find someone to take care of her. Take care of us. She never did, but the absence of that person felt like a giant fucking shadow over our entire life.

And I'd become someone who, understandably, couldn't be relied on.

I came and went as I pleased, and never, ever let myself get in a position where my actions might cause disappointment.

Look at how well I did there.

"I know you did, Poppy," I said. "But you have to give me a chance to catch up here, okay? I'm a little..." I clawed for the right word. "Thrown."

The rigid tension in her shoulders deflated, and the spark of heat died from her eyes. "I know. I'm sorry. I really didn't want this to happen in front of an audience."

"Your sister might murder me the next time I turn my back."

Poppy's mouth lifted in a wry grin. A tiny one, but it was there. "No, she won't. I won't let her."

"You gonna protect me now?"

"No one messes with the pregnant sister, trust me. Not even Greer." She smoothed a hand over her small bump. "I have the ultimate trump card here."

My eyes locked in on that movement, and my chest thumped uncomfortably. There were a million things to discuss, details that wouldn't even cross my mind until I'd had more time to process this. But that, that tiny person inside her wasn't a discussion point. Wasn't one of a million details.

It was my child.

Our child.

"Do you ... do you know what it is yet?"

She shook her head. "My next appointment is in four weeks. I can—we can," she amended slowly, "do an ultrasound then, if we want to know. If you'd like to come, that is."

My gaze flew up to hers, but I didn't say anything.

Poppy's cheeks were so pink as she stared up at me, her eyes so wide. God, what she must be thinking. What she must have felt, keeping this a secret for months. She'd done that to protect me if I was honest about it. And I hadn't done a damn thing to deserve it if I was honest about that too.

Wade came through the back door, eyeing the distance between us. "Poppy, sorry to interrupt, but they decided I was the only one safe to come back here in case they heard something that would require acid to be poured down their ears."

I sighed, rubbing a hand over my mouth. "What is it, Wade?"

"Sheila said you two had lunch plans with someone, and she wanted to know if you wanted her to reschedule."

Poppy glanced at her watch, brow pinching when she saw the time. "Shoot, okay. I'll be right there." She glanced at me again. "Can we … can we talk soon? We've got…" Her eyes fluttered shut, and her hand fluttered to her temple while she sighed. "We've got a lot more to discuss that we shouldn't get into now."

I nodded tightly, crossing my arms again, watching her lay a hand on Wade's arm as she passed. He kept his eyes locked on me while she did.

The silence stretched. And stretched. I exhaled heavily. "You got something to say, Wade?" I asked.

Like he had all the time in the fucking world, Wade pulled the unlit cigarette from where it was wedged underneath his beat-up fishing hat. His favorite lighter, a bright blue metallic thing he always carried with him, hissed to life with the flick of a button, and he took a slow drag, blowing the smoke up to the blue sky.

"If I was Tim Wilder," he said slowly, "I'd haunt your ass until the day you die."

Pretty sure my eye twitched as I stared at him. "Thanks. That's helpful."

"I'm talking flickering lights. Breaking shit when you're not looking. Wake you up in the middle of the night by giving you nightmares. All of it until you slowly lose your mind."

I slicked my tongue over my teeth. "You done yet?"

He blew out another stream of smoke. "Greer's ready to castrate you. Ian's talking her down, but Cameron still hasn't said a damn word." He eyed me carefully. "I think you're the unlucky bastard to be the first to rock their world since he died, you know?"

Just the position I always wanted to be in. Trigger an already protective family and launch those instincts into the stratosphere, fueled by grief and missing their dad's steady presence.

"It wasn't … I didn't plan any of this. It was just one night," I told him.

He held up a hand, eyes pinching shut. "I do not want details, kid."

I nodded.

Wade let out a long sigh, glancing back inside the store, where the sounds of tools and conversation filtered outside. "I think you should take the afternoon, Jax. Go clear your head. Let them do the same. Maybe try to talk to Cameron after he's done with work and less likely to…"

"Dismember me?"

"Basically." His mouth edged up in a ghost of a smile.

Since high school, Cameron was one of the solid rocks in my life. He'd never tried to change who I was and always accepted me, flaws and all. This was the single worst way I could've betrayed his trust, and still, I knew him well enough to know he'd do his best not to lash out until he could get his thoughts settled.

I could give him the afternoon.

"Yeah. I'll do that," I told Wade.

"You do right by that girl, Jax," he said, voice harder than I'd ever heard it. "It's the only way you come out of this intact."

He disappeared back into the house, and I sank onto the picnic table bench, let my head fall into my hands, and tried to figure out what the fuck I was supposed to do now.

Chapter 13
Poppy

Remember when I thought it sucked having the entire town of Sisters staring at me, wondering who went and knocked me up?

Feeling your family's eyes on you was a million times worse once they knew. Really, actually knew who'd done it. In a messy corner of my jumbled brain, I told myself that it wouldn't have felt like this if I'd been prepared, but despite the fact that Jax ostensibly fell off the face of the planet for months, I wasn't really prepared for what I'd do when I saw his stupid, handsome face again.

An atomic bomb just went off at the forefront of my entire existence, blooming so high in the sky that it dwarfed everything around it, and the only thing that was left to do was deal with the messy fallout. We'd be feeling the effects of this for a long time, and that was if Jax and I could figure out a seamless way to co-parent.

If.

If.

If.

I didn't even know for sure if he wanted to come to my appointment. That was *one* small question. A thousand more were behind it.

So many ifs in my life since I showed up on his doorstep. Where was Patrice now when I needed her sage advice?

I went the long way around the front of the store, trying to avoid Cameron and Greer, hoping they were back inside working. But I wasn't quite so lucky. My mom was waiting by the car with her arms tight around her middle and a deeply thoughtful look on her face. Greer leaned against the passenger door, but her eyes locked on mine the moment I came into view.

She opened her mouth, and I held up a hand. "No," I said firmly. "Not now, Greer."

My big sister, one of my very best friends in the world, sucked in a sharp breath and blew it out oh-so slowly. "You don't even know what I was going to say," she replied softly.

"I don't." My stomach trembled, and everything inside my head felt like I was a Tilt-A-Whirl. "But not now, Greer. Please. I know I lied, and it was fucked up, but it wasn't just him. I was there too, and... I can't talk about this now," I finished in a trembling voice.

Slowly, she nodded, then wrapped her arms around me in an impossibly tight squeeze that helped settle that unsettled swirling of my thoughts. Judging by the look on my mom's face, she and Greer shared a look over my head, and once I'd pulled out of Greer's embrace, I slid into the car and dropped my head back on the seat.

Once my mom was behind the driver's seat, she took her time hooking her seat belt, and the weight of her concerned gaze almost broke me. Everything inside me wobbled like a tower of cards. The slightest pressure and I might crack.

His face.

Oh, his face when we stood outside.

Not once in all the years that I'd watched Jax had I ever seen him look lost. Overwhelmed. Like he was going to pass the hell out.

"Do you want to go home instead of lunch?"

I pinched my eyes shut and nodded. "Please."

Mom pulled out her phone and sent a quick text. We'd planned on meeting one of her friends she'd met in a grief support group, someone I hadn't met yet.

Looking over at her, I studied her face, wondering if she was feeling the Jax-bombshell effect, but she looked surprisingly unruffled. "You can still go if you want," I told her. "I'll probably take a nap once we get home anyway."

Mom smiled gently. "No, it's okay. She'll understand. I'd rather be home if you want to talk."

I didn't, though. Not yet, at least.

Once we were back at the house, I immediately went upstairs and burrowed straight under the covers, the tears that I'd held back threatening with a mighty vengeance. Mom tapped her knuckles against the door and crept in when I didn't answer. Maybe she heard the pathetic little sniffle from underneath the covers.

She smoothed a hand over my back, pulling the blanket away from where I'd clutched it to my face. Her smile was small, but it was there.

"You used to do that when you were little," she said. "Hide your face in the blanket when you napped."

"I did?"

She hummed, playing with the strands of hair around my face. The gentle brush of her fingers had my eyelids fluttering closed. "You told me once you could focus on sleeping more when you couldn't see things to distract you."

"I have a lot more to distract me now," I whispered. "Think it'll still go away if I hide?"

"No, sweetheart." The warm weight of her hand moved to my shoulder, and she squeezed, comforting and soft. "Is this the part where I tell you I'm not really all that surprised?"

A big, hot tear slid out of the corner of my eye, running over the bridge of my nose before it dripped into the pillow. I didn't wipe it away. Neither did she.

"I just can't talk about it yet, Mom. I thought … I thought I'd have time to figure out what to say to everyone, what to say to *him*, and this whole day has just gone upside down so fast."

Mom rubbed my back, and the tension ebbed from my frame. Her soft shushing noise helped too. It was the kind of noise you'd make if a baby was crying, rocking them back and forth to try to make them feel better.

Except I was the one who needed consoling. Not because Jax had reacted badly, but holy shit, it was a less than ideal way for him to find out. For my family to find out.

I wanted to ask her if everyone would somehow be disappointed in me because I'd lied for so long, but I couldn't make the words leave the base of my throat. They just sat there, and I'm telling you, if slightly hormonal, mildly insecure questions had a taste, it would be something bitter and chalky.

My entire life, I was one of those kids who never got in trouble. Always had good grades. Showed up whenever someone needed me. And my crush on Jax was almost unilaterally viewed as a "poor Poppy" type situation, like I was something to be pitied because I couldn't quite move on.

Curling in a tighter ball, I settled my arm around my little bump and tried to imbue happy, low-stress thoughts down to the nugget. Could they feel what I felt? Today, I really hoped not.

Without saying anything else, my mom leaned down and brushed a soft kiss over my temple. "I love you."

"Love you too," I murmured, giving her a grateful smile. With a wink, she tugged the blanket back over my head, and I was fast asleep within a few minutes.

A couple of hours later, I woke with a dry mouth and a screaming bladder, and when I shuffled down the hallway to pee, I couldn't hear any noise coming from downstairs. The house might have been quiet, but I didn't have any texts on my phone from Mom letting me know she'd gone anywhere.

What I did have, though, was texts in our sister thread, and I groaned when I saw the first couple.

> Greer: Okay, just tell us how you want to proceed. Do you want to talk about it? Not talk about it? Jax left for the afternoon, so I'm a little calmer now.

> Adaline: OMG, did you threaten someone again? GREER.

> Greer: Listen, it was one little hammer, and if the man can't handle it, maybe he shouldn't have boinked the little sister.

> Ivy: The little sister can read these texts, you know…

> Ivy: Also, I, for one, would like to know how the boinking was after so many years of buildup.

> Adaline: Who let you in this chat, Ivy?

> Harlow: I did. We need some non-Wilder blood. I also wouldn't mind knowing. Call it author research in case I write this into a book someday. The angst would be off the charts.

> Greer: I swear, nothing is sacred anymore. I don't know what my brothers see in you two.

> Ivy: I'd answer that question, but I don't think you want the answer.

> Harlow: The sex aside, no one would be able to put up with Ian, which works out nicely for me.

> Adaline: I'm covering my ears. And eyes. Feel free to redirect this conversation ANY TIME, Pops.

A quiet laugh escaped despite my best intentions, but I didn't reply right away. I wandered downstairs, and no answer came when I called my mom's name. I sat at the kitchen counter and sank my head into my hands. What did I need right now? What would help?

I wasn't even sure what to say or how to address my big, certifiably insane family about any of this. They were nosy. Overprotective (especially of me). Loud with their opinions. Louder with their love. And now all of those things were one big, messy knot that needed to be untangled before Jax and I could move forward.

My hand grabbed for a notebook and a pen, and I took a deep breath before I started scrawling things down on the paper. I didn't think about what I was writing or worry about anyone seeing it. I just word vomited everything I could think of that would help make this better.

After a couple of minutes, I read back through and already felt a settling in my brain.

I needed structure.

I needed control.

And I needed everyone to shut the hell up and listen to me before they jumped to conclusions and over-the-top reactions that we were already known for. The fact that this town had survived us for so many years was honestly one of its best features.

> Me: Sorry, I took a feelings nap.

> Me: This is what's going to happen, and it's not up for discussion, okay?

> Ivy: I find it so hot when you get bossy.

> Me: Family meeting tomorrow at seven thirty. If you're in town, it'll be in the big conference room at the warehouse. If you're not, I'll send you a Zoom link.

> Greer: Yes, ma'am.

Me: NO WEAPONS, GREER. I'm serious.

Greer: I know, I know. It wasn't my best moment. I'm really sorry.

Me: This will not be a particularly in-depth part of the meeting because I physically cannot stand in front of my brothers and talk about it, but I was the one who showed up at his house, okay? He wanted me to leave, but it was storming, so I couldn't. There's no need to cast him as the villain.

Ivy: I wasn't. I knew you'd wear him down eventually.

Adaline: Honestly, I'm impressed you got him to cave.

Ivy: Were you naked under a trench coat when you showed up or something? Men have a tendency to lose a few IQ points when that happens.

Adaline: IVY.

Greer: Can we vote her off the island?

Ivy: I'd love to see you try.

Ivy: Poppy, just remember I live half a mile away if you want to tell me stories your sisters don't want to hear.

Harlow: We can't get rid of Ivy. She's the only one who's as scary as Greer when we need backup.

Me: I love all of you. No one is voting anyone off the island, and no, I wasn't naked when I showed up, but there might have been alcohol involved. That's all you get for now. I'm putting away my phone and getting a snack because the baby is hungry, and I need to make my meeting agenda.

> Ivy: AN AGENDA ABOUT YOUR NIGHT OF
> SEX WITH JAX. This will be the best meeting
> we've ever had.

With a short laugh and a shake of my head, I tapped away from the thread with my sisters. I saw another unread text and muttered a curse when I saw it was from Dean. Oh God, what was I going to say to *him*? My heart.

> Dean: Started to worry when I didn't hear from
> you after the appointment. Hope everything's
> okay.

> Me: Appointment went great. Sorry it took me
> so long. Went to see the store and took a nap.
> I'm pretty wiped today, so I think I'll stay home
> tonight. Call you tomorrow?

> Dean: Of course. Xx

In the jumble of the day, my boyfriend—sweet and kind and driven and almost unbearably attractive—completely slipped my mind.

Nicely done, Poppy.

Before today, I'd never actually felt like a horrible person before. Sure, I had moments just like everyone else—snappy moments and judgey moments and gossipy moments. But I still felt like, at my core, I was a decent, non-shitty human being.

Until today.

Tears welled in my eyes again, and I dashed them away ruthlessly.

No, I did not get to cry over this.

The list materialized in my head before I could stop it.

Lies to family.

Lies to boyfriend.

Forgets boyfriend's existence the moment I laid eyes on Jax again.

140

Sits back while my family lays the blame at Jax's feet without saying a word.

There was no denying that one hurt worse than all the others, a visceral shooting pain straight through the heart. But I wasn't that woman, you know?

I wasn't that person who spoke without thinking. I wasn't the one who unleashed her temper without a script. Maybe to my detriment, I thought just a little bit too much before acting. Made sure that whatever those actions were, the waves I made as a result wouldn't cause any damage.

And here I was. Hurricane fucking Poppy. Leveling the immediate area and leaving nothing but a heaping pile of drama in her wake.

With a groan, I got up from the table, notebook tucked under my arm and the pen between my teeth. The kitchen was clean, a plate of freshly baked muffins sat on a cooling rack underneath the kitchen window, and when I glanced out into the front, Mom's car was still parked in its normal spot. In the fall, Cameron built her a fancy chicken coop, and she loved spending time out there, so with the safe assumption that she was with the chicks, I sliced up an apple and some sharp cheddar cheese, broke a muffin in half, and went out onto the front porch to wait for her to come back.

I always chose my dad's favorite chair when I sat outside, which was maybe a silly way to feel closer to him on days when I missed him most, but it helped.

With the plate sitting on the side table, I ran my hands over the arms of the chair, felt the dings and scratches from years of sitting and taking his coffee there. I let my eyes flutter closed at the warmth of the sun on my face.

"Oh, Dad, if you could've seen this one," I said with a tiny smile. "I'm sure you would've been the one making me laugh right now. God, Greer had a *hammer*."

I always liked the idea that he could hear us. That he knew what was happening. Maybe it was naive, but sometimes the simple act of saying something that I'd want him to know out loud helped ease some of the twisting ache coiled in my chest since he died.

I'd asked myself a million times over the past few months what he'd think about all this. If he was alive, if I'd have confided in him about Jax. It was so easy to say that I would have. That if I'd had his calm, steady presence, I might have made different decisions. But the truth was much more complicated than a few simple questions, even if he had asked them.

There was a level of uncertainty that still clouded big decisions without my dad. How do we proceed? Who's taking his place for this event and that event? That massive, empty spot where he always stood, who was going to fill it? At Christmas, there was a stilted moment of pause before Ian stood and slowly picked up the carving knife when Mom unthinkingly laid it next to the turkey and took her seat.

My hand curled around the notebook in my head, thinking about how many times Dad caught me making a list to help move through a situation that was stressing me out.

"Feel better now, Popsicle?"

He'd kiss the top of my head and pat my shoulder.

I laid my own hand on my shoulder and squeezed. It didn't feel the same.

"Not yet," I whispered to no one but the trees. "But hopefully soon."

He'd have calmed everyone today. I knew it. He'd have spoken up in a way that I couldn't quite manage, the sheer magnitude of how overwhelming it was to see him weighing my tongue down like an anchor, muting any words that I might have said if I was a little more prepared.

Protective to a fault, my family was. Usually just to put people outside of our circle.

This was someone inside it. Very inside of it. Maybe, somehow, that made all of this even worse to my siblings, no matter how much they loved Jax on any given day. No one, and I mean *no one*, saw this coming.

My phone dinged, and I pulled myself from my looping, swooping thoughts.

> Jax: Are you home?

> Jax: I'm heading to talk to Cameron, but I'd like to stop there first if that's okay with you.

My heart stuttered at the sight of his name popping up on my phone's screen.

"Better get used to it," I muttered. I was staring down the barrel at years of interactions with Jax. *Years.* And that was before you started thinking about graduations and college and weddings and grandkids someday. I'd need *eight thousand* notebooks before this was over.

"Oh God," I whispered shakily. "Settle the fuck down, Poppy."

Maybe, *maybe*, I had a tendency to go a little overboard with my long-term projections.

> Me: I'm home.

Doing my best calm pregnant person impersonation, I waited for Jax to appear, methodically eating the apple and cheese so there were no hungry freak-outs upon his arrival. It wasn't that I didn't trust myself to stay levelheaded, but until you feel those pregnancy hormones, you didn't even *know* how little you were actually in control.

But the exact moment I heard the rumble of the motorcycle engine, that whole calm pregnant person was exposed for the utter bullshit it was. Would there ever be a time that I wasn't so thoroughly affected by his presence?

I sat still, hand over my bump, watching him astride that beast of a machine, his eyes covered by aviator sunglasses and his jaw coated with dark hair. I'd never seen Jax with a full beard, but I was a *fan*.

"Knock it off, Poppy," I hissed under my breath. Weren't those the kinds of thoughts that got me in trouble in the first place?

Honestly, though, what could they hurt? It's not like I could get *more* pregnant.

Jax eased his bike to a stop in the gravel driveway in front of the house, and from behind those mirrored lenses, I could feel the weight of his gaze. Patience was required in spades for this interaction, deep wells that I'd never accessed before. He had a point earlier at the jobsite. I'd had months to get used to the idea of this, but on that first day I found out? I was a hot-mess express.

When your life takes a sudden U-turn, it takes some adjusting. I'd had my family to lean on, but they'd had time to adjust as well. The only person who didn't was the man whose super swimmers got us into this mess.

Okay, fine, me crawling into his bed kinda got us here too, but I digress.

Extending grace to him wasn't just the kind thing to do. It was the only real option I had in order for us to move forward. We had time to make plans, and months to figure out the best course of action.

Maybe we could start just by being … friends. The thought helped, because I knew that despite Jax's epic reserve, he was a good friend to Cameron.

Yes. I could totally, one hundred percent do this. Friends with Jax Cartwright.

Hell, he'd probably be relieved when I told him about Dean.

The sound of the engine cut off, and the sudden silence had me pulling in a deep breath. Instead of joining me in the empty chair on the other side of the table, Jax walked up the steps to the porch and leaned his big frame against the railing, tugging off his sunglasses with the tips of his fingers, then letting them dangle by his side while he studied me.

Unlike earlier, there was much more weight and attention to this look. Instead of the overwhelmed, lost glint to this eye, now Jax seemed focused and determined, and I couldn't deny it had my heart racing just a little bit.

I waited for him to say something, anything, and he just … didn't.

He just stared, at my face, at my bump, and all the while, those sunglasses tapped against the side of this thigh.

"What?" I finally asked when I couldn't bear the thick silence anymore. "I know you didn't come here just to stare at me."

His lips were almost always in a firm line. The man was allergic to smiling. But if those lips softened even a tiny bit, if the edges of them hooked up into a hint of a smile, it never failed to make my stomach flip weightlessly, just like it did now.

"You were right earlier. I wasn't lying when I said I didn't want a family." He swallowed, finally dropping his gaze to the floor. "It's not something I've ever imagined for myself."

Why, I wanted to ask, but I tucked the questions away and just let him have his time to say what he needed to say. We had so much time for other questions, and this wasn't it. In the space of the silence that followed, the discomfort of this entire exchange was almost impossible to sit with.

It wasn't like this when I showed up at his house. There was an ease to that entire night, something we'd never really had to chance to explore, and as I waited not very patiently for him to find his big boy words, I desperately wanted that ease to return.

I didn't know how to interact with Jax like this.

And he was probably feeling the same.

This was the man who'd avoided being alone with me for years. The man who kept his distance and worked very hard not to string me along. This was sober Jax, as well. That was one huge difference. But it was more than that. It was more than the absence of alcohol.

Maybe he didn't know how to deal with me either. Didn't know how to talk to me with this giant life change hanging over our heads like a guillotine.

Yet I kept watching the slight fidgeting, the darting eye contact with a growing sense of curiosity.

I was used to him being quiet. Used to him being a little grumpy. This was neither of those things.

The *tap, tap, tap* of those sunglasses was the thing that kept clueing me in. The way the thick line of his throat moved in a hard swallow. Then his eyes locked on mine.

Jax was *nervous*. I'd never seen Jax nervous in my entire life.

The realization hit like a lightning bolt, nothing short of awe cracking my chest wide open. As it did, he locked his eyes onto mine, and the determination I saw there sucked the air straight from my lungs.

I wanted to ask him what was wrong, but all the words got trapped somewhere in my throat.

His chest expanded on a deep breath, and he blew it out in a sharp puff.

"I think we should get married."

Chapter 14
Poppy

Welp.

Something new just got added to my to-do list.

Research pregnancy-related hallucinations was on the very top because there was no way on God's green earth that Jax Cartwright just said what I thought he said.

Over the pounding in my ears, I sucked in a shaky breath. "I … what?"

His jaw flexed, eyes darting to the side before settling back on my face again. His chest expanded on a deep breath. "I think we should get married."

Nope. That was really real. Those were the actual words that came out of his mouth. Not once.

Twice.

Like hearing it a second time helped anything.

For a long moment, all I could do was stare because the absolute fricken irony of this was just too much.

I stood slowly, notebook clutched in my hand, papers crinkling in the tight grip of my fingers.

Think, Poppy, think.

Even in my wildest dreams when it came to this man, matrimony felt like it was anchored somewhere in a different stratosphere.

The older I got, the more I watched him move through life, the further and further away it got as a possibility. Jax was thirty-five, and never once had he showed a single inclination toward marriage, let alone more than one date with the same woman.

A couple of years ago, I'd made peace with the fact that if his ass ever got married, it would be one of those marriage-of-convenience deals where he needed a bride for some hidden fortune he never knew about. A choked laughter born from sheer hysteria slipped up my throat, and I swallowed it down. Barely.

It felt like the pressure of that laugh was ripping open my insides, but holy shit, if I let it out, tears would come right on its heels.

And then I'd sit here and sob, and he'd look at me like I was losing it, and it would be a whole thing. But honestly, what else was a girl supposed to do?

Think.

Think.

The notebook anchored me, and I pinched my eyes shut, pulling in a slow breath through my nose, then let it back out again.

"Jax, can I ask you a question?"

He didn't answer right away, and I peeled my eyes open to gauge his facial expression. The nerves weren't visible anymore, but his brows were in a deep V over his dark eyes.

And the eyes? Oh God, those were ripping my insides open too.

He looked tortured.

Eventually, he nodded.

With cautious steps, I walked closer to him. "When you woke up this morning, did you have a sudden, overwhelming desire for matrimony? Or was this a recent development?"

Jax pushed his tongue against the inside of his cheek while he held my gaze. "Recent," he said in a rough-edged voice.

My ribs creaked dangerously, the force of all the things I was holding inside pressing against the seams.

I attempted a small smile, my mind whirling at a million miles an hour. "You know, before this," I said, gesturing to my bump, "I never would've called you impulsive, Jax. You hide it well," I said lightly. "What brought you to this conclusion since the last time I saw you?"

His jaw flexed. "Fucking Wade," he said in a tight voice. "He … he said I better do right by you, and if he was your dad, he'd haunt me for eternity."

A loud, shocked laugh burst from my mouth, and when Jax gave me an incredulous look, I slapped a hand over my mouth.

"Sorry," I said, wiping that shaky hand over my forehead. "God, this day. I wish I'd had a little heads-up when my alarm went off." He gave me another look. "Right. You too, huh?"

With another deep breath, I stared out at the trees lining either side of the long driveway that led to the house.

Carefully, I spread my fingers open over the back of the notebook, an idea unfolding in my jumbled brain. Every step we took now had to be made with intention. With thoughtfulness.

I'd tried to do that, setting this meeting with my family, but as usual, Jax had a way of bulldozing through even the best of my intentions.

It was always him, wasn't it?

Even when it shouldn't be. Even when it hurt me to keep a hold of him at the back of my mind. Just like I'd done when I agreed to my date with Dean, I made sure that the thing binding me to Jax wasn't hooked deep anymore, wasn't erasing any ability for logical thought. It had for years, hadn't it?

I'd never been able to logically explain why my whole body angled toward him when he came into the room. Why my eyes were always drawn to him. Why my soul recognized something in his that couldn't ever be named.

It was time to set those childish things aside. My hand coasted down my belly again, and I took a deep breath. It wasn't about me or the feelings that plagued me for so long. And he knew that too. My feelings were probably the reason he offered in the first place—some misguided attempt at chivalry.

Chivalry had its place. But between me and this complicated, mysterious man, marriage did not.

"I think we should make a pros and cons list," I said decisively, my shoulder barely brushing his as I came to a stop next to where he stood against the railing. His entire frame was taut with tension, a low level vibration seeping from his skin to mine, and I could only imagine how hard this was for him.

Jax glanced up at the sky wordlessly.

My fingers tapped a frantic rhythm against the front of my bump, and for the briefest of seconds, his eyes locked onto the small, nervous gesture, then moved away again.

"Pros," I said in a steady voice. "I think we'd get along well. I mean, we don't hate each other." His chin dropped to his chest, the biceps in his arms popping with the force of how tightly he held himself. "But I'm not sure that's a reason for marriage," I added lightly. "I'd very much like to enter into that particular legal arrangement with the belief that it will last forever, and will be for love." Somewhere in my chest, my heart thumped unevenly—a bruising sort of pain buried deep in that irregularity. It was another moment before I spoke again. "And I don't think you're in love with me, Jax."

Under his breath, Jax muttered a curse word so softly that I couldn't hear it. He pushed off the railing, and in a few long-legged strides, he gave us both some space while he braced his hands on his hips and stared out at the trees too.

My chin rose an inch, eyes locked on his harshly beautiful profile.

"Cons," I continued, steeling myself for the reaction. "I have a boyfriend, and I'm not sure he'd understand me getting engaged to someone else on such short notice."

Jax's head snapped up in my direction, his eyes blazing so fiercely that the force of it sucked the air straight from my lungs.

"You what?" he rasped.

It sounded like his voice was wrenched from deep in his chest, some painful, battered place, and a corresponding spot in my own body felt it like a blow.

"His name is Dean," I told him. "We met just before you left on your trip. He's ... the vet in town and responded remarkably well when I had to inform him his girlfriend was pregnant by another man about a month after we started dating."

Jax dropped his chin down to his chest again, leaning forward to grip the porch railing. I couldn't tear my eyes away from the way the skin on his knuckles went white from the force of it.

His rib cage expanded on deep, uneven breaths, and the veins on his muscled forearms were just another glimpse into how tightly he was holding himself together.

"I'm sure you'll meet him eventually," I said steadily.

His eyes stayed locked on the ground. "Can't wait."

The dangerous edge to his voice had me standing straighter. "Jax, even if I hadn't met Dean, us getting married because I'm pregnant is a terrible idea."

The line of his throat moved on a swallow, and he pushed back from the railing, crossing his arms again as he faced me.

"When I get married, it's going to be for love—because he can't imagine not marrying me because being apart sounds like punishment." The thick press of emotion clogged my throat. "Not out of obligation." His brow furrowed, and his mouth pinched into a straight line. The look in his eyes almost made it impossible to speak, but I was not going to let this day pass without letting this be said. "I know you're trying to do the right thing, but this? This is not what I need from you."

In an instant, his face went blank. Like a wall slammed shut behind his eyes, blocking his thoughts from view entirely. He blinked a few times, clearly gathering himself from whatever that disconnection did inside him.

"I know you don't," he answered. The rough, low tone of his voice threatened to pull me under the surface, and I mentally planted my feet and refused to let it. "I shouldn't have…"

He gritted his teeth and had the distinct look of a man who'd punch a wall if given the opportunity.

"It's okay," I told him with a tiny smile. "It's not a bad story to say that I finally got you to propose to me. Took you long enough."

Jax stared at me, a plaintive light in his eye that had my heart skipping a beat.

I blew out a slow breath, dragging my gaze away from his sternly handsome face.

"What do you need, Poppy?" he asked carefully.

I really, really needed him to shave that beard, but I decided to keep the request to myself.

It was impossible to answer right away, hearing those words from his mouth almost more than I could handle after a really hard day.

What did I need?

Not what I *wanted*. Not what would magically make my life easier.

Giving the question the full weight of the past four months, I answered just as carefully as he'd asked.

"I need us to be friends," I said softly. Risking a glance at him, I could see exactly how stunned he was. "I know that's a lot to ask, but … I think it's the best option."

Jax ran a hand over his jaw. "Friends," he repeated.

Vulnerable words crept up my throat unbidden, and I decided to risk not swallowing them down. "It's all I can handle with you right now."

The bend in his brow at my answer looked a lot like pain, but Jax gave me a short nod.

I pressed a hand to my cheek, the skin underneath my palm was tellingly warm. I took a few long, deep breaths before speaking again.

"So," I said after my heart calmed down a little bit, "you're heading to my brother's house?"

Jax nodded. "Can't say I'm looking forward to getting my teeth knocked in."

I laughed. "He won't punch you."

He raised a disbelieving brow.

"He won't," I said firmly. "Cameron knows you. He'll be fair. And if he's not, just remind him that it's horribly sexist to assume that I wasn't the sexual instigator."

"Fucking hell, Poppy," he muttered under his breath. "Yeah, I'll get right on that."

I managed to hide my smile by turning to the side.

Jax slid the sunglasses back on his face, and the moment his eyes were covered, I felt like I could breathe just a little bit easier.

With the promise of talking soon, Jax swung his leg over the bike and the rumbling engine made my chest bone rattle when he turned it on. I could feel his eyes on me as he backed away, then I let out a slow breath when he turned and headed down the path toward Cameron's house.

I sank back into the chair and stared out at the trees.

"Well," I said to absolutely no one, "didn't see that one coming."

Chapter 15
Jax

This isn't what I need from you right now.

If there were ever a phrase to knock my ass back into reality, it was that one.

What was I thinking?

That was the point, though, right? I *wasn't* thinking.

She was just there, looking up at me with those dark eyes, and I lost my fucking mind.

Do something.

Do *anything.*

Turned out anything could absolutely be the wrong thing. The moment the words came out of my mouth, I knew, I *knew* they were the wrong ones.

All over again, I felt like a little kid clutching a beat-up bouquet of daisies, the crumpled plastic practically disintegrating underneath my grip.

Intentions didn't matter for shit, not when I laid something at her feet that looked a lot like pity. Like obligation. Like a sacrifice I'd make in order to do the right thing.

My hands tightened as I took the curve to Cameron's place. A screaming part of me wanted to make a sharp U-turn and tear in the opposite direction, feel the wind on my face and the roar of the engine while the road disappeared underneath me.

Leave.

Go.

Don't make anything worse.

If there was a devil on one shoulder and an angel on the other, the latter looked and sounded a lot like Poppy. The devil, however, was a voice I was used to hearing whispered into my ear.

Today, for now, I ignored that little son of a bitch.

The roofline came into view, and I slowed my bike as much as I could, my pulse racing while I tried to cram everything I was feeling into a dark, locked place in the back of my mind.

A boyfriend.

She had a fucking boyfriend.

My teeth clenched, thinking of the stupid letter in my stupid duffel bag, and my stomach churned with the unfamiliar feeling of regret. Of longing.

The undeniably bad timing of my feelings for Poppy was almost comical, if it didn't all feel so fucking tragic right now.

Cameron's house—a large A-frame cabin with floor-to-ceiling windows overlooking the wooded lot—sat about half a mile away from his mom's place. I'd spent so much time there over the years, watching football or basketball. Having beers on the deck. Since his girlfriend, Ivy, moved in, it was less frequent, but even with the unrest churning inside me, it still felt like home as I pulled my bike in behind where his was parked.

Like a stone-faced executioner, Cameron was sitting on the deck, legs spread and his hands folded over his stomach as he watched me approach. Next to him on the patio chair was Ivy, her legs tucked up against Cameron's lap. Her expression wasn't so much guarded as it was terrifyingly thoughtful.

As much as I liked Ivy, she was undeniably intimidating,

and I'd never felt it quite as much as when Cameron spoke low in her ear, and her eyes turned to mine as I got off my bike and walked up the steps.

She stood, giving Cameron a soft peck on the mouth before turning to me. "You know, before I hooked up with this guy, before I was all disgustingly happy in love or whatever, I might have glared you off the front porch. Threatened your manhood, something fun like that." Ivy paused, a regal arch to her brow. "Or I'd have reminded you that Poppy is one of the very few people I'd risk prison for, even though orange isn't my color and I'd make a terrible prisoner."

I blew out a slow breath. "But you're not going to do any of those things anymore?"

Ivy merely smiled. "No. I actually think this is a fairly interesting turn of events, even if I think the entire male species is punching way above their weight class when it comes to her."

"On that, we agree," I said evenly. "You feel that way about her boyfriend too?"

Giving me just a slight arch to her eyebrow, she turned and disappeared into the house without a response.

Cameron watched me silently as I took a seat in the chair opposite of his. After a few minutes, my skin crawled with the need to say something. Anything. But he merely kept his hands folded. His face even. His eyes on me.

"I think it would be easier if you just punched me," I said.

"I don't want to punch you, Jax. I'm not letting you off that easily." He leaned forward, his gaze hard and unyielding. "I never judged the way you were with women. Never cared because you weren't hurting anyone, and you were always clear with them about where you stood. And I *never* worried about Poppy's crush on you because she was the *one* woman in the world I trusted you not to touch. The one you *promised* me you'd never touch."

I rolled my lips over my teeth and let his disappointment hit me like a tidal wave.

"I don't know what happened with you two that night, and I *really* don't want to hear details. But I'm telling you this right now, Jax, if you cannot handle the responsibility of being a father or giving my sister whatever it is she needs to feel supported by you, then leave."

The breath left my lungs in a hard whoosh, like he'd socked me straight in the gut. My head reared back as I registered what he was saying. "What?"

"Leave before you make anything worse for her. Before she thinks you'll swoop in and turn this into some fairy-tale ending because you know that's what she's always wanted more than anything."

Anger had my skin going hot. "I'm not fucking leaving, Cameron. That's my child too. Maybe you're not giving your sister enough credit, because trust me, that is the last thing she's expecting me to do. I have no intention of making her do this alone, so fuck you for suggesting it."

His brows crawled high on his forehead. "Fuck me? Fuck *me?*" he yelled. Slowly, he stood, fists clenched. "You slept with my little sister who's been in love with you forever, got her pregnant, left for *months* while we watched her deal with the fallout, and you think you get to curse me out for trying to protect her now?"

It was my turn to stand, my heart thudding uncomfortably in my chest. "I didn't *know* she was pregnant when I left, Cameron. I wasn't thinking about anything like that when I decided to go."

He gave a sharp, uncomfortable laugh that I felt in my gut. "You never do, do you? The whim hits you, and you're off on the next adventure."

"It wasn't a whim," I said as evenly as possible. "I've wanted to do that trip for years, and I needed time to get my head on straight, and I couldn't just stay here after—"

Understanding dawned on his face, and it was like someone gripped their hand around my fucking throat, slicing off the path for any more words to escape.

"That's why you left," he said, brows bent over his eyes. Cameron's chin dropped into his chest, his hands spearing into his hair as he gripped the sides of his head in disbelief. "Holy *shit*, that's why you left for so long. Because of *Poppy*." He took a step closer, eyes blazing and frame tense. "I asked you if something happened, and you lied to me, didn't you? You left the country for over three months to get your *head on straight* after you fucked my little sister," he yelled. "Am I getting that right?"

Holding his eye contact was the hardest thing I'd ever done in my entire life because his anger cut me to the fucking bone.

My voice came out like someone had wrung my entire body dry—resigned and empty. "Yes, that's why."

He exhaled a harsh puff of air, shaking his head as he stared at me like he didn't recognize me. "Does she know that?"

"No."

There was a haunted quality to my friend's face that I'd never seen before, not even after his dad died, and that cut just as deeply as anything else. "I don't know what else to say right now, man." He held his arms out and let them drop by his side. "You've spent your entire adult life avoiding anything that could make you beholden to a woman, to anyone other than yourself, so I'm not exactly filled with confidence that you'll do right by my sister."

Over and over, it seemed I'd be forced to come face-to-face with the fallout of my choices. The good and the bad, no matter how much sense they made to me at the time. Being alone was the only thing I'd ever wanted out of life. Being able to make decisions that were only rooted in my own wants and needs, desperate to break the cycle I'd watched play out in front of me over and over and over, desperate to prove that I didn't need anyone. That I wouldn't ever need anyone.

It all felt painfully hollow now.

"I'm trying," I ground out. "I have had less than a day to wrap my mind around this, all right? Cut me some slack."

He let out a harsh laugh, a sound I'd never heard from him before. "Believe me, cutting you some slack is all I've been doing today. If I wasn't, I'd probably have broken your jaw by now."

I pinched the bridge of my nose, dropping back down into the chair while I took a few deep breaths. "I'm trying to do right by her," I said again. "And I'm not saying I'm doing a good job of that yet, but God, I don't blame you for being pissed, okay? I spent months beating myself up for what happened. I knew it was stupid to let her in the house when we'd both been drinking."

Cameron let out a harsh exhale and sat back down too. "I can't hear this, Jax. I *can't.*"

"Sorry." I tipped my chin up and tried to breathe.

He shook his head. "She showed up at your place," he said quietly, running a hand down his weary-looking face. "I swear, it's hard to think about Poppy as a grown woman sometimes. She's *Poppy.* She's the kid who always wanted me to put Band-Aids on her skinned-up knees if Mom wasn't around because Dad didn't do it right." He sank his head into his hands for a moment. When he lifted it again, he looked about ten years older. "I don't know how that same little girl is even old enough to be the one we're talking about. We've all been protective of her for so long, and with Dad gone, I think we all just … held on to that a little bit tighter than we should have."

It made sense. But that didn't mean it didn't fucking sting to be the one aimed in their crosshairs.

I gave him a beseeching look. "Do you really think I'd have left if I'd known?"

It took him a long minute to answer as he studied my face,

jaw tight and eyes conflicted. "No," he said eventually. "I don't."

My shoulders deflated, the pressure on my chest easing slightly. "Good."

Cameron eyed me carefully before speaking again. "She was finally moving on from you," he said softly.

"Yeah, I heard about what's-his-name." It sounded so much more bitter than I'd expected, but I felt slightly bitter about his entire existence.

"Dean," he corrected firmly. "His name is Dean, and he's a great guy."

Of course he was.

He saved puppies, for fuck's sake.

"Yeah, I bet everyone loves him."

Cameron's mouth softened in a hint of a smile. "Ivy doesn't."

"Well, Ivy is incredibly smart, so…"

His smile grew. "He beat her in chess. She's been a little salty about him ever since."

Oh goodie. He was a chess prodigy too. This kept getting better and better.

Cameron sighed. "So what are you doing to be there for her?"

I scratched the side of my jaw. "She wants me at her next appointment. We're going to try being … friends," I said slowly, tasting the word as it came out. It was strange. I fucking hated it. I hadn't earned the right to hate it, but I'd never claimed to be the most rational guy in the world.

"That was your idea?" he asked, brows climbing high on his forehead.

My mouth flattened into a line. "No, it was your sister's. I, uh, sort of asked her to marry me."

Cameron's jaw went slack.

The slider door flew open. "You what?" Ivy yelled. "You did *what?*"

Cameron's eyes fell shut. "I should've known you'd be listening."

"Of course I was listening. You're terrible at telling me stories after the fact. You never give details or facial expressions or proper inflection." Ivy crossed her arms, pinning me with another fierce glare. "You proposed to her? Are you *trying* to break her heart?"

"No," I yelled, then instantly deflated. "I thought ... fuck, I don't know what I thought, okay?"

She scoffed.

Cameron rolled his eyes. "You're an idiot, Jax."

"Yeah, well, I get that now, okay?" I folded my arms over my chest. "Believe me, your sister had no qualms about telling me how opposed to that idea she was."

Ivy smirked. "Good." Cameron gave his girlfriend a quick, loaded look, and Ivy held up her hands. "Okay, okay. I'm going back inside now."

"Door shut all the way this time, Ivy," he warned.

She let out a disgruntled sigh. "Fine. But you better have all the details."

When the slider closed firmly, Cameron shook his head, a hint of a smile on his lips. "She drives me insane sometimes."

It was so strange to watch him with her, watch the perfect balance of their opposite personalities. For years, Cameron had been just as single as me. The difference between us was that Cameron didn't have the time or energy to sleep around in his single state. Until one day, he met Ivy, and he just ... knew. After that, he had no compunction turning his world upside down. Isn't that what Poppy wanted? Someone who would set their world on fire for her love.

I rubbed at my chest, wondering if I was even capable of the kind of thing she dreamed of. Everything inside me felt cold. Empty. Only slight flickers of heat with the right person.

More than flickers of heat with her. The times I noticed her and didn't want to. That night. In the weeks and months after, too. I kept waiting for them to dissipate, for those flames to fizzle out. But they didn't. Not once. Not even a little.

I had to ignore those too. More importantly, I had to not fuck this up.

"I'm sorry, Cameron," I told him. I hung my head, bracing it in my hands. "I should've kept my distance, and I didn't. And if you can't trust me after this, I don't blame you." I lifted my head and met his gaze. "But I won't let her down. If I've ever promised you anything, I'll promise you that."

"I love you like a brother, Jax, and I'll get over it eventually," he said, then he sighed. "But right now, I hate that it's you."

The naked honesty in his voice cut just about as badly as you'd think, scoring down the edge of my ribs as it flayed me wide open.

But I gave him a steady look instead of flinching away. "I know you do."

"Fuck," he muttered, swiping a hand over his face. Cameron leaned his head back on the chair and stared up at the sky. "Dammit."

There was no point in apologizing again, so I didn't. This time, the silence didn't stretch out in a painful, thick way. It was the kind of silence that comes with acceptance.

Eventually, he dropped his head back down and leveled me with a tired look. "Want a beer?" he asked. "I think I need one."

I exhaled a quiet laugh. "Normally, I'd say yes, but jet lag is killing me. I should get home to eat something and go to bed."

He gave an understanding nod, standing from his chair as I stood from mine. "You still might want to wear a cup the next time you're around Greer."

I managed a grim smile. "Believe me, I will."

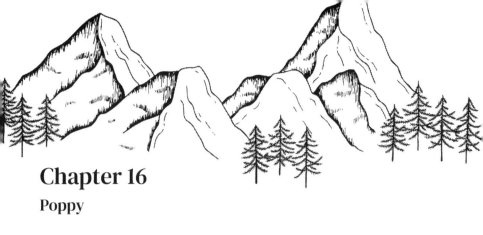

Chapter 16
Poppy

Did I cater in delicious baked goods to butter up my siblings for this family meeting?

You bet your ass I did.

Mom was only slightly affronted when I didn't ask her to make anything, but she got over it pretty quickly when she tried the chocolate croissant.

In front of me were my small stack of colored notecards, the agendas I hadn't passed out yet, and three colored pens in case anyone made a really good point I needed to write down.

On the large screens at the back of the room, my sister Adaline and brother Erik were patched in from their respective homes in Seattle. Adaline had clearly just crawled out of bed, still yawning into her coffee mug. Parker's square was still ominously black. I'd only texted him five times, but hey, sure … live your life, Parker.

"You know," Greer said, "that back bedroom that used to be Parker's would be the best nursery."

Mom nodded. "Best view of the yard."

Greer pursed her lips thoughtfully. "It did have the best view. Why did Parker get it again?"

"Because he was my favorite the week we decided," she said smoothly.

Ian snickered into his coffee.

Greer sighed. "Figures." She turned her face toward me. "What room are you thinking, Pops?"

"I—" I shifted the edge of a notecard that moved out of place. "I don't know. I may not ... I might find a place, actually."

Greer's, Mom's, and Cameron's heads all swung in my direction. The others were chatting among themselves and hadn't heard.

"Why?" Cameron asked. "You have a free place to live and built-in help."

Greer shared a look with Mom. "And built-in help," she repeated, eyes wide.

Mom's facial expression was more curious than anything. "You never said anything, Poppy."

Weird. Maybe because you couldn't get a freaking word in edge-wise when your family had dozens of people in it, all talking at the same time.

"I don't blame you for wanting space," Ivy interjected. "Now that Jax is back, you're part of the hottest love triangle since…" She tilted her head. "I don't even know what cultural reference to make right now because I spent too much time studying in college."

I rolled my eyes. "It's not a love triangle. It's a ... different shape that doesn't have three points. It's a line. I'm in a line relationship because there are only two people." I started handing out the agendas. "Please, I promise all this will get covered. Living arrangements is on the list."

Cameron's eyes widened as he read the sheet in front of him. "Family boundaries?" he whispered. "Does our family know what those are?" he asked Greer.

She shrugged helplessly.

"Good morning, everyone. Let's get started."

Cameron raised his hand. "We're not waiting for Parker?"

The square reserved for his Zoom screen was still black,

and I tried not to glare at it too badly. "Nope. If you note the top of the agenda, it says seven thirty a.m. It's now"—I glanced at my watch—"seven thirty-two, so I think we've waited long enough."

Ivy smiled. "Take it away, boss. It's your meeting."

I'd stood at the head of the conference room dozens of times in the past few months, running meetings about distribution updates and shipping data and discussing strategy of what needed to be done when. Most of the time, my siblings sat in the chairs just like they were now—Ivy and Cameron to my left, his hand underneath the table on her leg. Greer was on my right.

Ian didn't usually attend these meetings, but he and his wife, Harlow, sat in the middle across from Mom.

I picked up the first notecard and opened my mouth to talk.

"I like your dress, Poppy," Adaline said through the screen. "You look really pretty."

I blinked, looking down at the white sundress with little red flowers on it. "Oh. Thank you."

"Did you get that in town?" Greer asked. "I might need to see if they have other colors."

"Yes, I—"

"You do not have the chest to fill that out," Adaline told Greer.

Greer narrowed her eyes at the screen.

Cameron dug the heels of his hands into his eye sockets. Ivy rubbed his back with a slight smirk on her face.

I stared down at the first notecard. Point 1- Firmly address why I didn't tell them. Do not apologize.

"Are you feeling okay, Pops?" Erik asked. He had the computer screen tilted too far away from his face and he looked like an alien.

With a smile, I nodded. "Tired today, but good, thanks, Erik."

He leaned in closer. "Lydia wanted to know if you got that link she sent you about the baby stroller she wants to buy you."

Ian rolled his eyes. "Adjust your monitor, old man. We're looking straight up your nose."

With a grimace, Erik did as instructed, glaring when Cameron let out a low snicker.

Ian opened his mouth to say something, and I nailed him with a fierce glare that shrank him back in his seat. Notecard in hand, I looked around the room and found my mom's face first. Her smile and encouraging wink had my tense shoulders relaxing.

"Thank you for coming," I told them. "I'll try to keep this brief because I know everyone has a busy day ahead of them." I smiled at my sister-in-law. "Except Harlow, who told me the longer we talked, the less she'd have to try to write today."

Harlow raised her coffee mug in salute, earning a dry smirk from my brother at her side.

I smoothed a hand over my belly. "First and foremost, I know you're probably all wondering why I didn't tell you it was Jax," I said quietly, my eyes moving to each face around the table. "It wasn't because I was ashamed or afraid. And I never wanted to lie. But I refused to let him be the last one to know because it's not fair. Believe me, what happened yesterday was pretty much worst-case scenario for me."

Cameron's jaw tensed. Ian kept his gaze down at the table. Greer shifted in her seat.

"Most importantly, I won't apologize for not telling you," I said. "You may not understand, but I feel really strongly about that. And you know, women have this tendency to feel like we always need to apologize, right? Even if we haven't done anything wrong." My pulse hammered as all my siblings watched me like an animal in an exhibit. "And I wasn't wrong by wanting to tell him first. Even if it didn't happen the way I'd imagined."

Cameron cleared his throat, shoulders moving as he took a deep breath.

As soon as he was done doing the *big brother annoyed because I'm not in control right now* shifting, I held his eyes for a moment, then moved to Greer.

"I do, however, expect you to apologize to him for how you reacted," I added quietly.

My sister's eyes glossed over. "Poppy, I'm so sorry if I made you feel worse."

"I appreciate that, but *I* don't need the apology. He deserves one, though." My eyes burned too, but I refused to drop her gaze. "I should have spoken up yesterday, but there were a million people watching us, and I felt like"—my voice wobbled slightly—"like everything was exploding around me, and I didn't want to say the wrong thing or…"

Greer reached over and grabbed my hand, squeezing my fingers tightly. "I'll talk to him today."

A sigh of relief came out in a rush, and I nodded.

Erik cleared his throat. "I wasn't there, so I can only imagine what Greer did—"

"There was a hammer involved," Ian answered.

Greer grimaced.

"Of course there was," Erik said dryly. My oldest brother, stern and serious, gentled his tone when he shifted his attention back to me. "Listen, Poppy, I think we all understand why you didn't tell us about Jax. It makes sense." My relief was short-lived because he wasn't quite done. "But it's not a bad thing that your siblings are protective of you."

I notched my chin up. "I know that. But there were two people involved in this situation. Jax didn't seek me out, and he didn't seduce me. In fact, he was very against me being there in the first place," I explained. "He swore a *lot* when I first showed up, but my Uber driver was already gone, and we'd both been drinking. I mean, I was one bottle deep when I showed up, so…"

Cameron dropped his head in his hands and emitted a low groan. Ivy patted his back.

Erik slicked his tongue over his teeth, looking very unimpressed. "All the more reason that he should've kept his distance. You're ten years younger than he is, Poppy. Ten years. And not only that but he was more than aware of your crush on him. It was reckless, at best."

I tilted my head. "And how much younger than you is your wife?"

His jaw tightened, and he looked away. "That's—"

"Different," I finished for him. "It's always different for the rest of you than it is for me."

Cameron lifted his head, deciding it was time to insert himself. "We're allowed to be worried for you, Poppy. That's part of being a family. Even if it wasn't Jax, we'd be worried."

"I'm not telling you not to be worried," I said. My notecards got tossed onto the table because we were officially off the damn script. Acceptable family boundaries was third on my meeting agenda, not first. My head started spinning. "This isn't what I wanted to be talking about right now, okay? I just…" I paused, steadying the emotions that threatened to swamp me. "I just want you to listen."

"We are listening," Adaline added gently. "We can do all those things at the same time. Worry about you, and care about you getting hurt, and we can listen to what you're trying to tell us."

"Are you listening?" I asked. "Because right now it feels like everyone is just talking over me."

Everyone went quiet, and I noticed my mom covertly brush a finger under her eye.

"I know I'm younger than Jax. That I'm younger than all of you," I said. "But I'm twenty-five. I'm not a kid. Yes, it was impulsive to go to his place. I know that, okay?" I speared

Cameron with a look, and he returned it steadily. "I'm not perfect. I'm just me. And I'm trying to figure this out as I go, but it is unfair for you guys to cast me in some helpless role like I can't take care of myself. Should we talk about the shit you guys got into when you were my age? Or older?" I asked.

Erik's eyes dropped.

Greer shifted in her seat.

"I never judged any of you," I said hotly. "I never freaked out when you up and moved away and didn't come home for years," I said, eyes shifting pointedly between Erik and Ian. "I didn't yell or threaten anyone when you married a stranger," I said to Greer. "Or when you slept with *your* first crush, knowing he was leaving the next day," I said to Adaline. She dropped her gaze.

The far left screen flared to life. Parker's sleepy face filled the screen as he yawned, stretching his muscled arm over his head. "Am I late?"

My eyes narrowed. "Oh, don't even get me started on *you.*"

He blinked. "What did I miss?"

Ian swiped a hand over his mouth, spearing our youngest brother with a stern look.

A part of me wondered if I should take a break. Do some breathing exercises. Maybe some meditation in the hallway. And then, honestly, I just said fuck it, and let my rarely shown temper take the freaking reins.

"Everyone in this family has screwed up over the years, but I'm the only sibling who seems to warrant special treatment, like I can't make my own fucking decisions," I said, voice a touch louder than was comfortable. "I knew what I was doing when I slept with him. That he wouldn't want more, and I was okay with that. I knew that it was a risk and I might get hurt, but that's *life*. I didn't want to wake up one morning and wish I'd missed a chance to know if he ever felt the same. Or what it would be like to pretend he was mine for one night. And yes, it hurt when he left, but I'm still here. I didn't crumple, I didn't break, and I'm doing my best in a really complicated situation."

A single tear spilled over, and I let it fall. "Every single one of you has made decisions that the rest of us might disagree with, but when you made them, I listened to you when you wanted to talk. I never made you feel like you couldn't handle whatever was going on in your life. And I loved you through all the shit you've pulled over the years."

When I finished, I was breathing hard, and my hands were shaking a little, but holy shit, did it feel good to say all that.

That was the thing about being the steady, easygoing sibling at the back of the pack. I might only get one freak-out per year, but I would make it *count*.

My mom was the first to speak. "I'm proud of you, Poppy. I think it was brave for you to face us all like this."

"It was," Adaline agreed. Greer was quietly crying in her chair, and Ian gave me an encouraging nod.

"Did I miss the first agenda point?" Parker whispered. "I'm really lost."

"Maybe set your alarm next time," Cameron snapped.

"I did," Parker said. "I swear, it got turned off."

"By who?" Erik asked.

Parker grimaced. "Never mind."

Greer took a deep breath. "You're right, Pops. We should've trusted you to handle it yourself. And no matter what you said earlier, I think we do owe you an apology for earlier." She managed a tiny smile. "I really am sorry."

Cameron met my eyes. "I'm sorry, too."

Parker cleared his throat. "I wasn't there, so … I don't think this is a moment I need to add anything."

Erik rolled his eyes.

"Forgiven," I told them. I picked up the agenda and exhaled a laugh. "Well, the agenda was a nice idea in theory."

Mom smiled. "Anything else you want to let us know?"

I swallowed. "I don't know what this will look like for Jax and me as co-parents or the types of decisions I might make. But unless I ask for your advice, I need you to respect the way he and I move forward."

Everyone nodded.

Wearily, I sat back down in my chair, resting a hand on the top of my bump. "I think I'm done."

Ivy raised her hand. "May I have the floor, boss?"

"I'm pretty sure you're the boss, Ivy, at least in this building. But sure."

She waved that off. "While we have the whole family here, I think this is the perfect place to discuss your promotion."

My head reared back. "What promotion?"

Ivy leaned back in her chair, studying me with a shrewd look on her face. "I've been thinking about our plan to have you manage the store, and I'm not sure it makes sense anymore, what with the forthcoming bundle of joy and all."

Cameron cut his girlfriend a curious look. "When did you decide this?"

"Right now," she said, never taking her eyes off me. "Managing the store isn't very flexible, and it's not like you're going to bring one of those baby cages into work every day."

"Baby cage?" Parker asked in a horrified whisper.

"Do you mean a playpen?" Greer asked, fighting a smile.

"Sure, whatever it's called," Ivy said dismissively. "But as the Wilder House Director of Operations, you could work from home a few days a week if you wanted." She tilted her head, glancing around the room. "What do we think?"

Cameron smiled. "It's a yes from me. Poppy is ten times more organized than any of us here."

Greer nodded. "Yes from me."

We all turned to Mom. She owned Dad's and her shares in the company, and with a big smile, she nodded too. "As long as I still get to babysit a couple of days a week, it's a yes from me too."

My throat was tight with emotion as Ivy's face spread with a satisfied grin. "Thank you," I told her. I picked up the agenda and shrugged one shoulder. "Well, I guess that's it if you need to get to work now."

Parker yawned. "Not me. It's the offseason. I'm going back to bed."

"Maybe go work out instead," Erik said. "You looked slow last week in that video you posted."

Parker flipped him off, winked at me, and his screen went black.

Cameron shook his head. "Greer, let's go. You've got an apology tour to make."

After hugs from both of them, then Ian and Harlow, and a minute later, Adaline and Erik logged off. It was just Mom, Ivy, and me.

Ivy watched my face carefully, and that always made me a little nervous. From the moment I met her, she had an uncanny ability to read me. Sometimes it was good, and sometimes, like now, it made me want to hide under the freaking table.

"So," she drawled, "I hear you've shifted Jax Cartwright into the friend zone as of last night."

I ran a hand over my belly and smiled. "Yup. We talked last night. He asked what I needed, and"—I shrugged—" that's pretty much it."

"You talk to Dean about him yet?"

Slowly, I shook my head. "I'm going to call him later when he's off work."

Mom's eyebrows rose slowly. "What do you think he'll say?"

Ivy snorted. "Captain America will have the perfect response, as per usual. God, he'll probably want Jax's autograph or something."

I chucked a wadded-up agenda at her head, and she

172

caught it with a neat snatch of her hand, eyebrows raised like, *can't you do any better than that?*

"You're as bad as Parker," I told her. "I think it's admirable that he has firm personal boundaries."

"Is it also admirable that he cheats at chess?" Ivy muttered.

"That boy beat you fair and square, Ivy," Mom said.

Ivy screwed her lips up, and I coughed to cover my laugh.

"I bet they'll get along just fine," I said.

Mom and Ivy traded a loaded look.

"Stop it," I told them. "They will."

"Sure," Ivy said condescendingly. "You and your love line, non-triangle love triangle. I can see it now, Jax and his working vocabulary of seven words sitting with Dean while he waxes poetic about his renewed V-card."

I tried to mimic her boss-bitch glare, but I had a feeling it wasn't quite as effective, especially when she simply smiled innocently.

Mom chuckled. "Why don't we do this," she said. "I'll have everyone over for dinner in a couple of nights. That way, Jax doesn't feel like there's too much pressure on meeting Dean." She shrugged. "Just a normal night at the Wilders."

"Dinner with Jax," Dean repeated slowly, his bright eyes trained firmly on mine. "Dinner with Jax in front of your entire family?"

I risked a small nod. We were sitting on the back deck of his house after dropping my little news bomb about the baby's surprise paternity and his sudden reappearance in town. I did call him, like I'd said, but this was no conversation to be had over the phone. I needed to see his face. He deserved that, if nothing else.

Maybe this was what Jerry Springer felt like. It was awful —delivering world-altering news, yet again, knowing he'd probably feel like I was yanking the floor out from underneath his feet. I was on a roll this week, honestly. Jax and my family and now Dean. You'd think it would get easier, but it really hadn't.

It was one thing to accept the baby, but *surprise*! He was my brother's best friend, so he was around all the time, and *double surprise*! I had a *Titanic*-sized crush on him my entire life.

Out of anyone in this situation, Dean was the innocent bystander. He didn't have the front-row seat to my crush on Jax like my family. And he certainly wasn't complicit in the same way Jax was.

It never felt good to hurt the innocent bystander. To tell them you'd lied.

His unwavering support, his genuinely big heart and obvious feelings for me made this a bit like plucking the wings off a butterfly. Honestly, he was so beautiful it wasn't even fair. And the deep-seated goodness inside him was even more beautiful.

In a strange way, seeing him be a little discomfited by this was a relief.

"Holy shit, Poppy," he said, swiping a hand over his mouth and leaning back in his chair. After a moment, he stood, setting his hands on his trim hips and staring out into the backyard. He was still wearing his bright blue scrubs, and I'm telling you, a man and his ass had never looked as good in scrubs as Dean Michaelson.

Which was what made it even worse that I didn't feel those things when I watched him. The tingly things. The press-my-thighs-together things. The heart turning over in my chest things.

"If it makes you uncomfortable, I can tell my mom it's not

a good idea," I told him. "If you need time to make peace with this, it's okay."

Dean tilted his head back and took a seat again, angling himself closer to me as he sighed. "No, I don't need time. It's … it's the right thing to do." He slid his big hand over my thigh and squeezed. "I can be an adult about this."

I reached for one of his hands with mine. His eyes fell closed at my touch, but he didn't pull away. If anything, his grip was tight and possessive, like he was unwilling to let me back away now that I'd initiated.

"Should I be worried?" he asked lightly. "About this man who's taken up your thoughts for so long."

I sucked in a quick breath, choosing my words carefully. "Jax is a good man who wants very different things than I do. He's always been very up front about that. He doesn't want marriage or a family. I think he'll support the baby— financially at least—but I don't have any expectations from him beyond that," I answered truthfully. "I want to be friends with him. It's something we've never tried to do before."

Dean searched my face, and I could see his belief in me stamped as plain as day across his handsome features. He slid his hand over my cheek, brushing his thumb along my lower lip. "Okay," he murmured, brushing his lips over mine for a tender kiss. When he pulled back, Dean wrapped his arms around me, and I melted into his embrace. "Okay," he said again. "Then let's have dinner tomorrow night."

I pinched my eyes closed, letting the warmth of his body be louder than any of the other doubts running through my head.

Chapter 17

Jax

"What's this?"

Cameron tilted his head, mouth moving as he read the message waiting for me on my phone.

"Ahh. I believe we call those text messages."

My facial expression didn't budge.

Cameron grinned. "Looks like my mom got your cell phone number."

I set my jaw, glancing down at the text again, like I hadn't read it a dozen times.

> Unknown number: Jax, it's Sheila Wilder. I'd love to invite you over for a family dinner tonight at six if you don't have any plans. I apologize for the late notice. I meant to send this yesterday, but the day got away from me. If you can't come, please know you're always welcome in my home.

Cameron's eyebrows popped on his forehead. "What about this confuses you?"

I stared at him. "Your mom is inviting me for a family dinner."

"Good Lord, what nefarious thing could she have planned

for you?" As he brushed past me, he slapped me on the shoulder.

"I don't appreciate your sarcasm," I said to his retreating back.

"You never do. It's a real shame." Cameron stuck his fingers into his mouth and let out a piercing whistle. The whirring sounds of machinery died down. "Sorry to interrupt, but I'm about to head out to the Redmond site to check on some things. We'll be posting if we can't find anyone, but we're looking to hire a couple of new people if you know of anyone who's willing to learn and likes working with their hands."

Wade eyed me over the circular saw. "Maybe if Jax stopped taking so many European vacations, we wouldn't need a new person."

Cameron gave him a firm look. "If I hadn't been able to spare him, you and I both know he wouldn't have been gone. This is more for what's coming down the pipe, Wade. Once the store is done, we've got two large builds we'll be balancing, and this is a great time to do some training."

I wandered around the saw and clapped Wade on the back. "Maybe if Wade wasn't so old and grumpy, he wouldn't scare off the new guys during his training."

Wade rolled his eyes. "Not my fault if they can't handle me."

In the back of the room, Rob raised his hand. "I might know of someone, Cameron."

Cameron lifted his chin. "Yeah? Who is it?"

"My buddy, Trevor. College isn't his thing, you know? Real smart, though. He's like … *deep*. Hates sitting around doing nothing. He's been trying to find some work and hasn't had any luck yet."

Wade eyed Rob skeptically. "Your friend anything like you?"

I gave Wade a look. "He did say he was deep, Wade."

Rob laughed. "Nope, nothing like me, old man."

Wade grunted. "Good."

Cameron chuckled under his breath. "All right, give him my email address, I'll set up an interview." My friend nodded his chin toward the door, gesturing for me to follow. When we cleared the doorway, he crossed his arms, studying my face. "You gonna come to dinner?"

Discomfort must have been rolling off me in waves because I didn't say a word, and Cameron sighed, reaching up to scratch at the back of his neck.

"It's just dinner, Jax."

I glanced sideways. "Is it?"

My disbelieving tone had him chuckling. "What else would it be?"

"A Wilder family firing squad aimed right at my balls, maybe."

His smile faded. "Fuck, Jax, I shouldn't have said I hated it was you," he murmured, staring off down the street. "I was upset. At you. At Poppy. Wishing my dad was here to keep us all steadied out. It's like we're all still trying to figure out how to navigate big shit like this without him." His eyes met mine. "But I shouldn't have said that. Or told you to leave." Cameron extended his arm. "I'm sorry."

I clasped his outstretched hand in mine and shook it. "Forgiven. Honestly, if this had happened to her by anyone else, I would've been saying the same shit."

The words came out unthinkingly, and I kept my face even.

Cameron didn't answer, simply hummed quietly, then gave me one last look before he descended the front steps. "No pressure or anything, but you'll break my mom's heart if you don't come."

I flipped him off, then, to the sound of his laughter, I sighed, tapped out a quick reply to Sheila Wilder and headed back in to work.

By the time I was done, had gone home, and showered, I found myself driving toward the Wilder House, anxiety building by the second.

Was I supposed to bring something?

A dish to pass or something?

Wine.

Maybe I could bring her a bottle of wine. Or some flowers.

My stomach went ice cold. Anytime I thought about standing in front of that cheery fucking display, buckets overflowing with flowers, I wanted to break something. No. No flowers.

But I could pick a bottle of wine.

Turning the truck into the parking lot of the grocery store, I sat forward when I noticed Poppy walk inside, her dark hair swinging from a high ponytail, and her legs bare underneath a swishy blue skirt that stopped above her knees. An elderly couple stopped her just before she went into the store, Poppy smiled easily with a hand resting on the top of her small bump. They talked for a minute before she waved and headed inside.

I leaned my head back against the seat rest after she disappeared.

The cheery awning over the vet's office across the street caught my eye, and I fought a scowl.

I thought about seeing her again in front of her family, and I wasn't sure it was any easier than seeing her like this—when she wasn't expecting me.

It reminded me of the letter. Because I was a chump, I'd pulled it from my bag and shoved it in the console of my work truck. Carefully, I pulled it out and held it in my hands. The edges of the envelope were battered and bent from all the times I'd clutched it just like this.

What if I'd just sent it from Spain? Not knowing what was

waiting for me when I came back. If she'd known that my feelings had changed.

That they'd shifted into something else.

Something bigger.

The first time in my life when I waited—when I curbed an impulse brewing under my skin—and it seemed now like I'd waited too long.

Fucking figured.

The man I was when I scrawled my thoughts out onto paper wasn't even recognizable anymore. It was almost impossible to stay the same when the landscape of your life shifted so quickly. But the thoughts I'd put on paper, the feelings that plagued me every single day we were apart, those were still just as true.

Dear Poppy,

I'm not good with words, so forgive me for how this might come out. I can't stop thinking about you...

"Enough," I said in a harsh whisper, smacking the back of my head against the seat rest.

We were friends now.

I didn't know how to be friends with Poppy any more than she knew how to be friends with me, which was really fucking clear in our interaction on her parents' porch. We had no basis for this. No foundation to build on.

I didn't know her favorite food or if she was a morning person or not.

I didn't know if she took naps during the day or if she was craving weird foods.

God, how I wanted to know all those things. Not because we were friends, but because being around her set me on edge in a way that felt amazing and uncomfortable. Still didn't know how to label it, if I were being honest.

There were people in the world who balanced multiple friendships with ease, juggling them without breaking a sweat.

Good friends and work acquaintances and neighbors, all whipping through the air flawlessly.

For me though, each single relationship in my life was like the concrete footings we built houses on. You couldn't move them quickly, couldn't demolish them easily, and you only needed a few strategically placed to keep everything standing.

But I wasn't juggling shit.

I had Cameron. And now, I thought with a deep sigh, I had Poppy. Not in the way she'd always wanted me but in a way that was far more vulnerable. Because now, I was the one sitting back in the stands, watching her live her life, fighting against a burgeoning sense of longing that threatened to take me over.

Because that longing was futile. It was energy crawling through my body with nowhere to go.

The telltale signs of an anxiety attack crawled quick and lethal through my veins, and I ran my hands up and down the tops of my thighs. It was so much simpler when I didn't notice her. When I forced myself not to see.

Things that were easy for other people weren't easy for me, and instead of easily being able to shift things aside to make *some* room for Poppy, to be thankful that we had this tentative truce between us, there was this screaming instinct to swipe everything off the table until she was the only thing there.

I didn't want to just make room. I wanted to give her every fucking inch of my life, and I didn't know how to do less. When the baby came, maybe this wouldn't seem so complicated, but for right now, all I could hear were her family's justifiable threats ringing in my ear, and all I could see were her big brown eyes staring up at me when I asked her to marry me. When she told me she had a boyfriend.

A knock on my passenger side window had my eyes flying open, and Poppy's smiling face had my heart thudding uncomfortably. I leaned over, unlocking the door, and she leaned her shoulder against the doorframe after wrenching it open.

"You stalking me, Cartwright?"

"No," I growled. "I just … saw you go in, and thought …" I wiped a hand over my face when my cheeks felt suspiciously warm. "I don't fucking know what I thought, Poppy."

Her teeth dug into her bottom lip while she studied me, and after only a moment of hesitation, she climbed into the truck and closed us in together with a slam of the door.

That smell.

Damn, that smell. That would be the thing haunting me for the rest of my natural born life.

She situated herself in the corner of the truck so she could properly stare me down.

"What's got your knickers in a twist, Jax?"

At her phrasing, I gave her a dry arch of my eyebrow. "Nothing."

"It's something," she answered so very patiently. "No marriage proposals in the works today, I presume?"

"Wasn't planning on it."

There was a hint of a smile on her face, there and gone in less than a heartbeat, and for the first time all day, I didn't feel like a failure. Didn't feel like I was completely inept at all these new things being thrown at me.

The bag on her lap crinkled when she dug her hand into it, and when she pulled out a giant box of sour candy, my eyebrows popped up.

"You eat that shit?"

"Constantly right now," she answered. Poppy dug into the box and fished out a few of the colorful pieces, sighing happily when she chewed the first bite. "So fricken good. Want some?"

I eyed it suspiciously. "No thanks. Don't really have much of a sweet tooth, actually."

"Good, because I was just being polite. I'll have this box

gone before dinner." She ate another piece, her lips puckering up at the sour. Then she gave me a look. "You eat cookies when I bring them to work."

"Cookies are not that," I said, gesturing to the candy. "You know what they do to that shit to make it those colors?"

"Yeah, they create happiness from thin air, that's what." She ate another couple of pieces, and then settled back against the seat. "So … why are you sitting here being grumpy?"

"I'm not being grumpy."

Her attention shifted to the crumpled envelope in my hand, and my heart thumped erratically when she studied it curiously.

"What's that?" she asked.

"Nothing," I said quickly. Too quickly. Her eyes narrowed.

Could I stuff the envelope back in the console without her getting suspicious? Unlikely. Poppy was curious about everything.

"Bad day at work then?" she asked.

When was the last time anyone asked me about my day?

It was so … mundane. Normal. And holy shit, did it make me feel twitchy.

I grunted. "Work was fine. And I'm not sitting here being grumpy, I just…" I let out a sharp breath and decided honesty was about the only way this would work. "I saw you and wasn't sure how the fuck we're supposed to be friends. That's all. I don't have girl friends."

Poppy snorted. "I noticed."

"Friends that are girls, angel," I clarified, crossing my arms and staring out the windshield. "I don't … I don't know how this is supposed to work."

She chewed slowly, a thoughtful look in her eyes that made me incredibly uncomfortable. "Being friends with someone is easy, Jax."

I rolled my eyes. "You would say that."

Poppy smacked my arm. "I'm serious. You find the things you have in common and talk about them. You text each other when you find something funny. Grab a drink if you've had a shit day"—she tilted her head—"or grab a water in my case, but whatever. You hang out. Give each other advice. Talk about the memories you have."

I turned in my seat, all those impotent feelings snaking up my throat, looking for a way out from where I'd been bottling them up. "And which memory of ours should we revisit in our new friendship?" I asked, my chest tight and hot. "The shots? When you crawled in my bed? The second time I fucked you because I woke up hard, and you smelled so fucking good that I couldn't stop myself?"

The words poured out fast, unstoppable as a tornado and whipping through the truck just as quick, and Poppy's cheeks were deliciously pink when I finished. Jaw tight, I screwed my eyes shut and faced forward again, pinching the bridge of my nose when I realized exactly what I'd said.

Embarrassment had my hands trembling when I wrenched open the console and shoved the stupid fucking letter inside, then slammed the door shut. Shame had me looking away for a moment, the residual feeling coating my skin, sticky and cold and uncomfortable.

I didn't deserve her. I don't know why I ever thought I earned a chance to try.

"I shouldn't have said that," I admitted harshly.

Her face was even, and the look in her eyes was filled with so much understanding, it made me want to scream. "No, you shouldn't have," she agreed.

"I don't know how to do this," I said again in a low, urgent voice. "And I don't want to ruin this, but it's hard for me to just … pretend we have some easy road ahead of us."

"I know we don't," she spoke softly. "But we can start small."

How many chances would this woman give me? How

many emotionally stunted transgressions would she forgive before this was over? Before we figured out a normal that, at the moment, felt like it was as out of reach as jumping from my truck and somehow landing on the moon.

With a small, incredulous shake of my head, I risked a glance in her direction. "Like what?"

She stared down at the box of candy, then slowly tucked it away in the bag. "Well, now I know that you really only like cookies if you're craving something sweet. I didn't know that before. And you know I like sour candy. If I'm having a bad day, you show up with these, and I'll love you forever." At the slip in her words, my eyes flashed over to hers. She blew out a slow breath. "Sorry, poor choice of phrasing. I'll be eternally grateful," she said carefully.

"Candy," I said slowly. "That's the basis of our friendship?"

Poppy shrugged. "I mean, to your point, it's either that or the sex, and that might not be the best place to start. It honestly would've been so much easier for me if you were bad in bed, but..." Her voice trailed off when I gave her an incredulous look. "What? You didn't have to be such an overachiever."

I leaned my head back against the seat and sighed. "You're right. We should stick with the candy."

Her laughter filled my truck, and I wondered briefly if the sound would absorb into the seats, something that would imbue the space with just a little bit of the happiness she always seemed to carry around with her.

"Are you coming over for dinner?" she asked.

I grimaced. "Can't say no to Sheila, can I?"

She grinned, that dimple peeking out again. "It's really best not to try. She's relentless."

"A family trait," I muttered under my breath.

Poppy smacked my chest, and I rubbed at the spot like she'd actually wounded me.

She tucked a piece of hair behind her ear, one of her nervous tells. "Dean will be there too," she said. Her big eyes watched my face carefully.

Ahh. Right.

This was one of those moments, wasn't it? Where you prove whether you're as good of a person as you'd like to think you are. When you're faced with the hard thing and you have to make a decision how to react. I'd already proven that I was capable of frustration laced bursts of emotion. That I was more than capable of unthinkingly offering up solutions that didn't actually help anyone.

But could I do this thing?

Meet the guy who'd filled a space in Poppy's life that I never had. That I'd never allowed myself to fill.

"A vet, huh?"

She nodded. "Mom played matchmaker for a while before we finally met. I think she might have done too good of a job talking me up."

I hummed. "Not sure that's possible."

Poppy's cheeks flushed a pretty pink, and she gathered the small bag in her hands. "He knows you're coming too."

"He gonna play nice?"

"I don't know," she answered, eyes so open and honest that it was almost hard to meet them. "He was ... shocked, to say the least. I think," Poppy paused for a moment, glancing out the front of the truck. "I think it was harder to hear about you than it was when I told him I was pregnant."

"Why?"

Her lips edged up in a rueful smile. "Because you're you, Jax. You're the man I compared everyone against."

I shifted uncomfortably in the seat. "Lucky for those guys."

Poppy ignored me. "Before, there wasn't anyone for him to compete with. But now..."

My gaze sharpened on her face. "Is it a competition?"

"No." She swallowed. "He thought it was just a stranger I spent one night with. Someone he'd never have to see, or get to know. Watch me interact with."

My heart galloped in my chest.

A sharp awareness split me straight down the middle. Having to see them, get to know him, watch her interact with him was no less than I deserved.

I was nowhere near earning the right to feel any sort of jealousy, but there was no explaining the hot surge of it in my veins.

But with her sitting there looking at me, begging for this platonic relationship for her own sanity, begging with those big eyes and that sweet smile that I could do this thing for her, I ignored the heat. Ignored the surge. Ignored all of it.

"Dr. Dean has nothing to worry about," I told her. "We're friends, right?"

Poppy let out a slow breath and smiled. "Right." She tilted her head. "I'll see you at my mom's?"

I nodded, keeping my face impassive while that fucking devil on my shoulder absolutely raged.

Do something.

Anything.

Leave.

Go.

You're not what she needs.

With a hard swallow as the truck door slammed shut behind her, I took a few deep breaths and waited for her to leave the parking lot in front of me, then yanked the gear shift and put the truck in reverse while I followed her out to the house.

Chapter 18
Jax

I thought maybe we'd get lucky and be the first to arrive.

As usual, luck was not on my side.

"Why is this family so fucking big?" I whispered, following Poppy's car down the last stretch of the driveway.

There were other cars parked at the house when Poppy and I arrived—I recognized Greer's and Cameron's, then noted a sleek black SUV that I didn't. It was a beautiful night, and everyone was outside.

Harlow sat on the front porch with Sheila, Harlow's daughter, Sage, running along the side of the house with Greer's stepdaughter, Olive. Greer sitting on the front porch steps with Ivy while a basketball game was played on the driveway to the left of the house.

Cameron and Ian tussled underneath the basket, a two-handed shove from Ian garnering some boos and claps from the porch. Dribbling the basketball in front of Greer's husband, Beckett, was a tall, wiry guy with golden-brown hair and a fucking jawline crafted by the gods.

He drove his shoulder into Beckett's chest and easily dribbled around Ian when he tried to block him, easing the ball up into the net with an outstretched hand.

Cameron gave him a high five, and I had to grit my teeth

against the vicious spike that drove straight through my head. Poppy got out of her car first, and the living Ken doll lit the fuck up at the sight of her.

He said something to Beckett and made the guy laugh, then stepped back and drilled a three-point shot, jogging over to Poppy as he used the hem of his T-shirt to wipe the sweat off his face. He had an eight-pack, for fucking fuck's sake.

I wanted to punch something.

Her face scrunched up when he teased her with the sweaty shirt, pulling back with a laugh when he ducked in to try to wipe his forehead against her shoulder.

Then with his big puppy saving hands, he cupped the sides of her face and ducked down to place a deep kiss on her lips. In the deepest cavity of my chest, a dark corner of my irrational, unfair brain, something growled dangerously.

A raw scream of warning that I needed to ignore. An itch to claim something—someone—that wasn't mine to claim.

The kiss ended quickly, and Poppy said something to him with their faces still close. He nodded intently, eyes briefly darting over to my truck before he said something back. When she pulled away, she wiped at her mouth and gave a small, rueful shake of her head.

He dragged his thumb over her bottom lip, and I dimly registered that my hands were gripping the steering wheel so tight that my knuckles went white.

I wanted to fucking rip his handsome fucking face right the fuck off.

This whole friendship thing was going *great*.

The kids ran inside, followed by Greer and Ivy. Harlow went after them, and Beckett gave me a nod through the windshield and then jogged up the steps to follow his wife.

Cameron and Ian talked while I slowly exited the truck. Ian shoved his brother good-naturedly from behind, and Cameron gave me a look like, behave.

I rolled my eyes, but nodded.

As I approached Poppy and Dean, the guy slid his arm around Poppy's waist, an easy possessiveness in his grip as they turned to face me.

Why were his eyes so fucking blue? God, I hoped he was wearing those fake contacts because that wasn't even natural.

Poppy was clearly nervous, and I attempted as much of a smile as I was capable as I came closer.

Dean lifted his chin, bright, freaky blue eyes as clear as the fucking summer sky, like he had no reason in the world not to trust me.

"You must be Jax," he said, taking control of the exchange by extending his arm. "I'm Dean."

I took a deep breath and clasped his hand with mine, both of our grips instantly tightening. I didn't flinch, but then again, neither did he.

It was a draw, as pissing matches went, but he still smiled. And why wouldn't he? He still had his hands on the girl.

That was my own fucking fault, and he knew that too.

"Nice to meet you," I said.

Poppy glanced between us. "This is fun and not at all awkward."

Dean glanced down at her and smiled—a dentist's fucking wet dream, this guy's teeth were. "So you were in Spain, right?"

When I nodded, Poppy's shoulders relaxed. Tension that I hadn't even noticed before, too wrapped up in my own spiderweb-tangled thoughts.

Cameron gave me an encouraging nod, and I let out a deep breath before answering. I could do this.

"There's this set of trails I've always wanted to do," I answered. "A pilgrimage, they call it."

His face lit up. "The Camino de Santiago."

Slowly, I nodded. "That's the one."

"Which route did you take?" he asked, his hand moving in small up and down motions along her side. She stared down at the ground for a moment before raising her gaze to mine. Her cheeks were pink.

He probably had a PhD in loving affection and emotional regulation, the pompous prick.

I had to force myself back into the conversation, tearing my eyes away from Poppy's in order to answer. "I took more than one, actually."

"You're kidding." He let out a quiet, shocked laugh. "I've wanted to take the French route for years, but I was too busy finishing school to even consider it."

"I started on the Northern route, actually," I said. "Took my time with it. Walked when I wanted to walk, spent a few days in a town if I liked it, and I did that a lot. Took a few weeks to rest before I took the French route back into Spain. Finished with a couple I met on the last stretch, ended the whole thing in Santiago de Compostela."

"Incredible," he breathed, shaking his head slightly. "I'm feeling a little intimidated right now that you managed both trails in one trip. That's ... what? Seven hundred miles?"

Poppy's mouth fell open. "Seriously?"

My mouth edged up in a wry smile. "More like eight hundred," I said. I didn't need to squeeze the fucker's hand to bring him down to his metaphorical knees.

"Shut *up*," Poppy exclaimed.

"You didn't know where he was going?" Dean asked.

She shook her head, incredulity stamped in her big eyes. "No. We didn't talk about it."

Poppy and I exchanged a quick, tense look, and I felt it down to my fucking toes. Wasn't much talking happening that night at all, really.

"I'd love to hear about it," Dean said. "If you don't mind sharing, that is."

Did I mind sharing, he asked. I didn't really want to share shit with this guy—the muscles and the big brain and blue fucking eyes and his stupid fucking hand on Poppy's hip

No, I didn't want to share at all.

From across the driveway, Cameron caught my eye and grinned. "Jax *loves* telling stories."

Ivy snorted into her drink. Ian cleared his throat.

Dean just smiled, either too genuine of a person to register the blatant sarcasm in my friend's voice, or he was just really fucking oblivious. "Do you?"

"Fucking love it," I answered, only the slightest growl to my voice.

"Great," he said. "Maybe you could tell me over dinner."

"I think my mom has you two on opposite ends of the table in case this little intro went badly," Poppy admitted.

Dean's face softened as he looked down at her, and hell if it didn't look genuine. My chest went tight, a thousand pounds of pressure while I registered the slight softening in her eyes too.

"No chance of that, babe," he said gently. "There's no reason for Jax and me not to get along." He moved his gaze back to mine, and for the first time, I saw the slightest challenge there, enough to lift the hairs on the back of my neck. "Clearly, we have something really important in common. That's enough of a reason, isn't it?"

Poppy pinched his side, and he laughed.

An angry restlessness skittered under my skin.

Do something.

Anything.

Leave.

Go.

You're not what she needs.

What was I doing here? What was I playing at? I couldn't be that guy. Who pretended to be part of the family, when my presence made everyone uncomfortable.

Would it always be like this?

Birthday parties. Christmas. Graduations.

Poppy and Dr. Dean, the picture-perfect partner with a

great jaw and saintlike job and a gold fucking star in emotional intelligence.

"All right, kids, let's go on inside," Sheila called from the front porch. "Food's ready."

Dean and Poppy turned, his arm anchored around her hip. For a moment, my feet stayed locked tight to the ground, unable to move forward at that casual display of ownership. Poppy glanced backward, giving me an encouraging smile, but I couldn't force myself to smile back.

When they were inside, I let out a harsh puff of air and glanced up at the sky.

"Sometimes life gives us interesting curveballs, doesn't it?"

The sound of Sheila's voice had my head snapping in her direction. I thought she'd followed them in, but she was still waiting on the porch for me, a patient smile on her gently wrinkled face.

I managed a short nod.

"You still coming in?" she asked.

There was no judgment in her tone, no command.

"Not sure I should, Mrs. Wilder."

She clucked with her tongue, then came down the steps to stand beside me. There was a book tucked underneath her arm, and she moved it into one hand as she stared up at the house, like I was.

"It's just dinner, Jax," she said. "You've been to enough of them that you know how it's going to play out."

"Not this one," I answered. "Can't tell me this one isn't a little different."

Sheila sighed quietly. "Maybe a little," she conceded. "But there's no one inside that house who doesn't want you there." The dry, sideways glance I gave her had her lips quirking up in a tiny smile. "All right, maybe one. But he's just a man trying to find his footing, same as you."

"Probably wants to put that foot up my ass."

Her answering laugh was quiet and short, but I heard it all

the same. "Don't go assuming the worst, Jax Cartwright. He might surprise you." Unlikely. Really fucking unlikely. That guy shoved his tongue down Poppy's throat simply because I was sitting there, and I couldn't even really blame him. "And there's no one inside that house who doesn't want you here."

Everything seemed so easy when she said it like that. But it wasn't easy.

Like Poppy asking if we could be friends.

Like Margot telling me to just write down what I was feeling.

Like my idiot self thinking that I could walk away from Poppy without telling her I wanted her.

Easy was a fucking myth. Not a single part of life was easy. Even the good things. Friendship or love or family. Because those things came with people, their baggage, feelings, and their past weighing it all down.

The best thing I could do was just not make it worse.

And the fear of that had me asking something I might not have if it was anyone else standing by my side.

"Am I making it harder on her by being here?"

Sheila's face softened in understanding. "No, Jax. You're right where you need to be. You're part of this family—her family—whether you're here or not. And I believe that you'll be a wonderful father, if you let yourself."

I scoffed. "Like I fucking know how."

She set a soft hand on my arm. "I remember your mom, you know."

My head snapped in her direction. "You do?"

"Of course. She was so young when she had you, wasn't she?"

Jaw tight, I nodded.

"Everyone does their best, even if it doesn't always look that way, and I think your mom did the best she could considering she was just a kid, and she was alone." Sheila pulled the book out from underneath her arm. "I brought this for you. Pulled it out of Tim's box of books."

Slowly, I took it from her, my fingers tracing the warped edges. "This was his?"

"Bought it when I was pregnant with Poppy because he was convinced we didn't remember how to do it."

The New Dad's Playbook

Exhaling a quiet laugh, I turned to the front inside page, my hand tracing over his scrawled handwriting. *Please return to Tim Wilder. I have too many kids to lose this thing.*

She chuckled when she saw it. "Always thought he was so funny."

"He was," I said quietly. "Thank you, Sheila."

The pressure in my chest eased when she carefully closed the book in my hands and took my other hand in hers, settling it on the top of the cover. "All you need to do is be willing to try, Jax. No one expects more than that, all right? If you're doing your best, that's fine by me."

"What if my best still hurts her?" I asked, voicing it even though the words ached coming up.

"The fact that you're willing to ask is why you deserve a seat at the table, Jax." She tilted her head toward the house. "You ready to come in?"

With a nod, I gripped the book. "Let me set this in my truck first. I don't want to forget it."

Chapter 19
Poppy

"Can you remind me one more time what you said yesterday?"

Ivy's whispered question had me jamming an elbow into her side, shoving her away from me. Behind me, there was so much commotion, but I blissfully ignored all of it and focused every shred of my attention on serving up a piece of pie.

"Olive, honey, did you want some pie?" I asked my niece as she skipped past the table.

She didn't even stop, and I grimaced. Honestly, where were the kids when you needed them to distract people? They were always gone.

Greer sidled up on my left, leaning in just as far as Ivy was on my right. "Am I the only one noticing what's happening here?"

I punched the knife into the edge of the pie, slicing down into a piece so big, I'd never, ever be able to eat it.

Did I still put it on my plate?

Sure did.

What good was being pregnant if you couldn't fill half your plate with apple pie?

"Poppy is noticing," Ivy answered in lieu of my silence. "She just doesn't want to admit it because she tried to tell me the other day she's not in a love triangle." Ivy carefully extracted the giant knife from my grip. "A line, right? You're in a love line?"

"What does that even mean?" Greer asked.

"It means that Ivy is full of shit and needs to stop talking," I said sweetly, snatching the knife back and setting it next to the pie plate.

The three of us turned in tandem, and when confronted with the reality of what was behind us, I shoveled a giant piece of pie into my mouth. Greer used her napkin to fan her face.

"Well, whatever the current shape of your love life, I am *supportive.*"

The pie wasn't enough. I'd need four more.

I tried desperately to think about a good metaphor for what was happening inside my brain, and came up blank. Tangles and knots were close, but it felt messier. More permanent.

So many people, including members of my family, did a bang-up job of compartmentalizing. Blocking out the inconvenient feelings in their life so they could function.

I was not one of them.

Wouldn't it be nice if I could lock my past feelings for Jax in a little box and throw away the freaking key? Why did I think I could navigate any of this with a few simple decisions?

I sat in a vehicle and told Jax Cartwright he was *too good in bed.* With a straight face.

No wonder I'd never managed to be friends with this man. Something about him scrambled my actual brain.

Which is why I had half a freaking pie on my plate.

"Who decided this was a good idea?" I hissed. "Who decided a *physical competition* was a good idea?"

"Someone very smart," Ivy said unashamedly, her eyes locked on my brother's torso as he passed the ball to Jax.

A friendly post-dinner game of touch football. Sure. *Just what we needed.*

Except it wasn't very friendly. Someone tried to suggest not keeping score, and it didn't go over well.

"Honestly, would it kill this family to drop the intensity just a little bit?" I asked.

No one answered because we all knew it was rhetorical.

The teams were … lopsided. Greer said she was too tired, Ivy hated organized team sports, and when I tried raising my hand as an option, everyone yelled *No* immediately, which I thought was a little excessive, but whatever. Thankfully, Sage —Harlow's daughter—volunteered as quarterback for the second team.

And Olive, God bless her, had no idea what she was supposed to be doing, but she agreed to play with Sage when she asked to have another girl on the other team.

So we had Ian, Jax, Parker, and Olive matched up against Cameron, Dean, Beckett, and Sage. The disparity in a few of the players provided mixed results. Olive was far more interested in plucking weeds from the grass, but would occasionally run when Uncle Cameron chased her. Ian played defense against the QB because he wouldn't let anyone else guard his stepdaughter and risk hurting her.

This meant he wasn't trying very hard to tackle her because I honestly thought he'd rather lose than see Sage not do well.

Parker and Beckett, as teammates for the Voyagers, they were the only two who could meet each other step for step.

And that left Dean guarding Jax.

I couldn't even tell you how fun it was to watch the two of them try to sprint past each other or the shoving that was just past the limits of polite during certain plays.

Jax caught a pass from Sage, snagging it over Dean's head, reeling in the ball for a beautiful catch. His teammates cheered, and I kept my pie-filled mouth shut, I'll tell you that much.

Their team lined up again, and my eyes locked on the two men on the end. Dean swiped at his forehead with the collar of his shirt, and the quick glimpse of his chiseled abs had me digging the fork into my pie again.

Jax had lost his shirt after the first play because he hadn't dressed for football. And it was not good for my sanity.

When he pulled his shirt off and tossed it on the ground, I kept my attention right the hell on my mother's face, and I didn't like how she raised an eyebrow in challenge. When I narrowed my eyes in a glare, she only laughed under her breath.

Not that I was doing anything laugh-worthy.

Because what I wasn't looking at was the light smattering of dark hair across his chest. I wasn't looking at the sculpted curves of his pectorals or the rounded muscles on his shoulders.

And I wasn't looking at the stacked lines of his abs either. Or the way the sweat glistened on those abs in the light of the setting sun.

Fuck, I mouthed silently, right before taking another bite.

Beckett snapped the ball to Sage and took off running, and so did Jax, spinning around Dean to cut into the middle. Olive stayed right where she was, pulling up a dandelion and holding it out to Cameron with a smile. He scratched the side of his cheek and accepted it from her, tucking it behind his ear with a wink.

"He's too tall," Sage yelled, trying to dance around Ian as he made a few half-hearted attempts to 'tackle' her with a simple touch.

"Better run faster then, kid," Ian said, darting around behind her, laughing when she ducked under his arm and shot forward. She set her feet and heaved the ball in the direction of Beckett. Parker swore when he realized he was a step behind where he should be.

Beckett caught it with a yell but whirled when Parker tried to grab him. He shouted for Jax, then pitched the ball sideways for a lateral pass. It was almost perfect, but Dean's long arm shot forward and knocked the ball out of the air.

He shouted, pumping his fist like he'd just won the Super Bowl. Dean turned to me and grinned happily. I waved, wondering when I needed to break it to him that winning this backyard game of football didn't *actually* mean anything.

Greer shook her head, chuckling quietly. "You know, in the olden days, men did shit like this all the time to gain a woman's favor."

Just as she said it, Parker lowered his shoulder and tackled Beckett onto the ground. Beckett laughed, shoving Parker off before he hopped back up to his feet.

"I didn't have the ball, Parker," Beckett said with a grin.

Parker gave him a steady look. "I know, you just looked like you needed to be knocked on your ass."

Beckett rolled his eyes, shouldering Parker as he passed. Parker shoved back. The two started tussling. Again.

"And we wonder why their life expectancy is shorter," I murmured.

Greer sighed, watching her normally very stoic husband wrestle our brother on the ground. Next to Beckett and Parker, Jax picked up the ball and tossed it back to Sage, who caught it neatly in one hand.

Dean strode past Jax without a second look. "That's game, right? We won?"

No one answered him, but he jogged up the porch steps and tried to give me a hug.

I ducked away with a laugh. "Yeah right, get that sweat away from me."

Dean's eyes were bright in his face, and he smiled widely. "Oh come on, you love it." He snagged a quick kiss, then hopped off the porch, picking up a discarded basketball and dribbling it around. "Anyone want another game?" No one answered. Dean drilled a three-point shot, his focus entirely on the hoop. "How about you, Jax?"

"I think I'll pass for now."

"Suit yourself."

My chest felt cranked too tight.

Jax's jaw tightened, and his eyes locked on mine for a breathless second. Then he glanced away and walked over to Cameron and Olive. Ian and Sage had taken a pause, talking to Harlow, where she sat on the front porch next to Mom. The dessert table was on the other side of the front door. Greer, Ivy, and I still huddled together while I shoveled pie in my face as a coping mechanism.

"What *happened* when they came out here?" Greer asked. "Dinner was good."

"It was," I told her.

"I bet Cameron fifty bucks they'd come to blows," Ivy said smoothly. "I'm happy to lose, for obvious reasons, but the evening is still young, apparently," she said smoothly, eyeing the tense exchange in front of us.

I rolled my eyes as Greer laughed.

It's not like Jax was chatty. He was still Jax, but it was polite with him and Dean on opposite ends of the table. Pleasant, even.

Over the years, I'd honed a supernatural ability to keep blinders on when Jax and I were sharing space. Greer told me once it was just good self-control, but honestly, it was more about self-preservation than anything. And boy, did the years of practice come in handy at that particular dinner.

Parker's surprise presence helped keep Dean occupied, they didn't know each other very well. Parker hadn't been home as much since Dean and I started dating.

Ian and Harlow kept Jax occupied, and next to me, Dean was his normal amiable self. We talked about his day. He kept his hand anchored over my thigh under the table, his big hand a warm, solid presence that I'd gotten used to having on me whenever we ate a meal together.

He was one of those guys, always wanting to sit on the same side of the booth or table when we went out to eat. Easier to hold my hand, he always said. And he did that often, content with his arm around me or his hand in mine, his palm and fingers draped possessively over my thigh.

It was that same hint of possession present in his kiss when I arrived too. I couldn't hold it against him, really. Knowing my history with Jax, any man would feel the slightest bit threatened, but watching the two of them on that football field gave me the sinking feeling that I would have to admit something that I didn't want to admit.

That possessive display, even if it was understandable, sat on my skin like an oil slick I wanted to wash away. It wasn't giving me butterflies, and there was a low-level buzzing that this was just wrong, wrong, *wrong*.

Greer nudged me with her elbow, and I blinked out of my snarly, uncomfortable thoughts.

"What happened?" she asked again. "Did you see, Ivy?"

She shook her head. "I was helping your mom set up the desserts." Then she perked up. "You saw the cookies I made, right?"

Greer and I shared a loaded look. "They're very nice, Ivy," my sister answered diplomatically.

The plate on the table held a large pile of flat, slightly misshapen cookies that no one except Olive had tried.

Ivy narrowed her eyes. "Aren't you going to try one?"

Weakly, I held up my serving of pie. "Not sure I should have any more sugar, you know?"

Greer took a conspicuous sip of her iced tea. When Ivy continued staring at her, she patted her stomach. "I'm stuffed, but, uh, next batch, I promise."

Ivy muttered something under her breath.

I fought a smile. "Nothing happened," I told them. "It was Ian's fault, really."

"It always is," Greer murmured. "We can't take him anywhere."

"What did he do?" Ivy asked, picking up one of the cookies from the plate and setting it back down with a slight grimace.

"He was dumb enough to put them on opposing teams, and apparently, that was all it took to trigger some dumb caveman switch in their dumb brains."

I swallowed hard, watching Dean abandon his lone game of basketball to pick up the football. He looked like an athlete, even next to Parker and Beckett. The long legs, arms roped with muscle, the trim hips and big hands. He tossed the ball in the air, then told Parker to run a route.

He heaved the ball, a perfect spiral, that landed into Parker's outstretched hands.

Jax was standing behind them, hands on his hips, his chest bare and the lines of his stomach glistening. My heart rate jumped, and I tore my eyes away.

"You'd think they'd have so much to bond over," Greer said lightly. "Given their shared sexual attraction to this very fine young woman here."

If looks could kill, my sister would be so freaking dead.

"Sexual attraction isn't enough," Ivy said thoughtfully, "Dean doesn't actually have any sexual *encounters* with Poppy."

Greer made a small *aah* sound.

My face was seven thousand degrees. "I'm never telling you guys anything ever again."

Greer patted my arm. "Yes, you will. None of us can help ourselves."

"Think about it," Ivy continued. "Jax has quite literally staked his claim on you."

"He really didn't," I said firmly. "There is no claiming of anything, and it's so much better that way."

Ivy ignored me because she was the worst. "He didn't just sleep with you. He left his seed inside you. His line is continuing inside of your body, visible proof of his virility for all to see."

The fork in my hand slowly lowered back down to the plate, the nugget inside me choosing that precise moment for a few little fluttery movements. My eyes pinched shut.

"I can quite literally feel the feminism leaving my body as you're saying this," Greer whispered. "It's bizarre."

I blew out a slow breath.

"Even if Dean's reasons for wanting to wait are valid and understandable, in the alpha male hierarchy, the boy's at a disadvantage, and he knows it."

"I don't need him to be in the alpha male hierarchy," I hissed. "That's not even a real thing."

"Yes, it is," they said in unison.

Jax chose that moment to pick up his T-shirt off the ground, the muscles in his stomach flexing as he pulled the shirt back over his head and tugged it back over his chest. My pulse skittered at the way his massive biceps curled under the surface of his skin. When the shirt fell back into place, the dark line of hair that split his stomach disappeared.

"Dean doesn't need to sleep with me to prove anything," I said, but the words sounded weak even to my own ears. "He's a good boyfriend. A great one."

"We know," Greer said gently. "And it's obvious he's crazy about you."

He was.

So why aren't you in love with him, a voice whispered at the back of my head. The past four months had been filled with so much good. Warm affection and easy laughs and excellent conversation. The lack of heat hadn't registered because the decision was taken out of my hands. But why wasn't I in love with him? Even thinking the question triggered an anxious tightening in my throat. It wasn't that I was afraid to admit that Dean wasn't The One. If I was honest with myself, I knew it even before Jax came home.

My fear was rooted somewhere else.

It was a list I didn't really want to make because seeing it in black and white felt like a road map to my own doom.

Jax jogged up the steps of the front porch and nodded as he approached. "Anything good left?" he asked.

With a grimace, I peeked at the empty pie plate. "Umm…"

Ivy grabbed the cookies she'd brought and displayed them with a flourish of her hand. "I brought these," she proclaimed. "Sheila's recipe."

Jax's brow furrowed as he studied the dark brown blobs.

"Are they?" Greer whispered.

I rolled my lips together to stem a laugh. "Jax *loves* cookies," I said. "He told me earlier."

Underneath his breath, Jax made a small growling sound, and damn if I did not feel that all the way down to my little toes.

It was heat. Licking at my skin, skirting the lines of propriety with how lightning-quick that fuse was lit. I could practically hear the clicking of a stove, just waiting for the flames to take.

"Ahh, so this is what it's like being Poppy's friend," he said casually. Then he leaned down to whisper by my ear. Helplessly, my eyes fluttered shut, and it felt like even my heart slowed as it registered his closeness, the slight scent of his skin. *Come closer*, I wanted to scream. Just a little. Jax spoke again, and I tore my thoughts from that very unhelpful place. "Complete and utter betrayal of my innermost secrets. Thanks, *friend*."

Uncontrollable heat—from a tiny little growl and the scent of his skin near mine—so big that it almost hurt, and my eyes fluttered shut as I registered an instinctive pressing of my thighs.

Shit.

Shit.

Shit.

Brain. Scrambled.

Thankfully, it was the dark use of that word that had me laughing despite myself, and I smiled up at him.

Jax's eyes darkened when I smiled, the muscle in his jaw working as he reached past me and took two cookies from the plate. He swallowed thickly, eyeing the cookies like they might explode, then took a tentative bite, chewing very, very slowly. "They're … really interesting, Ivy."

She beamed. "See? I don't know why everyone's afraid to try them."

"Past history?" I ventured with a sweet smile.

Ivy's eyes narrowed dangerously. Cameron calling her name from the yard saved me from any further retribution, but honestly, the woman was a complete menace in the kitchen.

Once the bite of cookie had disappeared, Jax picked up a bottle of water from the cooler next to the door and drained half of it in one long pull. While Ivy's back was turned, he quickly tossed the second cookie into the trash next to the table, and when he wiped his hand off on his gym shorts, the firm line of his mouth edged up in a wry smile.

"You're keeping that between us, right?" he asked.

Heart racing from that curve to his lips, I nodded.

His eyes tracked over my face before he left the porch, and I let out a surreptitious breath, staring down at my feet while he walked down the steps.

Friends.

Friends.

Friends.

I would be friends with this man if it was the last thing I did. I'd find a way to lock my feelings up, bury them seventy-four feet underground, and burn them to the ground because

206

if I wasn't careful, those feelings would be my downfall. Channeling every ounce of Wilder family stubbornness I knew ran through my veins, I lifted my head. Dean watched me carefully, his own brow wrinkled.

Friends, I thought.

I managed a smile, and Dean's face smoothed out before he turned to throw the football again.

The moment his back was turned, my smile dropped, my shoulders slumping and my mom came up beside me, carefully extracting the plate from my hands. "Pie will solve a lot of problems, honey," she said quietly. "But I don't think it'll solve this one for you."

"How do you see everything?" I asked her.

"Years and years of practice," she told me. Then she gently patted my bump. "Just wait. You'll see." She wrapped an arm around me. "I'll make myself scarce after everyone leaves, just in case you need some privacy."

"Thanks, Mom." I gave her a grateful smile, even though my chest hurt a little bit.

As soon as she walked away, roping my brothers into cleaning up the kitchen, I grabbed the pie.

Chapter 20
Popppy

When I was little, I told my dad that hurting people's feelings made my stomach feel like it was flipped upside down. It was in fourth grade, and I invited a couple of friends for a sleepover. But there was a girl in my grade who heard about it, and I saw her crying on the playground the next day. The rest of the school day, I was sick to my stomach, that this perfectly nice little girl had her day ruined because of something I'd done, even if it was unintentional.

We had her over for a playdate a few weeks later, but I'd never really forget the look in her eyes when I saw her crying, never forgot what it did inside me knowing I'd caused it.

I had that same feeling sitting in the family room watching Dean dry the last of the dishes, even though my mom told him he didn't need to help.

Resting my chin on my hand where it sat on the back of the couch, I thought about that girl in fourth grade. Whether she ever really forgave me. Or if she still thought of me as that girl who didn't invite her for a sleepover.

The muscles in Dean's back shifted when he set the last of the glasses into the cupboard to the right of the sink, and I tilted my head as I watched him move with ease in my mom's kitchen.

"You're quiet over there," he said, still not facing me. "What's on your mind, beautiful?"

The bridge of my nose burned before I could stop it—a bad sign for the upcoming conversation. Before I answered, I took a few deep breaths and willed it away.

"A lot of things," I answered honestly.

Dean slung the towel over his shoulder and finally turned, leaning back against the counter while he looked across the room, gauging the expression on my face. Whatever he saw had him sighing deeply.

"I, uh, got a little carried away after dinner, didn't I?" he asked sheepishly.

My smile was fleeting. "A little."

Dean blew out a breath through puffed-out cheeks, then tossed the towel onto the counter and came to join me on the couch. He sat opposite me, easily pulling my feet toward his lap so he could dig his thumbs into the arches like I liked.

"That's not why we need to talk," I told him.

Dean was quiet, and I loved that he never rushed to say something, even in the quiet. He was thoughtful and good, and my heart ached that I couldn't feel more for him. That the touch of his hands and the simple act of his nearness didn't set me on fire.

"I feel like I'm losing you," he said quietly. His eyes didn't meet mine at first, and I watched him with a growing sense of understanding of how we'd ended up here. How, for months, we both settled into a comfortable rhythm in an uncomfortable situation.

Dean was driven and smart and kind, and he liked the fact that I wasn't fawning over him. I wasn't trying to tie him down. And for me, Dean was the kind of safety net I'd never had before. But we both deserved better than that.

"Dean," I said quietly.

He pinched his eyes shut as I pulled my legs back, because

honestly, his foot massages just might sway me not to say what I needed to say. "Poppy, I'm sorry. I'll do better next time."

"I don't expect you to be perfect." I smiled. "Lord knows I've screwed up so much in the past few months."

Finally, he looked up, and I was surprised to see the pain in his bright blue eyes. "It was harder than I thought," he admitted. "Seeing this guy that you…" He paused, searching for the right words. "It was easier when there was no one for me to picture."

I looked down at my lap, staring at my intertwined fingers. "I know."

He eased forward, tugging my hands between his. "I can work on this, Poppy. I don't have anything to prove to that guy, and I just forgot my head a little bit when we were playing football. It felt like … like everyone was comparing us all night." The earnestness in his eyes was almost my undoing. "Like you were too."

I didn't know how to answer because it was so hard to admit that I might always do that.

What did it say about me that I couldn't dislodge this one tiny thing from the deepest parts of who I was? That I couldn't dislodge the idea of one person from the core of my being?

"I don't think it's fair for me to pretend Jax being back doesn't change things," I told him carefully. "It's hard for me in a different way."

Dean swallowed thickly. "How?"

I blew out a slow breath, pulling my hand back to run it through my hair. "When he was gone, it was like … I could pretend that I was this different version of myself. The girl who moved on," I said in an emotion-choked voice. Dean's jaw tightened, but he didn't interrupt. "And I wanted to move on. I promise you, I did."

In the silence that followed, Dean nodded slowly. "But you can't."

"I told Jax that I want us to be friends, and I mean that." My throat felt locked tight with regrets and frustrations and the weight of the absolute chokehold that man had on me. "But it's not fair for me to put you in the position of being my safety net."

Dean's brow furrowed as he processed that silently. "Is that what I was?"

"Not always," I answered honestly. I shifted forward, my thigh resting easily on his while I cupped his face. "You made me feel beautiful and wanted, and that's exactly what I needed when we met. You made me feel like it was possible to move on. I have loved our time together."

Dean gently wrapped his hand around my wrist and pressed a soft kiss to my palm. My fingers curled up helplessly when he rolled his forehead against my hand. "Is that time over?" he asked.

There was no point beating myself up anymore for not feeling the right things for him because there was no right or wrong in any of this. We were all just doing our best, and the worst thing I could do was string him along. Use him to hide from the things I didn't want to feel.

"I think it has to be."

He deserved better. So did I.

If I expected my family to take me seriously, then I needed to act like an adult and do the hard thing. The thing that didn't feel good, leaving me open to a different kind of vulnerability.

His eyes went a little red, but he didn't tear up. I did, though. Dean rolled his lips together and studied my face. "I knew this was coming the second he got out of that truck."

"Why?"

"You looked embarrassed that I kissed you."

Shame had me dropping my gaze. "I'm so sorry."

"But I made you feel safe?" he asked. "Before that, I mean."

Slowly, I nodded. Dean brushed a thumb along my cheekbone, dragging it down my jaw to my chin. His hand eventually dropped back down into his lap, and I knew that was probably the last time he'd touch me.

"If he'd been home this whole time," Dean said, "would you have stayed with me this long?"

There was a look in his eye, the kind that told me he already knew the answer. So did I.

The first tear fell, and as I brushed it away, I got that feeling—the weightless, uncomfortable turn of my stomach flipping in on itself.

If I were in my bedroom, with that chipped mirror on the wall, I wouldn't want to meet my own gaze because it was horrible to face the consequences of such a deep-rooted thing inside you. The kind that caused pain for someone else.

But no matter what, he deserved my honesty.

"Probably not," I whispered. "And I know how unfair that is. How unfair I've been."

Dean sat back on the couch and tilted his chin up to stare at the ceiling.

"I should go," he said, standing up as he did. I pushed off the couch, ready to walk him to the front door. His next words stopped me though. "I hope being friends with him is worth it."

"What do you mean?"

Dean shook his head. "I think no matter how this plays out or how badly you want to be friends with him, Jax will break your heart."

"You don't even know him," I said, brows furrowing.

Dean smiled softly, and somehow the kindness and understanding in that smile made it so much worse. "I used to be just like him. Running from anything serious. Ready to bolt when things got too hard. Couldn't let myself settle into anything." He paused before he opened the door. "You're too smart to keep waiting for him to change."

All right then. So there'd be no sweet hug or beautiful shared tears over the experience we had over the past four months. It was a parting shot that struck somewhere deep, clanging and clanking as I swallowed it down.

I set my jaw and held his gaze. "Goodbye, Dean."

He let out a deep breath and slipped out the door. I sank onto the couch and speared my hair with my hands, elbows braced on my thighs. The baby did a small flip, and I glanced down, one hand coasting over the front of my bump.

"Hopefully, you're in the mood for some more pie because we are gonna need it."

Standing from the couch with a groan, I tried to decide how much longer I could get away with eating my feelings. At least a couple more months because if there was one excellent thing about pregnancy, it was those extra calories per day.

If I wanted to fill those calories with a bag of Sour Patch Kids the size of my face, there wasn't a person in the world who could stop me.

Mom's bedroom door cracked open, and her head poked out. "Can I come out? I wasn't eavesdropping, I promise."

I really needed my own place.

Still, I managed a smile. "Yeah. He just left."

As she left her room, she tied the ends of her fuzzy blue robe around her waist, the one she wore every morning and every night. "You okay?"

"I don't know." I yanked the covered pie tin from the fridge. Eyeing the two generous slices left, I opened the drawer in the island and pulled out two forks. "Want some?"

She eyed me carefully. "I think I'll let you have the rest."

"Wise move." There was no need to cut myself a piece because we both knew I'd be finishing that pie. Stabbing a bite with the fork, I narrowed my eyes and took a slow bite, thinking about what Dean said on his way out. "You know what's bullshit?"

Mom pulled a stool out and took a seat, watching me

demolish another bite of pie with a slight smile on her face. "No, but I have a feeling you're going to tell me."

I gave her a brief rundown of the conversation, and she listened without interruption.

"And what part of that is the bullshit?"

"The bullshit is that last parting shot about how I'm too smart to think Jax will change." I dropped the fork in the aluminum pie tin and set my hands on my hips. "I never said I expected Jax to change. I'm not begging for his attention, but it's like my feelings for him are a reflection of some weakness on my part. A character flaw that I should apologize for."

Mom sat back, her eyebrows rising slightly as she gestured for me to continue.

"How many books have we read or movies have we watched where the hero pines for the heroine, and there's no one for him but her? It's so romantic and swoony, and we celebrate it," I said fiercely. Oh yeah. I was worked up now. Pregnancy hormones flashed hot, and if someone gave me a mic, I would've brought the freaking house down preaching this to anyone who would listen. I waggled a finger in the air. "But if the woman can't get a man out of her head, it's *sad*. She's *too smart* for that."

Her eyes were wide, but she chose not to interrupt as I paced the length of the kitchen.

"The insinuation is that she's being stupid for feeling those things in the first place! And it's bullshit, Mom. Misogynistic bullshit." I set my hands on my hips, my breaths coming in short, embarrassing pants. God, what a mess I'd be by forty weeks. Maybe I should start working out again if a little angry rant got me out of breath. "It's like no one believes I can actually be friends with him. That I'm still sitting back hoping he'll fall in love with me."

Mom's face softened. "And just to be clear, you're not?"

"No," I said firmly. "Breaking up with Dean was the right thing to do for many reasons, and only one of those reasons is the way I felt about Jax. But those feelings don't make me weak or stupid or silly."

She leaned forward, eyes fierce. "No one thinks you're any of those things."

Something was comforting about hearing my mom come to my defense so thoroughly. It didn't matter that she'd always done that with us and loved us so deeply that she always wanted to see the best in us.

Beyond that, everyone knew Sheila Wilder would call us on our bullshit so fast, it would make our heads spin. But she wasn't calling me on this, which meant—unfortunately—I might have to call myself on it.

Hurt my own feelings. Just a little bit.

The words clawed their way out, past my flip-flopped stomach and a throbbing chest. "Maybe I worry those things are true about me," I said, voice hardly more than a whisper.

In the following silence, I worried that I'd admitted too much, that I should have kept that locked down tight, but Mom let out a quiet sigh. "All you kids are so different, you know? It kept our life interesting when your dad and I first got married. Six little people with huge personalities in one house, and juggling that was hard enough before we added you into the mix."

Slowly, I took a seat, the raw honesty of the conversation draining a little bit of my righteous indignation.

"I don't know if I added anything exciting to the mix," I said ruefully. "I'm just … me."

"That's because we have a big family, kiddo, and it's easy to get lost in the mix when you're not an extreme personality."

"Great. Does this mean I get lumped in with Ian and Greer?"

She laughed. "No, Ian stood out because he was openly distrusting, and it never bothered him to let people see it, but once you get to know him, he's a giant mushball." She paused.

215

"Greer is … occasionally terrifying," she conceded with a slight tilt of her head. "And always wonderful."

I grinned reluctantly. "They all are."

"Cameron, though," she added quietly, her eyes warming immediately at the mention of my other brother—the one she loved as if he was her own. "He got lost in the mix too, I think."

I nodded, chest tight as I thought about the way he quietly took care of everyone when Dad was the most sick. Whether he wanted to admit it or not, he was the glue. "He did."

"You're a lot like him, you know." Her eyes traced over my face. "You think about others before you think about yourself. Adaline, too. You three would be the people on an airplane who ignored directions and helped little kids with their masks before putting your own on because you literally wouldn't be able to stop yourself."

I leaned forward. "I always thought that would be impossible. What if I have some cute little old lady next to me who can't reach her mask?"

Mom laughed. "The way you love your people blows my mind. All of you kids. But I think something is extra special about the quieter ones who love so fiercely." Her eyes glossed over with tears. "You will be such a great mom, Poppy. Not once since all this started have I ever doubted that. That second we found out, I knew you'd move heaven and earth for that child because that's what good parents do."

My eyes might've been a little wet too. "I had really good parents to learn from."

She swiped at a tear on her cheek. "Who your partner is someday is not what will make you great at this, Poppy. That's your heart, sweet girl. You see straight to the core of who people are. Like when you meddle with your siblings because you have this radar for what will make people happy, it's deep in your bones."

"I wouldn't call it meddling," I hedged.

Her eyebrows rose slowly. "You literally dropped Harlow off on Ian's porch with no way to leave so they'd be forced to see each other."

With a wince, I sank into my chair a little. "Okay, well that might have been a teeny bit meddlesome." Then I brightened. "But look how that turned out! They're married, and Ian is so much nicer now."

"He is," she admitted with a grin. It faded to something softer. "I don't think you should be so hard on yourself for any of this, Poppy."

"Are you kidding me? Being hard on myself is what's justifying all this pie."

She laughed. "Breaking up with someone good is a rite of passage. Just consider this a merit badge for your twenties."

"Being an adult is wild," I said. "I had Froot Loops for dinner last night, and I just earned a hypothetical prize for dumping the biggest catch in town. Where does the excitement end?"

"Oh, don't worry, this family will always have something keeping us on our toes."

I patted my stomach. "I have us covered for a while."

With a hum, Mom leaned forward to snag a bite of my pie. "I have a feeling you're not the only one," she said with a meaningful look in her eyes.

On a gasp, I leaned forward. "Who?"

"Harlow, I think." She grinned. "Saw Ian touch her stomach after dinner and give her a kiss."

I glanced down. "See? Now you've got a cousin your own age. Isn't that exciting?"

"Maybe I'll have enough grandkids coming where I won't need to buy some goats to keep me busy," Mom mused.

After scooping the last bite of pie, I let my fork fall with a clatter into the pie tin. "Great. Just what this family needs. Some fucking goats in the mix."

Mom and I shared a look, then burst out laughing.

Chapter 21
Jax

"Don't make me do it," I begged.

Cameron pushed his tongue into his cheek and studied me with shrewd eyes. "Wade trained Rob, which means it's your turn."

Next to me, Wade had his arms crossed and a shit-eating grin on his face.

"Don't gloat," I told him. "It's rude."

Wade chuckled under his breath. "Oh, I can't wait to watch this. If you make it one week without losing your mind, it'll be a fucking miracle."

A tool dropping loudly on the floor had all three of us turning to look. Rob's friend—I didn't know his name—slowly bent over to pick up the tool belt he was supposed to be hooking around his waist.

At our notice, he paused, eyes wide and a sheepish grin on his baby face. "I, uh, missed the first buckle."

Rob slapped his back. "Don't worry, we all had a first day at one point."

"I didn't," Wade muttered. "I didn't *ever* have a first day where I didn't know how to put a tool belt on."

The friend tried to line up the hammer in its slot, missed, and it clattered back to the floor.

Wade's eyes fell closed, and he pinched the bridge of his nose.

Rob shoved him with a laugh. "You dipshit," he said.

"He has experience?" I asked skeptically.

Cameron sighed, scratching the back of his neck. "A couple of summers ago, he helped his uncle in Michigan on a job while he visited." Both Wade and I swung around to stare at him. He held up his hands. "I *know*. Greer liked him. She said he'd bring a good energy to the jobsite."

The kid sauntered over, his long, scraggly hair swooping down over his forehead. He had to do this weird head toss to keep it out of his eyes, and I set my hands on my hips.

"I'm Jax," I told him. "I'll, uh, be training you, I guess." The kid leaned forward, staring into my face like he was searching for something. Unthinkingly, I backed away. "What are you doing?"

His eyes were a vivid green, and then he straightened after another second. "You have a red aura." He lifted his hands, motioning around my body. "Some orange too. Interesting."

Cameron choked on a laugh.

I stared at him for a few seconds, waiting for him to elaborate. "What now?"

"Red is very passionate. Grounded. Physical. But orange is an adventurous spirit. Hard to settle down."

Rob settled a hand on his friend's shoulder. "He's very good at reading people's energies."

"Dipshit is?" I asked.

Wade snorted.

"That's not his name." Cameron sighed.

"It's what Rob called him." I hardened my jaw and studied the kid head to toe. "That's what I'm calling him."

Dipshit nodded like this made a lot of sense. "You were right, Rob. He's got a very hard exterior. What was your childhood like, Jax?"

Immediately, I turned to Cameron. "No. I cannot do it."

Cameron was still staring slack-jawed at the kid. "I—"

"It's all right," Dipshit said patiently. "We'll work through it. I'm an empath, so it's really easy for me to read people's energies and adjust accordingly."

This was it. This would be the day I quit and walked away and told Cameron he was on his fucking own because it wasn't worth the paycheck anymore.

I closed my eyes and took a few deep breaths, then slicked my tongue over my teeth and started walking away. "I'm not waiting for you, kid," I called over my shoulder.

"That was a great day," Dipshit said on a sigh. He was stretched out on the bed of Rob's truck, staring up at the cloudless sky. "Physical labor is incredibly grounding."

Rob sat on the tailgate, a cold beer in hand, nodding like that made sense.

It was one of our traditions—Cameron brought us a beer at the end of someone's first day. He'd had to leave for a meeting, but Ian, Wade, and I took part with some other guys. I drank half of mine and tossed the rest into the metal trash bin next to the house's frame.

Wade stood to the side, taking a long pull from his cigarette. "You break anything?"

Dipshit smiled. "Nope."

"Almost," I corrected.

"But I didn't," he said, sitting up and stretching his arms over his head. "You're a good teacher, Jax, even if you pretend to hate it."

Wade's brow raised so sharply that the bill of his hat moved.

I gave Dipshit a steady look. "What did I tell you about reading my aura at work?"

Rob laughed. "Come on, man, we should go. Cameron said you needed to drop off that paperwork at the office."

"We do paperwork for this job now?" Wade asked.

"Not you," I answered. "You're too old, and you've been here too long."

He smiled begrudgingly. "Tim pretty much said, hey, want a job? And then he started paying me cash at the end of every week."

"Bro, that's such a boomer thing to say."

"I am a boomer," Wade said dryly.

"You're my favorite boomer, Wade."

The sound of Poppy's voice had me snapping up straight. It was a good thing I wasn't in the middle of drinking my beer because I had the distinct feeling I would've choked on it.

Wade smiled easily. "Don't tell your mom that."

Poppy laughed, her eyes catching mine as she entered our little circle. "Hope it's okay I'm interrupting the first-day tradition."

Rob made room for her on the tailgate, but she waved that off with a grateful smile, one hand on her bump.

My awareness of Poppy felt like an electrical current. The moment she appeared, a low-lying hum of energy filled the space, tugging at the hair on the back of my neck.

Almost instinctively, my gaze traced over her face—the lush curve of her lips and the arch of her cheekbones, the dark brows over her dark eyes, the white of her teeth when she smiled at Wade.

God, it was like she brought the fucking sun with her. This sense of warmth and kindness soaked the space around her, and I wasn't even sure she knew how powerful that was.

Years earlier, this would've sent me into a tailspin, and triggered that irrepressible urge to run and hide from it, but even though she wasn't mine to want, I let myself settle into the way it felt.

To know and admit it because, eventually, it would fade.

Eventually, it would pass.

It had to, right?

Her hair was pulled off her face today, a high ponytail that highlighted the length of her neck, and even though the simple cotton dress she wore covered her shoulders and down to her knees, it left a deep V of her chest open. My stomach tightened at the sight of her cleavage. It was noticeably bigger, pressing against the line of the dress.

Don't think about Poppy's tits, I thought viciously. Like she could read the train of my thoughts, she gave me a curious glance, and I met it evenly, wondering what color her cheeks would turn if she had any fucking idea where my brain was dragging me.

I wasn't a caveman. I did have control of myself.

Except with her, apparently.

And now I knew what they looked like and tasted like and the sounds she made when I used my mouth on them, which made it all so much worse.

I swear, I was going to burn in hell for the type of person I was when I was around her.

Next to me, Ian cleared his throat pointedly.

I blinked, shifting my gaze down to the ground.

"You doing okay, Pops?" Ian asked, eyeing his sister carefully.

"Of course," she said simply. "It's a beautiful day, isn't it? Why wouldn't I be okay?" The unspoken subtext was heavy in her answer, and she gave him a wordless look that had me narrowing my eyes.

Ian hummed, taking a sip of his beer.

Fuck, I wanted to ask. Those freaking Wilders could have an entire conversation without exchanging a single word. I'd seen it a million times since I became friends with Cameron.

I'd seen them exchange entire sentences without a sound uttered. Encouragement. Understanding. Death threats.

Siblings were weird.

She cleared her throat when she realized everyone in the circle was watching their interaction. "I was just driving by and thought I'd stop and meet Trevor. I think you have some paperwork for me. Saves you a drive over to my office."

"Who's Trevor?" Wade asked.

Dipshit raised his hand. "I am."

"I like Dipshit better."

Poppy rolled her eyes. "You guys are the worst. Whose idea was it to call him that?" Everyone looked at me, and I pushed my tongue into the side of my cheek. "Oh," she said, fighting a smile.

Dipshit looked at Poppy with a slight tilt to his head. "Blue. Very blue. You have incredibly calming energy."

"I'm sorry?" she asked, brows furrowing slightly.

"Don't ask," I told her.

Trevor grinned, walking over to the front seat of Rob's truck to get the papers Poppy asked for. Handing her the papers, he was pleasant and kind, and had her laughing in only a few seconds.

As much as I didn't want to, I had to give the kid credit because he was completely unfazed by my sniping, which is probably why our first day of training wasn't complete hell on earth. He was eager to learn and clearly wanted to work hard. He reminded me of a puppy. Bouncy energy, nothing seemed to bother him.

My chest clenched, thinking of Henry. How patiently he'd taught me everything.

As he walked back to the truck to hop up next to his friend, I gave him a slight nod. "You did good today."

His features morphed into a pleased smile, his chest puffing out slightly. "Thanks, Jax."

Poppy watched us curiously, then tilted her head toward

the front of the house where she must have parked. "Do you mind walking me to my car?"

I'd walk with you wherever the fuck you wanted to go, I thought with a desperation that took me by surprise. But I simply nodded. Ignoring the looks from every guy around us, I followed Poppy with my hands tucked safely behind my back.

She waited with a smile as soon as we were out of view of the group. "I probably could have messaged you, but I really did need to get the papers from Trevor."

"No, his new name is Dipshit. If we call him Trevor, he'll feel like he won, and we can't have that for at least a year into his employment. The power will go to his head."

The sound of Poppy's laugh was like fucking bells or wind chimes or something light and pleasant and magical. Irrationally, I wanted to slam something over my ears to block it out because hearing it made me want to tear something down with my bare hands. It was that electricity again, a writhing pulse straight from her that sent a jolt of energy through my whole body.

She was a force, and she had no idea.

Had it always been like this? Had I just so effectively blocked myself off from it that it didn't even register? Suddenly, I wished for the ability to travel back in time. One year or two or three, to watch Poppy and myself from a distance. The times where she was clearly watching me and I ignored it, leaving the room or pretending I didn't feel her eyes on me.

Even then, I felt it, but it was muted. Blocked behind the forbidden nature of who she was, the impossibility of anything happening between us.

It wasn't muted now.

On her front porch.

In my truck.

At her mom's.

Every little snippet of time we spent together felt vivid and rich and deep, in a way that I couldn't even make sense of except for how powerful it was.

Friends.

Friends.

Friends.

I reminded myself.

She reached into her purse—a giant bag with hidden depths—and pulled out a manila folder, handing it to me with an expectant smile on her face. "I made a list of things we should really start discussing."

"How did that fit in there?" I asked, eyeing her bag.

"Oh, I can run the world with what I have in this purse."

"Uh-huh." Exhaling quietly, I flipped open the folder, my eyebrows climbing sky high. The list was long. "Holy shit, Poppy. How long did this take you?"

She tilted her head. "About an hour."

"All of this was just … ready to go in your head?"

"Yes?"

There was a blue section and a green section, orange and red, with timelines for each and an inexplicable pros and cons list on the side discussing different parenting styles.

"Wh-what do all the colors mean?"

"Oh, umm, that's priority level. Blue is lowest level of priority, then green, then orange. Red is highest level of importance. You know, sort of angry and pressing and needs to get taken care of soon."

"Like my fucking aura," I muttered.

"What's that?"

"Nothing."

"What's unschooling?" I asked, my head spinning a thousand miles a minute. Was I supposed to be thinking about all these things? God, I was so behind already.

Why didn't I read that fucking book from Sheila when I got home from dinner last night? I should have.

The section on discipline styles made me slightly nauseous.

"Oh, I was just throwing that in for comparison, I don't think it's right for me." She tapped the other side of the paper. "On this side here you can see that we don't need to worry about that for a couple of years, but it still warrants discussion. I assumed you wouldn't feel strongly about homeschooling, but your opinion is still just as important as mine, you know?"

I wasn't sure my opinions were worth shit in this situation because I didn't know what the hell any of this meant.

Slowly, I closed the manila folder and leaned against the side of her car, staring at her with a growing sense of awe. "How are you so calm all the time? I feel like I'm ... like I might have a heart attack reading all that."

Poppy closed her eyes with a soft smile, then turned and leaned against the car, her shoulder almost brushing my arm. A single inch, and it would be.

What would she do if I leaned in?

No. I couldn't. I wouldn't.

There was no world where I could let myself touch her again unless it was a freaking emergency because I was already struggling with a wobbling sense of discipline. I almost punched her fucking boyfriend in the balls when he purposely tripped me during our game to keep me from catching a pass. The yard full of witnesses was all that held me back.

The feel of her skin on mine was absolutely off-limits, even accidentally, so I kept still and made sure not to move a single inch.

"I wasn't calm at first," she admitted, staring straight ahead. "Not even a little."

Turning my head, I studied the lines of her profile. "How did you find out?"

She blew out a slow breath. "It was Parker, actually. He was home visiting after their playoff loss, and it was pretty rough for him. I thought I was sick. I'd never been that tired in my whole life. And he said something to me like, you're not pregnant, are you?"

My eyes fell shut, imagining how scared she must have been.

"And you knew," I said.

"I was pretty sure, yeah." She ran the tips of her fingers over the front of her stomach, the sweet smile on her face almost too much for me to bear. My chest felt cracked wide open, the messy feelings for her mixing with the strangest sense of awe that I'd have a child with someone like her. Someone good and kind and amazing.

The thought of a little girl just like Poppy sent a bolt of longing and fear so potent that I almost fell to my knees. With her smile and her hair and her eyes.

I'd be a fucking goner. I'd give her anything she wanted. Turn my world inside out just to make sure she was happy.

Sort of how I felt about her mom.

"Parker got me a million pregnancy tests," she continued. "And when I saw the positive test, I cried. A lot."

I dropped my chin to my chest and breathed through that image. My hands curled into helpless fists, the urge to reach for her so strong I could hardly think of anything else.

"The list has been slowly building in my head for the past couple of months," she admitted. "I knew you'd be home eventually, and we'd have to talk about things like … money. Health insurance. Custody," she added delicately. Her eyes darted to mine and held. "Do you want split custody? I don't even know how you feel about wanting to be a hands-on dad."

Anxiety sat like a block of ice on my chest, worries compounding bigger and bigger and bigger until I could hardly breathe through it.

I thought about my two-bedroom house with no personality. Thought about trying to have a kid there every other weekend and split holidays. Is that how it would work?

What did I feel about being hands-on? Could I handle a baby on my own?

I'd never changed a diaper in my entire life. Never rocked

a kid to sleep. Never handled them during a tantrum. Never tried to calm them when they had a nightmare or cried because they dropped their ice cream on the floor.

Pushing off the car, I paced around it for a few seconds, trying to let that initial prickling, cold wave pass. She watched patiently because, of course, she'd had her days and weeks to cry. I was the one who was behind.

Always, always behind on figuring this shit out.

What had my mom done when I cried? When I spilled ice cream on the floor or had a tantrum?

My mind was blank. Nothing. I couldn't dredge up a single memory of any of those things.

All I could think of was her handing me a strip of condoms when I was sixteen. "Keep those in your wallet. Believe me, you'll want to wrap it up or you'll end up with a whole lot of regrets, kid. Trust me."

I pinched my eyes shut. A different memory pressed through, insistent and unwilling not to be remembered. Sitting on Henry's back deck, eating a bowl of ice cream after we painted his front porch. "Tastes better after some hard work, doesn't it?" he said. And it had. It was the best ice cream I'd ever had in my life.

I had good memories. I had examples that I could pull from, and it was important to remember that.

Prying my eyes open, I turned and faced Poppy.

"I don't know," I answered honestly. "I don't know how… how to do anything for a kid, Poppy. Never thought about wanting one. Never imagined having one."

"That's okay," she said earnestly. "We have time, Jax. None of this needs to be decided now." Her smile was wry. "I know my lists don't always help—"

"Your lists are fine." I interrupted, stepping forward and keeping my eyes locked on hers. "I thought about them while I was gone, actually."

Her eyes lit up. "You did?"

"How they help you make sense of your thoughts."

Of feelings that didn't make sense. Helped carve a path through something big and scary that seemed far too daunting to face.

"You should see the notebook on my desk," she admitted, a sheepish grin lifting her cheeks. "It's slightly neurotic."

"What's in it? Tell me one of your lists."

The fact that I asked had her staring up at me with a shocked sort of awe. "I ... you really want to know?"

"I do," I admitted in a low voice. I wanted to know everything.

Poppy licked at her bottom lip, looking down at the ground for a moment as she seemed to come to a decision. "Well, I made a list about you once," she said quietly. "And it ended with me on your front porch in the rain."

God, I wanted to kiss her.

I wanted to slide my hands into her hair and slant my lips over hers, absorb the sounds she'd make, soak in the taste of her lips and the feel of her tongue. It would be good.

It would be amazing.

And it would destroy her, if I pulled her into some dark, selfish space with me.

"Hopefully that's a list you don't regret," I said.

Her smile did something to my insides. Something permanent and unmoving.

"I already told you I could never regret you," Poppy answered.

"And you still mean it?"

She gave me a small nod.

Maybe there was a past life I'd lived before this one. Perhaps I'd done something really fucking incredible to deserve this woman's trust, to deserve her unwavering admiration because it sure as hell wasn't anything I'd done in this life.

To deserve her.

Not that I did yet. Not that I even had the chance.

I looked down at the folder and sighed. "Can I keep this? Think it over?"

"Of course." Poppy took a step forward. "I know it's a lot to decide, and our decisions might change as time passes, but…" She smiled, her hand pressing to the side of her belly and her eyes lighting up. "*Oh*, they're doing backflips in there."

Don't touch.

Don't touch.

Touch.

Touch her.

"Yeah?" I asked, throat closing up. I wanted to fall to my fucking knees and press my forehead to that impossible little bump holding that impossible little person. But I couldn't.

I'd wreck everything.

She reached for my hand, and I pulled away before she could grab my wrist. The self-preservation was so strong, my muscles reacted before I could hardly take a breath to think about the ramifications.

Poppy's face showed a momentary shock, but she recovered well. "I shouldn't have assumed…"

My jaw was clenched so tight, it was hard to breathe. "It's fine, I just—I…"

How was I supposed to tell her any of this in a way that made sense?

I could hardly make sense of what I was thinking and how to walk through this, keeping our tentative, delicate friendship intact.

The one thing she told me she needed was that.

"Well, I have a feeling whenever you are ready … they'll only get more active. It's still new to feel it this hard." Poppy pressed her hand on her belly again, lips curling in a secret little smile. "Maybe you wouldn't have even felt it yet. The other day, I tried with my mom, but she couldn't feel anything."

I managed a short nod, cursing the spiderweb of emotions tangling up my chest.

"It's the size of a pear," she said.

"What?"

She held her hands out, cupping her palms together to create a reference point. "About five inches long. The baby is the size of a pear. Isn't that crazy?"

Staring down at Poppy's hands, I felt my heart turn over slowly. So small. Too small.

Where would they sleep?

What would they look like?

How was I supposed to help with something that tiny and breakable and important? I didn't know anything.

Do something.

Go and do something.

God, I hope they looked like her.

Poppy's phone rang, and she glanced at the screen. "Shoot, it's my mom. I told her I'd pick up some dinner while I was downtown." Her smile was sweet and a little mischievous. "It's really just because I was craving a burger from the pub."

"Cheeseburger with mayo, ketchup, and lettuce?" I said.

Fuck. Ing. Hell.

Her lips fell open on a gentle O, snapping shut in the next instant, and I cursed my fucking mouth. "Yeah," she said slowly. "Am I that predictable?"

Admissions stuck fast at the back of my tongue, and I pushed them back down where they belonged. "You better go get your food," I told her gently. "I have some work to do tonight."

Eyes curious, Poppy nodded. She paused by the car door, mouth open to say something, when Rob and Dipshit came around to the front of the house, laughing loudly. Ian was a few steps behind. She closed her eyes on a quiet laugh. "Never mind."

"It'll keep," I told her.

Poppy's gaze was so direct. How had I ever hidden from this woman?

"Can we talk soon?" she asked. "Maybe … maybe more than a random run-in or a family dinner where fifty people watch our every move."

"So I'm not the only person who felt like that?" I asked.

She laughed. "No."

"That sounds good," I told her, nerves cycling lightly through my stomach. It sounded intentional, something we'd never quite mastered, had we?

I held the door open for her while she settled in the driver's seat, carefully closing the door as she adjusted her safety belt over her bump.

Stepping back, I felt Ian approach while Poppy drove away.

"What was that about?" he asked.

I held up the manila folder. "I have five years' worth of decisions to make."

He laughed under his breath. "Sounds about right."

Her car disappeared, leaving with me the strangest sense that I'd be watching that happen a lot. Hadn't I earned that, though? Poppy had years of watching me live my life, and now I was watching her live hers.

Do something.

Go. Go now.

In the wake of her departure, the energy she brought didn't dissipate; it simply changed. The unused current was shifting into a twitchy sort of restlessness under my skin. I would've packed my bags in the past when I felt like this. But now, I had to plant my feet and figure out a different way to release it.

I thought about lists and pears and backflips that I

couldn't feel. Tiny little hands and feet. Wide smiles and pretty eyes and undeserved trust and trying to be what she needed.

Not what I wanted. Something even more important than that.

"Ian, do you have a few minutes? I need your help with something."

Chapter 22
Poppy

"If you were a murderer, do you think you'd break into a woodshop before you broke into the nearest house?"

Parker sighed so loudly, with such annoyance, that I rolled my eyes, even as I poked my head out from behind a tree to stare at the lights coming from the shop behind the house. The *supposed to be empty and locked and dark* woodshop.

"What are you talking about?" he asked. There was loud thumping in the background like he was at a club.

"There's someone back here in the shop," I hissed.

"What?" he yelled. "I can't hear you."

Cupping my hand over my mouth, I spoke louder, eyes locked on the way the flashlight bounced around inside the window. "Someone is in the shop. I saw a light coming from the windows right before I was going to go to bed, and maybe it's just Wade or something, but then why wouldn't he tell me he's stopping by? He always tells me when he's stopping by, and no one comes out here at night."

The noises faded in the background, and I heard the closing of a door. "Pops, if you're worried about a break-in, call Cameron or Ian and make them come check it out."

"Cameron and Ivy are out on a date in Redmond. Mom, Ian, and Harlow are at Sage's flag football game."

"Then call your boyfriend. Or better yet, call the cops."

I winced. Right. Law enforcement hadn't crossed my mind. Downfall of a big family, I guess. "Dean is … unavailable for those types of calls."

"Why? Off delivering horse babies or something?"

"Foals," I corrected. "They're not called horse babies. And I have no idea if he is or isn't."

"Oh." Parker cleared his throat. "And has Dr. No Sex been sidelined due to a certain someone's reappearance?"

"Dean was sidelined because I freaking knew better than to keep dating someone when my life was a giant mess of crazy." I stared at the moving light with narrowed eyes. "Do we have to recap this now? What if I'm about to get murdered?"

"You realize I live in Portland, right? I'm not going to be much help," he drawled. My eyes narrowed because the drawl sounded a little slurred. Parker never drank.

I was about to ask, but the flashlight moved again, swinging past one of the windows, and I ducked back behind the tree. Why was it so dark outside? Why had I decided to read one of Harlow's thrillers instead of watching a nice, happy, fluffy romance like a normal hormonal pregnant woman who wasn't getting any sex?

Let's not dive into the psychology behind that decision—where a creepy fricken stalker story felt safer than watching someone else getting laid. But of course, the downfall was that now I felt like someone was breathing down my neck, icy nerves prickled along my skin, and sure, I had the Taser from my purse, but that shit still had to be used in *very* close proximity.

Not my first choice, if a serial killer was finding a giant piece of wood to clock me over the head.

"I *know* where you live," I said. "I just wanted someone on the phone in case I get attacked."

"Or maybe you don't go out to the shop and call someone

from the safety of the locked house," he said so obnoxiously that I had a vivid fantasy of punching him in the throat if he were in front of me. "Call Jax. He'll come check it out. Isn't that part of his baby daddy job now?"

"No," I hissed. "He doesn't have any … baby daddy jobs."

"Well, it looks like you need a keeper, so maybe he should." The door opened, and music flooded the background again. "Go inside. Call someone local, and text me when the murderer has been apprehended."

"You are *no* help."

"That's what brothers are for," he said in an annoyingly level voice.

The call disconnected with a click, and I growled under my breath. Thumb tapping the side of my phone, I considered my options. If I called the cops and it was nothing, everyone in town would know.

Through the eerie darkness of the trees, there was a crack of a branch, and I sucked in a sharp breath when, from the tree directly above me, a previously invisible owl let out a low, bone-chilling hoot. Emitting a high-pitched shriek, I whirled, black Taser facing forward.

My breath was coming in embarrassing pants, but nothing was in front of me. I let out a shaky exhale and winced when the baby kicked down toward my bladder.

"Lord, I can see it now," I whispered. "Pregnant woman— too friggin curious for her own good—accidentally tases rare owl and then pees her pants."

Fumbling my phone, I decided to take Parker's advice and call Jax. Eyes locked on the windows so I didn't miss anything, I watched the flashlight pivot to the side, and his deep voice filled the line.

"Poppy? What's up?"

"I'm not sure," I said slowly. The nerves made my voice tremble a little and I winced.

"Are you okay?" he asked sharply.

"Umm, I think so. Do you have a minute?"

There was nothing but deathly silence on the other end of the line for a few seconds. All I could hear was my pulse roaring in my ears and a slight exhale from Jax. "Yeah, of course."

"You're not … out, are you?" The following hesitation had me wincing. It was a Friday night.

"Sort of," he hedged.

The image of him at a bar, or even worse, walking *out* of a bar *with* someone, sort of made me want to curl up in a ball and hide. But hey! At least I wasn't thinking about a murderer standing two feet behind me because that image made me want to shoot fire at some invisible woman who may or may not exist.

Pregnancy hormones were so, so fun.

"Never mind," I said miserably.

But no. There was no never mind-ing happening. "What do you need, Poppy?"

The flashlight was stationary now, and I backed up a couple of steps now that I had an actual helpful person on the phone. "Well, it's probably nothing, but Parker yelled at me when I was going to check it out myself because everyone is gone right now, but I think maybe someone's breaking into the woodshop," I said in a tumble of rushed words.

It was a strange time for Jax to practice breathing exercises, but that was what it sounded like. The house seemed like it was a mile away when I glanced over my shoulder, and sure, if I ran for it, I could probably get there quickly, but I hadn't run voluntarily in ages.

"Poppy," he said slowly.

The flashlight clicked off, and my breath snagged ice cold in my lungs.

"Oh shit," I whispered. I whirled again, foot poised to

break the land speed record for a pregnant person. The sound of the shop door opening had my heart seizing, and I rushed forward, far, far too fast, definitely far too loudly, just as he spoke again.

"Poppy, calm down. It's me."

My head snapped around. "What?"

I could hear his voice behind me. And in my ear. And Jax in surround sound was just too much for my poor, overwhelmed body to handle. "I was in the shop looking for something."

That was when I tripped, my foot snagging on a root, and I pitched forward hard, knee slamming into the hard ground first, followed swiftly by the heel of my hand as it broke my fall when I threw my arm out in front of me.

"Dammit," he bit out, "you were out here?"

I rolled to my backside, cradling my wrist against my chest, my heart jolting unevenly when he jogged over to my side. "Owww," I moaned.

Jax crouched by my side. I could hardly make out his features in the dark, but his smell—clean and crisp and woodsy—had my eyes fluttering shut briefly. "Where did you fall? Did you hit your stomach?"

I shook my head. "My knee and…" A razor-sharp pain sliced through my wrist, then I tried to move it, and I hissed, "Oh, my hand. It's my wrist, I think."

Jax stood, sliding his big hands underneath my armpits. "Okay, we're going to stand slowly. You feel any pain in your leg or knee when you put weight on it, and I'll carry you."

I swallowed. Hard. The immediate vision of him striding through the dark woods with me in his arms was a little too historical romance-come-to-life for my current state, and I said a silent prayer that my leg and knee would be just fine.

Thankfully, I was able to stand, only the slightest ache in my knee. He kept a hand hovering just behind my back, no longer touching me once I stood, and he clicked the flashlight onto his phone again, aiming down at the ground. The bright white light bouncing off the dirt threw his sharp features into view.

His face was close to mine, and I couldn't really tear my eyes away from the concerned wrinkle in his brow. "I'm okay," I whispered.

Jax's jaw clenched, a shadow appearing in the hollow of his cheek from the reflection of the light. He hadn't shaved yet.

I really liked that he hadn't shaved yet.

"What are you doing out here?"

I let out a groan. "Being that person I hate when I watch movies or read books. You know, the too stupid to live one who's like, oh! I'll be fine. I'll just check it out myself with my trusty Taser." I glanced down at the ground. "Oh shit, I dropped my Taser."

Jax's answering sigh was so full of long-suffering that I almost cracked a smile. He cast the light from his phone in the direction of where I fell, then leaned over to snag the device in question. One dark eyebrow arched high when he handed it back to me. "Try not to hit an innocent bystander with this one, all right?"

"I almost got an owl," I told him as we walked shoulder to shoulder back toward the house.

"Sure you did."

"I'm not sure I like how doubtful you sound. Did you see how quick my reflexes were? I turned and fell the exact moment you opened that door. It's impressive, actually."

"Yeah, I'm sure I'll think about that stunning athletic display all night."

Another tree branch appeared in our path, and Jax cupped my elbow in his hand to steady me as we stepped over it, disappearing just as quickly. His fingers were so long. Wasn't that such a strange thing to think about? People could be similar heights. Similar weights. And one man could have short, stubby fingers. Another man could have long, almost graceful fingers.

Dexterous fingers.

Strong and calloused. Capable of … a lot.

Was I breathing hard again?

I rolled my lips between my teeth and yanked the reins on wherever that train of thought was going to go.

We cleared the branch, sidestepping toward a clearer path back to the house, and Jax's fingers disappeared from my skin, the heat lingering after he'd dropped his hand back to his side. The walk from the shop wasn't long, and we ascended the porch quietly, him walking just behind me as I opened the door to the house.

Jax paused in the doorway and looked at the scene I'd left behind—quiet music playing on the speaker in the corner, a fire crackling in the stone fireplace that dominated the center of the wide open space between the kitchen and the family room. My book was tossed on top of a big fuzzy blanket.

"One of Harlow's?" he asked.

I nodded slightly. "That's probably what got my imagination going a bit too well when I saw the flashlight. Of course I chose her freakiest book." I ran my good hand through my hair because God knows what it looked like. My pajama pants hung beneath my bump, and a plain light pink sleep tank—too small for how far along I was—was practically shrink-wrapped to my chest and stomach. At least I was wearing a bra. A flimsy one, but it was something.

"First-aid kit?" he asked.

"Umm, the bottom drawer to the right of the sink." I tried to rotate my wrist and winced. Maybe not.

He cut me a sideways glance when a hiss of pain left my lips. "Leave it steady. You should go in and get it checked tomorrow."

"I don't think it's broken," I told him.

"I must have missed the time you gained X-ray capabilities with your eyes."

"Perk of pregnancy." I tilted my head. "And aren't you a giant hypocrite? Remember when you slashed your arm open on a jobsite, rinsed it off with water and told Wade to put some duct tape on it when it clearly needed stitches."

Jax pushed a few things aside in the cabinet, eyes locking briefly on mine. "And look at how well that turned out. Arm didn't fall off or anything."

"That's your barometer of success?" I snorted. "It's an actual miracle that you're still alive."

"No argument there," he muttered. Arms flexing underneath the kitchen lights, I watched through lowered lashes as I tried to pinpoint why this felt different.

No safety net. That was a big one. But there wasn't one the day before either when I gave him The List.

God, was I a secret control freak? Maybe it was the times I didn't expect him, and didn't have time to prep what I was going to say or do that we had moments like this. We'd never be like Cameron and Ivy with sharp, witty banter because it would make my brain hurt to keep that up all the time, and we weren't Harlow and Ian with an entire lifetime of shared memories. We were somewhere in the middle.

Always hovering between labels.

For years, we were nothing.

Now … now we were something.

In the daylight, when we were surrounded by people— friends or family or coworkers, it didn't seem to matter—it was so much easier to keep this compartmentalized. Keep him compartmentalized.

In his neat, tidy little box where my sanity demanded he stay.

Jax pulled the big plastic kit from the drawer and motioned me toward the sink. "Come here."

The quietly spoken command was an awful lot like he yanked on an invisible string tied around my spine. My steps were quiet as I joined him by the counter and presented my hand. The skin along the meat of my palm was scraped, red, and angry but not actively bleeding.

Jax motioned for me to come closer with his chin, and I did, angling my hand over the sink while he flipped open the bottle of hydrogen peroxide. The cold liquid on my skin had me sucking in a breath, and it bubbled immediately, washing out all the dirt and grime.

I bit down on my bottom lip when he added more. My shoulder brushed against the warm wall of his chest as he bent his head over my hand. He didn't touch me. Hadn't touched me since we came back into the house, and it felt intentional, with his hand hovering just beneath mine, like he'd step in if necessary.

Instead of staring at the hard line of his jaw or the gentle way he cleaned my hand, I kept my gaze on my injured palm.

Jax set the bottle down and snagged a clean piece of paper towel, gently dabbing at the leftover white bubbles on my scrape until it was dry. For a moment, he paused, staring down at my hand like he was trying to make a decision. His chest expanded on a deep breath, and he slid his fingers underneath the back of my hand.

The tips of his fingers were rough with callouses, a detail I'd chained up somewhere in the back of my mind. Goose bumps prickled along my forearms, and I prayed he didn't notice. Jax brought my hand up to his mouth, blowing softly on my skin, and my skin went warm, my stomach weightless.

Even when he stopped, Jax didn't drop my hand, and I could hear my pulse roaring in my ears. Slowly, he lowered it again, removing his hand from underneath mine.

My fingers tingled after he did.

"Sit," he said quietly.

With a hammering heart, I listened.

Jax pulled another chair so that he was facing mine, sliding closer after he set down a bandage and the nude-colored athletic wrap. The air was thick and tense when he moved my arm, settling it onto the table so that he could maneuver it easily. Adding a small dob of antibiotic gel to the bandage, he smoothed it over my skin with deft movements, and if I hadn't been studying his face so closely, I might have missed it.

The tightness in his jaw, and the slight catch in his breath when my fingers curled inward, brushing the rough skin on his knuckles when he lingered for just a second past what was necessary.

The first couple of passes with the wrap had me filling my lungs and holding my breath, eyes closing at the dull, throbbing pain radiating up my arm.

"Sorry," he murmured.

"It's okay." The more he tightened the fabric, the less it hurt. But still, he gentled the way he pulled. Those long, graceful fingers angled my hand as he worked, just whispers of pressure like I was made of glass.

"Wh-why were you out there?" I asked, cursing the slight hiccup in my voice at the tenderness he was showing.

Jax didn't answer right away and simply made a few more rotations with the tape. "Needed to borrow something from Ian for a project." His eyes locked on mine for a moment. "Should've told you I was coming. Didn't mean to scare you."

"Oh, I wasn't scared," I said airily. "I had the Taser, after all."

The firm line of his mouth gentled, but it wasn't quite a smile.

Jax tugged my hand up toward his mouth again, using the edge of his teeth to snap the end of the tape. My belly swirled dangerously as he licked his lips. Thank God he wasn't watching me, because I slammed my eyes shut, needing to snap that visual.

If my sanity needed Jax in a locked box, then that box was

blown the hell open. My ribs rattled on each deep pulled breath, and I conjured every ounce of restraint in my possession.

I could do this without a safety net, agenda, or clear, precise plan.

I could do it because it was necessary—not just for me but also for the baby and for Jax too.

"I need to say something," I started, "and I just need you to listen because I don't want to make things weird."

Because he was looking down, replacing the roll of tape in the kit, his cheeks lifted on a smile that I couldn't see, his hands still moving the wrap around my wrist. "Go ahead."

"I know I threw a lot at you yesterday, and I think I have a tendency to hyperfocus on the things I can control when everything else feels … too big, I guess."

"Did stuff feel too big for you yesterday?"

"A little," I admitted. I kept my eyes on his face and willed him to look up at me. I needed him to understand this, and said a little prayer that I'd be able to explain this in the right way. "I broke up with Dean after the family dinner the other night."

Jax froze, his hands on the first-aid kit and every inch of his big, muscular body bowstring tight. "Why?"

I wasn't sure what made me tell him. I hadn't even really made the decision beforehand. There was no requirement to clear my personal relationships past Jax.

The rough edge to his voice had my hands trembling slightly where they now sat in my lap. "It wasn't because of you," I assured him quickly. "And I know the timing of it seems like it was, but…" I floundered when he continued to sit eerily still in front of me, "I broke up with him for the same reason I said no to you when you proposed."

Finally, finally, Jax lifted his head, the dark intensity of his eyes making me sit back in my chair. "What's that?"

"He was a very, very well-timed distraction. It was wrong

of me not to face that earlier, and I hate that it took me four months to do it. Dean is still a good person, and he will make someone very happy, but he's not what I need right now either."

The line of Jax's throat worked on a swallow. "What do you need?"

Three days to sleep.

Seven pounds of Sour Patch Kids.

And the kind of sex I hadn't had since the man sitting one foot away from me shared his bed.

My exhale was shaky as I pushed those immediate, illogical wants behind a wall of more rational thoughts.

This wasn't about what I wanted. It was about what I needed.

Through the thick, crackling tension clouding the room, I somehow managed to breathe. "I need the same thing as before. For us to be friends. Might even need it more now than I did when I said it."

Why did the look in his eyes make me want to burst into tears?

"Is that why Ian asked if you were okay yesterday?"

Slowly, I nodded.

He let out a small noise of understanding—half hum, half groan—pinching his eyes shut and pushing away from the table. While he put the first-aid kit away, I could practically see the resolve on his face.

"And are you?"

I blinked. "What?"

"Are you okay?" He shifted, taking a deep breath. "Or do you need to, like, talk about your feelings or whatever."

"You want to talk about my feelings?" I asked, doubt coloring my tone.

"Or whatever," he bit out.

I bit down on my bottom lip to hide my smile, but it was too late. Jax made a small scoffing noise when I couldn't contain it, and he crossed his arms tight across his wide chest. "It felt like something a friend might ask."

Tilting my head, I stared at the tense way he held his body, the darting eye contact that couldn't rest on mine for more than a few seconds. A nervous Jax Cartwright was my crack, and that was a dangerous realization. "And if I said I wanted to sit and watch a sad movie and cry because it would make me feel better? Would you do that?"

His jaw tightened, grim resignation filling his face. "If that's what you needed, sure."

"*Titanic* is my go-to cry movie."

"Shit," he muttered, swiping a hand over his mouth. "I'm out. Call one of your sisters. That's fucking torture."

Laughing, I sat back in my chair.

His entire frame relaxed, and he gave a slight eye roll. "You're evil, woman."

"A for effort," I told him seriously. "But I promise, I'm fine. I think single is a good look for me at this point in my life." Slowly, I stood from the chair, hand on my stomach. "We've got enough going on right now, don't we, nugget?"

The smile faded off my face when I looked back up to find Jax staring at me intently.

"That's a good look for you too," he said quietly.

"What?"

"Pregnancy." He swallowed, the tops of his cheekbones flushing a slight pink. "It looks fucking incredible on you."

My heart raced, and I tried to ignore it. "That something a friend would say too?"

Jax merely held my gaze for a long moment, then the side of his mouth hooked up in a slight grin. "Yeah, it is."

"Thank you."

He nodded, pausing after he opened the front door. "Can you do me a favor the next time you think someone's breaking in?"

I grinned. "What's that?"

His eyes traced over my face. "Call me before you leave the house, all right?"

Slowly, I nodded, pulse racing as he disappeared through the door. Thank God the chair was directly underneath me, because I immediately sat back down.

"Right then," I whispered. "I can totally do this."

Chapter 23
Jax

Margot: You've been awfully quiet.

Me: Always am, Margot. How's Robby?

Margot: Misses you terribly. Did you get my email with the pictures?

Me: Haven't checked my email since I got home. I'll do it later, I promise.

Margot: It's a Saturday, what else have you got to do?

Me: You wouldn't believe me if I told you.

Margot: Try me.

With a sigh, I leaned against the bench along the back wall of my small pole barn. The work bench in front of me was covered in spindles and stain samples. Set along the side was the large bottom piece, the edges sanded down to a rounded lip. Tacked up on the wall behind it was the simple sketch I'd started with, Ian's scrawled notes in the margin almost completely illegible.

> Me: Working on a project for a friend.

> Margot: Suitably cryptic. You give the girl the letter yet? Living out your happily ever after?

> Me: Were you always this nosy?

> Margot: Yes. You were just too tired to notice. Come on, give an old lady something to be excited about. I might die tomorrow and then you'll feel like shit.

I pinched the bridge of my nose, that hollow ache behind my sternum blossoming into something big and uncomfortable. I'd gotten used to it since I'd arrived home, almost able to ignore its presence, but it was screaming at me now.

> Me: It's complicated.

> Margot: How?

> Me: Came home. Found out she was pregnant. It's mine. She had a boyfriend while I was gone, she just broke up with him and the one thing she needs from me is friendship. So.

> Margot: My goodness. You're joking, right?

> Me: I am not. Got any parenting book recommendations because I finished the only one I have right now. Stayed up until 2am reading last night.

> Margot: Did it make you feel better?

> Me: Not even close. I feel like I'm going to throw up all the time.

> Margot: Should I call you and be a kindly voice of reason right now?

Me: Please don't. If you're mean to me right now, I might cry.

Margot: When have I ever been mean a day in my life?

Me: Weren't you the one who told me to quit my 'whinging' and pull my head out of my ass when I wanted to take a break on the second to last day?

Margot: Yes well, that was necessary. I find men respond much better to firm instruction.

Me: I'm not touching that statement.

Margot: I can send you some book ideas. Our neighbour just had a baby and she read everything. But Jax, it's really quite simple. You feed it when it's hungry, rock it when it cries, keep the nappy dry, and don't drop it on its head. Even you can manage that.

Me: Your confidence in me is inspiring, thank you.

Margot: What are you going to do about the girl?

Me: Nothing. I won't fuck this up by pushing her if it's not want she wants.

Me: And don't come at me with your kindly voice of reason right now about why I should take a chance. Respecting what she wants is the best way for me to handle this. The safest.

Margot: Safest for who?

Me: Margot.

Margot: All right, I'm done. I promise. Will you call me if you want to talk?

Me: Yeah.

Margot: No, you won't, but I appreciate you saying so.

Margot: Robby and I would make excellent British grandparents, you know. Maybe we can come visit you someday, and you can show us your mountains over there.

After telling her I'd love that, I set my phone down and stared across the barn, the sound of birds filtering through all the noise in my head.

The safest for who?

A question I didn't really want to answer.

You, a voice whispered in the back of my head. It's safest for you.

Ignoring that, I stood back up and finished staining the finished spindles. Walking back to the house about an hour later, I pulled up my email and smiled as I scrolled through the pictures from Margot and Robby.

I hadn't even been home for two weeks, and on a day like this, it felt like a fucking year. That was the best and worst thing about those kinds of experiences. The moment you remove yourself from your day-to-day life, the days stretch out longer and slower. I always felt like I could breathe differently the precise moment I got away. Think clearer. Center my thoughts.

Like Poppy and her lists.

Her thoughts and mine had always been on different trajectories. Mine were locked tight into avoidance of anything that could hurt, anything that could dig its claws into my life, any situation where I might do the hurting instead.

And hers ... I had a feeling that Poppy's thoughts, at least when it came to me, were aimed at something else. She'd made peace with them, almost like she considered her feelings for me as an extension of herself. When we were in the same room, she didn't fight for my attention, she didn't ever try to change my mind. Instead, she was keenly aware of what it was between us, and what it wasn't.

I showered, trying to keep any thoughts of her out of my mind, to limited success. God, I couldn't even think about her wrapping her injured wrist without getting half hard.

That's how bad it was.

I'd probably see athletic tape and immediately get a boner because I'd think about the bones in her wrist, the graceful length of her fingers, the impossibly soft skin and the blue veins running underneath it when I wrapped her hand.

Bracing my hands on the shower wall, I let my head hang under the scaling hot water, viciously wrenching the handle to the right when those thoughts veered past her wrist.

No.

This wasn't happening.

Because I was an adult, and adults had self-control and didn't fucking jerk off to thoughts about their friend who was carrying their baby.

When the cold water did the trick, I hopped out of the shower, toweled off, and quickly dressed. By the time I was done, there were some texts from Margot—books her friend said I should read. I glanced at the clock and decided to head into town to get some groceries and stop at the library to look for the recommendations.

I decided to take the truck since I'd have food and books. I patted my bike seat when I passed it because it was a gorgeous day—perfect for a ride.

The library parking lot was quiet when I walked under the tall wood-arched entryway, and I was thankful for it. Just what I needed was some gossipy old lady seeing me check out a stack of parenting books.

At the front counter, a friendly-looking clerk in her mid-thirties asked if I needed any help, and I shook my head, content to wander the aisles rather than tell her what I was looking for. The first row I entered was the romance books, and I grimaced when she tilted her head out to the side to watch what I was doing.

A kiosk held a computer at the end of the row, and I pulled up Margot's text, punching the computer keys with my pointer fingers until I could search for the first of the books. My mouth moved quietly when I found the location information, scanning the end caps to see where I needed to go next.

An elderly couple passed me at the end of the romance aisle, the wife's arms stacked high with options.

She smiled at me. "Gotta stock up for the weekend, don't we?"

Her husband patted her back. "Don't think he's getting the same books as you, sweetheart."

The woman winked. "You never know. These young men nowadays are more in touch with their feelings."

With her free hand, she patted my arm, and my lips edged up in an unwitting smile.

Wandering down the rows, I finally found the area I was looking for, crouching down to the bottom shelf where my finger traced along the spines. As I did, I felt someone's gaze on me, and ignored it.

Just as I was about to pull the first book out, I couldn't shake the feeling that I was being watched, so I glanced over my shoulder at the front desk. The woman working was on the phone, her eyes trained on her computer screen. The elderly couple was out of sight.

Shaking my head, I exhaled quietly, and tipped the book off the shelf, flipping through the pages. There were diagrams, and I grimaced at some of the illustrations of childbirth. My eyes snagged on the words *mucus plug*, and I carefully set the book back on the shelf, deciding maybe this one wasn't for me.

"What the fuck is a mucus plug?" I whispered.

What did it plug? Why would it fall out at some point?

I probably didn't want to know.

The hairs on the back of my neck stood, and I glanced to the side again. Scanning the big room, I saw a mom with some young kids heading into the children's area, two teenage girls sitting at a table in the middle of the room looking at a laptop, and then by the entrance near the community board, I saw her.

Her dress was bright green today, hair down around her shoulders, her eyes aimed right at me. When our gazes locked, Poppy's dimple appeared with the easy curve of her lips. My throat went dry as she started walking over, and I stood slowly, making sure all the mucus plug books were safely out of view.

She reached the end of the row and leaned her shoulder against the bookshelf. "Weekend reading?" she said, nodding her chin at the section of pregnancy books.

My cheeks felt fucking hot, and I cleared my throat. "Just browsing."

I snatched blindly in front of me and pulled something else off the shelf. When Poppy leaned forward to look at the cover, the scent of orange blossoms had my eyes falling shut.

No.

No.

No sniffing the hair of the friend carrying your baby. That was right underneath *no jacking off in the shower to thoughts of her mouth* on the list of things I definitely should not be doing.

"That's the book you were looking for?" she asked, an innocent widening of her eyes. Curious, I looked down at the cover and clenched my jaw.

The Seed: Infertility is a Feminist Issue

When Poppy bit down on her bottom lip to stem her smile, I gave her a steady look, then gently pushed the book back into its place on the shelf.

"I mean, now I'm curious," she said, tapping her finger along the spine. "Maybe I'll try that one next. Will you let me know how it is?"

In response, I cut her a dry look.

She laughed under her breath. "What are you doing here?"

"Some people come to the library to get books," I told her.

Poppy sighed. "Okay, smart-ass, don't answer me then."

We walked toward the entrance, and I kept my hands tucked behind my back. Between us, there was hardly any space, and the ends of her hair tickled along my upper arm. "What about you?"

"Some people come to the library to get books," she answered smoothly, gently nudging me with her shoulder.

I sighed heavily, and Poppy laughed. The clerk at the front desk gave her a stern look, and Poppy whispered she was sorry.

The elderly couple from the romance section appeared around one of the front displays, and she leaned into her husband, whispering something into his ear when she caught sight of me and Poppy.

"The books were for her, then?" she asked.

My eyes cut over to Poppy, who stared back with raised eyebrows. "Uh, no. I didn't … I wasn't getting any."

She must have sensed my discomfort, shifting her attention to Poppy as she stepped closer. "How far along are you, honey?"

"Just about eighteen weeks," she said. "Starting to feel some kicks."

The woman's eyes bounced between Poppy and me. "Do you have any names picked out yet?"

The awkward pulse of silence was probably only noticeable to Poppy and me. I gave her a quick look, and she smiled. "Not yet."

The husband puffed his chest out. "We waited until our kids were born. Got a look at their faces before we decided."

His wife patted his arm. "Only one of the four stumped us. Took about twenty-four hours to pick that one."

After a little bit of small talk with Poppy, they smiled and continued their browsing. Following after Poppy, I found myself watching them walk away.

"What is it?" she asked.

"It must be you."

"What?"

"No one ever stops me to chitchat."

"Didn't she talk to you earlier?" Poppy asked.

"Besides that one time, no one does that. It has to be you."

She patted my shoulder. "That's because you never smile at anyone, and you look sort of terrifying."

"Do I," I said dryly.

"Especially with the beard." Her eyes widened when I arched one eyebrow. "It works, trust me. But you are sort of intimidating."

I sighed. "That settles it. If it saves me from small talk, I'm never shaving this off."

Poppy laughed, and it occurred to me that she thought I was joking.

"What were you doing here?" I asked her. "No books for you either."

We stopped in the lobby, and she tilted her head toward the community board. "Greer told me I should look here."

The board was filled with brightly colored advertisements and hand written notices with slits cut in the bottom for tear-away phone numbers. There were ads for everything—litters of puppies. Flower bulbs. Furniture and cars for sale. "What for?"

She tapped on a piece of neon pink paper marked with big black letters. "I've been looking for a place, actually."

My eyebrows shot up. "Really?"

Poppy nodded. "My mom has a bunch of friends over this morning—a monthly brunch thing she's doing with some women she met in her grief group. And I love it for her, but it's a good reminder about why I want my own space, you know? I forgot they were coming over, so I walked downstairs today wearing only a sleep tank and no bra, and it was *awkward.*"

Don't think about it.

Do not think about it, you asshole.

The night before, she'd had on a pale pink sleep tank, her baggy pajama pants hanging underneath her bump, a sliver of skin visible when she walked. The image of a sleep-rumpled Poppy in just that tank top would haunt the ever-living fuck out of me.

Bare legs. The curve of her ass peeking out from under the hem. What kind of panties would she be wearing? All I remembered was the tight, sleek length of her body under my hands and mouth in the dark of my room and fuck if I didn't want to see her now too.

See her in the light.

Study every fucking inch.

Worship every fucking inch.

Memorize the changes, because God, my mouth was watering thinking about them.

My skin hummed, and I took a deep breath, keeping my eyes locked on that pink paper tacked to the board. It was a two bedroom home in a decent area of town, but the rent was astronomical. Her hand reached up to pluck one of the numbers off, and I smacked my hand down on the listing before she could grab one.

Her eyebrows shot up. "Do you mind?" I didn't move, and Poppy's head reared back slightly. "Jax, move your hand."

"That's a fucking rip off."

"You haven't even seen it, maybe it's really nice."

I spoke before thinking. "I have a better idea."

Her eyes narrowed. "I swear, if you tell me that I should move in with you, I will punch you in the throat."

A shocked exhale that was just short of a laugh escaped

through my mouth, but Poppy didn't so much as crack a smile. "I wasn't going to," I told her.

"Good. And don't give me some giant lecture about why I shouldn't move out because believe me, I've heard it all from my siblings, and I want my own space." Her chin jutted up defiantly. "I have enough money to afford something nice, and I just want … I just want someplace I can call my own." Her hand coasted over the front of her bump. "Now can you please move your hand?"

Slowly, I lowered my hand, keeping my eyes steady on hers. The idea took root quickly, and that ache under my sternum shifted into something else. Something good.

It wasn't impulsive, and I could do this in a way where she still felt independent. Self-sufficient. Where I knew she'd be safe and taken care of.

"I have a better idea," I repeated. "Will you come with me if I show you something?"

Poppy sucked in a sharp breath, her dark eyes flitting between mine like she couldn't figure out my angle.

The white of her teeth bit down into her plush bottom lip. "What do you want to show me?"

"I'll tell you when we get there."

Her lips curled. "Ahh, we're being mysterious again, are we?"

"Don't tell me you don't like that, angel," I said, immediately freezing at the way the nickname slipped out. Her mouth fell open, but she snapped it shut just as quickly. "Probably shouldn't call you that anymore, should I?"

I wanted to, though.

The deep, rough quality to my voice had her swallowing, pulling her gaze away from mine momentarily.

When she looked up again, her eyes were clear and her cheeks flushed. "Well … why don't you show me this better idea."

Chapter 24

Jax

"It's a house."

"Glad to see pregnancy hasn't robbed you of your observational skills."

I could sense the eye roll more than I could see it.

She let out a shaky breath, pushing the sunglasses back onto the top of her head. "Whose house is it?"

"My friend Henry used to live here."

"Used to?"

I managed a short nod.

Memories crowded my brain, the day he left the house for the last time, agitated and restless and confused why he couldn't stay.

Take care of it, kid. Just make sure someone loves it like I did, all right?

Hands tucked in my pockets, I rocked backed on my heels briefly while she continued to stare. The yard was freshly mowed, something I'd done the night before, which is why my jaunt to the Wilder shop had happened in the dark.

Since the house had been empty, I usually swung by on Friday afternoons just after work, but hadn't had the chance the night before because I was working in my own barn, only derailed when I realized I didn't have the right kind of small lathe necessary for some spindle work.

Ian was usually the master carpenter for anything to do with Wilder Homes, but no one was going to touch this for me.

Poppy rubbed an absent hand over her belly, the wheels clicking in her head so loudly that I could practically hear the gears as they chugged through the millions of questions.

"Want to see the inside?" I asked.

She swallowed, dancing her fingers over the front of her bump. "Yes." Then she cut her eyes to mine. "But I need you to tell me why first."

I held her gaze without answering.

She let out a small huff. "Now is not the time to lose your words, Jax."

Nerves had my chest tight the longer we stood there staring. Yes, it was impulsive, but it was different. I could handle this differently. Do it right.

"I think you know why."

Poppy muttered a quiet curse under her breath, lips twisting up as she drank in all the details of the home. "This doesn't feel like one of those situations where I should assume anything."

I crossed my arms over my chest and jerked my chin toward the house. "You want your own place, right? Here's an empty one."

"And you just … happened to have the key. And know it's empty."

Words balanced on the tip of my tongue, straddling an invisible line I really didn't want to cross. "I take care of it for Henry. He asked me to."

"Typical. Has a freaking house sitting in his back pocket just when I need one," she muttered under her breath. Her hands rose and fell in a helpless drop. "Look at it. It's *perfect.*"

The cheery blue siding was freshly painted within the last year, something I'd done when the fading started to get under my skin. I hated the thought that Henry's house looked old. That it reminded me of how long he'd been gone, and just how much I missed him—missed the role he filled. How thoroughly he'd changed my life when he took me under his wing.

A two-stall garage anchored the left side of the house, and if I closed my eyes, I could still see his car parked in the middle of that pristine garage, ready to be backed up so we could do our Saturday car wash. Leading off the right side of the driveway was a small sidewalk leading to the front porch— big windows on either side of the glossy red door. I painted that too. The second floor had three tall windows overlooking the front yard.

It was tucked back in the cul-de-sac, a large swath of undeveloped land behind it, filled with wildflowers and tall grasses. It got more sun than her mom's house did because there weren't as many tall trees filling the neighborhood, which was why there was actually enough grass to mow regularly. Up one side of the street and down the other, neighborhood kids rode their bikes and played basketball in their driveways.

Briefly breaking my rule to never, ever touch Poppy Wilder unless it was an emergency, I settled my hand along her lower back and nudged her gently. "Unless you've developed X-ray vision, it's gonna be tough to see the inside from the driveway."

She gave me a sidelong glance. "Someone's full of it today."

The edges of my lips tilted up briefly, and her eyes snagged on my mouth before she looked away. Wouldn't I have done the same thing?

The chemistry between us was as natural as breathing since I'd been back. The floodgates opened that couldn't be closed again. Everything about her made my head spin, and it was impossible to imagine a time when that wasn't true.

We walked up the step onto the front porch, and I held out my hand, gesturing for her to go ahead. Poppy sucked in a quick breath and walked inside the house.

It was clean and bright, the room empty and smelling like lemon cleaner. She took in the spacious family room with beams running across the ceiling and the flagstone fireplace with a chunky wood mantel in the center of the room. The hearth was big, and at Christmastime, Henry would line it with thick green garland covered with colored lights. I thought it was the prettiest thing I'd ever seen.

She wandered through the dining area that overlooked the huge backyard, and paused at the slider, fingers touching the glass. The meadow behind the house was bursting with color —pink and yellow and white blooms tucked between the tall grasses. Poppy stood at that spot for a long time, staring at the flowers with an unreadable expression.

"Henry doesn't have any kids?" she asked.

I shook my head. "Never married either. When I was about ten, I thought he was the coolest guy I'd ever met. Told me he was a lone wolf, but it was fine for two lone wolves to hang out together sometimes." I rubbed the back of my neck. "I wanted to be him when I grew up."

Poppy's brows lowered over her big, dark eyes, and after a long moment, she looked over at me. "Looks like you were successful," she said lightly. "I've never met anyone who likes to be alone as much as you."

God, it hurt hearing her say that. Only truth could cause that kind of sharp pain under your ribs.

Poppy dropped her gaze, sucking in a fortifying breath.

After one more lingering glance into the backyard, she turned into the kitchen, running her hands over the edge of the island, and I saw the slightest tremble in her fingers when she did. Wordlessly, Poppy checked out the back of the house

—a full bathroom connected to the laundry room, and another door that led to the two-stall garage.

It wasn't until we walked upstairs and she saw the first of three bedrooms—painted an eye-bruising neon green—that she finally spoke.

"I think I need some more information now."

Poppy leaned against the wall, a clear signal she wasn't looking at anything else until I told her something. Anything.

"I grew up across the street," I told her first. Her eyebrows arched gently, and I nodded to the window. "See that little red house?" Poppy didn't answer, but her eyes skimmed the small home. "That's where my mom and I lived. Henry lived here. He was ... I spent a lot of time here on the weekends and in the summer."

When her gaze sharpened, practically brimming with questions, I had to fight the urge to back away from this. From her. Letting her into this space felt like pulling open my skin and seeing those hidden parts of me that even her brother didn't know.

"And..."

"And what? It's been empty for about six months. The last family moved out before I went to Spain. Hasn't been advertised anywhere, so it's still empty now." I held her gaze. "Doesn't have to be, though."

Poppy licked her lips. "And Henry is fine with you deciding who rents it?"

"Yup."

"How much is it?"

I quoted her a number—high enough that it wasn't an obvious scam but low enough that it was a really good fucking deal. Her eyebrows shot up on her forehead. "For a fully updated three-bedroom house in a great neighborhood with a huge backyard?"

Wordlessly, I stared back at her.

Poppy's chest rose and fell on increasingly short breaths,

her hand moving over the front of her belly. She did that a lot, especially when she was thinking about something.

Her eyes narrowed. "Who would I write the check out to?"

"Emerson Enterprises," I answered honestly. "It's Henry's business name. You know all those car dealerships in Redmond of the same name before they sold a handful of years ago?"

Her eyebrows lifted. "That was him?"

I gave her a short nod.

There was a slight pause before Poppy covered her mouth with her hand and continued staring around the room.

"You think you'd like it here?"

After letting out a disbelieving laugh, Poppy glanced around the first bedroom. "I mean, the green has to go before anything else happens. I'm assuming you didn't pick this color?"

I shook my head. "That would be the fourteen-year-old girl who used to live here. Her name was Bree, and her parents let her pick whatever she wanted."

"Clearly, they loved her a lot."

I couldn't help but smirk. "Do you want to see the other bedrooms? The primary is across the hall."

She held my gaze for a breathless moment, and I felt like she was trying to pry straight into my thoughts. But then she blinked and walked past me out into the hallway.

The primary bedroom was even larger than the first, painted a soft, calm blue, with big windows overlooking the backyard and the meadow. She paused at the far window and glanced down at the way the sun streamed across her body. "This would be a perfect place to read in the morning," she said quietly.

I could see her there. Could so easily imagine the way she'd fill this space with her warm, loving energy. How she'd wake in the middle of a big bed set in the center of the room, sleepy and warm, cuddling under a blanket with her book and her coffee. And for a split second—almost viciously, heartbreakingly clear—I saw myself in bed watching her.

It was the first time I'd ever walked through the house and imagined myself there too, but I ruthlessly snipped the thread holding on to that idea.

Poppy continued through the room, and I pulled in a sharp inhale of orange blossoms through my nose.

The main bathroom got a quick, appreciative glance—especially the large soaker tub tucked into the corner next to the big shower and long vanity. We left the main bedroom quietly, me trailing after her like a lovesick fucking puppy. The third bedroom was the smallest, but when she walked in, her eyes got all big and soft.

"Oh, this would be the nursery," she breathed.

The way she said it had my chest cracking wide fucking open. Because Poppy could look not that far into the future and see all of this so clearly. Where the baby would sleep and where she'd read in the morning. She could close her eyes and imagine being a mother as easily as breathing, while I was hanging on by the skin of my fingernails with no clue how this would work or if I'd know how to do any of it. From the moment she showed up at my door, I was following her lead, wasn't I? I was so fucking lost, and the only thing that made sense was her.

"Yeah?"

My voice was rough, but she didn't seem to notice.

"Yeah. You can see the cherry tree in the backyard. And it's got the best view of the meadow, too." She closed her eyes, spreading her fingers wide over her stomach and breathing deeply. "Jax, this is…"

But she didn't finish.

And I didn't need her to.

It was perfect. She'd love it. She'd make it a home, and Henry would've loved that too.

Because I knew exactly how big this thing was that I was offering her. And fuck, did I want her to take me up on it. There was so much I couldn't do. So much I couldn't be for her, no matter how much I wanted.

This I could do, though.

"I need to think about it," she finally finished, opening her eyes. They were bright and glossy, but no tears fell. "I can't rush into big decisions."

"Why not?"

She laughed.

I held her gaze unflinchingly. "I think this is the right place for you. Can't you feel it when you're here?"

Poppy blew out a slow breath. "Yes. So do you … would you be the property manager?"

"Sort of."

"I'm starting to think you are genetically predisposed to cagey answers." She shook her head.

"Oh come on, I think that's one of my most interesting traits."

Her eyes searched mine. "No one warned me how stubborn you are underneath all that quiet."

My heartbeat stuttered in my ears, loud and erratic. "I think you already knew."

Her smile was mysterious—Sphynx-like and so intuitive that my hands ached to reach for her. "Maybe I did," she murmured. "But it's nice to know we can still learn things about each other, right?"

Now, it was my turn not to answer. There were too many things I wanted to say.

Wanted to. Couldn't.

Wouldn't.

"Can I walk you out? Or do you want to keep looking?"

She took one last glance around the room. "No, I think I've seen enough."

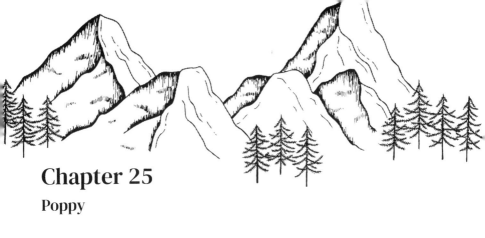

Chapter 25
Poppy

"This looks like a very serious endeavor."

At the sound of my mom's voice, I closed my eyes, clutching the notebook to my chest.

An hour of staring at it, at all the things I'd written down hadn't given me the peace I quite needed.

Prying my fingers away from the metal spiral edge, I glanced down at the neatly written letters in silver pencil lead. It didn't matter how decisively I'd written each one, how precise the curves and lines of each word were.

Down to my bones, it felt like I was still waiting for a piece to click into place, something just out of reach.

"You know when something feels like it should be an easy decision, but once it actually comes down to making it, it's really freaking hard?"

With a thoughtful hum, Mom eased herself into the chair next to mine on the front porch. Instead of looking at me, she focused her attention out into the yard. "That sounds pretty familiar, kiddo. Want to talk through what you've got on that list there?"

Handing it over to her was harder than I thought, so for now, I kept it tight in my grip. "Jax showed me a house this morning," I said quietly. "It's his friend's or something."

"Ahh." Her eyes tracked over my face. "Did you like it?"

My throat was thick as I nodded slowly.

"Is the rent fair?"

Again, I nodded. "Cheaper than I expected. And I have about a million questions about why he's the one showing it and where his friend lives, and…" I blew out a slow breath. "It's bizarre to realize that a man I've crushed on for half my life can be really, genuinely surprising after all this time."

Mom laughed. "Poppy, that's a beautiful thing, isn't it? Everyone in our life has the capacity to surprise us. We don't walk around with signs on our backs explaining why we are the way we are, all the details that make for a single, complicated person."

"We should. That would be so much easier."

"I don't think you mean that," she said sagely. "I think because it's him, it's making you feel differently."

"I can't figure out if his involvement makes things better or worse," I admitted. "There's something I can't put my finger on."

Mom tilted her head. "Like what?"

My fingers played with the edge of the paper. "You've known Jax as long as Cameron has."

She nodded, brows slightly lowered. "Of course. I remember the first time he came to our house. Serious," she said. "Very polite. Reserved, of course."

"I thought about stopping by Cameron's to ask him some questions," I said. "But I already know he won't tell me anything good."

Mom laughed easily. "And you know why."

"I do." My lips pushed out in a slight pout. "Because I should let Jax tell me."

"And this is information you need in order to make a decision about this house?"

This was harder to put into words, harder to put down on a concise list, but my heart screamed it all the same, jumbled thoughts and a whisper-thin kind of feeling that I couldn't nail down.

"He's already everywhere." I ran my hand through my hair and sighed. Inside my belly, the little nugget rolled, and my lips ghosted up in a smile. "And I can't figure this out, you know? Can't figure him out. He's got this house he takes care of for his friend? No one ever knew about it. Or at least I didn't."

"I didn't either."

"Jax is still this walking mystery that I want to solve more than anything." God, that hurt coming out. Even after all this, after all the ways I'd worked to have a healthy, balanced relationship with him, he was this living, breathing ghost—something strong and vital and so very alive—that wouldn't stop haunting me. "I can't help it. The things he says and does, I know there's so much more to him than he wants to let on. I think he's afraid to be a dad, but he doesn't want to say it out loud," I told her.

"That's a justifiable fear," Mom said. "Being a parent is terrifying. I remember when I left the hospital with Erik. He was tiny, and they just … let me walk right out the doors, assuming I knew what the hell I was doing."

I laughed quietly. "I think he's afraid I'll judge him for saying it. He seems to watch his reactions very carefully around me, especially since he proposed."

"Not his best idea," Mom said with a wry smile. She took a slow sip of her iced tea, rocking her chair back and forth with a simple push of her foot on the ground. "So that's one of your cons?" she asked. "The fact that he's the one watching the house?"

"That's somewhere in the middle." Staring down at the list again, I shrugged one shoulder. "I don't know if it's a good thing or a bad thing."

"What else?" she asked gently. Even without saying another word, of course she knew there was more. I'd never quite understood how they did it, but my parents had this eerie knack for seeing the truth written all over their kids faces. No matter what we got into, no matter what harebrained plans we came up with, no matter what was weighing on our hearts, they could take one look at us and know.

Would I be able to do that?

God, I hoped I could. I hope that was something stamped in my genes, like the hair color from my mom and the smile I got from my dad.

Chewing on my bottom lip, emotions clogging my chest, I handed her the notebook and waited for her to skim through my list.

Pros
Location
Rent is perfect
The house is beautiful
Big backyard

Undecided
Jax's involvement?

Cons
Leaving Mom alone

"Oh honey," she said, her eyes glossing over. "You can't pass this up because of me."

"When I think about you alone in this big house, I can hardly take it," I whispered back, voice full of tears. "I don't want to be the reason you're sad."

A single tear slid down her cheek as she turned, clutching my hand with hers. "I won't be," she said fiercely. "You haven't brought me a single moment of sadness since the moment I knew you existed, sweet girl. And that won't change, not as long as I live."

"Are you sure?" Hope swelled dangerously, a sweet and cool relief mixed with the bittersweet feeling of inevitable change.

"I'll miss you," she admitted, tears falling more freely.

"You know I love seeing your face every morning. You've taken such good care of me in the last year. I hope you know that. But taking care of you is the most important thing now."

"Everything's changing," I said, voice catching on a sob that threatened to break free.

She leaned forward and cupped the side of my face, swiping her thumb at the tears that coursed down my cheeks. "Life is supposed to change, Poppy. We're supposed to change with it, too. And I would never expect you or any of your siblings to pass up something meant for you, not because of me. Your dad wouldn't have either."

"I know." I sniffed loudly, dashing a hand over my cheeks.

"Is this what was making it so hard for you?" she asked.

Slowly, I nodded.

As she handed the notebook back, she hummed. "I understand more than you know, sweetheart. The hard decision that should be really easy."

Studying Mom's profile, I tried to straighten out my thoughts before I spoke again. "When did that happen to you?"

Her smile was immediate—soft and a little sad. "Giving your father a chance when we first met."

"Really?"

"Oh yeah. We had more baggage than a 747, Poppy. He buried a wife he loved, all while taking care of those three boys. I had a husband walk out on me and three young kids. You know how hard it is to trust someone with your heart when it's already been crushed?"

I angled in my seat to face her more fully, leaning my head against the back of the chair. "But you still did it, even if you knew."

"He was pretty impossible to resist," she said, voice wavering slightly. "But I did. Even if it was crazy, and even if it didn't make sense to anyone else." She tapped her temple. "My head was the thing telling me to be careful. Telling me I might get hurt again." She tapped her chest. "But in here, I knew he was exactly what I wanted. This is the thing we need to listen to with these big, scary, should-be-easy decisions." Mom searched my face. "This isn't really about the house, is it?"

Slowly, I shook my head. "I don't mind the idea of change," I told her. "We've had enough of it in our lives. And I know the house is perfect. Staying home always made me feel like I'd never quite grown up. I feel good knowing I can do this, and make a home for baby. I can provide for us, even if I'm getting help along the way." My eyes closed firmly. "I finally feel like I know what I'm doing in life, you know? My job, the baby, and now this. "

"But…"

My stomach somersaulted over the question I was trying to answer with no real clarity and no real exit plan. "What if … what if after all this time—being heartsick over him for so long, telling myself that it was just one night, and trying to be friends—what if he's the one thing I can never outgrow? If I'll sit here and watch him leave over and over again, disappear when I least expect it, and I wait and wait and wait for him to want something more?" Tears slid silently down my cheeks. "Why is it so hard not to feel anything for him? It should be easy."

Mom made a small tsking sound with her tongue. "That's your problem, honey. Those should'ves will drive you crazy, and you need to let those stay in the past where they belong."

My eyes rose to hers. "What do you mean?"

"I don't think you want someone easy to love, Poppy." She held my gaze, open and honest and the slightest hint of challenge. "Of all my kids, you and Cameron are the most alike. Not only do you have supernatural patience, but I think you want the challenge, like he did with Ivy. You want to love someone who won't open easily because you are the kind of person who knows exactly what's waiting underneath when they do. Probably better than that person knows, actually." She leaned forward and set her hand over mine, gripping my fingers tight. "You've always known what's inside that man, and maybe I can see that more easily than the rest because I'm old, and I've had so many years to watch how people love, what happens when they run scared, and what happens when they don't. It takes incredible strength to look someone's fears in the face and decide to love them anyway," she said, her eyes firmly on mine, and I felt that eye contact rip through my skin. "As a friend. Or more."

Chewing on my bottom lip, I stared down at the notebook in my lap and tried to filter through what was happening in my heart, that stubborn organ that went in direct contradiction to my much more logical head.

"Can you love him as a friend or more, knowing what's underneath?" she asked. "Can you figure out a way to co-parent with him through that too, knowing he might never face the fears that hold him back?"

Mom didn't wait for an answer. She merely smiled at whatever she saw on my face as she stood from the chair. She paused to plant a kiss on the top of my head.

"And don't worry, I'll find a use for your room before the last box is packed," she whispered.

Through my quiet tears, I managed to laugh. Waiting for them to ebb, I finally set the notebook down on the side table and swapped it out for my phone.

I pulled up Jax's number and carefully tapped out a message.

Chapter 26
Jax

"Which one do you like better?" she asked.

I squinted. "You cannot tell me those colors are even the slightest bit different."

She rolled her eyes, tucking the paint swatches back into the display. "I knew I should've asked Greer to help me with this."

The delicate smell of orange blossoms was too addicting to ignore.

I leaned closer, dropping my mouth closer to her ear. "Yeah, but then you'd have to deal with Greer, and I'm so much more pleasant, aren't I?"

"You're something," she muttered.

With a grin that I knew she couldn't see, I backed away. The older gentleman working behind the paint counter watched us with a knowing twinkle in his eyes. "Picking nursery colors?" he asked. "We've got some brochures over on the left side if you want to take a peek."

Poppy and I locked eyes, hers dropping first. "Eventually, yes, we will. Today is just a spare bedroom." She nudged me with her elbow. "Someone allowed it to be painted a really horrid neon green color."

He smiled. "Ahh. You might be wanting some color-blocking primer then," he said. "Why don't I show you where that is."

Poppy pushed the cart behind him, chatting warmly as he asked her a few questions about the project. I didn't follow right away, instead studying an end cap filled with roller covers and brushes. I picked a package of covers, tucking it under my arm while I settled on a two-inch brush. I had my own set of paintbrushes, but it would be smart for Poppy to have her own at the house too.

With that in mind, I picked out another smaller one, a four-inch roller and some covers, along with a few rolls of painters tape. My hands were full when I approached them in the aisle over.

She gave me a curious glance when I dumped everything into the cart, but I ignored it and kept wandering.

I studied the contents of a basic tool set with a bright pink cover with narrowed eyes. What good would something like this be if she had an emergency in the middle of the night? I sighed, striding back to the front of the store to grab a second cart. Extra light bulbs. Emergency flashlights. Batteries. Small camping lanterns in case she lost power. Every new section of the store had me running through an exhaustive list of what she could possibly need in any given scenario. Maybe an extra Taser or two couldn't hurt either. My chest pinched, and I rubbed at it.

Fuck, had it always been so dangerous to live alone? I'd made it down three aisles, adding more and more, until she found me trying to decide between two different power drills. Quickly, I stepped away from the cart because she'd probably think I'd lost my fucking mind.

"You really should start wearing a bell around your neck," she said easily. "And here I thought a kid wandering off some day would be my biggest issue." Poppy's cart bumped the front of mine, and her eyes widened when she saw the contents. "My goodness, I didn't peg you as an impulse shopper. Are we facing down an apocalypse I don't know about?"

I ignored her, lifting my chin toward her cart. "Did he sell you shit we don't need?"

"Undoubtedly. But he was so sweet, I couldn't say no."

"Not sure I've ever had that problem," I told her.

Poppy rolled her eyes, but a glint of affection was buried in her expression, so I decided to take it as a compliment. She walked around the carts to show me two more paint chips, each one starting with light sky blue and ending in a deep, rich navy. "What about these?" she asked, tapping on the middle color of each swatch.

"Whatever you want," I said.

Tilting the swatches toward the light coming in through the front windows, Poppy didn't notice the way I was staring at her. The light dusting of freckles over her nose started to come in more during the warm weather, a sure sign she spent more time in the sun. There was one above the right side of her mouth, and my pulse sped up the longer I studied the lush, pink curves of her lips.

What would they taste like?

Sweet. I knew that for sure.

Sinful. Didn't doubt that one either.

Poppy would taste like forever, and the truth of it terrified me to my core. The way I wanted it did too.

What would she do if I curved my hand around the back of her neck and simply … kissed her?

God, the way my chest ached the longer I thought about it. What if I went my entire life and didn't know the feel of her lips on mine?

It was inexcusable. Unpardonable.

If I'd missed that opportunity out of habit or fear or some ridiculous notion that kissing her would somehow make it easier to let her walk away.

"This one," Poppy declared.

I blinked. "Sure. It's great."

She glanced up at me. "Did I lose you there?"

"Just thinking about something else."

Instead of sweeping away that disappointed feeling, I let it settle deep under my skin, knowing full well that if I ever had the opportunity to kiss this woman, I'd be fucking taking it.

Poppy smiled. "Dreaming of a blue bedroom, are we?"

Tugging the paint swatch from her hand, I checked the name on the one she'd chosen. Smoke. A bit farther down the chip, I studied the deepest color and made a small humming noise. "I wanted a dark room like this when I was younger," I said. My thumb rubbed against the dark greenish-blue on the bottom.

"You didn't get it?"

Lost for a moment in the memory, I shook my head. "My mom thought I'd get sick of it after a year. Didn't want to hassle with it." I swallowed hard, the memory crawling up my throat like a spider coming through a pipe. "Couldn't blame her, really. My mom worked two jobs most of my life. She was always busy and tired."

The money to buy paint and the time necessary to do it were a luxury she didn't really have.

Poppy's shoulder brushed against my bicep when she shifted out of the way of someone going down the aisle, my eyes falling closed at the feel of her skin on mine.

"Does she live around here?"

"No."

The thoughtful twist to Poppy's lips told me this conversation wasn't quite over. "Would you want me to invite her to the baby shower my sisters are throwing this summer?"

A cynical laugh threatened to slip past even the staunchest of my defenses, but I swallowed it down. "Not sure that's necessary, no."

The way she glanced up at me made me feel like she was trying to crawl into my brain. "You don't see her?"

"Nope. Last I heard, she was living in on the east coast with husband number four, so hopefully he's got the patience and the bank account to stick around longer than the last three."

"Probably why I've never heard her mentioned," Poppy said lightly. "When did she move away?"

God, were we doing this in the middle of the hardware store? It was like prying the lid off a jar that had been rusted shut for a decade or more. The groan of disuse practically echoed through the aisles when I tried to fumble for an answer.

"When I was eighteen." Reaching forward, I pulled a canvas drop cloth off the shelf and tossed it into her cart.

"And you stayed?" she asked with the slightest tilt of her head. "Why?"

"Henry," I answered easily. "He was more my family than she was. And maybe your brother too. Can't get rid of the prick now, even when I do something like get you pregnant and ghost for three months."

Poppy let out a shocked laugh. "Are we joking about this now?"

I stared down at her, feeling the slip in my defenses, the way she dug her graceful fingers into them and yanked and yanked with all her might. "Maybe."

She hummed, arching one dark eyebrow.

Waiting to see if she'd ask any more questions about my mom was agony, but my jaw unclenched when she dropped the subject. I handed back the paint chip. "It's a good color," I said.

Poppy stared down at it, eventually nodding. I pulled the color-blocking primer out and set it back on the shelf. She scoffed.

"I'm telling you, we don't need it with the color you're picking. It's dark enough to cover." I ambled next to her as she started pushing the cart back toward the paint counter.

Reaching forward, Poppy grabbed the primer and set it back in the cart. "He'll feel bad if we don't take it."

"Saying no to people is liberating, trust me."

As we walked, she gave me an inscrutable look.

I shifted, hands tightening on the handle of my cart. "What?"

"I'm not sure I should say it," she admitted quietly, her eyes deep and dark under the harsh fluorescent lights.

"Well now you better."

Her lips ghosted up in a smile. "*Sometimes* you have a problem saying no to people."

I snorted. "Like when?"

The smile faded, a heart-crushing sincerity left in its wake. "You didn't say no to me," she said quietly.

The rapid thrumming of my pulse was anything but even. My stomach churned with the way she said it, my throat closing tight with all the words I was shoving down.

Because I wanted you too bad.

Because you're fucking perfect.

Because that night was everything good and right, and if you'd let me, I'd keep you.

Because when I close my eyes, you're mine.

"I didn't," I replied evenly.

Poppy's breath caught in her throat, like I'd said all those other words out loud. And for a clock-stopping moment, I had to remind myself that I didn't.

"I'm going to get the paint," she said unevenly. Poppy didn't wait to see me nod slowly, just left me with the cart and didn't wait to see me drop my chin to my chest as I struggled to breathe.

When she left the aisle, I let out a slow exhale, feeling so wildly out of control that my hands clenched so tight around the handle I was surprised I didn't crush it flat.

With a backward glance, I studied the full cart I'd left behind, and flagged a worker wearing a cheery red shirt.

"Hey, can you set that aside for me? I'll be back for it in a little bit."

The woman nodded, took my name, and I waited for Poppy to appear with two gallons of paint. When I eased them out of her hand, our fingers brushed, and she cleared her throat as we approached the register, side by side.

A pimply-faced teen rang everything up, bagging the items into brown paper bags. He glanced between us and said the total.

My eyebrows shot up. "What the hell do they put in paint these days?"

Poppy elbowed me in the side, smiling sweetly at the kid behind the counter. "Ignore him. We all do."

The kid gave me a nervous, wide-eyed look, and I sighed. Poppy reached for her purse at the same time I reached for my wallet.

We both froze, gazes clashing.

"Not a chance," I told her.

Her jaw edged out mulishly. "Jax, I'm the one who wanted to paint the room. I'm paying for it."

"No, you're not."

The dark brown of her eyes sparked hot, and I felt a corresponding tug deep in my gut. "This is not a thing we're doing," she said firmly. "It's for my house, I'm paying for it. You don't just get to pay for stuff simply because you're with me."

I arched an eyebrow, handing my credit card over the counter without dropping my gaze a single inch. Her mouth fell open on a quiet, scoffing noise.

"I'm giving you some cash," she argued.

Slowly, I leaned down and spoke quietly next to her ear. Her whole body went stock-still. "Try it and I'll rip up every fucking dollar."

Poppy inched away until she could look me in the face again. Those high cheekbones held a blush of pink, and her chest was heaving. I held my breath, waiting to see what she'd do.

The kid looked around nervously.

"Thank you," she said quietly.

"You're welcome. That wasn't so hard, was it?"

There was a dangerous narrowing of her eyes, and I hid my grin because I didn't fancy getting punched in the throat.

After paying, I carried the boxes out to Poppy's car and settled them in the trunk, waiting for her to leave before I jogged back into the store and purchased the other cart.

Back at the house, I found her waiting patiently on the front step.

"Goodness, I had no idea you were such a slow driver."

I arched an eyebrow. "Were we racing? I didn't know."

Poppy merely smiled, batting her eyelashes. "It's always a race. At least in our family. The first person back home gets dibs on the remote for the night."

I shifted the box in my arms and handed her my keys. "The blue one," I told her. "I have your copy inside."

She fished it out from the others and unlocked the door, pushing it open and then standing back to let me go through.

"I can't believe this will be mine," Poppy said quietly, turning in a slow circle in the family room. Her hand coasted down the front of her bump. "Ours," she added quietly, and the bittersweet pang that sent through my bones almost took me to my knees.

After a few attempts to swallow that down, I handed her the first box. "This has prep stuff. If you don't mind bringing it up there. I'll get the rest."

"Do you want me to start taping the trim for the primer?"

I gave her a flat look. "We're not using that primer."

"Why not? He said we needed it."

"We don't, I promise."

"Poor Ralph," she sighed. "He's just trying to do his job,

and I can only imagine what kind of men ignore him all the time because they don't like following directions."

"You know his name?"

Poppy's responding facial expression was all incredulity. "Don't you? He's worked there for ten years."

I rubbed my forehead. "I don't make it a habit of … talking when I go in there."

"Really? How surprising."

With a slight roll of my eyes, I went back out to my truck, unloading the rest of the items in a couple of trips. Before I went upstairs, I took the box of tools and emergency supplies into the laundry room, quickly tucking them into the empty cabinets above the washer and dryer.

The two gallons of paint were at the bottom of the other box, and I slipped them out, carrying both in one hand as I walked upstairs. When I turned the corner, she wasn't in the green bedroom, but I could hear her across the hall in the room that would be hers.

She played some music on her phone, humming softly while I heard the occasional snap of the measuring tape. Having this sort of uninterrupted time with her was soothing in an incredibly foreign way.

"I think I'll move in midweek if that works for you," she called out. "Gives me a few days to pack and figure out some furniture. Ian and Cameron won't be gone, so I'll have hands for heavy lifting."

"I'll be here too," I told her, unwrapping the canvas drop cloth and laying it over the floor. I finished that, then moved on to uncovering the new brush. "Just text me what time."

"'Kay," she said.

I gripped the small metal can opener in my hand and ran it under the lip of the first gallon of paint. When I pried the loosened lid off, I simply stared for a few seconds.

"What the…" I whispered.

From the doorway, I felt Poppy's eyes on me. When I

glanced up, she was biting down on her bottom lip to stem her growing smile. "It's a good color," she said with a slight shrug of one shoulder. "Someone should use it."

What was she doing to me?

Did she have the slightest fucking clue?

I was still staring at the empty doorway when she turned and walked back across the hall, my eyes burning and my head spinning. There was a distant ringing in my ears as I dipped the pristine paint brush into the glossy, wet paint.

The first pull of the brush left behind a thick swath of the deep, rich color, exactly the way I'd imagined it for so many years.

Before I dipped the brush again, I saw the label printed neatly in black marker.

Jax's Blue.

Chapter 27
Jax

It didn't take long, and the radioactive green was slowly covered, replaced by the deep, rich bluish green.

"I can reach the top of the wall if you'd let me get up on the ladder," she huffed.

She had blue speckles on her arms, and a chunk of hair tipped in blue, but she didn't seem too bothered by it. She stood with arms crossed, eyes alight with stubborn heat.

"Not happening, angel," I answered evenly, dipping my brush into the small container I had set on the top of the ladder, then angling the brush to cut in with one smooth line.

When she showed me she could manage it, she'd been rolling the walls with her good hand, coming behind me after I did the cutting in against the trim and ceilings. But she couldn't reach the top third of the walls, so when she finished as much as possible, I'd set my trim brush down and come down the ladder, relieving her of the roller so I could finish the rest.

On one of those occasions, she'd left to get us some lunch and buy some staples for the house—cleaning supplies, toilet paper, and paper towels. I could hear her downstairs in the kitchen, opening and closing cupboard doors as she made a dozen fucking lists about where she wanted to put things.

She worked on one of them while we sat on the floor of the bedroom and ate the subs she'd picked up in town.

"What about Holland?" she asked, wiping her thumb in the corner of her mouth.

I arched an eyebrow. "What about it?"

"As a name," she said.

"That's not a name, it's a fucking country."

"I think it's cute," she stated.

Setting my sub down, I motioned for the paper in her lap.

With a tiny eye roll, Poppy pushed the notebook in my direction. There was a girl column, in bright pink—Evelyn, Holland, Gemma, Cecily, and Rosie. My eyes snagged on the last name, thumb brushing over the letters, and my brain did that thing again, picturing a button nose and big brown eyes. Dimple in her cheek, just like her mom.

Thinking about a little girl named Rosie with those eyes and that smile, knowing how thoroughly I'd be tied in knots over her, a wild sort of emotion clawed up my throat, and I tried clearing it out. Tried and failed.

"Boys are on the other side," she added. The weight of her gaze on my face made my skin feel hot, but I ignored it for the time being, turning the paper over to find a deep blue ink with another small list of names.

Isaiah, Miles, Lucas, Hayes, and Griffin.

My brow lowered.

"What?" she asked.

"Not Timothy, after your dad?"

Poppy closed her eyes, resting her head against the wall, and I saw how much effort it took for her to swallow. When she opened them again, her eyes were red and a little glossy. "I'm not sure I could handle a first name," she admitted. "A middle name, maybe. Whenever I see his name on something, I feel a little pinch of sad in my heart. Something that's just for him, you know? Like I want to protect that feeling as long as I can." She sighed. "Grief is weird. Some days I can go hours without thinking about the fact that he's gone. It wasn't like that the first couple of months. It just changes one day, and you don't even realize how it happened. It sneaks up so quietly, this invisible barrier that slowly stretches out the amount of time between those thoughts. And then you go, oh yeah, I'm still *really* sad about this."

When the first tear slid down her face, I had to force myself to stay still because the urge to gather her up in my arms eclipsed my common sense in no more time than a heartbeat.

Poppy sniffed, using her lunch napkin to dab under her eyes. "Sorry. Sometimes I don't know whether I should blame hormones or if it's just … me."

"Don't apologize," I told her, voice rough and heart raw. "You should miss him. I think any time we lose someone that important, missing them is what makes us know we're not dead inside." Invisible fingers strangled my throat, trying to keep those words down, and Poppy's eyes glinted with instant curiosity. I kept talking because the last thing I wanted was more questions. "Not many people can put up with all the shit your siblings used to pull and still keep their head, but he was one of them."

Poppy emitted a watery laugh, another tear escaping down her cheek. She didn't wipe this one away.

I'd always admired her ability to feel out loud, the absolute fucking bravery that it took to wear her heart on her sleeve. Most people didn't feel safe enough to do that, but Poppy did. In her grief, in her optimism, in the ownership of her flaws, even in her years of misguided feelings toward me, she showed a strength that ten of me wouldn't have been able to master, and for once, because of her, I wanted to know what that felt like.

Do something.

Do something.

This wasn't the same kind of restless energy that had me

wanting to sprint and run and go somewhere to clear my head. It was something deeper, pulled from a vital place inside my head, urging me into action that might obliterate the firmly defined line she'd drawn.

It was a worthwhile risk because the thought of her being so sad was more than I could bear. Staring down at her, chest in knots, I moved my hand without permission and caught that tear with the edge of my thumb.

Her skin was so fucking soft, even damp from her tears, and I swallowed hard, cursing my own weakness. There was the slightest catch in her breath, and I ignored it as I pulled my hand back to the safety of my lap.

"There's a lot of people in this world who aren't worth your tears, angel, but your dad is one of them."

In the delicate notch at the base of her throat, I could see the fluttering of her pulse.

When she moved one of her legs, Poppy's notebook fell off her lap, the pencils hitting the floor, the melancholy mood efficiently snapped.

I blinked down at the ground, and Poppy seemed to be gathering herself as well.

Which was good because we needed to be … gathered.

My gaze lingered on her neat handwriting. The lists were such a fascinating glimpse inside her head, and I found myself wanting every single one.

"Good grief, Poppy, how much shit you got on that list?"

"A lot," she sighed. "I just don't want to forget anything. My brain is like a sieve these days." She tilted the page toward me, and I tugged it closer, shaking my head at what I saw. "You should see my lists at work," she added ruefully.

I took the last bite of my sandwich and stretched my legs out in front of me. "Pretty sure your job would be perfect punishment for someone like me."

She laughed lightly, wadding up the paper from around her sub and mine, then shoving them in a bag for garbage. "I love it. Keeping track of all the little details is the thing I love most. I'm not like Greer or Ivy. I can't come up with the big picture ideas and concepts like they do. But if someone gives me that idea? I can immediately figure out the hundreds of steps we need to get there."

"That's why you're good at your job."

Poppy's cheeks flushed pink, that addicting soft wash of color that always gave away her embarrassment. Or pride. Or desire.

I wondered if she hated that she did it, hated that she couldn't control it.

For someone like me, who needed clear signs of where her head was at, I loved that little tell. Loved it, even if it got my head in trouble, leading it down paths it really shouldn't go.

How far did that blush travel down her body?

Clearing my throat, I yanked my thoughts somewhere safer.

"You glad you went to school instead of starting with Wilder Homes earlier?" I asked. Cameron and Greer had taken over the family business from their dad early. Cameron was twenty when he started moving into the general contractor position, easing some of the responsibilities from his dad. Greer worked as the head designer in tandem with getting her degree. Poppy was the only one who didn't start with the company until after her degree was finished.

No matter how much I didn't want to admit it, I'd been paying attention to her a lot longer than I realized.

She nodded. "I liked being in school. Liked learning. I didn't really need the Master's in Management, but I'm glad I have it now that I'll be overseeing Wilder House too." She leaned her head back on the bedroom door and sighed, her hand moving over her stomach again. "I can't imagine ever working somewhere else, but it's nice to know I have the education to back up what I'm doing, if I did." I found myself fidgeting with a straw that went unused with our lunch, and her eyes lingered on the movement of my hands. "You glad you didn't go to school?" she asked.

My answering nod was easy. "College wasn't for me. Took one semester because Henry thought I should try." I smiled a little, picturing the day I came back here and told him I was dropping out. He was so pissed. "Hell, if it hadn't been for Cameron helping me, I probably wouldn't have done as well in high school either. I can't handle sitting anywhere too long. I'll go crazy."

She shifted, a slight wince on her face as she adjusted her growing body. "A trait this child has picked up."

"Yeah?"

Poppy nodded. "They've been moving a lot today. This baby will grow up on jobsites, just like I did, won't they?" She smiled. "In the back storage rooms of Wilder House, and knowing how to frame a house before they can drive. Isn't that weird to think about? That's how I was too, I guess." She smiled. "I've never given much thought to what you were like when you were a kid. I bet you were serious back then too, in a little red house dreaming about a dark blue bedroom." Poppy paused, her chin raising slightly as she searched my eyes. "What else did you dream about, I wonder."

I took a deep breath, my gaze holding hers for a long beat. The space between us seemed to shrink with every second that neither one of us looked away.

Her brow furrowed. "What?"

I dropped my gaze. "Nothing."

"Jax."

For the rest of my life, I'd be able to conjure the memory of her saying my name in a variety of ways. It wouldn't be a tangible memory, an action, or a specific moment. But the way she said it now—the clear want of something from me—would be my downfall.

Because I couldn't say no. No matter what she asked of me.

Slowly, I stood and held out my hand to help her up. The confusion on her face was plain, and I let my fingers wrap around hers while I pulled her to standing.

She didn't let go right away, and neither did I.

My eyes traced over the tiny blue speckles on her shoulders, and even though it was stupid and I fucking knew better, my thumb reached out to touch one on her jaw. Her eyes fluttered shut. "I was a serious kid," I told her. "Sometimes I think the only way I've changed is that I've gotten bigger. Still don't know what the hell I'm doing most days."

Poppy's eyes opened, and she licked her lips before speaking, like her mouth was dry. That flash of her pink tongue had my mouth dry too.

"That's not true," she said.

I sucked in a slow breath, the edge of my finger brushing over the impossibly soft curve of her chin. Her chest rose and fell on a choppy breath, but she didn't pull away.

"Yeah it is," I whispered. "You learned different lessons growing up than I did, angel. Yours were the good kind."

I learned how to be alone. How to be self-sufficient. How to take up less space in whatever my relationships were because I was less likely to hurt someone. Learned what I didn't want—that reckless chase for someone to fix everything that was wrong in my life.

But no matter how hard I pretended otherwise, no matter how much I didn't want it to be true, she'd shown me that I wanted someone in my life to be mine. That I wanted someone to love and take care of.

Wanted someone sweet and warm and thoughtful and kind to fill up all those empty spaces in my life that I'd guarded with clenched fists and a closed-off heart.

And it wasn't just someone. It wasn't just want. I needed *her*.

We were so close. Poppy swayed toward me, and her fingers brushed along my side when she tried to brace herself.

The space between us was practically nothing, and when I dipped my head, I could drag the tip of my nose along the top of her hair. That sweet, intoxicating scent filled my lungs, and God, did I breathe it in.

Why was it that every time I got within arms reach of this girl, the air went thick with tension? Maybe that had been the key for years of safe interactions with Poppy Wilder—I never got close enough to know. Never got close enough to feel what it was like.

I wasn't even sure how this happened, how that innocent conversation led us to this place. The only thing I knew for sure was that Poppy and I proved over and over that we didn't know how to undo what we'd done. We didn't know how to be in the same space without feeling this electric connection, this invisible, iron-clad link that neither of us could shake.

The only things that held us back were a rapidly fraying sense of honor because she'd never forgive herself if she crossed that line when she wasn't ready to. And I'd never forgive myself if I was the reason she did.

I swallowed hard, lifting my head away from Poppy.

Poppy let out a shaky exhale, her hand dropping from my side. "I ... I need to go," she said, eyes on the floor as she backed away. "Can you, umm, finish painting while I run a couple of errands?"

My heart thundered erratically, but I nodded.

Before she left the room, she paused and finally dragged her eyes up to mine, and I wanted to scream at what I saw there.

Worry. And the slightest hint of regret.

"Poppy," I started in a low, urgent voice. "Wait."

She held up a hand, shaking her head almost immediately. "It was nothing. It was just—"

"It's not nothing," I interrupted hotly. "Don't say it's nothing."

Her eyes were huge in her face, the color draining from her cheeks. The pink was gone in a heartbeat, and that pale version of her face hurt.

But instead of nodding, instead of conceding to this being *something*, she held my gaze. "It *has* to be."

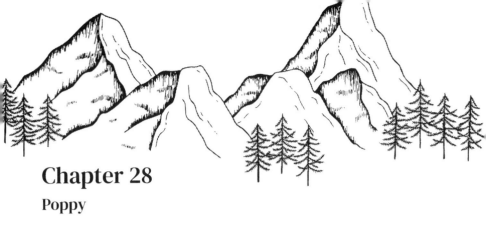

Chapter 28
Poppy

The very best thing about a house full of Wilders was that there was no shortage of distractions.

My house—I'd finally started calling it such a couple of days before I moved in—was a few trains shy of Grand Central Station for all the noise, chaos, and people filing in and out. Because I was pregnant and thereby viewed as useless for heavy lifting by everyone in my family, I stood at the front door, directing the traffic with my notebook in hand and my phone ready for scanning.

"Stop," I yelled at Cameron as he tried to go past with a big box.

"I can read, Poppy," he said. "It says *Main bedroom* right on the top."

Ignoring his complaints, I ran my finger along my master spreadsheet and double-checked the number on the box with the number on the sheet. "Main bedroom," I said sweetly.

He rolled his eyes as he walked past me through the door, his big boots pounding on the stairs as he delivered it to the correct place.

"Told you," he yelled over his shoulder.

"There's a system for a reason," I yelled back. "Measure twice, cut once, right?"

My brother muttered something, but he was too far up the stairs for me to hear it.

Ian followed him, a smug smile on his face. "There is literally nothing I love more than someone throwing Cameron's own life advice back in his face."

Behind him, Harlow paused, arms full of grocery totes. "Nothing you love more, huh?"

He gave her a heated look, and she ducked her face closer to his so he could sneak a sweet kiss. "Almost nothing," he murmured against her mouth. "You're a close second, at least."

She gave him a mocking glare, ignoring his smirk as she brushed past him to deliver the food into the kitchen, where Greer and Adaline unloaded dishes.

I double-checked the sheet for Ian's box and tapped the side of it. "Laundry room," I said.

There was no need for a moving truck, but my driveway and the cul-de-sac were lined with Wilder Homes work trucks, each packed to the gills with boxes earlier that morning before we departed from my mom's house.

After my brothers left, Greer and Adaline followed in another big vehicle. Mom and I took a moment alone in my suddenly empty room. The walls were now devoid of all the artwork I'd accumulated over the years—family photos and splashes of color in the art I favored. My closets were bare, and so were the bathroom drawers across the hall. My dresser was in the back of Ian's truck, the mattress and bed frame in Cameron's. They'd unload those first, then return for the boxes lining the front porch.

While I took a moment to say goodbye to the room I grew up in, in the only home I'd ever known, my phone dinged with a text.

> Parker: Heard I'm missing all the fun today. Does this mean your bedroom is up for grabs? I could really use an off-site trophy room...

> Me: Oh, do you have trophies to display now? I must've missed that.

Parker followed that up with a middle finger emoji, and I laughed under my breath, tucking my phone away and allowing that moment of levity to act as an anchor on a day when my emotions were rioting.

Over moving, over moving *on*, and which one was clawing to be at the forefront of my mind. Leaving something big in your past was gut-wrenching, even if good was to be gained from it.

A bedroom. A house. A person.

Packing up my entire life over the past week made me feel like someone entirely new was the one making the move across town. I could hardly recognize myself now, not just because of the physical changes, but also through the intentional setting aside of things that I knew weren't good for me. Things that weren't right for me.

It was that little piece of hard-to-swallow wisdom that had me viciously blocking out that moment with Jax, the tiptoeing of a necessary line.

There was no room here for big, heart-breaking errors between us, and he knew it as well as I did. When I looked down the road at all the ways we'd need to be there for each other, I couldn't handle the thought that a brief flare of heat from some untapped chemistry would be the reason we couldn't coexist well.

It didn't even really make me feel any better to know that I wasn't the only one feeling it. Somehow it only made me feel worse.

All of it heaped on an already very emotional day had me crying before a single box was unloaded into the new house.

My mom had her arm wrapped around my shoulders as I cried silent tears standing in the middle of that room. The mirror stayed mounted on the wall, and while I leaned my head against hers, I touched my finger to the chip in the bottom right corner.

"You sure you're going to be okay?" I whispered.

"Oh honey," Mom said, "that's supposed to be my question to you when I leave your house later tonight, you know."

I closed my eyes and sniffed piteously. "I know, but I'll still worry about you."

With firm hands, Mom turned me to face her. Then she cupped my face, drawing her thumbs along my wet cheeks. "This is what's supposed to happen, my darling girl." Her eyes were bright with unshed tears as she wrapped me in a tight hug. "This will always be your home, Poppy. Just like it'll always be home to Cameron and Ian and Parker, to Erik and Greer and Adaline. Doesn't matter how old you get, or how far away you move, or what changes in your life." She pulled her face back and smiled through her tears. "Even better is that you'll have more than one. You have the home you'll create yourself, and you have the one that will welcome you back whenever you need it."

Pregnancy hormones didn't stand a chance against a Sheila Wilder pep talk, and I melted into her embrace again, and the two of us cried for a few minutes. Mourning the inevitable change in our lives, and just how different everything looked now than it had a year ago.

By the time I pulled up to my house, our eyes were dry, and we were ready to work. The bed got set up first, my dresser moved in next, followed by the couch and two chairs I'd found at a cute little secondhand store in Redmond.

Greer and Adaline tackled making my bed with clean

sheets and a gorgeous white bedding set I'd splurged on from one of our suppliers at Wilder House, moving downstairs into the kitchen once that was done. Ivy took it upon herself to unpack my clothes in the double closets while the boys returned to Mom's house to get the rest of the boxes.

Jax joined them on that second trip, and I only allowed myself one—just one—lingering glimpse at the pop of his arms and the hard line of his jaw when he carried a box into the kitchen. At the look in his eyes as he actively avoided glancing back in my direction. I hadn't seen him all week, the longest stretch we'd gone since he arrived home, and all friggin day, my eyes had the horrifying tendency to seek him out when I entered one of the rooms.

We made it two hours.

Two hours and nine minutes.

I walked into the family room, sidestepping a couple of boxes next to the base of the stairs, just as he was walking out. He stopped dead in his tracks. So did I.

When Jax's eyes met mine, everything else around us disappeared in a great big whoosh, a sudden vacuum of sound so staggering that I could only imagine what we must have looked like. Standing on opposite ends of the room, we were unable to look anywhere else.

Would it always be like this?

Would there ever be peace in my heart when it came to this man?

After this many years, I should be immune to something as simple as a look, but I *wasn't*. I could hardly find a thread of logic in any piece of my reaction to him, and I hated that more than anything.

I broke first, yanking my gaze away from his.

"I, uh, have the first rent check," I told him. "I stuck it on the fridge with a magnet. You never gave me the address for where to send it."

His brow was slightly furrowed when I glanced back. "It's a … PO Box downtown. But I'll grab this one today."

I managed a short nod over the thundering of my heart, turning toward the kitchen when Greer asked me a question about where I wanted my cups. Jax's footsteps receded quickly like he couldn't leave the room fast enough.

Running a hand over my forehead, I swallowed against a bone-dry throat and a tidal wave of frustration before answering. "Umm, that one in front of you is fine."

Her brows furrowed. "You feel okay, Pops?"

I couldn't answer for a minute because my thoughts felt so messy in my head, which kept clear words from forming.

Adaline came up behind me, wrapping her arm around my waist. "Do you need to rest?"

"No," I said. "I'm just a little overwhelmed, I think."

She smoothed her hand up and down my back. "I think they've got that reading chair in the spare bedroom upstairs. Maybe take ten minutes in there?"

Eyes heavy with exhaustion, I nodded.

Greer stopped me with a hand to my arm. "Side note. I didn't know you were going for dark, sexy, and moody."

Oh fuck, was I that obvious? I blinked, not so much as a single word able to climb past the block in my throat. "What?"

She gave me a strange look. "The color you chose in that room. I thought you were going light and airy."

I laughed—but the sound came out like I was choking on my own spit—and my sisters shared a telling glance, like I was losing my mind.

Wasn't I, though?

"I, uh, had a change of heart at the hardware store."

Greer smiled. "It was a good change. Sometimes our gut leads us somewhere very unexpected."

"No shit," I muttered under my breath.

"What was that?" Adaline asked.

I glanced up to find them both watching me with that awful big sister sharp-eyed look.

It was knowing.

Big sisters who thought they knew things were the worst because more often than not, they were right. Which led to smug, knowing, obnoxious big sisters.

"I don't need to rest," I told them. "I promise."

Greer finished loading the glasses. "We're almost done anyway," she said. "Cameron is helping Ivy with your clothes. I think Jax was doing some yard work, Ian was going to hook up your TV, and Mom went back to the house to watch Sage and Olive and make some dinner. Do you want to join us or bask in your empty house without all of us watching your every move?"

An empty house, I thought with a bone-melting sigh of relief.

I'd have an empty house every single night.

The sisters heard that sigh too, and their smug, knowing grins widened into something else.

They were happy for me.

Adaline squeezed my arm. "Enjoy it," she whispered, kissing me on the temple.

We worked in the kitchen, finishing up the last box, and I wandered upstairs to find Ivy flattening the last of the wardrobe boxes. "All done."

I stared at my closet with my mouth hanging open. "Holy shit, Ivy. How am I ever going to keep it looking like this?"

Cameron gave her a look. "See? I told you."

Ivy sniffed. "It's a highly logical organization system, and you are the kind of person to appreciate it, so don't even pretend you don't." She swept her hands over each section of clothes. "Sleeveless here, then short sleeved, then long sleeved, then dresses, grouped by color within a subsection. In the mood to wear a black sweater?" Ivy did her best Vanna White impression. "Look no further. How about a purple tank top? It's right here."

"You are very impressive," I told her. "Thank you." Then I smacked my brother's arm. "And you zip it, just because you've never organized anything in your entire life."

"Except his toolbox," Ivy whispered. "He's really particular about that. I borrowed one of those wrenchy things once and put it back in the wrong spot and it was a whole ordeal."

Cameron rolled his eyes, gently setting his hands on her shoulders. "Come on, let's go see if Ian needs help downstairs. Plugging in that TV might tax his brain too much."

Ivy laughed, and they left me alone in my bedroom. I could tell Greer had spent some time in here because it was the room that looked the most finished. The soft white bedding was perfectly fluffed, a furry blanket draped just so along the foot of the bed. A mountain of pillows in different shades of white and cream looked so inviting I almost cried.

Above the bed, she'd mounted the framed painting she'd done for me when she was in art school, a watercolor of mountains and towering green trees, an abstract representation of what we'd see from the front porch at Mom and Dad's house. And on my dresser, a framed picture of the whole family a few weeks before Dad died.

My eyes filled with tears as I traced the image of his face. He was so thin, so tired, and so happy.

"I wish you could see all this, Dad," I whispered.

And for the first time, I had a breath-stealing thought. If he'd still been alive, it was entirely possible that none of this would have happened.

Not my night with Jax.

Not the baby.

This house or Dean or the tension with my siblings. The house that already felt like it was mine down to my bones.

None of it.

There'd be no building of this messy, little life. No glimpses of a future that I could see without trying very hard.

And the force of how wrong that all felt, to even *think* it, had my knees feeling weak. With my hand gripping the edge of the dresser, I tried to breathe steadily, because the last thing I needed was to toss myself straight into a existential panic attack.

If I'd gone home from that date and had my dad to talk to … I never would have gone to Jax's. Never would have talked myself into that, hanging that decision on the precipice of avoiding regrets.

There was nothing I'd undo about this. Not one piece, no matter how unclear things seemed, how quickly they changed, and how much it was forcing me to learn about myself.

No matter how much this was tilting my nicely planned world on its head.

The baby executed a strong kick, and I pressed the tips of my fingers to the side of my belly.

"You are worth everything," I whispered. They moved again, and I laughed. "You've been quiet today, huh?" I rubbed my palm over the press of a little foot or an elbow or something, wondering how much they could feel when I pushed back. "I know, it's a lot of excitement."

I tilted my head back, willing the tears to go back the hell wherever they came from.

A burst of laughter filtered upstairs, and I smiled. As much as I was ready for the quiet, ready to lay on the couch and stare at the ceiling in complete and utter silence, I knew to cherish nights like this.

I wasn't scared of this change. Wasn't afraid to live on my own or worried about locking doors or anything like that. But it was a little daunting when you've lived your whole life with a revolving door of your loved ones constantly in and out, to be faced with nothing but silence greeting me when I came home.

With a sigh, I straightened and brought a small box of makeup into the bathroom, eyeing the bathtub with a slight whimper. Later. When everyone was gone, I was filling that bitch with epsom salts and lighting some candles and I was going to soak out all the soreness screaming in my feet and hips.

What I needed was a massage. Head to toe.

Gone were the days when I could be on my feet all the time, that was for sure. They felt puffy when I leaned over to stack clean towels in the cabinets opposite the shower. To the right of the cabinet was a small box, and I eyed the marker on the side.

Laundry room.

"Oh sure," I muttered. "*I know how to read*, he says." I whipped out my phone and scanned the QR code on the side to make sure it was correct, rolling my eyes when a list of laundry items came up. "No one wants to listen to me. I'm just the one who came up with the system."

The box was small enough that I didn't think I'd get yelled at for carrying it downstairs, and thankfully, everyone was busy enough that they didn't even notice. In fact, the main floor was empty when I got to the family room. A slight twinge in my lower back and a dull ache through my hips had me groaning a little bit.

It wasn't until I walked through the kitchen and caught a glimpse of Cameron, Ivy, and Greer in the backyard talking to Jax that he caught my eye through the big window.

The actual time of eye contact was quick. Nothing more than a few seconds. And I felt the weightless dip in my stomach like he was doing that thing he'd done the other night —the slightest brush of his nose against my hair.

Dammit.

I steeled my mind from backsliding into sex thoughts, striding as confidently through the kitchen as I could manage, given the slight waddle to walking from my screaming hips. The laundry room was a long rectangle, with a small stretch of counter to the right of the machines. Above the counter, as well as the washer and dryer were upper cabinets, painted a creamy white color. The walls in this room were a soft pale green that reminded me of spring.

With a slight grunt, I set the boxes onto the counter and backtracked into the kitchen to find a pair of scissors to slice through the packing tape. Just as I found one, the slider opened, and Jax let himself inside the house.

My throat went dry because I'd lost all my loud, distracting family members.

What good was it having them here if they couldn't interfere in moments like this, when my traitor brain and traitor hormones had a field day with his presence. I swear, I could smell him the moment he came inside and closed the door behind him.

"I can take care of those boxes," he said.

"It's fine," I told him. "Knowing you, you'll put the detergent too high up and my short ass won't be able to reach it when I go to do laundry."

I said it teasingly, but the man stopped, blocking my entry to the laundry room.

Arching my eyebrows, I ignored the way he held his hand out for the scissors. "Can you move, please?" I asked.

"No."

I scoffed. "Jax, move. I can unpack them myself." With the hand not holding the scissors, I tried to push him aside, but holy shit, it was like trying to uproot a very stubborn tree. "You cannot be serious."

He crossed his arms, and the ink rippled with the sudden bulge in his biceps. My skin went hot, and there was a dangerous tremble under my skin that I wanted gone.

No man should look like him, I thought frantically. They shouldn't look so appealing with no smile and no people skills, and the overbearing tendency to ignore me when I just wanted to unpack a fucking box.

It was the eyes. As I glared up at him, I couldn't help but

register the slightest hint of amber around the edges. And it was the jaw—covered with dark hair because he still hadn't shaved since he got back.

"Move, please," I tried again, voice softer this time. There was a flicker in his eyes, and I fought a triumphant smirk. Yet he still didn't move.

"Isn't there something else you can work on while we're all here?"

"No," I said in exasperation. "I'd really like to work on this, so that the kitchen and laundry room are done."

He held his hand out again. "Great. I'll do it. You go sit and rest."

Under my breath, I growled.

"Cute," he said. "You sound like an angry little kitten."

I pointed the scissors at his stupid face. "Move."

Jax swatted my hand away. "No. Let me take care of this for you."

You know what was horrible? When your traitor brain and traitor hormones felt a swell of skin-tingling attraction at really inopportune times. It was like a warm, prickling wave from the top of my head to the tips of my toes. All ten toes. All the hairs on my head too.

"This kind of overbearing caveman bullshit isn't cute," I whispered fiercely, but there was a slightly breathless quality to my voice that gave me away.

That was a traitor too.

"It's not meant to be cute," he said. "You're tired. I can see it in your face. You need to sit."

I tossed the scissors onto the counter, where they clattered uselessly to the floor, then I wrapped both hands around the unforgiving muscle of his arm and pulled. Hard. He set his jaw, the muscle bunching at the edge, unfolding his arms to gently pluck my hands off him.

I deflated. "This is ridiculous." I gestured to the scissors a mile away on the ground. "And now I have to bend over. You have no idea how hard that's getting already because your giant, somersaulting baby has wrecked my center of gravity."

Jax's lips twitched, like he was fighting a smile, and with a slight eye roll, he stepped forward to snag the scissors off the floor.

"Ha," I yelled, edging through the opening he left and darting into the laundry room.

He muttered a curse under his breath. I snatched the scissors from his hand before he could yank them away, sliced the box open, and pulled out the first laundry detergent container.

My hand curled around the cabinet knob of the door farthest to the right, and Jax slammed his hand on the edge. I turned, gaping up at him.

"*What* is the matter with you?"

His jaw was still tight, and gawd, with the way he *loomed* over me, I felt positively engulfed by heat and the crisp clean smell, the highest hint of fresh cut grass from whatever he was doing outside. Looking down at me, his eyes were hard, yes, but there was a slightly panicked edge that had me dropping my hand. "Just let me do it," he said.

"No," I said—again, with the breathy thing. I was so annoyed with myself I could scream. "This is insane."

The only logical reaction to that kind of insanity was measured violence. It was either that or I was going to whirl in place and do something really stupid like press my nose against his chest and just … inhale him. I jammed my elbow into his stomach, and he dropped his arm with a shocked gust of air.

Wrenching open the cabinet, I felt a sick thrill of victory, but my hand froze in midair, then slowly lowered until the detergent sat on the counter.

"What…" I whispered.

The cabinet was full already—perfectly organized bins with printed labels on the front of each. Mouth hanging open, my eyes scanned over the brand new items that I recognized from the cart next to him at the hardware store. The cart he'd walked away from, so I assumed it was someone else's.

Jax stepped back, the loss of his body heat almost immediate.

"What is all this?" I asked.

One of his hands hung off the back of his neck, and he could hardly make eye contact. "It's just … I kept thinking about how you'd be alone. And I know everyone is close, but when the weather is bad or something happens, you can't always wait for help, you know."

His cheeks were slightly pink, and my heart turned over in my chest—a slow, unsteady roll.

"Why didn't you want me to see it?" I asked.

Jax clenched his jaw again, his thumb tapping rapidly against the countertop. The thick line of his throat worked on a swallow, the light in his eyes so hot and intense that I could hardly breathe. He licked at his bottom lip, and that small, insignificant movement drew my eyes to his mouth.

This was so wrong. Knowing how wrong it was didn't stop it from feeling so incredibly right either. Like he wrapped his hand around my spine and pulled, I felt the tug toward his body, and I swayed as my eyes fluttered shut.

A knock on the front door had me yanking back. Jax backed up a step too, but the look on his face didn't move a single centimeter. The blazing heat, the staggering desire I saw in his face had my pulse tearing sky high.

"Poppy?"

My mom's voice had me blinking down at the ground. "Back here," I called.

"The kids and I decided to bring some sustenance."

Olive and Sage ran around the corner, oohing and aahing about the house and big backyard.

"You have a meadow," Olive gasped, pressing her little face to the slider. "Can I go look at the flowers?"

"Of course, sweetie. Knock yourself out."

Sage yanked the slider open for Olive, and they ran into the backyard. My mom came around the corner, carrying two bags of food in her hands. "Everything looks wonderful, Poppy."

She wrapped me in a hug, and even though I wanted to look away from Jax, I couldn't.

My heart galloped in my chest the longer neither one of us broke the breathless eye contact. I thought Jax would smile. Thought he'd do something to ease this discomfort pressing against the seams of my entire being. But he didn't.

He just stared right back.

My whole body trembled, and my mom must have sensed something was off because she hummed, tightening her arms like my only tether to the ground. "You okay?" she whispered.

Instead of answering, I buried my head in her shoulder and let out a slow, deep breath.

No. I wasn't okay.

When I opened my eyes again, Jax was gone.

Chapter 29

Jax

If this Monday didn't feel long enough, the two idiots on either side of me were determined to make it feel ten times longer.

"She text you back?"

Rob nodded, tossing his phone to Dipshit. "Acted like she hadn't ghosted me for the whole fucking week."

Next to me, Wade sighed. Heavily. I pressed the nail gun to the frame, hitting the trigger three times as quickly as possible.

I'd nail every square inch of the framing if it would drown out the sound of the voices.

Dipshit glanced at the phone and whistled. "That's what she said?"

Rob gave him a look. "You see what I said back?"

"*Bro.*"

I growled, slamming the nail gun down onto the work horse. "If you two don't zip it, I'm going to staple your mouths shut."

Dipshit's eyebrows shot up. "That feels like an excessive reaction."

"I just want to get our work done, and you two never stop talking," I yelled.

Rob leaned closer to Dipshit. "He's been in a bad mood the past few weeks. You missed a lot before you got hired."

"What did I just say, kid?" I snapped.

Rob grinned. "He came home from this big long trip because he gets four times more vacation than the rest of us, found out he's gonna be a daddy with the boss's sister, and his panties have been in a wad ever since."

Dipshit's eyes widened. "Greer?"

Wade muttered something under his breath. I slicked my tongue over my teeth, pinning him with a glare so potent that I hoped it shriveled his balls.

Rob burst out laughing. "Can you imagine?" He wiped at an imaginary tear under his eye, then shook his head. "The other one. The one who was here last week."

"No cap?" Dipshit asked.

Wade's brow furrowed. "*No cap*? What does that mean?" He looked at me for clarity. "Last week, they said Ian had a great flow, and I don't know what that means either, but it makes me want to gouge my eyes out when I hear it."

"Hair, man," Dipshit said. "It means his hair."

I pinched the bridge of my nose. "I swear, you two have a death wish."

Dipshit ignored me, looking suitably impressed at what he'd just discovered. "Poppy, huh?"

"I know, right," Rob said knowingly.

"Fucking legend." Dipshit gave me an appraising glance. "Banged the boss's little sister, huh?"

Chest roaring, I took a step forward. "You say *one* thing about her, and I will make you spit nails for a week."

He held up his hands. "Hey, more power to you. She's hot."

"What did I just say?" I yelled.

"It's a compliment," he said, backing up defensively.

"Didn't feel like one," I growled. "How about you go work elsewhere right now?"

Instead, he leaned up against the wall and gave me a head-to-toe study. "You seem to get very angry when the subject of Poppy comes up."

Wade flicked him a pointed look. "I think he gets this angry every time you open your mouth actually."

I took in a deep breath. Three more hours. I could keep my composure for three more hours. Dipshit nodded his head like my reaction was giving him all the information he needed. "I know exactly what's happening here." He glanced at Wade meaningfully. "My mom's a spiritual healer."

"I can't do it, Wade." I dropped my chin to my chest in defeat. "Make it stop."

Wade didn't make it stop. He *couldn't*. It was like a runaway fucking train, and at this point, I'd step in front of that train just to make this entire conversation go away.

"Do you feel like something in your life is out of alignment? Like, with the universe."

Rob nodded, face serious. "That makes a lot of sense actually. He's never happy."

I leveled him with another glare and snatched the nail gun off the table again. "Are you still talking?"

Dipshit looked between Wade and Rob. "It's more common than you think. Our bodies are a walking energy field. When our vibrations are low, we seek control in the wrong places, feel stress and anxiety and depression. But if you simply shift your thoughts," he said, laying a hand on my shoulder, "you can manifest the life you want once you're back in vibrational alignment."

Lifting my chin slowly, I held his gaze. "What's your name again, Dipshit?"

He smiled. "It's Trevor."

"Trevor?" I said slowly.

"Yeah?"

"If you don't take your hand off my shoulder, I will break it."

Smile fading, Trevor swallowed, carefully retracting the grip he had on my arm.

"Thank you," I told him calmly. "Can we get back to work now?"

The two of them moved away, thank God, and Wade snickered under his breath.

"What are you laughing at? You're probably vibrating at the wrong frequency too, old man."

Before he could answer, my phone rang where it was tucked into my back pocket. A familiar number popped up, and I stepped out of earshot before I answered.

"This is Jax."

"Jax, it's Molly over at Mountainside Living Center. Is this a good time?"

Rolling my neck until it cracked, I walked a few steps farther away from any of my coworkers. "Yeah, go ahead. He okay?"

"That's why I'm calling, actually. He's having a really good day today." My heart rate spiked when she paused. "He asked about you just now. Thought maybe I'd see if you had time to come for a visit."

It hardly registered that I told Wade I had to leave, and I ignored the shocked looks on everyone's faces, but I was jogging out to my truck as soon as I hung up the phone, blood humming with a strange mix of anticipation and apprehension.

The drive to the living center was one I hadn't taken in a long time, and the lush, green scenery passed in a blur, the silence in my truck a welcome reprieve from all the noise in my head—thoughts of almost kisses and forgotten conversations, of how fears lock down the rest of our world when we hardly even realize it.

Tucked back behind some towering trees, the brick covered building came into view, tall wooden beams holding up the covered portico that led to the locked entrance. I cranked the steering wheel into a spot at the back of the half-empty parking lot. A Monday afternoon wasn't a very popular time for a visit, and even though I'd been sitting for the better part of half an hour, I was completely out of breath while I waited for someone to buzz me inside the second set of doors.

Molly, the charge nurse for Henry's unit, lifted her head from where she was standing in front of a med cart, her wide smile setting something at ease in my chest. "Goodness, you didn't waste any time."

Vaguely, I shook my head. "How's he doing? Besides the good day."

She leaned against the cart with a rueful smile. "That man is as healthy as a horse. He'll probably outlive both of us."

Exhaling a quiet sigh of relief, I nodded. "I'm sorry I haven't been here since I got back. It's been … I've had a lot going on."

She waved that off, tucking her long braids behind her shoulder. "He did just fine while you were gone. We never needed that emergency number, so don't you even worry."

The last few times I was here, my presence seemed to agitate him more than anything, my visits thinning out because making it worse, even if he didn't understand why, was something I couldn't handle. I couldn't remember the last time he'd looked at me with even the slightest flicker of recognition. At least four years.

Glancing around the other residents in the dining room, I noticed quickly that Henry wasn't among them. Around the corner from the nurses' desk, the big space split off into two distinct rooms. One was the gathering area for large groups, with couches and chairs, and a big TV mounted on the wall with a piano set in the corner. Off to the other side, there was a room full of activity stations—almost like what you'd see for kids to be able to play make-believe.

But instead, this was for the residents, allowing them a space to do a job, something that made them feel good, feel needed and feel important. A woman wearing a bright red dress and matching lipstick sat in a rocking chair with a baby doll in her arms, patting the doll's back like she was trying to burp her after a meal. To her right was a changing table and a small bin of toys, like she was sitting in a nursery.

Empty today, but someplace I'd often found Henry was a worktable like you'd find in a garage—realistic-looking tools lining the pegboard wall, things he loved to tinker with, imaginary items he could fix.

Just to the side of that was a small office setup, and I recognized the Black gentleman sitting at the desk, shuffling through papers and using a large calculator. His frizzy white hair was longer than it was last time I was here, and just like the time before, he was sharply dressed—a crisp press to his white dress shirt, expensive looking suspenders and a smart bow tie around his neck.

It was Molly's uncle, and she told me once he used to be a high-profile prosecutor, then a circuit county judge.

He looked up at my entrance and smiled, heavy wrinkles bracketing his friendly eyes. "Do we have a meeting, young man?"

"Not today," I told him. "But I know you're a busy man."

His nod was slow, his eyes going distant for a moment. "Indeed, indeed."

Molly smiled at her uncle, then set her hand on my arm and tilted her head down the hallway that led to a securely fenced yard. "Henry's back there."

"Thank you," I told her.

With a gentle, understanding smile, she patted my arm. "Let me know if you need anything."

The rooms were quiet as I passed, only the occasional hum of a television show or some low level conversation filtering through opened doors. Each room looked like its own small front porch. Fake plants and flowers in big pots sat in front; a different color on each door made it look cheery and welcoming. Number seven—Henry's room—had a bright red door, something I'd asked for before he moved in because I hoped he'd recognize it from his old house. The flowers I'd brought before I left for Spain still looked fresh and new, and I let out a deep breath as I passed by, approaching the door to the outside space. A nurse's aide was walking with him, holding on this arm and pointing out things beyond the tall black iron fence.

He was nodding, and the clench in my chest grew when he tipped his chin up and laughed at something she said. There were only small whisps of white hair left on the top of his head, combed over in a neat line. Even though it was warm and sunny out, Henry wore a maroon cardigan over a blue dress shirt, his khaki pants hemmed to perfection over his brown leather dress shoes.

When I opened the door to join them, Henry glanced over his shoulder, his brow furrowing slightly. My heart was in my throat while I took slow steps in their direction, fixing my face into a pleasant sort of neutral, just in case the earlier moments of lucidity had ebbed.

"Nice afternoon, isn't it, Mr. Emerson?" I asked.

"Beautiful," Henry said, still staring at me with slightly curious eyes.

I let out a quiet exhale, relief easing some of the pressure under my ribs. We were already off to a better start than my last few visits. I gave the aide a slight nod, and she withdrew her arm from Henry's to give us a bit of space.

"You've got a nice view here," I told him, easing my hands into my pockets and standing shoulder to shoulder with him. "I like all those flowers."

Henry wasn't looking at the flowers, though. He was staring at me.

"I know you, don't I?"

A big, unnamed emotion trembled and groaned under the weight of this interaction, and I managed a slight nod. "You do," I said, risking that piece of information because of how much I missed him.

Briefly, he looked away, staring sightlessly at the beautiful meadow beyond the edge of the fence. "You're a lot bigger now, little pup."

The nickname hit me like a blow to my sternum, and I swiped a hand over my mouth, trying to contain the aching sound of relief before it escaped in a messy sob. It took a moment before I could look at him safely. "A bit, yeah," I managed.

Henry turned, settling his hand on my shoulder. "You still keeping my car clean? Keeping the house nice?"

I attempted a short nod, but a tear escaped before I could stop it. I cleared my throat and looked away, dashing a palm under my eye so he didn't notice. "Got someone new that moved in a couple of days ago," I told him.

"Family?"

"A woman about to have her first baby," I said, my voice tight with everything I was keeping on a trembling, taxed sort of leash. "You'd like her a lot."

"Good," he said. "That's good. That house needs someone to love it."

"She will," I whispered. "She'll make it a home. Did the moment she walked in."

"She pretty?"

"Beautiful," I told him. "Most beautiful woman I've ever seen."

His eyes were cloudier now than they used to be, surrounded by deep wrinkles and age spots, but when he turned them on me, I felt so stripped bare that suddenly I wanted to hide.

"Does that scare you, little pup?" he asked, as lucid as I'd seen him in years.

How badly I wanted to keep that admission buried, like letting it be said to someone somehow gave it more power.

"Terrifies me to the fucking bone, Henry."

His slow nod made me feel like that was the answer he expected.

"Probably means she's important then. The important ones always do that to you." He shuffled closer to the fence, wrapping one hand around the black iron, staring at those flowers like he used to when we played checkers out on his back deck. "I had someone like that once, I think. She left before I could tell her. Married someone else."

"You did?" I asked, head spinning. I knew better than to ask why he never told me before. These bursts of lucidity were few and far between, a mysterious, confusing gift of time that I knew better than to question.

He blinked a few times, and I fought the urge to push.

"You give her flowers when she moved in?" he asked. "Women like flowers."

"Not yet." My throat was scratchy and dry, my eyes felt like someone raked them with twenty grit sandpaper. "You think I should?"

"Good ones, too," he said. "Those pretty wild ones that you can't get in a store."

"I know just the kind."

His hand shook slightly as he removed it from the fence. "I have a field behind my house," he said. "Do you know where it is?"

I dropped my chin to my chest and fought for composure, unable to look up again until I could unclench my teeth and breathe through the pain of watching him slip away again. "I think so, yeah."

Distractedly, he nodded. "Good. That's good."

Tipping my head up, I stared at the blue sky until my eyes burned.

"You shouldn't be scared of her, you know," Henry said quietly. "Whoever she is."

Rubbing the back of my neck, I gave him a long look. "No?"

"Nah. Because if you're this scared, then she probably is too." He tapped a finger to his nose. "That's the key to knowing. We only run scared from the things that matter. And every time we do, they just get bigger in our minds until we can't see anything past that. Until you wake up one day and realize that whatever you're afraid of isn't bigger than the thing you want. Don't have that moment too late, Jax. Believe me."

The sound of my name on his lips had me pinching my eyes shut, the frame of my body trembling dangerously as I tried to keep everything in.

"You're always right, Henry," I told him when I managed to open them again to look at him. And even though this terrified me to the fucking bone too, I set a hand on his shoulder. "You mind if I get a hug while we're out here? I think I could use one."

His face wrinkled in a smile, the kind I hadn't seen in years, and when he wrapped his arms around me, I held him as tightly as I could manage without hurting him. He smelled like Old Spice and slightly musty clothes, and all the tension in my muscles ebbed as we stood there.

"You were the best thing in my life until her," I whispered. "I hope you know that."

Knowing I might never get him like this again, I felt another tear escape, and I rolled my lips together, fighting more that wanted to follow it.

Henry patted my back lightly, pulling away to tap the side of my face like I was a kid. "Right back at you, little pup." His eyes traced over my face. "Maybe … maybe you could shave before you bring her those flowers. You look like a yeti."

I barked out a laugh, and he smiled, still absently patting my arm as we started walking back toward the building.

"You gonna go see her tonight?" he asked, pointing off

toward the west, where some dark clouds were rolling heavy across the sky, still a far ways off but ominous all the same. "I think those storms might be headed our way."

An idea hit me like a lightning bolt—clear and bright and perfect. "Maybe I will."

"You want to stay for a game of checkers first? And maybe dinner too?" he asked. "I think they're doing grilled cheese today. It's not half bad."

"Yeah," I answered softly. "I'd like that."

Chapter 30

Jax

The absolute worst thing about working with Rob and Dipshit were the stupid words they used, and how quickly they'd been burned into my brain. Tonight's word of choice?

Simp.

I had to google it when they used it the first time because they both thought it was so fucking funny. So in the safety of my truck, without their nosy asses anywhere close by, I tapped my big thumbs on the too-small screen of my phone.

Simp: to show excessive devotion, or longing, for someone or something.

With a small grocery bag clutched in my hand, letter shoved into the back pocket of my jeans and hair damp from the walk from where I'd parked, I knocked on Poppy's door. She didn't answer right away, but I knew she was up. There were lights on inside when I drove by before parking next to the garage.

The porch light flipped on, then the sound of the dead bolt disengaged. When she cracked the door open, it was her widened eyes that had me thinking about that fucking word again.

"Jax?" she asked. "What are you doing here?"

The honest answer threatened to bolt from the tip of my tongue.

Simping. I was fucking *simping.* And even if someone paid me a million dollars, I'd never admit that I used that word, even in my own thoughts.

But God, it felt right. Being here, simply because I was thinking about her, wanting to be near her, it felt so fucking right. I was pretty sure I'd fall to my knees if she asked, and do it with a smile on my face.

Hadn't she earned that after all this time?

Instead of saying any of that, I held the bag out without a word and waited for her to take it. The door opened more fully, and damn if I didn't devour the sight of her like this.

She was in a soft-pink pajama set, a tank top tight over her chest and belly, short shorts riding high on her legs, and fuzzy pink slippers covering her feet. Poppy was wearing a bra, but not much of one, and through the pastel cotton, I could see the slightest shadow of her nipples. I tore my eyes away, fixing them instead on her face as she studied the bag like it might explode if she touched it.

"It's not going to bite," I told her wryly.

A crack of thunder made her tense, and her eyes pinched shut as she set a hand on her chest and laughed under her breath. "Sorry, the storm has me jumpier than I thought."

"I thought you might be." The words came out lower than intended, a slightly desperate edge making my voice husky like I'd chewed nails on my ride over.

Her brow furrowed delicately as she studied me, then slowly reached out for the bag gripped in my hand. Her fingers brushed over mine, and she swallowed visibly before opening it up.

Poppy's mouth fell open as she stared down into the bag. "How did you…?" She shook her head a little. "How did you know?"

"You told me."

Her eyes snapped up to mine. "I did?"

I nodded. "When you got to my house that night." I cleared my throat. "You told me about you and your dad and storms." The edge of her white teeth dug into her lush, pink bottom lip as she stared up at me. "I didn't want…" I paused, trying to figure out how to say it. "I hated the thought of you sitting here alone when it started storming."

The words didn't come easily, but I said them instead of locking them up or holding them back. Each step forward felt a little bit less scary.

"So you drove in the middle of a storm to bring me ice cream," she said slowly, like she was trying to understand exactly what was happening.

With a tight jaw and an ache in my throat, I managed a nod.

Poppy's eyes were huge in her face, searching mine so deeply that it dissolved that ache, melting it away bit by bit by bit.

"Will you come in and have some with me?" she asked, chin tilted and gaze direct.

I think she expected me to say no. That I was just dropping it off, and I'd retreat behind the safety of our established lines.

I took a step closer, and she sucked in a sharp breath at my nearness. "I'd love to," I said roughly.

Poppy's eyelids fluttered slightly as she backed up, a tiny shake of her head like she couldn't quite get her bearings.

I left my boots by the front door, and I followed her into the house, breathing in the scent of her that already lingered in the air. The couch and chairs faced the flickering TV over the mantel, and the fuzzy blanket tucked in the corner told me where Poppy's favorite seat was. Behind one of the chairs, she had a soft lamp on, which cast a warm light over the room. She'd lit a candle in the kitchen—something clean and citrusy. Boxes were still stacked in the dining room behind the circular table, but the house already looked like a home.

In one day, she'd managed to fill the space with some inviting energy that I'd been unable to master in the twelve years I'd been in my place.

Poppy set down the bag and pulled open the drawer in front of her, laughing quietly when she had to open the one next to it. "Still don't know where my silverware is," she said, handing me a spoon. She fished a couple of bowls from the cabinet to the left of the sink, and as she reached up to grab them, I couldn't stop myself from admiring the curve of her backside in the shorts, the lean length of her legs. Her hair was pulled back in a messy bun at the nape of her neck, tendrils of dark hair around her face and shoulders.

"What sounds good?" she asked, eyes locked on the two containers of ice cream.

You. I'll take you on the counter.

Roughly, I swallowed, tapping the top of the cookie dough. "That one, please."

"I should have known," she said lightly. "The one with cookies in it."

"You know, I never thought I could be turned off from cookies, but Ivy came really close to proving me wrong."

Poppy exhaled a laugh, shaking her head as she pried the top off the first container. Using an ice cream scoop with a mint-green handle, she dished up a couple of scoops into a bowl and pushed it toward me, sucking a small spot of ice cream off her thumb.

There was no tearing my eyes away from that mouth.

As she dished up the chocolate into a second bowl, I noticed her rotating her ankle with a slight grimace on her face.

"What's wrong?"

Her eyebrows popped up. "Oh, nothing. My feet just hurt from moving this weekend. I didn't wear the right shoes to

322

work, and I was in the warehouse more than usual today. We had drama with some of the new software, which was messing up all the shipping processes."

Dropping a spoon into each bowl, then setting the ice cream scoop into the sink, Poppy turned to put the ice cream into the freezer. I stepped back to let her lead the way.

The lightning flashed bright in the room, illuminating her profile as she tucked herself into the corner of the couch. In the dim light of the room, her eyes were liquid and dark, leveled right at me while she tried to gauge what was happening. I fought the urge to blurt everything out, but deep in my gut, I knew letting it unfold slowly was better.

"Do you want to start a movie?" she asked, pulling the blanket up over her legs, covering most of her chest as well. Which was good for my sanity, if I was being honest.

I shrugged between bites of ice cream. "I'm not the one with control of the remote. That's you, boss," I pointed out.

Her lips curled around the spoon, which she aimed at me after she cleaned it off. "That is a new nickname I can get behind."

I held her gaze. "You'd miss it if I stopped calling you angel."

The low timbre of my voice had her blinking rapidly, and she dropped her eyes, taking another bite of the ice cream. When she glanced up again, she watched me with a curious twist to her lips. Thunder rumbled outside, but the sound was farther away, the storm moving past us slowly. The rain hadn't abated yet, and the consistent pattering on the windows made the room seem smaller and more intimate than it would have been during the day.

"You left without saying goodbye on Saturday."

Ice cream gone, I set my bowl down and hummed, stretching my arm along the back of the couch, leveling my gaze to hers steadily. "I did."

"Even Cameron didn't know you'd left."

"Your brother is really dramatic when he feels left out."

She laughed. "I just wish I could've thanked you for all your help."

I dropped my hand, nudging her knee where it was tucked up against the couch underneath the blanket. "I'm right here."

Poppy ducked her face down, drawing up an edge of the blanket to cover her mouth. Which was a fucking shame because I could stare at her lips all day.

"Thank you," she said quietly, playing with the edge of the blanket with the tips of her fingers. "We got so much done. I still can't believe it." Then she groaned. "My feet do, though. It's been a couple of days, and they still hurt."

Knowing full well it was a bad fucking idea and might derail my entire plan, I slid my hand down and tapped her ankle.

Her brows furrowed. "What?"

I angled one leg toward the back of the couch and settled one of the eighteen throw pillows in my lap, easing her legs forward until her heels rested on the pillow. Carefully, I pulled the first slipper off and tossed it onto the floor, followed by the second.

The room was so quiet, I could hear the thud of my heart in my ears. Maybe she could too.

"Jax, no, you don't have to," she started, then stopped when my thumbs dug into the arch of her foot, her head lolling back onto the couch with a groan. "Never mind," she moaned. "Keep … keep doing that, please."

My lips curled into a faint smile, and I pressed my fingers in deeper, pushing along the ball of her foot. I used both hands on one foot for a few minutes, watching the flickering reactions on her face when I'd hit a particularly tender spot.

The silence in the room was punctuated by her slight shifting on the couch, and she sucked in a breath when I moved to the other foot, dragging both thumbs down the arch.

"Oh," she breathed. "That's good." Poppy rolled her lips between her teeth, like she was trying to keep her reactions quiet, and I questioned the sanity of telling her to stop doing that, stop holding it in. Telling her I wanted to hear everything.

I clenched my teeth and pushed my thumbs back up, pressing into the balls of her foot, rolling in small circles to relieve the tension. Or *that* tension, at least.

The other one would have to wait.

I was hard as a fucking rock from touching her feet. Months without sex would do that to a guy, apparently. Or maybe it was just because it was Poppy. Because I was in so deep and no desire to be anywhere else.

I wrapped my palm over the top of her ankle to hold her leg in place, and the moment my fingers brushed over her ankle bone, I noticed the shift in her breathing. The blanket shifted down, and my mouth went dry at the curves on display.

"I have an idea," I said evenly, dragging my thumbs firmly down her arch again, using pressure from where I held the top of her foot, watching the rise and fall of her chest.

"Mm-hmm," she hummed, almost unable to lift her lashes.

"We should play a game."

Her eyes snapped open, her whole body going still. "What?" Poppy pulled her feet back toward her as she sat up, the blanket pooling in her lap. "What game?"

The storm outside had nothing on us, because when I shifted forward, stretching my arm out along the back of the couch, the tips of my fingers brushed against the wild mess of her hair and that slight touch felt like it rocked the foundations of the entire house. With my thumb and forefinger, I tested the silky softness of the strands and hummed quietly.

Waiting until she fixed her slightly unfocused gaze back

onto mine, I breathed in the heady sensation of electricity that bounced back and forth between me and her.

Lightning bolts.

Dangerous and wild, highly unpredictable. I wanted to absorb it into my skin and let it ratchet up this moment between us.

Intensity rolled between us, sprawling across the room, a slight crackle in the air that I could feel over my skin.

Do something, I thought. *Do the scary thing.*

So I did.

"Truth or dare," I said simply, winding that tiny piece of hair around my finger, then letting it fall. "I'll go first."

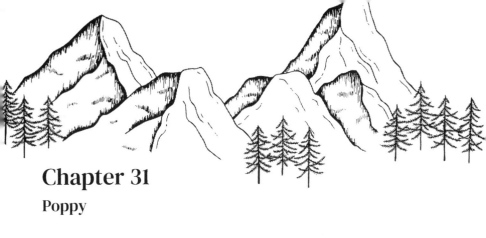

Chapter 31
Poppy

I was off the couch before I registered the decision to move, heart thrashing, brain scrambling for clarity.

When the distance between us was something that allowed me to breathe, I turned, hands digging into my hair as I stared at him. "Truth or dare," I repeated in a whisper.

Jax's eyes bored into mine—so bright and intense that my lungs were frozen trying to pull in air. "That's what you wanted, right?"

My eyebrows arched, a disbelieving scoff escaping my opened lips. "Yes, when I was drunk. My decision-making was not at its best that night."

Jax stood slowly, his gaze never dropping from mine. "Beg to differ, angel." The sharp rise and fall of my chest was pronounced, mainly because I was having a very hard time breathing, but his attention never wavered from my face. "Which is it, Poppy? Truth or dare?"

The room spun, my head spinning with it, and I desperately wanted it to land in one place.

Both options felt terrifying because everything at the base of this—his surprise presence, the way we'd danced over the line in the sand lately, the ice cream, the way he was looking at me—was as scary as anything I'd ever imagined between us.

One of my hands settled lightly on my hammering chest, and he took another careful step, erasing precious inches between us. "Or do you want to go first?" he asked. "Because I'm happy to do either."

Inhaling sharp through my nose, I watched him warily, lifting my chin in a dare. "No matter what I ask?"

"Try me."

What did I want to ask Jax? A million questions flashed in tandem, the bright pop of a camera bulb, and I tried to see through it, a little blinded by all my options. Brow furrowed, I stared down at the ground for a minute.

He took another step, and I forced myself not to retreat equally. Not because I was scared and not because I didn't *want* to be closer, but because the moment he came within touching distance, it felt like we were doomed.

Like there was no alternate end to this scene where it didn't end with us touching each other.

But I wanted more. I didn't want a limited flare of heat and the sating of an unquenchable thirst. I wanted his heart, and nothing less than that would do at this point.

"I know you've got something in there," he said gently. "A pretty list of things you've always wanted to know."

"That would've been smart," I whispered. The edge of his delicious mouth curled up, and the flickering heat I felt in response had my toes curling. Licking my suddenly dry lips, I tried to sift through everything I'd ever wanted to know, anything I'd ever wanted more clarity on, and came up entirely short, because there was really only one thing that mattered. One thing that would give me enough to press forward. Holding his gaze, I took a small step forward, and the flare in his eyes—triumph and desire—was exactly what I needed. "Okay, I'll play."

The muscle in his jaw flexed while he waited for me to continue.

"Truth or dare," I said.

There was no hesitation as he spoke. "Truth."

The thrumming of my pulse was all I could hear as I did too.

"Why did you come here tonight? Not the ice cream. Not the storm. Why are you doing all this?" I asked.

My heart was in a tight-fisted grip while I waited for him to answer, years and years of watching him from the sidelines melting into this one breathless moment of waiting. And the worst part, the very worst part, was the warm slide of hope that I felt climbing up my ribs.

It was unstoppable.

So powerful that I was helpless against it.

He knew I didn't want one night. Knew that anything less than everything would break my heart.

He knew.

And that knowing was the catalyst for all my yearning, and there was no stopping the way it spiraled high and hot, an overwhelming wall of heat that scorched me to the bone.

Jax's face was a thing of beauty while he searched for the right words to answer me—harsh in his features, handsome and hard and stern and so precious to me that I wished I could put it into words.

The space between us shrank again as he took another step, and I fought a wave of tears at the tender shift in his eyes. "I'm doing this because the chance of being with you is more important to me than anything I could possibly be afraid of."

A pin drop would've sounded like a scream in the pulse of silence that followed, and right on its heels, the violent crack down the middle of my chest at what his words did to me.

A tear slid down my cheek, but I didn't brush it away. "What are you afraid of?"

Jax watched that tear absorb into my skin, his frame expanding on a deep breath.

"That no matter what I do, no matter how hard I try, I'll

never quite be what you need. That I'll disappoint you or hurt you." He stepped closer again, sliding his fingers down my arms until his fingers ghosted over my knuckles. Skin tingling with the spring of goose bumps, I glanced down at the way he slid his rough, calloused fingers between mine. "That I'll give you the sad wreck of this heart in my chest, and it won't be enough to make you happy. And God, if anyone has ever deserved the perfect love, it's you, Poppy." His voice was so full of heartache and tightly leashed emotion, and when I looked up into his face, I felt another tear at the edge of my lips. "And I'd have to go the rest of my life knowing you'd wasted all this time on someone who doesn't know how to love the right way."

That hope clashed mightily with the urge to fling myself into his arms, but I held myself in check, a roaring bark of self-preservation interrupting the movie-perfect ending of this night.

"You're afraid of getting hurt," I said. His hands tightened in mine, and eventually, he nodded. "So am I," I whispered brokenly. Jax's brow furrowed. "Hearing you say all this is…" I stopped, disentangling my hand from his and laying it on my chest. "It's what I've always wanted. But I have this awful voice in the back of my head screaming *why*. Why now? Is it just because of the baby? Is it—"

"It's not because of the baby." He interrupted firmly. His eyes were blazing, and my heart wrenched sideways, a dangerous squeezing of that fickle hope again. "Truth or dare, Poppy."

I blinked a few times. "What?"

He dipped his head, the edge of his nose following my hairline, his ribs expanding on a deep breath that made my pulse dance. "Truth or dare, angel. I suggest picking the second."

"D-dare," I said quietly.

"Smart girl," he said in a growling whisper against my

skin, an onslaught of heat right on its heels. Jax withdrew his other hand from mine and reached into his back pocket, holding out a cream-colored envelope with battered edges and my name written on the front. "I dare you to read this, angel."

With trembling hands, I took the envelope from his grip, curiosity and a heartsick sort of joy threatening to swamp me. Unfolding the paper, my breath caught when I saw the date, a Spanish hotel letterhead, and the sight of my name in messy block letters in blue ink.

"What is this?" I whispered.

He didn't answer. I probably wouldn't have heard him anyway because the sound of my thrashing heart roared in my ears.

Dear Poppy,

I can't stop thinking about you, and I don't know what that means. Instead of trying to find the perfect words to explain the mess in my head the past three months, I'll make sense of this in a way that makes sense to you.

Times Poppy Wilder has literally scared me into hiding

-on your 21st birthday, you wore a blue dress. I saw you from behind at the bar, not knowing it was you. Do you remember? I approached while you weren't watching and told the bartender I'd buy your next drink. When you turned, I felt it like a punch to the gut. That was the first time I ran. Not the last, though.

-the next Christmas, you knit everyone scarves.

They were terrible. You were the only one to give me a present that year. Mine was blue and white and gray, and when you gave it to me, it was the softest thing I'd ever felt, and the look in your eyes when I opened it is why I left for two weeks after the holiday. I kept the box on my kitchen table for six months, where I could see it every day because when I saw it, I pictured your face. Every fucking day.

-When your car broke down the following spring, and Cameron and I picked you up after class. You were singing a song in the back seat. It was the first time I heard you sing. I left for a week, and I listened to that song in my tent. Every fucking day.

-On your twenty-third birthday, you organized that fundraiser for the animal shelter. I told Cameron I couldn't go, but I drove downtown anyway. You were walking three puppies, and one kept trying to eat your shoelaces. You sat in the middle of the parking lot and laughed while they climbed all over you. It made my chest hurt, seeing that kind of goodness. I left for two weeks after that.

-Every time you come to the jobsite, it's like you bring the sunshine with you, and I don't know if you realize how powerful that is. You're kind to everyone—listening to what they have to say, not

332

bullshit fake listening, but like you actually care. You laughed at something I said to Wade once, and it was the first time I heard someone's laughter and wanted to hear it again and again and again. I left after that too.

I could give you a dozen lists, Poppy. The parts of you that are kind and good and thoughtful and why you're the most beautiful woman I've ever met. Things I see in you that make me want more. Want everything. And when you've spent your entire life avoiding exactly that, it made you the most terrifying thing I could be around. I made excuses every single day for why it wouldn't work and why I didn't really feel those things, and why it would pass. Why it should pass.

But it didn't.

It hasn't.

I find myself wondering if this is what it was like for you all those years. If you picked apart every moment, every word exchanged. Because that's what I do. What I've done for three months. Twelve weeks. Eighty-four days.

The way you looked at me. The way you laughed. The smile that you gave me. The way you felt in my arms. How incredible it was to wake up with you next to me.

Poppy, every time I roll over in the middle of

the night, in that in-between space of being asleep and being awake, I wanted the warmth of someone, and it was never there. Even when I wasn't alone, I never found that moment, the click of a puzzle piece. Until you.

I don't know what I'm ready for, but I know that I want you.

More of you. In whatever way you're willing to give me.

With a hand covering my mouth and my heart *wild*, I scanned the words again, making sure I wasn't dreaming this, some mind-fuck hormonally fueled dream that would disappear if someone pinched me.

My cheeks were wet with tears when I clutched the letter to my chest and finally lifted my gaze to his. "You've … you've had this with you since you got back?" A sob threatened to break free. "When I got in your truck at the store, this is what you had in your hand?"

He nodded, eyes clear and direct and earnest.

"Y-you left all those times because of me?" I whispered brokenly.

At my stunned realization, at the stunning truth of it, his gaze filled with so much warmth it almost took me to my knees.

"I think I couldn't let myself look at who you really were because once I did, you were the only thing I'd see."

This was real.

Oh God, this was *real*.

Jax's hand coasted up my arm, over my shoulder, until his big palm was anchored at the back of my neck while his eyes locked breathlessly on mine. "I don't just want more of you,

Poppy. I want all of you," he said in a rough whisper, something torn straight from his heart. "If you need time, if you need me to prove to you that I mean this—that I'm not going anywhere—then I'll wait, Poppy. I'll be patient because fuck, have you earned my patience. I'll be whatever you need me to be in your life, but I couldn't let a single day pass without you knowing what's in here." Gently, he picked up my free hand and settled it on the warm wall of his chest. "*You* are in here." When I curled my fingers into his shirt, refusing to let go, he slid his palm down my arm, splaying his big fingers wide on my bump. "And you," he whispered.

I melted into him, my forehead resting against his shoulder as he withdrew his hand from my neck, curling it around my shoulder to pull me closer. He exhaled heavily, pressing his mouth against the top of my hair.

And my heart. My heart, shaking so mightily that it threatened to burst, only started to settle once he had me in his arms. I snaked my arms around his middle, the warmth of his body seeping deliciously into mine while we stood there and breathed each other in.

From my belly, a mighty little kick smacked right where his hand was, and both our heads snapped up.

"Did you feel that?" I whispered.

Jax's mouth hung open, and he stared down at my stomach. "Holy shit," he breathed.

I exhaled a shocked laugh, shifting his hand a little to the right and pressing it down further.

Bump.

Bump bump.

Jax let out a short burst of air, easing to his knees in front of me so he could cradle the sides of my belly with both of his hands. Eyes full of awe and jaw hanging open, he stared in front of him like it was the most incredible thing he'd ever seen. My heart was too big for my chest, unable to hold all these big, incredible feelings, and I was happy for the momentary reprieve. Gently, I sifted my fingers through Jax's hair while he set his forehead on my belly.

"Hello in there," he said quietly.

I smiled, and when he tilted his face up, setting his chin on my belly, the look in his eye made my heart quiver with anticipation.

"Our game got derailed," I said softly.

He hummed, lids heavy and gaze heated. "It did. Do you want to keep playing?"

"Maybe."

Jax took a deep breath and stood again, towering over me in a way that, with any other man, it would've felt claustrophobic or threatening. But it didn't because it was him.

One of his hands came up to cup my face, the tips of his fingers tangling in my hair. His thumb brushed over my cheekbone, and I closed my eyes at how good it felt.

How good and how right and how perfect. I tried to imagine waiting for any of this, waiting so that he could pass some invisible test.

There was no freaking way.

What I wanted and what I needed were finally, finally in alignment.

"Truth or dare," I asked him, hands curling into the front of his shirt.

"Dare," he said, an urgent sort of edge to his voice that had me narrowing my eyes.

"Yeah?"

Jax nodded, cradling my jaw with his other hand now too, the edge of his thumb tracing the line of my bottom lip as he exhaled shakily.

"So many options," I murmured, my eyelids fluttering shut at the gentle, inciting touches. "How will I ever choose?"

Jax made a delicious humming noise from the back of his throat that lifted every tiny little hair on my arms.

"Remember what you told me that night?" he asked, eyes

tracking over every inch of my face like he couldn't get enough. Like he couldn't get enough of *me*. "You stared down everything that scared you, and it was so fucking brave, Poppy. I couldn't have done that."

I smiled, curling my hands around his wrists. "You're doing it now," I reminded him.

"Then dare me again," he said, his voice lowering to a pitch that had the hairs raising on the back of my neck because it was heavy with want. "What you wanted to do that night, angel. Do you remember?"

If I wasn't so fucking turned on, I would've laughed. If I wasn't anchored so tightly to the bliss of this entire conversation, I might have cried. But I didn't do either. I was clear-eyed and ready. So was he.

In the feeble cage of my chest, my heart pounded.

My grip tightened on his wrists, and I held his gaze unflinchingly. "I dare you to kiss me."

Jax dipped his head further, his nose brushing against mine for a moment, then finally, finally, his lips ghosted over mine as he spoke. "Do you know how long I've wanted this, angel?"

I smiled. He pressed the heat of his chest along mine, one arm wrapping tightly around my waist while he tilted my face up with his other hand, the pressure of his thumb along the line of my chin a sweet sort of prelude to this earth-shattering tipping point we'd been riding for days and weeks and months.

I cradled his jaw with one of my hands and pulled back to meet his fiery gaze, a spark of courage flaring hot in my chest. "Buddy, you're just catching up. I've been waiting a lot longer than you," I told him.

Jax's face split into a wide, happy grin as he laughed—the straight white teeth against his stubbled jaw, the brackets around his mouth, and the faint lines around his dark, dark eyes had my heart soaring, my soul stretching into some blissful, sweet place that I'd already dreamed of.

His smile faded, replaced immediately with heat and toe-curling intent. And then finally, *finally*, Jax Cartwright—the man who I'd loved for as long as I knew the word—dipped his head, slanted his mouth over mine, and with a chest-rattling groan, he kissed me.

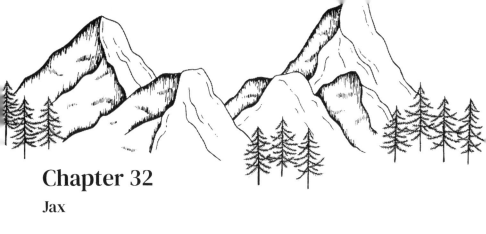

Chapter 32
Jax

One thing was exceptionally clear. Every second I spent not kissing Poppy Wilder was a monumental fucking waste of time.

Tilting my head to lick into her mouth, I felt a shiver wrack my frame when the wet heat of her tongue slid around my own. Her lips, just as soft and sweet and firm as I'd imagined, pushed and pulled against mine while we traded breaths, traded sounds of pleasure and longing. I sucked on her bottom lip, and her quiet whimper lit that feeling under my skin, the fierce drive to take more, kiss deeper, touch harder.

My hands shook where I clutched her body to mine, sliding over her back, filling my palms with the firm curves of her backside while she writhed against the thigh I had wedged between hers.

Every inch of her body was warm and soft and curved, and I could spend all night just mapping the spaces that I hadn't spent near enough time on during her night in my bed. There were freckles along her shoulders and collarbone, each tiny dot something that should be counted and memorized, kissed and kissed and kissed.

I dragged my nose along the edge of her jaw and inhaled

deeply while she curled her hands around my shoulders and held me tightly to her. Taking her mouth again, everything in my head distilled down to this perfect fucking kiss. Poppy arched her back and moaned when I speared my hands into her hair and fisted the silky strands.

Now I *knew* I'd done something really great in another life. Saved a city from destruction or cured a disease or stopped a war because it sure wasn't anything I'd done in this one to deserve a moment like this. To deserve her. To deserve anything like what I felt just by kissing her.

The world expanded in a heartbeat, growing to something so big and stunning, a dizzying kind of desperation had my hands clutching her tighter, wanting to feel more and more and more as I pressed her sweet, curved body against the wall behind us.

What was this feeling clawing at my chest?

I wanted to fuck her.

I wanted to hold her.

I wanted to kiss her for hours and feel her weight in my arms, and I'd be the happiest I'd ever been in my entire life.

I wanted to love her for the rest of this life and into the next one and the one after that. For as many as I'd get with her.

Ripping my mouth away, I sucked in a sharp breath and studied her kiss-abused lips and blown-out pupils, the high color on her cheeks. I rolled my forehead against hers and gently kissed her top lip, then her bottom, helpless admissions climbing up my throat that I did nothing to stop.

Not anymore.

"You are so beautiful, it hurts," I said, the words aching as they escaped.

Everything ached, actually. Whatever piece of my heart she'd claimed for her own, it whittled away all my reservations and pumped blood through my veins to the sound of her name. Poppy's eyes glossed over with tears, like she could hear all my thoughts, and for a moment, I wondered if she couldn't.

If anyone was able to slice past my reserve, my inability to put voice to the things I wanted, that I feared and craved, it was her.

With a steadfast heart that couldn't be swayed and a determination that could crack through the firmest of walls, this beautiful creature had chosen me to love, and I'd spend the rest of my life being worthy of it.

"Don't cry, angel," I whispered.

"I'm happy," she whispered back. She kissed me deeply, a relieved moan slipping from her mouth to mine. Poppy pulled away and smiled, and I wanted to ink that smile onto my fucking soul. "I'm so happy, it hurts."

My lips edged up in a crooked smile, the tips of my fingers roaming over the high, graceful cheekbones, the sharp cupid's bow on her pink lips and the dimple that appeared when she smiled a true, genuine smile.

They tracked down the line of her jaw, tracing the graceful line of her throat as she swallowed. A helpless shiver wracked her frame as my fingers moved to her cheekbones, edging along the curves of her shoulders, over the edge of her shirt and the heaving warmth of her mouthwatering cleavage.

I ducked my head and whispered soft, unintelligible words against her skin while my palms coasted over her upper arms and down the line of her waist, curving over her belly before ghosting over the hard tips of her breasts. With the backs of my knuckles, I teased her there until she threw her head back on a helpless gasp.

"What do you need, Poppy?" I asked.

With a dazed, shaky exhale, she gripped my biceps and tugged my chest flush along hers. "You, just you," she begged. "Please, Jax."

With a groan, I slanted my mouth over hers again, the groan from my chest echoing in the quiet room as I licked against her tongue. She rolled up on her tiptoes, twisting her tongue against mine with a tilt of her head, then nipped at the tip when I tried to withdraw it from her mouth. Poppy and I stood like that, wrapped around each other, trading fierce kisses that snatched the air from my lungs and the thundering heart in my chest.

I pulled away from the kiss and cupped her face in my hands again, locking my eyes with hers. "Will you take me to your bed this time?" I asked evenly. "Or do you want to wait?"

With a heartbreakingly earnest expression on her face, she wound her fingers between mine and looked up at me in a way that had my chest cracking open. "This is real, isn't it, Jax? I'm not imagining this or—"

I cut her off with a hard kiss, pulling away almost immediately. "This is real," I said fiercely. "You and me and that baby and however many more we make, because now that I've kissed you," I paused, the heaving of my chest making my ears ring, "Poppy, now that I've kissed you, you're mine, and I won't give you back."

The smile started in her eyes, something warm and soft and full of promise, and she tugged on my hands, turning us until she was walking in front of me, leading the way to her very big, hopefully very sturdy bed.

At the landing at the base of the stairs, she whirled, eyeing my chest. "Shirt off."

After a glance over my shoulder to make sure the curtains were closed, I reached behind my shoulder blades to fist the shirt in one hand, pulling it over my head and tossing it onto the floor. Her eyes devoured every inch of skin as I uncovered it, and she licked at her bottom lip, dragging her fingers over the slope of my shoulders and dancing down the front of my biceps.

I jerked my chin up. "Your turn."

She gripped the bottom of her tank top with two hands and peeled it over her head, her hair slipping down over her shoulders as she stood one step above me. The sight of her smooth skin and curves had my mouth watering. I slid my hands over her bump, holding her gaze while I placed a soft kiss just above her belly button. Poppy shimmied the waistband of her shorts down her hips, and I decided that just standing there without helping was incredibly rude. I tucked my fingers into the top and tugged, dragging my knuckles along the skin of her outer thighs, grinning when she kicked them off. Cut high on her legs were simple white cotton briefs.

I slid my fingertips to her inner thighs, watching with sharp-eyed interest while she tipped her head back and let out a gasping breath.

"I didn't taste you here last time," I said lightly, smoothing my fingers back and forth and back and forth along the front of her panties. Poppy rocked her hips, but I kept the pressure light. "Should I start here, angel?"

Her eyes snapped down to mine. "Later," she said fiercely.

"So demanding," I murmured. With my hands on her hips, I nudged her to take one of the steps, and she followed my direction, walking backward as I kept one step below her. I unhooked the belt holding up my work jeans, and the clink of the buckle had her swallowing visibly.

She stopped at the top step, gaze searing into mine while I pushed the jeans off and left them where they fell, left only in my black boxer briefs. Against the flimsy cotton barrier, my hardness strained above the waistband, and she sucked in a breath through her nose when she noticed.

"Your fault," I said with a wry arch of my eyebrow.

That heat in her eyes melted away when my hands drifted up her back and found the clasp on her pristine white bra. Carefully, I peeled it off, staying on the step below hers.

"Look at you," I whispered, tracing a circle along the edge of one hard-tipped pink nipple.

"Gently," she begged. "They're ... sensitive."

Low in my throat, I hummed. "Like this?"

I leaned forward and placed a sweet, sucking kiss there. She sighed, clutching the back of my head as I gently sucked her warm, soft breast into my mouth, tracing the tip of my tongue along the edge, then dragging my nose across her chest to the other, lifting it with my hand and holding her gaze. In contrast, I carefully dragged the edge of my teeth along the hardened nub—lightly enough that she shivered, hard enough that her hands tightened along the back of my scalp.

"Yes," she breathed. "Just like that."

Digging my hands down the back of her underwear, I filled my palms with the warm flesh of her backside, laving my tongue over the tips of her chest. "Delicious," I told her, holding her gaze as I brushed my mouth over her nipples. "Could do this all day. What about you, angel?"

"I can't," she gasped. "I can't take much more of this."

I stepped up, and she took the final step onto the second floor, whirling into the bedroom with my hand clutched in hers. I crowded against her back, holding her hips flush to me while I rocked against her.

"You think I can?" I whispered hotly against the back of her neck. "You think I'm not one touch away from losing my fucking mind?"

I slid my hands along the front of her hips and tugged on the white cotton covering her. It got as far as tangling around her knees, and I found the hot, wet center of her with two fingers, sliding back and forth while her head dropped back onto my shoulder, her body sagging with a helpless moan. I held her up with an arm banded underneath the lush, mouthwatering weight of her breasts.

"That's it," I told her as she worked her hips over my hand.

She let out a low moan and even if I lived another hundred years, I'd never forget what it sounded like. All my best fantasies come to fucking life. There was nothing that would ever come close, ever do to me what she did.

"Been dreaming about this," I told her. One hand between her legs, and one hand cupping a full, warm breast, I sucked at the skin of her shoulder while she writhed in my arms. "Been dreaming about this every night, angel. Want those sweet little noises you make and the way you clench so tight around me."

Her breath was coming in short pants, and she clutched my wrist when I didn't slide my fingers more than an inch inside her, circling just around where she wanted me most.

"Please," she begged.

My hands gripped her hips again, turning her so I could slant my mouth over hers for a brief, hot, tongue-tangling kiss. When we broke apart, I rolled my forehead to hers and fought the urge to take her fast and hot and hard.

Later, she'd said.

We had time.

So much fucking time.

First, I thought with a shiver wracking my spine, I wanted something else.

I sucked her lower lip into my mouth, biting down before I released it, relishing the prick of her fingernails into my back. That bite of pain had me rolling my neck, clutching at any shred of control I had left.

My mouth watered at the scent of her, and I wanted her to melt on my tongue and feel her thighs snap tight around my head.

I pushed her to her back on the bed, wrenching her legs open as she moved backward to make room. Wasting no time, I wedged my shoulders between her thighs and licked straight up her center with the flat of my tongue.

My eyes fell shut at the taste of her, a groan wrenched from the back of my throat. I kissed her there too, luxurious, wet licks of my tongue against the softest, sweetest parts of her while my hips rocked mindlessly against the mattress underneath me.

Poppy moaned my name, and I slid my fingers inside her, hooking them up as I watched her go slack-jawed and mindless.

Her back snapped up, a sharp curve to her spine and a helpless gasp.

I met her gaze from between her legs, and she sobbed my name as she broke wide open, writhing against my face.

After another slide of my tongue as she came down and a sucking kiss just because she tasted too good not to, I pulled away.

"I'll kiss you here every day if you let me," I promised in a rough voice. "Have you for breakfast if I'm fucking lucky."

With my forearm, I wiped at my face and prowled up over her lush body, slanting my mouth over hers and sucking at her tongue while she clutched at my back.

Poppy groaned into the kiss, and I tilted my head to deepen it.

This was us, wasn't it?

A filthy, perfect mix of her personality and mine. Fucking heaven.

I'd never want anything else for the rest of my life, if I could have this with her.

I rolled my weight to the side and gripped her thigh in one hand, laying her leg over my hip. She was sensitive from the first orgasm, and I kissed her gently while I gripped myself in hand and teased her with the tip, allowing her to rock carefully over my length without taking me inside yet.

Poppy was still gasping for breath, her cheeks and chest flushed and her eyes so fucking dazed that I wanted to pound my chest. I kissed her and kissed her, letting the small rocking motion of my hips bring her back up.

Wanted to kiss her forever, this perfect woman of mine.

"I missed you," I told her in an emotion-rough voice. "I missed you so fucking much."

Gripping my face in both hands, Poppy kissed me deeply, a decadent whimper slipping from her mouth into mine.

We got lost again, rocking against each other like we didn't dare go further, allowing the deep, messy clash of our mouths to work us both into a frenzy. Her arms were tight around my back, and I couldn't stop touching her everywhere.

I pressed her back into the mattress with the strength of my kiss, and she whimpered, sliding her hands into my hair and gripping tight.

Stopping the motion of my hips first, I had to stop the kiss too, because leave it to me to come like this. She felt so good. Too good. And I was feeling so much. Too much.

She took me in hand, and I hissed at the way she rolled her palm at the angry tip, working me with her tightly clasped fingers.

"Careful, angel," I warned, "I'm not trying to come on those pretty thighs just yet." I took her mouth in a ferocious kiss. "We can do that later."

Poppy smiled, devilish and beautiful, and she pushed with two hands on my shoulders, rolling me onto my back as she swung her legs over my lap.

At the sight of her above me, so fucking beautiful and mine, I let out a drawn-out, "Fuck, look at you."

Poppy tipped her head back, her full breasts on display, the curve of her stomach and her soft hips the perfect handle for my greedy hands. She worked her hips in tiny circles, sliding down inch by torturous inch while I gritted my teeth.

Better than anything.

This was better than *anything*.

When she was fully seated, she let out a decadent sigh, setting her palms on my chest, her fingernails digging into my skin.

"You gonna take what you want, beautiful?" I asked, keeping my hips still even if I felt like I might fucking die if I didn't move soon. "I'm at your mercy."

Her lips curled up into a smirk, and she tightened around me. I groaned, my hands gripping her hips so hard I might leave marks.

Then she started moving. Back and forth, slow circular motions of her hips, and I met her with movements of my own until her breath started getting faster and faster.

She rubbed her pelvis over me as she rocked, and I could feel the telltale tightening, could sense how close she was. Pleasure built and swelled down my spine, even though something inside me was screaming for fast and hard, some visceral joining that would bind this moment into something as wild as she made me feel.

Poppy rolled her hips again, and I groaned. "Damn, woman, you are evil."

She smiled, her dark eyes gleaming. "You know," she said breathlessly, "we're going to have to be a little creative with our positions from here on out."

"Yeah?" I moved my thumb between her legs, and she gasped, her rhythm faltering. "Tell me."

She held my gaze, teeth digging into her bottom lip while she changed the angle of her hips, and I groaned. "I bet you can guess," she whispered brokenly.

Tightening my hands, I allowed my hips to rock up just as she came down. "Can I have you on your hands and knees, angel?"

Poppy gasped, hands gripping mine. "Yes."

"Bent over the counter," I moaned. "In that shower. On your side while I hold you down and you can't move. Tiny little thrusts that'll drive you out of your mind. That sound good?"

"Jax," she sighed. Her hands slipped into her hair as she worked herself over me, her chin tilting up helplessly. "Hard, Jax. I need hard."

My fingers dug into her flesh when she lifted until I almost slipped free of her body. Her eyes locked on mine, bright with challenge and heat and love, and I clenched my jaw and slammed my hips up.

She groaned.

From beneath, with her luscious curves bouncing from the snap of my hips, I took her like we both wanted. Sweet could come later. Slow could come later.

I braced my feet on the bed and watched with nothing short of awe as she broke apart above me, my name in a hoarse scream of pleasure that inked itself on my heart. The heat grew and spread over the base of my spine, bleeding into my hips and cracking open in my chest as I tipped over the edge with a roar.

I sat up, gripping her hair in a tight fist as I took her mouth in a ferocious, tongue-tangling kiss, milking what remained of our pleasure with short, rolling motions of my hips.

Her arms hung limp over my shoulders as we kissed, slow and sloppy and wet. Her teeth dug into my bottom lip, and when she pulled back, she was smiling.

Thumb brushing over her cheekbone, I stared up into her face as I kissed her again. When I pulled back, her eyes were wet.

"I've never told anyone that I loved them," I whispered, my heart threatening to burst from my chest. "I think maybe I was saving those words for you, Poppy."

I didn't realize my eyes were wet too, until the first tear fell, and Poppy brushed it away with a gentle swipe of her fingers, cupping my face in both hands. The patience and understanding in her face had my throat tightening.

Never rushing me.

Never expecting me to be something I wasn't, say something I wasn't ready for.

What a gift that kind of acceptance was. What a gift she was.

"I love you," I told her, and it felt impossible that three

little words could hold everything that was pressed inside my rib cage for this woman. Saying them didn't lessen the pressure, only added a sweet sort of weight and anticipation that I'd never experienced before.

For the rest of my life, I'd get to love her.

Have the privilege of being loved by her in return.

Her eyes fell shut and she rested her forehead on mine as we sat there, tangled and sweaty and perfect.

"I love you too," she answered, her voice thick with tears.

With a sharp inhale, I wrapped my arm around her back and kissed her again, fingers tangling in her hair and my soul sighing with relief.

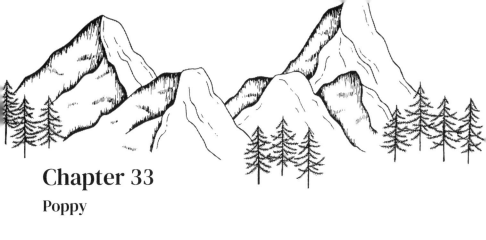

Chapter 33
Poppy

"Wake up, angel."

I groaned, unable to pry my heavy eyelids open. There was a weight banded around my back, something hot and heavy that prevented me from hiding fully under the blankets. Rough fingertips danced along my spine, tangling in my hair, and warm, dry lips brushed over mine, coaxing me into wakefulness.

Humming, I slid my hands up the wall of Jax's chest, keeping my eyes closed even as I sank into the sweet morning kiss. In one night, I could safely say that I'd kissed Jax Cartwright hundreds of times and it was not even close to enough.

He kissed me like he fucked me—with a tender desperation that made me feel like the most powerful woman in the world. Like he could never, ever get enough. Like something as simple as a kiss to start the day was the most important thing in the world.

His nose dragged along the edge of mine as he gathered me closer with the strength of his arms. The light brush of his tongue against the seam of my lips was a sweet demand for more, and with a sigh, I opened my mouth and gave it to him.

My heart wanted to burst from the billowing sort of happiness that bled into every corner of the room, filling the house to the seams. Filling me to the seams along with it.

It almost felt unfair, that this was real, and after so many years of wanting more of this man, I seemed to be in possession of every single piece of him.

Jax gentled the kiss, and I followed his mouth as he pulled back, which made him laugh low in his chest.

"Time to get up," he whispered against my lips.

"Noooo," I groaned. "Time to stay in bed."

To tempt him into exactly that, I slid my hand down between his legs and ran my palm against the front of his boxer briefs, where he was already hard and heavy. Even though I was *sore*, and my thighs wouldn't work right for a few days, I wanted him. Again and again. Jax's arms tightened around me, his hands immediately tilting my hips closer to him where we lay tangled up together on our sides.

"Work is overrated," I told him, angling my chin for another deep kiss.

His tongue slid over mine, wet and hot, and the sound pulled from the back of his throat gave me goose bumps.

I wanted to kiss him forever.

Jax pulled back, resting his forehead against mine while my hand moved up and down, slow movements with a firm grip, just like he'd taught me, and his brow furrowed, his eyes pinched shut, like he couldn't bring himself to stop me.

I didn't want him to.

"Poppy," he groaned, plucking my hand away from him, pressing a kiss to my palm. "Later."

"Later is so far away," I said with a pout.

He laughed quietly, giving me another lingering kiss that had me seeing stars.

We stayed tangled up in each other for a few more minutes, just kissing and whispering, trading easy touches and letting the embrace be the perfect start to the day.

When he pulled the sheet back and started easing his body down, I bit down on my bottom lip and wove my fingers through his hair while he dropped a kiss on each breast, then splayed his hands around each side of my belly.

"Good morning to you too," he whispered.

My eyes pricked with helpless tears as I watched him greet the baby. There wasn't much movement, but he pressed a kiss to the skin just above my slightly distended belly button.

"What can you feel right now?" he asked.

"Not much." I propped my head on my hand, elbow braced on the bed as he traced over the taut skin. Faint stretch marks had already started along my lower belly, and he kissed those too. "Sometimes, the movements are little. Like a flutter. Sometimes I can feel them poke me, like an elbow or a foot. It's the weirdest, coolest thing ever."

His face was full of awe as he studied my stomach. "Incredible." Jax's eyes lifted to mine. "Can they hear me?"

"Not yet." My fingers traced his brow, following the strong line of his nose. "I think that's twenty-three weeks."

"And you're ... how many?"

"Nineteen." I smiled. "Almost halfway."

Jax closed his eyes. "I missed so much."

Heart aching, I tugged him back up so I could kiss him again, and when we pulled away, I made sure he was looking straight at me. "You did your best. So did I. That's all either of us can expect from each other."

Jax dragged his fingers along my jaw and then my bottom lip. His eyes looked troubled.

"Talk to me," I whispered. "I see something in your face right now, and I don't know what it is."

Pinching his eyes briefly shut, Jax expanded his chest on a deep breath. "Doing my best doesn't seem like enough either. It's like I need to learn a new definition for that word."

"What do you mean?"

The subject of work was on pause because he kept

touching me, seemingly in no hurry to leave the bed. Taking his cue, I did the same, gently running my hands over his chest and shoulders, down the front of his biceps.

"My mom was young, as you know, and she was always looking for the next man to take care of us." He paused. "Take care of her, really. When I was ten, I did chores for neighbors and earned money so I could buy her flowers for Valentine's Day. When she saw them, she was getting ready for a date, and she told me I wasted my money. She didn't need that from me. She just needed me to be good and stay out of her way, essentially."

I kept my hands on him the entire time he talked, pain for a serious little boy making my ribs ache from the force of holding in my tears. "That must have hurt to hear," I said quietly.

His brow furrowed as he gave a short nod. "That's all she wanted from me. Be good, stay out of the way. Be…" he paused, searching for the right words.

"Smaller," I finished.

Jax nodded. "Smaller. Take up less space in her life because if I took up more, it would distract her from what was really important. Love, or the search of it, felt like a fucking death sentence. It was the height of being selfish. Of expecting someone else to take care of your shit for you. Henry told me there was no relationship in the world that could fix my mom's baggage. She needed to fix it herself. Which is why he never married. He kept that weight on his own shoulders."

"And that's what you did too," I said quietly.

He inhaled slowly. "Yeah. And I know that sounds like horrible advice to give a hurting little kid, but he was the only reason I didn't blame myself for how my mom acted. No one else looked me in the eye and told me that the way she acted was on her. And that I still had control in how I turned out."

Jax closed his eyes. "He never treated me like a burden, and I'm so fucking grateful for that."

Finally, I burrowed my head against his chest, allowing the strength of his arms around my back to hold me in place there. He kissed my temple and sighed.

"Everyone protects themselves in different ways, Jax." I kissed the notch at the base of his throat, where his pulse was steady and strong. "I think you did what you had to do. We all make choices to avoid hurt. Some people dive into it headfirst because they think embracing the pain makes them more immune to it. Some people avoid it through people pleasing or never asserting their opinion. You chose a different route. It's what you saw him do—this important person in your life. Henry was human, he was probably doing his best too." I pulled back slightly to meet his eyes in the dimly lit room. "Look at my family. Every single one of us reacted differently to my dad being sick, to knowing he was going to die at some point. It only becomes wrong or unhealthy when you start hurting yourself in the process. If you can't move out of that when it counts."

Jax tightened his arms, breathing in with his nose buried in my hair. "You're really fucking smart, you know that? You always read people so well."

I smiled. "Good thing you've got me locked down, huh?"

Jax laughed. "Yeah," he murmured, dipping his face for another kiss, "good thing. God, I hope our kid is like you."

"I hope they're like both of us," I told him, sneaking a quick kiss.

We managed to pull ourselves out of bed after a few more minutes, opting for separate showers for the sake of expediency and a complete lack of belief that we could get in there together—naked—and not get further derailed. I showered first while he brewed himself some coffee, and he hopped in while I was braiding my wet hair off my face, dressing in one of my cotton work dresses and some cute tennis shoes.

Slipping into the steamy bathroom to put on some makeup, I almost stabbed my eye out with the mascara wand when he turned around, holding my gaze through the fogged-up glass as he soaped up his magnificent body with brisk movements of his hands.

"None of that," I said, pointing the mascara wand in his direction. "I'm already dressed."

Jax smirked, rinsing the last of the shampoo from his hair and reaching for a fluffy white towel. With it wrapped around his waist, he exited the shower as I turned and leaned against the counter to watch him.

There was so much strength leashed in his tall, broad frame, the sheer expanse of his chest, the flat tapered waist, and the bulge of the muscles in his shoulders and arms had my stomach taking flight, a dizzying sense of rightness that he was mine.

Not because he finally *caught up* or because I'd waited so patiently but because we fit together. Because all the pieces of me—the good and the bad—locked tight against the pieces of him.

Any earlier in my life, and I might not have been ready for him. Any later in his, and he may not have been willing to step into this space with me. My hand curled over my stomach, and I smiled.

"What?" he asked.

"Nothing."

"If you're thinking it, it's not nothing," he said, his eyes catching mine meaningfully.

I bit down on my bottom lip as I stared at his face, the line of his jaw and the dark brows and the beard that I hoped never went away. I shrugged one shoulder delicately. "I like looking at you and knowing you're mine. That's all."

Jax stilled for a beat, eyes locked on me, unrelenting and hot.

"Say it again," he growled.

"What?"

"Say it again."

I inhaled shakily. "I like knowing you're mine."

Jax strode across the bathroom, gripping the sides of my face and stealing a hot, hard kiss that yanked a whimper from my lungs.

His skin was damp and fragrant, and the slick slide of his tongue against mine made me writhe in place.

"Five minutes," he growled. "We have five minutes."

His hands shoved at the hem of my dress, tugging at my panties while I laughed against his mouth.

"Better get to work then," I whispered against his mouth, then hopped up on the counter and split my thighs apart, tearing at the towel around his waist, and he swallowed the sound of my groan with his mouth as the bathroom echoed with the sound of *one more time*, simply because we could.

"Poppy, you have a delivery I need you to sign for, please."

The squawking voice from the phone on my desk yanked me from the list of vendor options that had my eyes crossing, and I had to blink a few times to get my head clear. "Can you sign for it? I'm right in the middle of something."

My day had flown in a blur of meetings and paperwork, and throughout the entire thing, I'd managed not to go into the middle of the warehouse and shout over the PA system—*Jax Cartwright told me he loves me, and we had epic sex all over my house.*

If adult merit badges were being handed out, I wanted one for that too.

Restraint was difficult when you finally got what you'd wanted your whole life.

"No, I think you should," she answered.

I blew out a breath and stood from my chair with a wince. No one, and I mean no one was prepared for the quad workout of a sex-a-thon. Three times in the span of twelve hours made it feel like I'd done a thousand squats.

No Poppy on top if that man was coming over after work. My thighs simply would not hear of it.

I skipped down the steps that exited into the main lobby of the Wilder and Co. distribution center—the new name and logo on the wood slat wall that Cameron installed a couple of weeks earlier to showcase the new umbrella company over Wilder Homes and Wilder House. Knowing Ivy, she'd add a couple more companies to it by the time we hit Christmas. I wasn't entirely sure when she slept, if I was being honest.

As I turned the corner, I stopped short.

Standing by the curved desk was Jax, his hands tucked into the pockets of his work jeans, his Wilder Homes T-shirt molded to his broad chest and a pleased, smug little grin on his face. On the desk was a huge, wildly colorful bouquet of wildflowers—the explosion of colors so bright and beautiful, and I couldn't help but exhale a quiet laugh. They were wrapped tight with a burlap ribbon and set inside a chunky square vase.

"A delivery," I said quietly.

His eyes never left mine. "Henry told me I should bring you flowers. The good ones. Not something perfect and curated and untouchable." He took a step closer, and nervously, I eyed the side of the lobby, where Kate and two of the warehouse workers were watching us with wide-eyed excitement. "Something wild," he said. "Something unpredictable."

My heart softened into a pile of goo. He'd told me about Henry while we talked in the middle of the night, about his visit, and knowing I might not ever meet the man who remembered Jax, I fought the urge to wrap my arms around him.

"That so?" I asked, touching my finger to a bright orange bloom right at the top of the bouquet.

He nodded.

I tilted my head toward where the women stood, watching us through the glass windows that separated the lobby from the warehouse. "They're gonna talk, you know."

Jax pulled in a deep breath. "That's why I'm here. I think we should go to Cameron's house after this. I want to tell him. Right away. No hiding it, no pretending." Another step and the space between us all but disappeared. "I want to look your family in the eye and tell them I'm in love with you."

My smile started somewhere in the vicinity of my throbbing heart. "Yeah?"

"Yeah." He grinned, the sight so boyish and unexpected that I almost threw myself at him right then and there. "Plus, Dipshit told me my aural energy had intertwined with someone else's, and all I could think about was whether there's a sex color that he could see, and I don't really want to hear him talk about it."

Tipping my head back, I laughed loudly. Jax reached forward and tangled my fingers with his. "Will you come with me, angel?" His eye contact was piercing, the want buried in those dark depths so tangible, I felt like I'd be able to hold it in my hand. "I want them to know."

Because I wanted to, because I could, I rolled up onto the balls of my feet, flung my arms around him and kissed him full on the mouth. The whistles and claps finally broke through the static in my ears from the kiss, and we were both smiling when we pulled back. "Give me five minutes, and I'll be ready to go."

He tilted his head, regarding me with a banked heat that had my heart turning over in my chest. "Is one ever ready to tell your best friend you're sleeping with his little sister and plan to do it for the rest of your life?"

I hummed thoughtfully. "Probably not."

Jax sighed. "That's kinda what I thought."

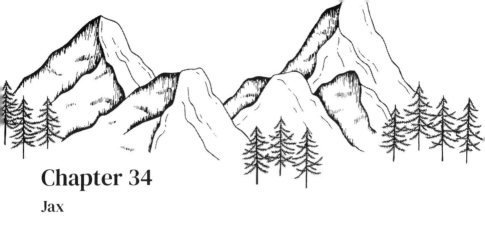

Chapter 34

Jax

Somehow, approaching my best friend's house for this visit was no less nerve-wracking. Less scary in some ways and more in others.

I'd expected his disappointment before. And now ... I wasn't quite sure how he would react. All I did know was that the woman sitting beside me was worth it.

Worth everything.

Poppy's hand was firmly clasped in mine, and she sat in the passenger seat of the truck, a content smile on her face as we drove down the curved driveway past her mom's house and back toward Cameron's.

Both Cameron and Ivy's vehicles were there, and Poppy gave my hand a tiny squeeze.

"Just make sure you knock really loudly," she said.

Looking over at her, I quirked an eyebrow. "Why's that?"

"Walked in on them once."

I winced. "When?"

"It was before this," she answered, gesturing vaguely at her stomach. "I saw my brother's ass, and I swear, if there has been anything in my life that might warrant therapy, it was that."

"Noted," I said, fighting a grin.

Through the massive windows framing the front of his home, there was movement in the family room as I parked behind Cameron's truck, and I exhaled long and slow as the front door opened and the two of them came out onto the front deck, also hand in hand.

Poppy unhooked her seat belt and gave me an impish smile. "Do you know how hard it is not to kiss you right now and let that be their sign?"

I hummed, eyes locked on her soft lips. "Don't tempt me."

The air hummed too, something thick and delicious building between us. She blinked dazedly. "Goodness," she whispered. "This has to ease up sometime, right?"

Since they couldn't see my hand, I eased it from hers and slid it down the firm skin of her thigh, my fingertips spreading wide until my pinky brushed underneath the hem of her dress. She exhaled a shaky laugh.

"Don't count on it, angel," I whispered. "Hold that thought until we're gone, yeah?"

Poppy's throat worked on a swallow, and she managed a jerky nod. "Top of my list."

I held her gaze and curled my pinky along the edge of her underwear. "Is it?"

"Yup. Do Jax Cartwright." Her eyes glowed. "Code red on the color scale."

I was still chuckling as we exited the truck, and Cameron watched me with a thoughtful expression on his face. Ivy was tucked into his side, her arm wrapped around his back.

"Wasn't expecting any visitors," he said, smiling curiously at his sister as she shut the truck door.

"Imagine how happy I am that you're fully clothed," she said.

He rolled his eyes. "That was one time, Pops."

"Personally, I love it when you're not clothed," Ivy stated.

"We know, Ivy," Poppy sighed, hand over her belly as she

came around the hood of the truck. Her eyes flicked to mine, and I saw the question there.

It wasn't a question of why now or why not her. It wasn't a question of whether we were going to do this.

She wanted to know how we were going to do this—the last big step into this new part of our life together. No secrets. No lies. No doubts.

No more fear and no more hiding.

With a hammering heart, I waited for her by the deck steps, slowly extending my hand when she came closer. On the deck, I heard the slight catch in Ivy's breath, but I didn't take my eyes off Poppy.

Her smile was wide and beautiful and that was all it took for the hammering to slip gears—something slow and steady and sure. Poppy's fingers wove easily between mine, and when I stepped forward, Cameron's eyes were locked right on that telling gesture.

Ivy's face broke open into a massive, shit-eating grin. "I knew it," she hissed under her breath. She smacked his chest. "Pay up, Wilder."

Together, we ascended the steps, and Cameron's frame expanded on a deep breath, his face unreadable. At my side, Poppy was a warm presence, glancing up at me with trust and love in her big brown eyes.

God, what a sight. And she was all mine.

My eyes closed a second, and I tightened my grip on her hand in a brief squeeze. When I opened them again, I was facing her brother.

"I'd like a word with you, if that's okay," I said to my best friend.

Slowly, he nodded, then glanced down at Ivy, who was still smiling. His face softened.

"Pops, how about we go inside?" Ivy said. "I have a new cookie recipe I tested out. You can be the first to try them."

Poppy's smile tightened at the edges, her voice taking on a forced brightness. "Oh. Great."

Cameron smothered a grin.

Before she walked away, I tugged on her hand, and when she tilted her chin up in my direction, I leaned down and brushed a soft kiss over her lips. Her cheeks were pretty and pink when she pulled back. "All right then," she whispered. "Guess you were tempted too."

I licked my lips as she tucked a piece of hair behind her ear and kept my eyes locked on her as she walked away.

Ivy shook her head, immediately hustling Poppy inside the house as she peppered her with whispered questions. Over her shoulder, Poppy gave me one last look, and I smiled gently in return.

"Holy shit," Cameron breathed when the door clicked shut. "I think you better start talking now."

We took our same seats, me opposite of him with a table between us. But this time, my soul was completely at ease, any of the initial nerves were gone, and I met his gaze evenly.

"I love her," I told him simply. "And I wanted you to know."

Cameron sat back in his seat, studying me intensely. "When did this realization come about?"

I let out a deep breath. "The first trip I took was the day after Poppy's twenty-first birthday. Do you remember that?"

His gaze sharpened. "Vaguely. You didn't stay long at the bar that night," he said slowly, like he was still retrieving the memory. "You came back from getting a drink and…"

Instead of saying anything else, I let Cameron come to his own conclusion.

His jaw went slack, and he exhaled a quiet, incredulous laugh. "What are you saying, Jax? That trip was about my sister too?"

I merely stared back at him, eventually giving him a slow nod in answer.

Cameron's brow furrowed, and his throat worked on a visible swallow. "Why are you telling me this now?"

Bracing my elbows on my thighs, I sat forward and clasped my hands between my legs. "I can't go to your dad for his blessing," I said quietly. "I know I could talk to your mom, but I have a feeling you'll be a tougher critic than she will." Cameron's eyes cut down to the ground for a moment, then lifted to mine again as I kept talking. "You're my best friend," I told him. "And I love her. I think I've loved her a lot longer than I ever wanted to admit."

He swiped a hand over his mouth and stared at me with a tight jaw as his hand dropped back into his lap. "What would you be asking my dad right now, if he was here?"

If this was hard for me, I couldn't even imagine what it felt like for him—the sense of responsibility he'd always felt to take care of his family, the weight he'd carried for years, even when he didn't need to.

"I'd ask his blessing to marry her someday," I said, emotion tightening my voice. "Not right now. But someday. Poppy and I are adults; we don't need permission to be together, but it's important to me—for her sake—that her family supports us. I'd want to know that he trusted me to take care of her. I'd want to know if he could rest easy knowing I'd love her in the way she deserves," I said brokenly. "You know I'd never say those words if I didn't mean them down to my fucking bones. Because I will, Cameron. I'll love her better than anyone ever has, I swear that to you."

Cameron's eyes were red, and he pushed his tongue against the side of his cheek while he glanced away and blinked a few times.

Slowly, he stood, chest expanding on a deep exhale. He held out his hand.

I stood too, and when I clasped his hand in mine, he pulled me in for a tight, back-bruising hug.

"I know you will." Then he pounded my back with his fist

as we pulled apart. His eyes were clear. "Blessing granted," he said thickly. "Because I know he would've given it to you a long time ago."

Any remaining pressure banding tight around my chest snapped, and I let out a sharp puff of air. "Thank you."

Then he smiled, small and restrained and genuine, clasping my shoulder with one hand and holding my gaze steadily. "I'm glad it's you, Jax," he said firmly.

The casually spoken statement had my throat closing up tight again, and I couldn't find the words necessary to try to answer, so I managed a short nod while I struggled to keep myself in check.

"If you cry, Ivy will never let you live it down," he said wryly.

I exhaled a laugh. "Don't I fucking know it."

Right on cue, the door opened, and Poppy came out first, her eyes locked on mine. I held my arms out, and she walked straight into my embrace. I sighed as my arms folded her close to my chest, allowing my chin to rest on the top of her head.

Ivy dabbed at her eyes as she watched us, and the flash of a large diamond on a very meaningful finger had me narrowing my gaze.

"Is that what I think it is?"

She froze, trading a sly glance with Cameron, who looked down at her like she hung the damn moon. Poppy was contentedly snuggled against me, so they must have talked about it inside.

"We would've gotten there eventually," Ivy said. "I'm tempted to believe he proposed to distract me from making him try my cookies, but I can't argue with the results. And I didn't want to steal your thunder when you walked up. We've only been waiting how long for this announcement?" she said, gesturing between us.

Poppy looked up at me and grinned. "Some of us have been waiting longer than others," she teased.

I quirked a brow. "You're never going to let me live that down, are you?"

"Not a chance, Cartwright."

Chapter 35
Poppy

What did it say about me that watching Jax do yard work felt like foreplay?

Who was I kidding? Watching him *breathe* felt like foreplay for the past couple of days.

And if the man wanted to spend his evening breathing and weeding landscaping beds wearing one of those really nicely fitted Wilder Homes T-shirts, who was I to say no?

It did wonderful things to his forearms every time he yanked one of those little suckers out of the ground, and I sat on the back deck at his place, a bowl of sour gummy worms in my lap while I unapologetically gawked.

He caught me once, rolling his eyes good-naturedly when I sat there grinning at the way he tugged his shirt up and wiped some sweat off his forehead, affording me a delicious glimpse of the stacked muscles on his stomach.

I could've been at my house doing something less fun than this, but in these early days of our relationship, we were both feeling a bit like time apart was dumb, and there was no point. If we were apart, there would have been no talking, kissing, sex, or staring at each other when we did mundane homeowner activities like weeding.

Before work that morning, he sat at the kitchen island at

my place, watching me make some eggs for breakfast. And boy, he was watching me in some sort of way.

It ended with my skirt pushed up around my hips, my underwear tangled around my knees, dried out eggs in the skillet, and Jax screwing me from behind while I held the very sturdy counter.

I was checking that position off on my list with a very enthusiastic thumbs-up and a note to add it to the rotation.

Maybe we had a competency kink. Was that a thing? I was a decent cook, and when the eggs didn't get forgotten in the pan, they were way better than his. Jax watching my complete mastery of simple breakfast foods might have turned him into a mindless brute. Not that I was complaining. Starting your day with a screaming kitchen orgasm was pretty high on my favorite things list now. Just like I'd probably end my day with yardwork-induced sex because of what this simple homeowner's task was doing to his forearms.

With a sigh, I bit off half a gummy worm.

"You eat those really violently," he commented, tossing a few weeds into a bucket next to him. "Makes me wonder if I should be nervous when your mouth gets too close."

Arching my eyebrow, I snapped off another chunk. After swallowing it down, I said, "Oh honey, I won't use teeth unless you ask nicely."

Jax gave me a heated look, tugging off the work gloves and dropping them to the ground while he ambled back onto the deck, settling his hands on the arm of my chair and stealing a long kiss from my upturned mouth.

"Delicious," he murmured.

I held up the bowl. "Want one?"

"I'd rather taste them on you," he said, sneaking another kiss before he walked back to his work.

"So I was thinking about something this morning," I said. "You know, after the ruined eggs and the sex and we were off doing boring work."

"What's that?" He dug into the dirt with the gardening tool, unearthing a particular stubborn weed with long, straggly roots.

"The trips you took. They weren't *all* about me, were they?"

Jax gave me a wry, subdued grin. "I can't tell which answer you'd rather hear."

I threw a gummy worm, hoping to nail him in the head, but it fell a solid two feet shy of the target. "The truth, mister."

Eyebrow arched attractively, he sat back on his haunches and gazed out toward his barn for a moment. "Most of them were, yeah," he said, glancing back at me. "You were too young. Too sweet. And I just … I thought that space would do the trick. Make it go away. And it did, for a while at least. Then something else would happen and I couldn't keep you out of my head like I wanted."

"But my brother never knew."

"That it was about you? Hell no."

As I processed that, I twisted my lips to the side and tapped a gummy worm along the edge of the bowl. "But he always let you go. Always. I'd get emails from him telling me that you'd be gone for two weeks, with a day's notice. How did you pull that off?" I held his gaze challengingly. "I'm the one who prints your checks. Or used to, until we expanded. I know what you make. How did you do it?"

Jax used his forearm to swipe across his forehead, expelling a forceful breath. "We'd get here eventually. Might as well be now."

I took a bite of my candy, watching him with narrowed eyes. "Where?"

Turning to face me, Jax was unexpectedly serious. "I need you not to freak out about this."

My eyebrows shot up my forehead. "Do you know that approach has literally never worked with any woman in the history of ever? The moment you preemptively tell someone not to freak out, they're already starting to freak out."

He exhaled a quiet laugh, his shoulders shifting uncomfortably. Then he set his jaw and met my curious gaze. "I don't actually have to work for your brother."

Tilting my head, I said, "Of course you don't *have* to. You could work anywhere."

"No," he said gently. "I mean that I don't need that job. Before Henry's dementia set in, he appointed me the executor of his estate. It's ... extensive, and he set it up so that I get paid a healthy salary to make sure his investments are taken care of, that he's always taken care of. This is just one piece of property he owns—his favorite, admittedly. When I travel around the Pacific Northwest, I can stay at any one of his places. He's got four or five in total. I sold a couple last year that were more trouble than they were worth. I'll probably sell a couple more this year, because they're worth so much, and I'd rather let someone else handle them." He paused, blowing out a slow breath. "And when he sold all the car dealerships, the assets grew tenfold. I made a percentage off that sale too."

Mouth hanging open, the gummy worm clattering onto the deck when it fell out of my limp hand. "You... what?" I breathed. "Wait, so I'm paying Henry, but I'm sort of paying ... you?"

He quirked an eyebrow. "You know I'm not touching a cent of that money. It's still going to Henry's estate. And yes, some of that funnels back to me, which will funnel back to our child. Every cent you give me is going to go right into an account for the kid. College or whatever."

I blinked a few times. "So you're telling me that all this time, you're like ... loaded?"

He smiled. "I've done all right," he said modestly. "But someday, hopefully not soon, when Henry passes away, it'll all be mine."

Not even sour candy would help with this. I sat back in my seat and stared at him.

There was only one question that felt important enough to ask.

"And you *choose* to deal with my brother and Greer every single day?" I shook my head. *"Why?"*

Jax laughed, and I marveled at how much more easily the sound seemed to come from him in the past couple of days. "I'd go crazy without something to keep me busy," he said. Staring down at the landscaping, he plucked another weed. "I like working outside. Like working with my hands. And your brother is probably the only boss who'd be this understanding."

"So *he* knows about Henry and all your hidden money."

Jax's teeth gleamed white against his beard as he smiled. "Yeah."

"No one ever tells me anything," I muttered.

Standing slowly, Jax flicks his eyes to me briefly. "Would it have changed your opinion of me?"

Because I knew he was asking seriously, I gave it serious consideration. "Maybe," I said after a long moment.

His gaze sharpened. "Yeah?"

I nodded. "I might have climbed into bed with you sooner."

Jax didn't laugh, but his eyes smiled as he watched me. "That so?" he murmured, the flex in his arms distracting my attention for a moment.

"Oh yeah. What a great baby daddy you've turned out to be. You give out orgasms like candy. You're independently wealthy. And you love me," I said simply. "What more could I ask for?"

"What more, indeed," he said, a ghost of a smile as he turned back toward the weeds. "Still don't know how to change a diaper, though," he added.

I tried to hide my smile, but it didn't work. "It's easy. You'll get the hang of it in no time."

"Aren't there like, multiple tabs and velcro and shit?"

"Yes," I said gravely. "And there is a correct way to put them on, but I promise, even you can figure it out. I'm sure there's a chapter about it in your pregnancy books you tried to shove in the kitchen cabinets when I walked in." I fluttered my eyelashes.

His face went slack with shock but recovered quickly. "I don't know what you're talking about," he murmured, a slight flush of pink tingeing the back of his neck.

I wanted to eat him alive. Briefly, I wondered if we could manage backyard sex without getting too loud. Five acres of land was a lot, but the right kind of sounds echoed.

"Mmmhmm," I said. "Don't think I didn't see those before you hustled me out here and distracted me with candy."

He grimaced and got back to work. Then he stopped, turning his face back to mine, and the determined light in his eyes had me tilting my head curiously.

"I made a thing," he said.

I arched an eyebrow. "You might need to elaborate."

Jax sighed. "It's not a crib. It's smaller. You put it in the bedroom with you when they're, you know, tiny."

A helpless smile curled my lips. "A bassinet?"

His cheeks were flushed slightly with a delicious pink, and he nodded. "Yeah. It's not ... I didn't finish it yet. Thought I would this weekend, but I got a little ... distracted."

I laughed. "Sorry about that." Jax gave me a warm look that told me how much he needed an apology for that. "Is that why you were in the shop that night?"

Eventually, he nodded. "Ian gave me some tips. But I..." He sighed heavily. "I wanted to do something. I kept thinking about how small they'll be when they're born. How they'll need a safe place to sleep." His eyes darted over to mine. "It rocks, too. So you can just lean over in bed and help them get back to sleep."

My eyes filled with tears, but I blinked them back. "Sounds like you thought through everything," I said lightly, my heart aching with the force of how much I loved him.

He swallowed, focusing his attention on a particularly stubborn weed. After a few moments, Jax's movements slowed, and I watched something play out over his face.

"Your ultrasound is soon, right?"

I nodded. "End of this week."

His brow furrowed slightly. "Do you want to find out what it is?"

"I don't think I do," I told him. "Is that okay?"

"Yeah," he said quietly. Then he nodded. "Yeah, that's okay. I like not knowing too." The line of his throat moved on a swallow, and he stared down at the ground. "God, it's going to feel so much more real, isn't it? Seeing them. A nose and hands and a mouth and a tiny fucking human that's ours."

Jax paused, pinching the bridge of his nose for a second before his hand dropped into his lap.

"What is it?" I asked.

When he looked up, his eyes were heartbreakingly earnest. "Do you think I'll be a good dad?" he asked quietly.

"Of course." I sat forward and held my hands out. "Come here. I don't like being so far away from you when we're talking about this."

Jax smiled softly, swiping his hands over his pants as he walked over. Settling his weight on the cushion next to me, he stretched an arm out behind me, and I turned, easily swinging my leg over his lap so that I could sit facing him. A few more weeks, and the logistics of a good lap straddle would be too difficult, but for now, it worked.

He eased his hands up the tops of my thighs, along the sides of my belly and around to anchor on either side of my hips. "Closer, as commanded," he said.

I cupped his face, my thumbs bracketing the sides of his mouth. "You're going to be a great dad, because you care enough to ask that question. Because you think about where they'll sleep and if they're safe."

I swallowed, watching the shift in his expression as he looked up at me. Somehow, my opinion had always mattered to this man. Far before I ever realized it, and more deeply than I could have imagined.

Having his heart in my care was such a precious gift, and nothing I'd ever take for granted.

"I thought maybe you were afraid to have a kid," I admitted. "When you didn't want to feel the baby kick."

Jax's eyes closed and he shook his head. "No, it wasn't that. I mean, I am afraid, but I think most people are, right? Aren't you?"

"Terrified," I admitted with a smile.

"I was afraid of you," he said simply. He settled one hand on the side of my belly, feeling for motion underneath the tight skin. I moved it up and to the right where I felt the baby, pressing his fingers in more firmly. When the baby did a tiny little kick, I raised my eyebrow and he smiled, closing his eyes at the sensation. "It's silly now, maybe, but touching you felt like I was tempting myself more than I could handle." He swallowed. "Thought I'd have to get used to seeing you with someone else. Someone better for you."

Bruises on our hearts were so slow to heal, and I knew that this one would take time for both of us. And that was okay. In conversations like this, open and honest and extending grace to the other person for however they might feel would make this relationship a lasting one.

It wasn't in having similar personalities because we definitely didn't have that, and it wasn't in the chemistry that helped us cross the first line. It was shared values, and it was understanding. Every day, it was choosing to see the best in each other.

I sighed, leaning forward to give him a soft kiss. Jax's hands tightened on my hips as his tongue brushed lightly against mine.

"There's no one better for me than you," I spoke against his lips, imbuing those simple words with every ounce of what I felt for him, the way I trusted him, the truth of who I knew him to be, the sheer rightness of the two of us together. "There never has been, and there never will be."

For a moment, we sat there, trading breath and staring into each other's eyes. We were so close, I could see every nuance of color in his eyes, see that all those reservations that had haunted him before were cleared away and gone.

Now there was just love. Perfect, sweet, head-spinning love.

Tilting his head, Jax took my lips in a fierce kiss, a deep, possessive groan rattling his chest and yanking the hairs up on the back of my neck. When his tongue licked hot against mine, I let out a small whimper as I snaked my arms around his shoulders and dug my fingers into his thick hair.

There was a devastating effect to kissing Jax Cartwright, how something relatively simple could slice through my very being. I'd never take this for granted. Never.

And I knew, as he kissed me so thoroughly, made me feel so incredibly wanted and sexy and confident, that this is how it was going to be between me and this man. Jax's hand moved up, and deftly, he filled his palm with one aching breast, handling it gently like I'd asked, soft, teasing brushes against the hardened tip until my hips moved restlessly.

My hands dug between us and pulled frantically at his belt while we panted against each other's mouths.

"Here?" he whispered, tugging at my bottom lip with his teeth.

"Here." I leaned forward and ran my tongue along the shell of his ear, relishing the way he shuddered. "Can you be quiet enough?" I whispered back.

Jax pulled his head back so that his gaze locked on mine, two blunt fingers moving between my legs to wrench my underwear to the side and sliding inside me. "Can you?" he asked with a daring lift to his eyebrow.

I rolled my lips together, my eyes fluttering shut. But I managed a jerky nod.

"Good girl," he whispered, nipping at my bottom lip while he did a thing with his wrist that had me gasping.

Withdrawing his fingers, Jax started helping with zippers and belts and things. He lifted his hips just far enough to shove his jeans down, and we both laughed when it was harder than we thought.

He took me like that—small, slow, torturous rocking movements as I canted my hips in time with his—with no one to see us but the tall, swaying trees and the blue, blue sky. He had one hand clamped tight on my hip, directing my movements, and the other fisted tight in my hair as he whispered filthy things against my lips.

This wasn't sex like a lightning bolt, fast and fierce and immediate. It crept up my body, sneaking up my veins so that I hardly noticed the build until my skin went tight and a decadent groan escaped my mouth.

"That's it," he moaned, licking up the side of my neck.

My orgasm was like honey left out in the sun—thick in my veins and delicious on my tongue, rolling over my skin sticky sweet. Jax followed quickly after, grunting through his own release into my mouth while we kissed each other through it.

I slumped against his chest and tried to catch my breath, sighing quietly while he smoothed his hands up and down my back. It was probably too warm to be cuddling like this, but neither one of us moved as we came down.

Gently, like he couldn't help himself, Jax brushed kisses over my temple, tangling his hands into my hair and pushing it over my shoulder as he held me close. Under my cheek, the steady thrumming of his heart mirrored the pace of mine.

A quiet hum left my mouth before I could stop it, and he tightened his arms around me, a protective, strong embrace that I could claim as my own.

"I like backyard sex," I murmured sleepily.

He laughed under his breath. "Probably shouldn't attempt it at your place. The neighbors might not like it."

"Fair enough," I sighed, closing my eyes and letting the warmth of the moment lull me into a near sleep.

It seemed bizarre, to find a moment of peace such as this after sex like that. My hands curled into his shirt, trying to find an anchor so my emotions didn't go flying into happy tears.

"Honey," he repeated quietly, gazing down at my hands where they gripped the front of his shirt.

"Hmm?" I sat up and arched my back, hissing slightly when Jax pulled himself out from inside me and tucked himself back into his jeans.

His grin was unrepentant, and I rolled my eyes slightly at the smugness on display.

Honestly, though, he'd earned it.

"Earlier, you called me honey." His hand reached for mine, and he ran his thumb over each knuckle, moving to the next, back and forth. "I've never had a pet name before."

I smiled. "Not sure that one fits right. We've got time to figure it out."

He hummed, tilting his chin up so his face was fully in the sun. "'Spose we do."

Weaving my fingers between his, I settled our joined hands on my thigh and studied his face. "What are you going to call me?"

"Come on, you had your nickname a long time ago, Poppy. You gonna get greedy on me now?" he asked, a teasing tilt to his lips that had my skin warm.

"Not that one," I said on a laugh. "I mean … am I your girlfriend? Your partner? Your baby mama?" I teased. "What are we? We haven't even gone on a date yet. Feels premature to say, *this is my boyfriend, Jax*. But you're…" I was feeling slightly vulnerable by the change of conversation.

Jax's eyes landed unerringly on mine, and I swear, I could see his entire heart there. "Everything," he finished. "You're mine. And you're everything."

I leaned forward, cradling his jaw with my hand, my heart squeezing at the way he leaned into my touch. "I like that," I said softly. He met me in the middle, our lips brushing decadently, the tease of his tongue at the seam of my lips had me opening on a sigh.

The breeze was cool and sweet on my face as we kissed, and eventually, he pulled his mouth from mine, tugging me closer into a tight embrace. My eyes burned with unshed tears at the slight tremble in his frame as he held me.

Everything, I thought, right here in our little corner of the world. We sat like that for a long time, with the sun warming our skin, until he took my hand and walked us back inside his house, miles away from where we started and with an entire lifetime ahead of us.

Epilogue

Jax

Five months later

When the entire Wilder family showed up for any single event, it was nothing short of a fucking circus. The first preseason game for the Portland Voyagers wasn't normally something we'd get a luxury box for, but given that Parker was desperately trying to pull his head out of his ass, there was no option but for the *entire* family to show up.

Although I'd been friends with him since high school, and Cameron had two brothers and now two brothers-in-law who played professional football, I'd never been to a game before.

It was loud. And there were people.

Normally, that was enough to deter me, but the woman standing at my side—wearing a blue Wilder jersey stretched across her very large belly—would get anything she wanted, if it was up to me.

So we were at the game. When she was forty-one weeks pregnant.

"I can't believe she got you to cave," Cameron said, eyeing his sister. She waddled more than she walked lately, and we'd had three rounds of false labor over the same number of weeks. We'd tried spicy food and long walks, more shower sex than I thought I'd ever have in a two week period, and we still couldn't trigger the real thing. Despite the fact that she was ready to rip the baby out herself if it meant not being pregnant anymore, she did not want to miss this game.

"Do you know how hard it is to say no to her when she really wants something?" I asked, leaning closer so Poppy didn't hear me. "I had to smuggle her OB in to the section right below us just in case she goes into labor."

"You didn't."

Jerking my chin up, I pointed at a seat two rows in front of our box. "The lady in the blue hat and white shirt."

"No shit," Cameron breathed. "I had no idea you were so paranoid."

"I'm not paranoid, asshole. I just don't want to have to deliver our baby in a car because we're stuck in fucking traffic trying to leave this stadium. Do you think I'd do well in that situation?"

"No," he said gravely. "I don't."

Crossing my arms over my chest, I sighed. "Glad we agree on that."

I'd been a ball of fucking nerves for weeks leading up to Poppy's due date. The house was ready. Beyond ready. Nesting, or whatever the hell she called it, had started about a month ago.

The nursery was painted a beautiful, calm green. On the far wall, Greer had painted a beautiful mural of a meadow, with tall grasses and leaves and an aspen tree.

There was a shelf full of books and little wooden toys that Ian made, and a closet full of impossibly tiny clothes. Under the changing table were bins full of diapers, and even though Poppy teased me, I practiced on one of Olive's dolls until I felt like I could manage it.

I'd all but moved in with her about a month after we started dating, because I decided it was really stupid to sleep in a bed without her when I had the other option in front of me. For the time being, we decided to keep my place, because with the amount of land I had, we could build something bigger if we decided Henry's house wasn't where we wanted to stay long term.

For now, though, it was home. And God, it was a good one.

Every morning, I got to wake up with her in my arms. Every day, I got to take care of her—lately, it was helping her put on her shoes and painting her toenails, which I was slowly improving at after slathering hot pink nail polish all over her toes.

Who created those tiny-ass little brushes was beyond me. They sure weren't meant for big, clumsy hands like mine.

And in those mornings and days and nights, we found a seamless rhythm that made it seem like we'd been doing that forever. That I'd been loving her forever.

Probably because it felt like I had.

She was so fucking smart. And insightful. A better listener than anyone I'd ever met. And the fact that our kid would have her as a mom was more than I could handle.

And she was also really, really loud when she was at her brother's games.

Parker got flagged for offensive pass interference, and Poppy cupped her hands around her mouth and booed. "Get your eyes checked, ref," she yelled. "He hardly touched him."

I settled my hand on her back as she rubbed a hand over her stomach and winced.

"Maybe the screaming isn't helping," I told her, dropping a kiss to her temple.

Poppy didn't answer, though, stilling immediately and staring down at the ground.

"What is it?" I asked, concern making my chest tight.

She sucked in a deep breath and looked up at me with wide eyes. "I think my water just broke."

"What?" I yelled. "Holy shit, I knew this was a bad idea."

Poppy laughed, dragging my face closer and giving me a

quick kiss. "It's fine," she said. "Childbirth happens all the——" she froze, face bending in pain. "Oh fuck a duck," she groaned. "That's a big one."

I felt her stomach, and the skin was hard. "Have you been having contractions?" I asked incredulously.

"I mean, sort of?" she hedged.

"Poppy."

"I thought it was false labor again, and they were way more than five minutes apart. I could still talk through them, so I didn't think it was anything to worry about." Looking into my face, she winced because my jaw was about hanging down to the ground. "Sorry?"

It was at that moment that I realized the entire suite was dead silent, eyes on me and Poppy.

"Is she——" Sheila asked.

"Holy shit, is she in labor?" Greer asked.

"I think she peed her pants," Sage whispered.

"She's wearing a skirt," Ian corrected. "She peed her skirt."

Poppy breathed out a laugh, hand over her stomach.

I was just trying not to have a panic attack in the middle of the box. "Yes, her water broke. We need to get out of here."

The suite erupted. Sheila grabbed all of Poppy's things, Greer bolted from the box to get security. Erik's wife Lydia was on the phone with someone, asking about prepping a private hospital suite. Cameron, Ian, and Erik watched wide-eyed as their sister was gripped with another contraction, and her legs buckled as she cried out. Heart hammering, I wrapped an arm around her waist and yelled for Cameron.

"Go get the doctor," I told him.

He ran from the suite as I eased Poppy onto a small sofa. "Breathe, okay? Deep breaths. You remember what she said in the birthing class."

Poppy did as she was instructed. "Oh that one came fast," she groaned.

"You'll be fine, angel." My voice came out calm and steady, which was a fucking miracle. My pulse was racing wildly, my heart trying to thrash out of my chest. There was nothing I could do. Not really.

Hold her hand.

Feed her ice chips.

Not stare at her vagina, which was a promise I'd made when we watched a birthing video in the class.

And it was that wildly out of control feeling that had me closing my eyes and fighting for calm. She squeezed my hand, and I opened my eyes.

There it was.

The calm, as it always was, was found in her.

She smiled. "We're gonna meet our baby," she whispered.

"Yeah, we are," I whispered back. "I can't wait."

Cameron jogged back into the room, and Poppy's head reared back when she saw her OB. "Dr. Beal? What are you doing here?" she asked.

Dr. Beal smiled from underneath her Voyagers hat. "Someone very generous purchased my ticket and heavily suggested I take in a preseason game."

Poppy laughed, turning to give me a kiss. "You didn't."

"You didn't leave me much choice, Poppy. It was either that or have them prep a delivery suite next to the locker room."

The doctor smiled, tapping Poppy's leg and having her lean back while she snapped some gloves on. "Why don't you head into the bathroom? I just want to see where we are before we head out to the hospital, okay?"

With my arm around Poppy's waist, I helped her into the suite's restroom and Poppy did her best, leaning up against the counter while Dr. Beal examined her. "Goodness," she said, eyebrows climbing up her forehead. "You're already at a five, my dear."

Oh yes. I knew what this meant. Centimeters. Learned that one in the class, where I also discovered—to my chagrin—what a mucus plug was. Could've gone the rest of my life not knowing it, but it was honestly shocking what I'd gotten used to at this point.

Poppy's face went white. "I am? Does this mean I can't get my epidural?"

Immediately, she started crying, and I brushed the hair back off her forehead, trying my best to calm her.

"You'll be just fine, sweetie," Dr. Beal said. "Let's just get you somewhere—"

The doctor was cut off as another contraction rocked Poppy and she made a low moaning sound that made me want to tear my chest out. Her hand was squeezing mine so tightly, I had to turn away and hide the slight wince of pain.

Honest to God, I thought she was going to break my fucking hand.

Dr. Beal whispered something to Poppy and then left the bathroom. I saw her talking to Greer and Lydia. Lydia was gesturing wildly, and they both had concern on their faces.

"What are they talking about?" Poppy asked, leaning her forehead against my shoulder.

"I don't know, angel. But you'll be just fine."

"You snuck my doctor into the game," she said. Her eyes were still wet from tears, and underneath her smile, I saw worry and fear.

I cupped her face. "I'd do a lot more than that to make sure you're safe."

Poppy melted into me, clutching at my shirt while another contraction rolled through her. She breathed through it while I rubbed her back.

Dr. Beal came back into the room. "Okay. New plan. A concert just let out across the street, and there's an accident on the highway we need to use to get to the hospital, so we're moving to plan B."

Poppy was breathing hard when the contraction was done. "What's plan B?"

The doctor smiled. "Well, you have two choices. We can use one of the ambulances here for the game and hope you can get past the traffic. Or … Poppy, how do you feel about being the first person to have a baby at a football stadium? There are EMTs on hand for the game, they're ready to assist and could take you in after the baby is delivered."

"What?" I gasped. "I was joking when I said I'd prep a room."

Dr. Beal cocked an eyebrow, and if she didn't look so calm, I might have lost my fucking mind right there. "There are worst places to have a baby, trust me. I think we'd do just fine if it comes to that."

And that was how we found ourselves thirty minutes later, in a treatment room turned into a makeshift delivery suite. Security and medical staff from the team escorted us into the lower level, and with Poppy's hand gripping mine, her entire freaking family trailing behind us, I wondered how the absolute hell this was actually happening.

The room itself wasn't bad—they'd loaded us up with clean towels and sanitized a cushy, expensive-looking examination table, plastic covering the floor underneath, and Dr. Beal used a long table along the wall to set up her equipment. She scrubbed her arms in a sink and pulled a gown from her purse to wear over her Voyagers gear.

On the table, Poppy did her best to weather the contractions, but they rolled through her body in a way that left her panting and sweaty. More than anything, I just wanted to take it away for her.

Outside the room, eighty-seven Wilders waited, and I tried my best to ignore the fact that we were at a football stadium and Poppy was about to give birth where her brother got massages.

"I hope they burn this table when I'm done with it," she groaned. Another contraction wracked her frame, and she turned toward me, gripping my hand while I tried to coach her to breathe. Dr. Beal spoke to the EMTs stationed in the room with us, an older Black man and a blonde who looked so young, she couldn't have been more than twenty-one.

"You got it, angel," I told her. "You're doing so fucking great."

"It hurts," she whimpered as the contraction came down.

"I know, love. I know." I brushed my lips over her sweat-damp forehead, only releasing her hand to get a wet washcloth for her forehead.

When I laid it on her skin, she sighed, but the relief was short-lived because there was another contraction right on the heels of the last one.

"We're close," Dr. Beal said. "This little one really wants to come meet you two."

Poppy yelled when she felt the need to push, and I stood at her shoulder, holding her hand and just generally trying not to make anything worse.

But just watching her, God, she was the most beautiful thing I'd ever seen.

She looked up at the ceiling as she struggled through her breathing exercises, and when it ebbed, she gave me a teary-eyed look. "Is it okay if my mom comes in? I need her."

"Of course," I told her.

The look of relief on her face was obvious, and I gave her a quick kiss before heading to the door. When I poked my head out, everyone's gaze snapped up, but I motioned to Sheila. "She wants you in there."

Sheila hustled in behind me, and just before I shut the door, I noticed Parker standing with his brothers, stripped down to a white T-shirt and still wearing his game pants and cleats. I gave him a quick nod.

"Tell her the whole team is taking bets on whether they'll be able to hear her scream in the locker room." He grinned. "And that if she wants me to win some money, she'll get really loud."

Every sibling around him turned to give him an incredulous look.

"What?" he asked.

Greer smacked him on the back of the head, and I blew out a slow breath before retreating back into the room.

The moment Sheila took a position on the other side of Poppy, my girl started bawling, the relief at seeing her mom had tears coursing down her cheeks.

"I don't know how to do this, Mom," she sobbed.

Sheila made a soft, shushing noise, running her hand over her daughter's cheek. "Sure you do, sweetheart. Your body knows exactly what to do. You just get to go along for the ride." They touched foreheads, and that was when I noticed Sheila was crying too. "And at the end of the ride, you get to hold that perfect baby."

Poppy sobbed again, blindly reaching for my hand on the other side. "I want to meet her so bad."

"Her?" I asked, voice suspiciously thick.

Poppy nodded, smiling wide. "I think it's a girl."

Another push stopped the conversation. Then another.

For twenty more minutes, Poppy was a fucking warrior, and it was the most incredible, terrifying, awesome thing I'd ever witnessed in my entire life.

Until *she* came out—screaming at the top of her lungs and with a shock of dark hair—and my whole world came to a screeching, heart-bursting stop.

"It's a girl," Dr. Beal said with a huge grin over her face. "You did great, Mama."

"It's a girl?" Poppy sobbed, holding my hand tightly while I kissed her full on the mouth.

Dr. Beal motioned for me, holding out a pair of scissors, and somehow I cut the umbilical cord without passing the fuck out. She wrapped the squirming, gooey bundle of skin and hair and tears and laid her on Poppy's chest, and I wrapped my arm around them both, kissing Poppy's temple while we both wept.

The tiny cries from that impossibly tiny body had my heart living somewhere outside of my chest, and I gently laid my hand over her back.

"She's so small," I said, awe choking my voice into something unrecognizable. "How is she so small?"

"She's perfect," Poppy said through her tears. Then she turned to me—sweaty and exhausted, mascara running down her cheeks—and I'd never seen anything better in my life. "I love you so much."

I laid a hard kiss on her mouth, rolling my forehead over hers.

Dr. Beal gently picked up the baby and brought her over to the EMTs, who examined her on another table.

Sheila wiped tears from her face and gave Poppy a hug while I wandered over to the table to watch what they were doing.

"Congratulations, Dad," the older male said. He had kind eyes, and with deft movements, he used some washcloths to wipe all the fluid off her tiny, pink little body. "Ten fingers, ten toes, and a strong set of lungs."

Dr. Beal patted me on the back. "You did great. I appreciate you not fainting because I would've had to leave you there while I tended to Momma."

I gave her a wry grin. "Understandable."

When the baby was clean, the EMT handed her carefully to me. A tear slid down my cheek as he instructed me how to cradle her head. Once she was settled in my arms, I blew out a hard breath and stared down at this little person who just blew my world wide open.

"Hi there," I whispered. She blinked up at me, eyes gray and lashes tiny little spikes against the translucent skin on her eyelids. The tiny squirming sounds from her bow-shaped lips had my heart racing wildly.

How could you love someone this quickly? I brushed my thumb over her tiny fist and breathed out a soft laugh when she blinked slowly.

"I think your momma wants to hold you," I whispered.

We walked back to the table.

"You look good like that," Poppy said tiredly. Sheila helped her sit up, adjusting the exam table behind her, and I eased the baby into her arms. "Oh, look at all her hair," she whispered.

"I suppose this means we need to name her now, huh?"

Poppy stared down at her scrunched little face, button nose, and I swear, I caught a hint of a dimple when she twisted her mouth up, ready to cry again.

"I have an idea," she said. "What about … Rosie? Rosie Emerson Cartwright."

At the sound of Henry's last name, my head snapped up, my heart exploding behind the frail cage of my ribs. "Really?"

She nodded, eyes brimming with tears. "I think someone should honor him, right? He's still here, but … someday, when he's gone, you'll still have a little piece of him."

I kissed her. With the baby squirming between us. Her mom standing next to us crying. Her entire family waiting out in the hallway to find out what was going on.

Because I couldn't not kiss her.

Finding someone who makes your life better in every single way, who understands you at your core and isn't scared of what's there, it was the greatest kind of gift.

"It's perfect," I said against her lips. "I love it."

She smiled, handing the baby back as the doctor still

worked between her legs. Sheila kissed her daughter's forehead, whispering something I couldn't hear, and she hurried off to tell the family.

As the door closed behind her, I heard the happy roar of a room full of Wilders—cheering and clapping and a burst of happiness that was tangible. I stared down at Rosie Emerson, and gently touched my finger to her upturned nose, feathering it over the impossibly soft skin of her cheeks, smiling when she turned toward the touch.

"Welcome to your new life, little pup," I whispered. "It's a really good one, I promise."

The End

Also by Karla Sorensen

(available to read with your KU subscription)

THE WILDER FAMILY

One and Only (Greer Wilder's story)

Head Over Heels (Cameron Wilder's Story)

Promise Me This (Ian Wilder's story)

Parker's story is coming early 2025.

WASHINGTON WOLVES: NEXT GEN

The Lie

The Plan (Erik Wilder's story)

The Crush (Adaline Wilder's story)

THE BEST MEN

The Best Laid Plans

The Best of All

THE WARD SISTERS

Focused

Faked

Floored

Forbidden

THE WASHINGTON WOLVES

The Bombshell Effect

The Ex Effect

The Marriage Effect

THE BACHELORS OF THE RIDGE

Dylan

Garrett

Cole

Michael

Tristan

THREE LITTLE WORDS

By Your Side

Light Me Up

Tell Them Lies

LOVE AT FIRST SIGHT
(Published by Smartypants Romance)

Baking Me Crazy

Batter of Wits

Steal my Magnolia

Worth the Wait

Acknowledgments

There's a really strange correlation between how many times I doubt myself in the process of writing a story and how much I love it by the time I get to the end. Poppy and Jax's story was a journey, and it changed immensely from initial plot to final product. I hope that their hard-fought HEA gives you the same butterflies that it does to me.

I could not get to that final product without a handful of people who are saint-like in their patience, support and encouragement—Kathryn Andrews, Amy Daws, and Piper Sheldon. These three went above and beyond in talking things through with me when I had the usual story breakdowns (so, so many breakdowns).

My husband, who talks about fictional people far more than he ever anticipated, and always knowing when to push me and when to listen. My boys for giving me pockets of encouragement right when I need it. My mom for MANY last minute school pickups when I needed one more hour to finish my word count for the day.

Kelli Collins and M.E. Carter in their developmental help and not taking it personally when the story changes massively from first draft to second draft (so, so many changes.)

A gold star for coming in clutch at the exact right moment and reminding me that my gut instinct about a story is usually right goes to Becca Syme. You are a GIFT to the author community and we don't deserve you.

Jenny Sims and Kelly Allenby for the polishing.

Najla Qamber and Jane Ashley Converse for a beautiful cover.

My agent Georgana Grinstead for the encouragement and support.

My readers—for everything.

"Set me as a seal upon your heart, as a seal upon your arm, for love is strong as death."
Song of Solomon 8:6

About the Author

Karla Sorensen is an Amazon top 10 bestselling author who refuses to read or write anything without a happily ever after. When she's not reading Dramione fanfiction or avoiding the laundry, you can find her watching football (British AND American), HGTV or listening to Enneagram podcasts so she can psychoanalyze everyone in her life, in no particular order of importance. With a degree in Advertising and Public Relations from Grand Valley State University, she made her living in senior healthcare prior to writing full time. Karla lives in Michigan with her husband, two boys and a big, shaggy rescue dog named Bear.

Made in the USA
Monee, IL
30 December 2024

75650136R00233